MISCHIEF AND THE MASTERS

MASTERS OF THE SHADOWLANDS
BOOK 12

CHERISE SINCLAIR

VanScoy Publishing Group

Mischief and the Masters

Copyright © 2016 by Cherise Sinclair

ISBN: 978-0-9975529-5-9

Published by VanScoy Publishing Group

Cover Artist: April Martinez

ACKNOWLEDGMENTS

First, a huge *thank you* to all of you who email, comment on Facebook, and/or participate in my discussion group. Uzuri's story came about because y'all insisted it was her turn. By your command...here is her book. I hope I did our li'l prankster justice.

A shout-out goes to the Shadowkittens in my Facebook News & Discussion group who serve up generous helpings of inspiration, weigh in on momentous decisions like "should this sex scene be kinky or all about the pain?", toss out ideas for new stories and characters, and just do what kittehs do best—be adorable and fun. I love you all.

You know, back when I started writing, I was clueless about how many people were needed to get a book into readers' hands. So here's a map of those involved.

First up are my beloved critique partners who bravely take on the first rough draft. Monette Michaels, Bianca Sommerland, and Fiona Archer—thank you!

I'm always stunned and grateful for readers who volunteer to help with a book. Huge thanks go to Angie-Leonie Hinckson, Eliana West, Natalie Jett, and Tracy Harris who guided me down the path of interracial romance with advice that ranged from hairstyles to lifestyle issues. Big hugs, my dears, and heaps of gratitude.

Once cleaned up, Red Quill Editing steps in for a myriad of back and forth copyedits and proofing—and during that time, my wonderful team of beta readers, Barb Jack, Lisa White, and Marian Shulman also check over the writing for all the goofs an author can make.

Meantime, April Martinez does her usual fantastic job of designing the cover art. So when the author (me) makes impossible demands like, "I love this photo for Uzuri and Max, but this photo is what Master Alastair looks like, so can you put them all together?" she somehow makes it work. Thank you, April!

When editing is done, Paul at BB eBooks formats the manuscript. Blessings upon you and your team, Paul, for both your speed and your attention to detail.

Finally, to get the word out to everyone, I have two promo people who help with the Facebook discussion group, sending ARCs to bloggers, and creating catchy memes. Thanks to Janet at JJS Marketing & Design, and Leagh and Lisa at Romance Novel Promotions for your hard work.

And finally, a big thank you to my wonderful dearheart who will drag me out of my writing cave and remind me that life isn't all work and no play. *I do love you so much.*

CHAPTER ONE

Coming "home" truly was the hardest part of each day.

As Uzuri Cheval pulled into her driveway and turned off her car, she looked at her one-story duplex. The dark windows appeared like hollow eyes in the white stucco. There were no dog toys in the yard, no laughter or music coming from inside. *Lonely*.

But, it was hers. Her refuge against the world, and one she needed right now. She'd had one crummy day.

Sometimes, she wondered if handing out burgers and fries wouldn't be easier.

At least a Mickey D's counter person wouldn't have her boss demand a marketing plan for spring swimsuits. She wrinkled her nose, remembering last year. All those skinny mannequins in bikinis and not one with a real woman's figure.

To make matters worse, the fall clothing stock wasn't selling as well as predicted, which was probably because the Florida summer had been scorching and showed no signs of slacking off, even well into September.

To top off her day, she'd had a close encounter of the ugly kind.

I should have stayed in bed. With the covers over my head.

1

Still...the fast food industry would have to limp along without her shoveling their fries. Being a fashion buyer with all its challenges truly was a dream come true.

Selling and buying and marketing? She was all over that like a bargain shopper on Black Friday sales. *Love it.*

Working with the advertising section on marketing strategies? *Super fun.*

She knew that bad sales figures happened occasionally. The merchandising manager had even admitted that climate change wasn't under Uzuri's control.

But...the ugly scene? Omigod, her encounter with Carole Fuller had been horrible. If only she hadn't visited the women's clothing section today. But it was part of her job to observe what clothing attracted customers, what they picked up, and what they considered and put back. While there, she'd noticed a sales associate repeatedly ignore customers needing help to fawn over better-dressed white women instead. That wasn't right. The sales staff was to give everyone exceptional service. *Everyone.* How many of those women who'd been slighted would never return? After all, Tampa had plenty of clothing stores.

When informed, the section manager had been furious. Apparently, Carole had already been warned twice to amend her ways. The manager had called the sales associate over for a final warning.

Not an hour later, Carole and her friends had entered the deli where Uzuri was eating. Uzuri shivered at the memory of the loud, ugly confrontation. Carole blamed her for the reprimand. Said Uzuri didn't know anything. After all, Carole had been selling clothing since before Uzuri was born. *She* knew how to sell far better than any new grad. At least, she hadn't said black new grad.

Uzuri shut the car engine off. Thank goodness, Carole wasn't male since Uzuri would probably have cowered. However, confronting a female was difficult, but not impossible, and Uzuri had responded in a firm, level voice. Okay, she'd totally pretended she was Master Z.

She hadn't let the older woman's sneer shake her. Of course, after returning to her office, she'd trembled for a good hour. A long internal debate later, she'd decided the confrontation didn't need to be shared with the woman's manager. Enough was enough.

Thank goodness, the day was over.

As she slid out of her car, the early evening heat plastered her suit to her curvy frame, reminding her of why the fall clothing line wasn't selling well. *I should have ordered extra shorts and tank tops instead, but who knew global warming would negate half of the fall season?*

The white stucco duplex shimmered with heat, and the stately line of curbside palms provided no shade at all. Catching the awful scent of rotting food, she wrinkled her nose. *Ewww.* Purse under her arm, she quickly crossed the driveway. *Air-conditioning. Need air-conditioning.* As she rounded the bushes, which concealed her recessed front door, the stench got worse and then she saw the cause. A heaping pile of...of *garbage* sat on her front stoop.

Fear stabbed her so hard she gasped. *No, no, no.* Fumbling for the pepper spray in her purse, she spun to check her surroundings.

No one hid behind her car or the trees. No one watched from across the street. There were no strangers in sight. Despite the sultry heat, cold fear-sweat trickled down her spine. As she fought for a breath, her ribcage refused to let any air in.

Down the street to her left, teenaged Duke Hernandez was mowing his lawn. On the sidewalk to the right, blonde Brenna rode her tricycle and sang some Disney tune in a high voice. The golden furry shape sprawled in the neighbor's yard was the Smith's retriever.

She found no hulking man with a patchily shaved scalp. No Jarvis.

Embarrassed, she huffed out a breath and stowed her pepper spray. *Way to overreact, girl.* Undoubtedly, some fun-loving brats had dumped one of the garbage cans that'd lined the curb this morning.

Surely, that was all.

Or was it? Over the past few months, other minor incidents had occurred. Her car window busted, a dead mouse left on a windowsill, her newspaper ripped to shreds, her electricity turned off. All since Jarvis had gotten out of jail.

But really, the instances were few and far between. She wasn't being stalked. Pranks happened all the time; it was just her turn right now.

"Uzuri, you're back." The quavering voice came from Mrs. Avery who lived in the other side of the duplex. Leaning on her walker, the elderly lady stepped outside. Stooped and shriveled with skin almost as white as her hair, she was one of the sweetest people in the world. "Such a mess. I saw it when Betty brought me back from grocery shopping."

"Did they dump anyone else's garbage?"

"It doesn't look like it, dear."

Just me? Yet, that still didn't mean the culprit was Jarvis. Maybe someone had targeted her for being black. Wasn't it weird to hope she was being harassed for her race?

But she couldn't bear to think of the alternative...

Mrs. Avery pursed her lips. "I talked with Mr. Hernandez. He will send over the boys with shovels and a garbage can to get that cleaned up. He said they owe you for feeding their dog and cats last month."

Uzuri's shoulders relaxed. "That will be a wonderful help. Thank you so much."

Mrs. Avery waved her hand in dismissal. "None of us could bear thinking of you having to deal with it. You work so hard."

Uzuri's eyes burned. Although she'd only lived here since last spring, her neighbors had taken her in as one of them. "Thank you."

"Go get changed now, dear. You'll want to spray the stoop after Duke and Roberto cart away the mess."

"You're right." She'd wash it and drench the area with Febreze. As Mrs. Avery returned to her half of the duplex, Uzuri stepped around the garbage and opened the front door, then stopped to listen.

Silence.

More silence.

With an exasperated breath, she forced herself to step inside.

Cool air washed over her. Everything was neat and tidy. Not like the destruction Jarvis had wreaked on her apartment in Cincinnati. The pale blue couch with bright floral pillows showed no wrinkles from someone's heavy body using it. From someone making himself at home.

The framed prints of fashion shows hung straight. Beneath them, various customized Barbie and Ken dolls strutted across the hanging shelf, attired in fall's seasonal clothing. None were disarranged, no heads or arms pulled off.

No vindictive intruder. *Honestly, girl, get over it.*

Jarvis was in Cincinnati, on parole, and unable to leave the area. He'd gone on with his life. He wasn't interested in her any longer. She needed to stop seeing him as a boogeyman and the cause of every trivial mishap.

That crawling sensation on her neck didn't mean anyone was actually watching.

CHAPTER TWO

The next afternoon, Uzuri encountered a new kind of anxiety as she waited in the reception area of the fancy-ass spa with three friends. At the desk, Andrea chatted with the scheduler.

"You know, I like a bit of pain, but this...this wasn't on my to-do list." Sally was in her mid-twenties like Uzuri with long, curly brown hair and brown eyes. Wearing ugly gray sweatpants and a red T-shirt that said, ZOMBIES HATE FAST FOOD, she had a crushing grip on Uzuri's cold hand.

A few years older, Kari and Jessica looked equally uneasy. Kari hugged herself, brown eyes wide. "I'm a schoolteacher. I don't do stuff like this. How did this happen?"

Jessica rolled her green eyes. Short, curvy, and blonde, she was also in sweats. "Maybe because you were as drunk as the rest of us?"

"Actually," Sally said judiciously, "I think she was worse."

"We couldn't let Andrea face this alone." At the Labor Day party, Andrea had whined about her huge pre-wedding task list—and how her very dominant fiancé had requested something terrifying. Thinking Cullen craved a new flogger or something, Uzuri had teased Andrea and said his request couldn't be that bad. Only Andrea hadn't been talking about a flogger. Oh noooo, Master Cullen wanted Andrea to try a *Brazilian wax*. Obviously looking forward to the honeymoon, he'd told his fiancée he loved how waxing left...things...extra smooth.

Seeing Andrea's worry, well, what could her friends do but offer to go with her?

Of Andrea's besties, Rainie begged off since she'd recently had her own waxing appointment. Gabi and Kim couldn't get away, and Beth was swamped with work and her two new children. And Linda...

"Why didn't Linda come?" Sally asked. "She always makes me feel better if she's around."

Uzuri nodded. Linda was the most motherly person on the planet. "She wasn't at the party, remember?"

"I saw her the next day and asked if she wanted to come. Oh, my God, she turned red." Jessica giggled. "Apparently Master Sam ties her down, heats up the wax, and tends to that little chore for her."

"Oh sweet heavens." Uzuri shivered. Master Sam was a hard-core sadist. He wouldn't try to make waxing less painful. On the contrary.

Sally shook her head. "I'm not sure whether to feel sorry for her or envious."

"We're going to find out all too soon," Kari said nervously.

"Is everyone ready?" Andrea's golden-brown complexion had turned an ashy pale color. She waved for them to follow the receptionist. "Everyone is assigned to a room. Let's go."

Jessica disappeared into a room. Then Sally.

Uzuri's turn.

As she entered the small room and saw the long padded table in the center, her heart started thumping way too fast. At least the esthetician, Maria, a middle-aged Hispanic woman with warm brown eyes, appeared reassuringly competent.

Maybe the woman would want to chat for a while first.

Maria handed Uzuri a towel. "Everything off from the waist down and climb up on the table. I'll be back in a couple of minutes."

Or not.

Uzuri fumbled her clothes off. The last time she'd been told to strip down had been in the Shadowlands and a lot more fun. There had been nipple clamps and...

She frowned. The table here looked far too much like a BDSM bondage table. Biting her lip, she climbed up on it and checked. No restraints. *Whew.*

When Maria returned, the position she asked Uzuri to take was familiar. Feet together, knees open.

"Good, your curlies are the right length," the woman said in approval.

Uzuri's "curlies" seemed awfully long at half an inch. Last weekend at the club, she'd actually left early in fear that a Dom would notice her stubble and give her grief about it.

With a little stick, Maria applied wax and covered it with a strip of fabric. Although Uzuri jumped, she decided the hot wax wasn't uncomfortable.

Then Maria took a firm hold on the strip—and ripped out the hair.

Fuck! Uzuri made a sound that wasn't pretty at all. Rainie'd insisted waxing felt like a Band-Aid being ripped off. Had the girl no nerves in her hoo-ha? Thankfully, the painful fireworks subsided quickly to a mild burning.

Maria patted her hand. "See? Not so bad. The first visit is always the worst. With each visit, the hair follicles shrink, and the pain gets less."

From the room next door came a screech. "*Madre de Dios!*"

Uzuri grinned. Andrea was usually so polite, but omigod, the Hispanic woman could swear a blue streak when she got upset. "Andrea, are you all right?"

"*Mierda, no!*"

"Hey, Andrea, are you still going to get married?" Sally called.

"I may murder the *cabrón* instead. The *hijo de puta*, he said this would hurt less than a flogging. He *lied*."

Silence fell over the entire section of rooms, and Uzuri saw her esthetician's mouth drop open. A second later, every Shadowkitten was giggling.

Even giggling didn't help the pain of the next rip.

Pussies now bare and beautiful, the entire group had pulled on clothes and fled to the bar across the street for alcoholic aftercare. Uzuri figured a few drinks would be far more effective than the soothing oil the esthetician had applied.

"I wonder how many of the waxing clients come here for alcohol therapy?" Shifting uncomfortably in her chair, Sally sucked her second drink down as fast as the first.

"Lots." Sitting next to her, Uzuri matched her drink for drink. All of her sensitive bits felt swollen and hot, as if she'd basked in the sun for hours with no panties on. And her nice dress slacks were way too tight. Why hadn't she worn droopy old sweats like Sally and Jessica? Vanity wasn't worth *this* kind of discomfort.

Jessica arrived with another pitcher of Screaming Orgasms, plopped down beside Uzuri, and turned to Kari. "Hey, what was going on in your room? I heard a lot of '*Oh, no*' noises."

Kari's face turned the florescent shade of red only white girls could achieve. "The esthetician had finished my...my mound, working downward, you know, toward the uh...center. I got worried and closed my legs and...um...the sides kind of stuck together."

Andrea's eyes widened. "*Dios*, you glued your *pussy* shut?"

Uzuri choked on her drink.

The laughter from their table turned heads throughout the whole bar.

"How about you, Jessica?" Sally grinned. "What were all those '*I'm so sorry*' comments for?"

Jessica rolled her eyes. "Let's just say eating bean soup for lunch was a really bad idea. That poor woman!"

"You didn't!" Uzuri was giggling so hard she couldn't catch her breath. "What did—"

"Hey, ladies." A couple of men stood right behind Uzuri. Looming over her.

She squeaked and cringed. Gripping the table hard, she forced herself to sit still. To breathe. *One breath. Two. Relax, stupid.*

The men were smiling, not attacking. A little drunk and a lot happy, they were simply two rednecks on the prowl. One hitched his pants up. "Y'all sound like you're having fun. Want some company?"

Andrea shook her head. "No, sorry. This is a girls only night."

The bearded guy with the torn-off sleeves whined, "Aw, c'mon. We're nice—"

"Don't waste your time with us. None of us can have sex tonight." Sally smiled sweetly and held up her Kahlua and Irish cream-laden drink. "This is as close as we're going to get to a *screaming orgasm* for a day or two."

The bearded guy shut his mouth with an audible snap, and both men backed away.

Andrea let out a hysterical whoop.

Uzuri gasped for breath. Omigod, she might die from laughing. "The looks on their faces..."

"Here, m'dear, have a nice orgasm." Kari tapped her glass against Sally's, and they both downed a good portion of their drinks.

Jessica had been laughing so hard her voice came out hoarse. "But what did you mean about no sex?"

Sally tilted her head. "The instructions said no sex right after a wax job. Didn't you read the brochure Andrea gave us?"

"Uh, no. I didn't think there was anything to learn. Hair gets ripped off painfully and... No sex, really?" Jessica bit her lip. "That might be awkward to explain."

Uzuri patted her hand. "Master Z probably...um..." She couldn't tactfully say that Master Z was so experienced with women, he probably already knew. *Change subject immediately.* "What did Master Z say when you told him about getting waxed as a way to support your friend?"

"Oooh, that jerk. He said if I was willing to undergo that much pain for a friend, he'd have to see what I would take for my beloved Dom. And that Master Sam probably had some interesting toys to borrow." Jessica scowled. "Between worrying about the waxing and what evil things Z might come up with, I didn't get any sleep last night."

"The thought of Master Z dreaming up creative ways to inflict pain is utterly terrifying." Kari took a large chug of her drink and turned to Uzuri. "What did you think of the waxing?"

"Actually... It hurt, but wasn't as bad as I'd anticipated." And when Maria had started ripping out hair on her lower folds, Uzuri'd gotten almost floaty. "But"—she lowered her voice—"I don't think anyone has looked at my hoo-ha so closely since...ever, and that last position, where she wanted me with my butt up and holding my cheeks open, was purely humiliating."

"Hey, mine didn't ask for that pose," Jessica said. "She kept me on my back and made me hold my legs up over my head."

"Yeah, legs up." Sally nodded in agreement.

"Oh, I had the ass upside, too!" Andrea hooted. "It was like anal sex without the grand finale!"

"*Shhh.*" Blessed Mother, everyone in the place had heard Andrea's loud comment. "Kari, take her alcohol away from her!"

But Jessica and Kari were laughing so hard they were worthless.

Sally clung to Uzuri, her shoulders shaking.

Giggling, Uzuri clung back.

Then her eyes filled unexpectedly...because she was surrounded by friends and laughter. When she'd moved to Tampa, leaving her beloved Cincinnati and everyone she'd known, she'd felt her life was over. Instead, her world had opened up in wonderful and unexpected ways, including gaining a slew of crazy friends who knew her more intimately than anyone had before.

A hand covered hers. Sally's brown eyes were concerned. "Okay, girlfriend?"

Uzuri grinned. "Oh, yes. Just having one of those 'I love you all' moments."

The rest heard her and expressions turned soft.

"I feel you, *chica*. Who else would have shared something like this?" Andrea lifted her glass up. "To my Shadowkittens."

Uzuri blinked hard, clinked her glass against the rest, downed her drink, and joined in the cheering.

Sally leaned back. "So, was that tweezing stuff at the end horrible or what?"

Uzuri grinned. Trust Sally to keep them from getting too mushy.

"What tweezing?" Jessica frowned. "I didn't have anything plucked."

"Oh. My. God. No one else did?" Sally looked indignant. "Mine pulled out the strays that way. I'm used to being looked at, not gone over with a magnifying glass...or tweezers! It was like something Master Sam would do just to hear a subbie squeak."

"I'm glad mine didn't do that. Ewww." Kari shifted in her chair, obviously looking for a more comfortable position. "What was the most embarrassing part for you, Andrea?"

"I wasn't all that embarrassed." After a second, she turned red.

"Well, not until I turned over, and I'd sweated so hard that the paper was stuck to my ass. *Mierda*."

"Oh, me, too. The same," Jessica said.

Sally swirled her drink. "Still, it wasn't that bad. I've never felt so smooth—like I've been exfoliated or something. If the hair grows back as slow and fine as I've heard, I'll probably switch to doing it this way. My demon Doms will like the smoothness."

"Demon Dom. There's a perfect label for any Master." Andrea gave Sally a pitying look. "I still can't believe you fell for *two*."

"Me, neither." Uzuri couldn't handle one Dom, and Sally'd married two. She frowned at Sally. "When you started to get all crazy-pants, someone should have given you some Prozac and counseling or something. Letting you get involved with two *Masters*? I totally failed you as a BFF."

"You totally didn't. Besides, I always did like two men at once..." Sally waggled her eyebrows. "You should try it sometime."

"No way, no how, not ever, never." She couldn't even manage one Dom sometimes, especially if he was taller than oh, five-ten or so.

Sally straightened, her gaze on something across the room. "Uh...Andrea, are you still planning to murder Master Cullen?"

Uzuri turned to look.

Like a steamroller in action, Andrea's fiancé was crossing the room. The powerfully built Dom had a rough face of blunt angles, shaggy brown hair, and green eyes. Getting him in good clothing didn't happen often, but the Dom totally rocked jeans and T-shirts.

He spotted them and his attention locked on his bride-to-be. Once beside her, he tangled his fingers in her hair and tugged her head back. The kiss he laid on her was long and lascivious, totally inappropriate to being in public, and so sexy that the temperature in the room skyrocketed.

Uzuri let out a silent sigh of envy.

Master Cullen caressed Andrea's cheek. His voice held a slight

Irish list as he asked, "So, love, are all your tender bits naked now?"

Her brows drew together. "*Sí*, you...you..." She burst out laughing again. "It hurt like hell, but I am bare as a baby's bottom." Her voice was still loud.

His eyes narrowed before he glanced at the empty Screaming Orgasm pitchers on the table. "You're toasted, pet."

She frowned at him. "No, *mi Señor*, they did not toast anything. They ripped all the hairs out of my—"

Roaring with laughter, he put his hand over her mouth. "I mean you're drunk, love. Time to take you home." He glanced at the rest of them. "I appreciate you joining her today. It's good she has friends to back her up."

Sally waved her glass in the air. "That's us, always available for kidnappings, bachelorette parties, counseling, and wax torture."

He snorted. "She's not the only one who's toasted. Do you all have a way home?"

"We're good. Dan is picking up me and Kari, and Vance is coming for Sally and Uzuri." Jessica smiled. "Take your woman home and pamper her a little. She suffered for you today."

Cullen grinned. "I'm sure I'll hear about it." His face softened, and he brushed his hand down Andrea's loose hair. "My sweet Amazon."

The love in his expression pierced through Uzuri so hard she felt as if something had cracked open deep inside. Tears filled her eyes, and she set a hand on her aching chest.

Cullen lifted his fiancée to her feet and kept her upright with an arm around her waist. Andrea chattered away. Her hands flew as she described the waxing, and his booming laugh filled the room. Steering her toward the door, he guarded her from any bumps. Andrea didn't even notice.

Uzuri did.

What would it be like to have a man to lean on?

Her mama had been the only person Uzuri had ever counted

on for support. And then for a few years, she'd been the one to support her mama. Before Mama had died.

Uzuri looked around the table. All her friends had Doms who loved, helped, and protected them. What would that feel like?

A longing sparked to life deep in her chest, and even a big gulp of her sweet, potent drink couldn't drown it out.

CHAPTER THREE

For Friday night at the Shadowlands BDSM club, Uzuri had dressed in all white—a white halter top, frothy petticoats that barely covered her ass, and white fishnet thigh-high stockings. Ben, the security guard had actually approved of her white lacy stilettos, and she'd gotten to leave them on rather than going barefoot.

She'd done her hair in a braided Grecian crown that circled her head and created what she liked to think of as a halo around her head. When she'd told Holt that this was her angelic look, her friend had laughed his fool head off. The dumbass Dom. What did he know, anyway?

Then again, he might still be grumpy about her signing him up for all those Viagra and male enhancement products. She grinned.

Time to start her barmaiding shift. As she headed toward the bar, she danced a few steps to "Mirrors" by Natalia Kills and checked out each roped-off scene area as she went past. One had a Domme flogging her male submissive; the next was a sadist caning his favorite masochist. Saxon had claimed the spanking bench. He had huge hands, and the woman strapped to the bench yelped with every smack.

A few people had gathered around the next area, and Uzuri stopped to see what had them so fascinated.

Oh. The Drago cousins were co-topping. Unable to resist, Uzuri stopped to watch. Who wouldn't?

With the brunette submissive named Alyssa tied to a bondage table, Alastair was dripping hot wax over her bare breasts while Max was using various vibrators on her pussy.

Two Doms at once. *"You should try it sometime."* Oooh, Sally should never have suggested the idea. Uzuri had dreamed about the Drago cousins last night and woke up terrified.

Although watching this scene was a little anxiety inducing, it was also hot. Okay, seriously hot. Maybe because Master Alastair was one of the Doms. Like Master Marcus who was a lawyer, Alastair dressed fine. Polished and stylish. He'd tossed his jacket and tie over a chair and wore a button-down white shirt with the sleeves rolled up. His skin was a few shades darker than Uzuri's, and he was...gorgeous.

And, truly, Alastair's rapport with his cousin was refreshing to watch. The two made an amazing team.

"I thought you didn't like Master Alastair." Sally appeared and slid an arm around Uzuri's waist. "Although if that's true, I'd have to question your taste. Every unattached submissive in the place adores him."

"Of course they do. Just look at him." Talk about male perfection. A couple of inches or so over six feet, he was all lean, rippling muscles and chiseled features. Although in the dark clubroom, his eyes matched his skin, in daylight, his eyes were an uncanny and beautiful hazel with the slightest Oriental tilt.

His deep, British-accented baritone was simply icing on the cake.

"I like the way he wears his hair now," Sally noted.

"Me, too." A while back, he'd stopped shaving his scalp, and now kept his hair barely long enough to show some crisp curl. A perfectly sculpted short beard framed his sensuous lips and jawline.

If only he were shorter...like well under six feet. She couldn't possibly be with a man who would tower over her.

"Did you two ever make up?" Sally glanced at her. "I mean, like, a year or so ago, you yelled at him that he was hung up on race issues. I'd never heard you yell at anyone before."

"You're right; I was rude. And...it wasn't true, either." As guilt gouged her conscience, Uzuri stared down at her shoes. "He was amazing, and I wanted to scene with him—even though he's awfully tall—but when I was restrained, he bent over me, and I got scared, and I kept panicking, and I couldn't explain it, and he couldn't figure out why since I was the one who'd wanted the scene."

"Oh, wow." Sally frowned. "But then..."

"He left town afterward, for months. When he returned and wanted to see if we could figure out why I panicked, I went off on him." She should have apologized. However, every time she'd thought about it, she'd chickened out. What if he got mad at her?

"Oooh. You yelled at a Dom. In public. And accused him of something that wasn't true?" Sally shook her head. "And now, he's a *Master*."

"I know." Masters in the Shadowlands were allowed to do almost anything they wanted. Uzuri brightened. "At least, I'm not a trainee any longer."

"Mmmhmm." Sally snickered. "Can I watch when you tell Master Z he's not...really...in charge of you."

Oh, Lord. Master Z considered all the submissives to be under his charge—especially the trainees—no matter how long ago they'd left the program. "You're a brat, you know that?"

Sally smirked. "So Galen and Vance keep telling me." Her gaze returned to the scene. "Wow."

Max and Alastair had upped the intensity. A sliver of envy ran through Uzuri. What would it be like to be at the mercy of two very experienced, very careful Doms?

Smiling slightly, Alastair splattered hot wax over the submissive's breasts as his cousin teased her pussy. Alyssa climaxed —again.

"God, they're good." Sally fanned herself. "So...back to my question. Did you ever apologize to Alastair?"

"No. I stay out of his path." Ever since that night, she'd avoided both him and his cousin, Max.

Having arrived with glowing endorsements from a Seattle club, Max had been a Shadowlands member for a few months now. Whether co-topping with Alastair or alone, he'd proven to be a talented and powerful Dominant. No one was surprised when Master Z recommended him for the Master title. The club had voted last week. Uzuri had voted for him—no doubt most of the members had, too.

Uzuri watched him deliberately teasing Alyssa. As with Alastair, if Max were an average size man, she'd have been interested.

He wasn't anywhere close to average.

In fact, in black jeans, boots, heavy black leather belt, and a tight black T-shirt, Max was more intimidating than anyone else in the room. His biceps looked like boulders, and the way the cotton stretched over his muscular chest was scarily mesmerizing.

He'd pulled his shoulder-length brown hair back in a leather tie, which emphasized his square jaw and high cheekbones. His eyes were an intense blue in his tanned face, his features strikingly chiseled. Like Holt and Alastair, he was model gorgeous. The difference between them was that Max's expression tended toward the menacing...until he smiled.

His smile could probably coax a *nun* into messing around behind the altar.

"Well, I think you should woman up and apologize and then do a scene with both Doms. Hey, you survived wax on your pussy hair. Wax dripped on your breasts by the tall, dark, and deadly

Drago Doms would make your whole month, right?" Sally shoulder-bumped her and headed back to her own Masters.

Wax on her breasts? With Alastair standing over her? And Max?

Arms around her waist, she watched Max drive Alyssa back to the edge of climax. Every time he eased off, his cousin would pour wax on the submissive's breasts, each time from a lower height thus increasing the heat. One Dom handed out pain, the other pleasure. Covered in sweat, Alyssa was shaking and begging.

What would it be like to look up into Alastair's odd-colored hazel eyes and beg? To know that he held all the control. To be the center of all that attention, not only from him but also from his equally powerful cousin?

As Uzuri actually dampened, she backed up a step and another...and bumped into someone. Firm hands gripped her arms, steadied her, and turned her.

She looked up into the silver-gray eyes of Master Z, owner of the Shadowlands.

"Easy, little one." His smooth, low voice soothed her fears, calming her.

"Excuse me, Sir," she said.

"There is nothing to excuse." He gave her a faint smile, his hand still on her shoulder. "What do you think of the scene?"

"The scene?" Heat still simmered inside her along with the desire to be the one they watched so closely and drove so crazy. But she also saw how they'd tower over her in a terrifying way. She averted her gaze. "Um. It's interesting, and wax play is nice, but... um, three-ways aren't my thing."

Master Z's eyes narrowed, turning even more unreadable. "I see," he said, his voice soft.

He saw too much was all she could think. Her attempt to edge away was defeated by his hand on her shoulder. "I better get moving. My shift starts now."

"Of course." He released her.

21

Hurrying away, she glanced over her shoulder. He'd resumed watching the scene with a thoughtful expression.

With a nicely sated submissive in his lap, Alastair Drago watched his cousin clean the bondage table and pack their toy bags.

Finished, Max stretched. "I'm ready for a drink."

Alastair deliberated. The long day at the clinic had left him knackered, and he'd considered not coming to the Shadowlands. However, the concentration needed for this scene, even without having sex, had blown his stress away like a gust of fresh air. A drink would be the perfect finish. He looked down at the woman in his lap. "How about you, love?"

"No, thank you, Sir. With your permission, I'll join my friends." Alyssa rose.

As Alastair followed suit, he gave her an evaluating glance. Steady on her feet, color good, muscles relaxed. "All right."

Max, having made the same automatic appraisal, nodded his concurrence.

Alyssa beamed at Max. "Thank you for the scene, Sir." She turned to Alastair. "Thank you, Master Alastair."

"Our pleasure, love." As she strolled away, Alastair shook his head. Beautiful woman, but not one he wanted in his life. If Z hadn't requested they do a scene with her, it wouldn't have happened.

As always, Max had followed his thoughts. "Hopefully, we've done our duty and can pick our own subbie next time."

To be perverse, Alastair commented, "She was nicely submissive."

"Too fucking submissive. No fire. No sense of humor." Max tilted his head. "An OCD, rules-driven Master would be delighted with her. Not me."

Max was a police detective, but the Dom didn't want

unthinking obedience. Alastair pulled on his suit jacket, pocketed his tie, and picked up his toy bag. "I believe you're right."

"Anyway, I choose the next submissive," Max decreed.

"It's your turn," Alastair said amiably. He'd enjoyed the scene with Alyssa more than Max had. As Dominants and cousins, he and Max enjoyed topping together, but their styles didn't match completely. Finding someone whose personality melded well with theirs had proven tricky.

In their last year at university, they'd lived with and shared a submissive. Alastair had not found any relationship as fulfilling since. When Max'd joined the Shadowlands, they'd returned to co-topping, but hadn't discussed anything more serious. Perhaps the time had come.

Max stopped to talk with a friend, then Alastair was halted as well. This late in the evening, many members remained simply to socialize. Several newer Doms had questions about the bondage demonstration he and Max'd done the previous week.

When they finally reached the bar, Cullen, who was tending bar, brought a bottle of Fat Tire ale for Max and a Tanqueray and tonic for Alastair. The Dom never forgot a member's favorite drink. Cullen grinned at Alastair. "Gotta say it was a pleasure listening to Alyssa moaning and screaming."

"Indeed." Z was seated on a nearby barstool. "Thank you for topping her. You did well."

"Good to hear. However"—Max set his jaw and made their position clear—"we're not interested in more scenes with her. We're not looking for permanent relationships for that matter."

Alastair stiffened. That had been true in his youth. However, he would now be pleased to find a woman for more than an evening's recreation. It was time.

Yes, he and Max needed to discuss their goals...soon.

Z tilted his head. "I agree that Alyssa isn't a good choice for either of you."

"Then why did you ask us to top her?" Alastair asked.

"With her desperation to be dominated, she was latching onto anyone with no thought whatsoever. Being topped by disinterested Doms like you gives her a chance to regain her equilibrium. Once she's able to make reasoned decisions, I'll introduce her to appropriate choices."

"You know, Z, you're a sneaky bastard." Max voiced what Alastair was thinking.

"Sneaky, perhaps; however, my mother insists she was wedded before I came along." Z's lips quirked.

"I'd dare anyone to suggest otherwise." Cullen slid a beer down the bar to a waiting Dom. "Madeline Grayson could give Mistress Anne lessons in intimidation."

"She would be pleased you think so." Z stood and rested a hand on Max's shoulder. "Since you're here, I have an announcement to make."

Knowing what was coming, Alastair grinned.

"If I might have your attention." Z's raised voice reached those in the bar area without ranging far enough to disturb the scene areas. "Last week, the members voted on a proposed new Master, and the tally was overwhelmingly in favor. Please congratulate Maximillian, our newest Master of the Shadowlands."

"What the fuck..." Max straightened in shock.

Cullen's laugh boomed out. "Congratulations, Max-i-millian." He drew out the name, thickening his faint Irish accent.

"Jesus." Max growled loud enough for everyone to hear. "It's *Max*. The next person, Dom or sub, who calls me Maximillian, will get ass-whipped."

Laughter broke out around the bar as a chorus of congratulations rose. Drinks lifted in toasts.

Alastair slapped his cousin's arm in congratulation before giving way to the well-wishers. There would be a lot. Despite the cop's sternness, he was well liked.

Waiting patiently, Alastair enjoyed his drink and studied the unattached women in the submissive's sitting area. Two of them were quite fit, but barely twenty-one. In his mid-thirties, he preferred to play with women twenty-five and over. There were two male subs—not his interest—and a masochistic bottom who needed more pain than he was willing to provide.

One pleasingly curvy brunette was unfortunately all take and no give.

The blonde at the far end wanted only non-painful, sensuous play. Alastair wasn't a sadist, but he enjoyed dealing out erotic pain, which was why he'd had fun with Alyssa. He'd driven her right to the edge. Watching her take it, pushing her, seeing her respond had given him back fully as much as she'd taken. The scene had wiped out any thought beyond what was happening right then and there.

It had been a bloody bad day. His jaw tightened. His last patient appointment had been an eight-year-old girl with wide brown eyes, a chuckling laugh—and leukemia. Acute lymphocytic leukemia, dammit. The tests had confirmed his suspicions. Her mother, a woman with no husband to help, had cried.

Being a pediatrician could fray a man's soul.

"You falling asleep there, cuz?" Max's rough voice broke into his thoughts.

Alastair saw the crowd had dispersed.

When Max stepped closer, Alastair could see concern in the sharp blue eyes.

"I'm—"

"Hey, Sirs." The submissive who stopped in front of them was a symphony of color and life, from her bountiful flesh, to the flower and vine tattoos, to her dancing eyes and streaked hair.

Alastair smiled down at her. "Rainie, how are you this evening?"

"Very well, thank you, Sir." She smiled and held out a stack of pictures. "An animal shelter in Citrus Park went belly-up from lack of funding, and the vet clinics in the area are trying to get the animals adopted. Why don't you look these over, and I'll be back to see which one you want."

Smoothly, she slid several photos into Max's hand and moved away before they could protest. Max stared after her and chuckled. "That one's got spirit to spare. Why couldn't she be unattached?"

"Because her Dom is a veterinarian, and she gets to play with puppies all day." Alastair frowned at the pictures. "Do we want a pet?"

His cousin's easy laugh was a pleasure to hear. For the first months after Max's move from Seattle, his laugh had been rare, his mood negative. He was finally back to his normal gregarious self.

Max flipped through the pictures. "A cat might be nice, but..." His voice trailed off.

"What?"

Max held up a photo of a medium-sized, shorthaired dog with floppy ears. Brown covered its head, shoulders, and flanks. Everywhere else was speckled. A German shorthaired pointer.

The pang of loss hurt Alastair's heart. "Looks like old Jeeves, doesn't he?"

"Yeah." Max stared for a second before reading the description. "Two years old. Owner was in his eighties and died."

"A dog would require more time than a cat," Alastair pointed out.

"True."

Twenty years ago, the ranch dog, Jeeves, had slept in Max and Alastair's bedroom and accompanied the boys everywhere. In the cold Colorado lakes, the dog had been the first to jump into the water and the last to come out. He'd led the way on trail hikes into the Rockies, protecting the two lads he'd considered his charges. Each fall, when Alastair had returned to his mother in London, he'd missed Jeeves almost as much as Max.

Heart hurting, Alastair stared at the forlorn eyes in the photo.

"Between us, we could give him enough exercise," Max said.

Most people seeing Max's grim features thought he was the sadist and Alastair the soft touch. Wasn't it odd how appearances could deceive? "This dog isn't Jeeves, Max."

"I know. But...you want to leave him in jail?"

Bloody softies, they were. "Of course not. Let's see what we need to do to free him and take him home." Alastair looked for Rainie.

She was talking to Uzuri, a curvy, petite, mixed race submissive whom he'd scened with a year ago when home from the South Sudan. In the scene, she'd panicked repeatedly, and he'd realized she had underlying issues. The challenge of helping her with them interested him, but she'd turned him down.

He'd asked her if she preferred white men, before recalling she'd initiated their first scene. In turn, she'd loudly accused him of liking her solely for her color. Quite insulting. Although he did generally select submissives of color for one-time scenes, for long-term relationships, he chose by personality, attractiveness, compassion, intelligence, and honesty. He dated all colors and ethnicities.

However, Uzuri had known he was interested in helping her for her own sake. Her behavior when turning him down was much like a cornered child. Nevertheless, she was an adult. Rather than apologizing, she avoided him like the plague.

In the beginning, she'd intrigued him. Everyone had problems; that hadn't been his concern. But, since she apparently had no intention of working through her issues, he'd written her off.

Max followed his gaze. "Cute outfit. Uzuri, right?"

"Correct." He remembered Max had met her at Nolan and Beth's party last September. "She's the type of woman you like." Dark, curvy, petite, fun. "No interest?"

"As you Brits would say, she's not my cup of tea. I'm guessing she's high maintenance, and I realized at the party she comes with a heavy load of baggage." His lips twisted cynically. "Been there, done that."

Max's marriage was long past. This bitterness had to be from something recent. Alastair frowned. "Are you going to tell me what happened in Seattle?"

"Yeah, I suppose. Maybe after some alcohol. Make that a lot of alcohol."

Interesting. "All right, then." He'd pick up a six-pack of his cousin's favorite Colorado brew. "Next weekend."

"Stubborn Brit," Max muttered and frowned.

Alastair followed his gaze to the submissive area where Rainie was trying her best to get Uzuri to take a dog or cat.

Uzuri felt cornered. When volunteering at the vet clinic, she'd seen Rainie in action. Although her BFF was the sweetest person in the world, when trying to place an animal, she turned into a bulldozer and would flatten any resistance.

"How about this one?" Rainie handed over a picture. "She's a sweet terrier mix."

Uzuri shook her head. Never, ever would she put another animal in harm's way. *Ever.* Jarvis was out of prison. Sure, he worked in Cincinnati and hopefully had forgotten her, but she couldn't take that chance. If he came here for revenge, he would target pets, too.

Her throat closed. In Cincinnati, she'd come home, but her happy, yipping, adorable dachshund hadn't greeted her at the door. She'd finally found little Hugo trembling behind her couch. Brown fur matted with blood, he'd cowered away from her. He'd whimpered when she touched his ribs.

Rainie's voice grew more coaxing. "C'mon, girlfriend, you have a nice little backyard and..."

Hugo had loved her backyard in Cincinnati. As if going into battle, he'd charge out the door, ears flying, tail high. Jarvis had liked Hugo. He'd said so. Although he'd threatened *her*, she hadn't believed he'd hurt a lovable, little dog.

He had.

Fighting guilt, she swallowed painfully. Hugo had recovered... although his innocent trust in humans had been destroyed. Her cousin in Minnesota had been delighted to take him, love him, and pamper him. Hugo was safe.

And Uzuri had cried herself to sleep every night for months. Eventually, she'd stopped listening for little paws, stopped expecting to be greeted at the door, stopped saving a bite of meat from her meals. But her heart still hurt.

Rainie held up a picture of a big-eyed poodle. "How about this—"

"No." As Uzuri fought against tears, her voice rose. "I won't take a dog or cat." When Rainie opened her mouth to argue, Uzuri couldn't bear it. "I don't *like* animals. At all."

"But you—"

"*No.* I hate pets. I hate dogs. They shed and lick and...and ruin my clothes." She shoved the pictures into Rainie's hands.

When Rainie took a step back, her shocked expression was like a slap in the face.

Uzuri held her hand out and whispered, "I-I'm *sorry.*" Her voice broke; her throat closed. Chest hurting, she looked away.

At the bar, Alastair was watching. His cousin stood beside him, his blue eyes sharp.

Max's glance at Alastair was cynical and easy to read—he hadn't expected anything different from her. It was insulting. Hurtful.

Choking back tears, she spun and headed in the other direction. Behind her came Alastair's deep resonant voice. "Rainie, if you have a moment, can you tell us something about this dog?"

An hour later, Uzuri's time as a barmaid was ending. With a list of drink orders and empty glasses on her tray, she wove her way through the sitting areas.

Earlier, she'd found Rainie and apologized. Her softhearted friend had forgiven her, and thank heavens, had promised not to push pet adoptions again. Uzuri sighed. Someday, she'd give Rainie an explanation for the outburst.

"Hey, girl." A blond man motioned her over. Sprawled in a leather chair, he was dressed in a black T-shirt with black jeans tucked into military boots. His gaze ran over her and lingered on her breasts. He licked his lips.

Be polite, she told herself. Master Z said submissives didn't have to like every Dom, but politeness was required. "May I get you something to drink, Sir?"

"I have a drink." When he leaned forward, she took an involuntary step back. "I like race-play. You into that at all?"

She didn't roll her eyes, but it was close. "You mean you want to treat me like dirt and call me names, like nigger bitch, coon cum slave, and black slut?"

"Oh, yeah." His ruddy color heightened, and his breathing quickened. "That's it exactly. I can—"

"No." She forced herself not to retreat, kept her spine straight, and pushed assurance into her trembling voice. "I suffer too much of that kind of behavior in day-to-day life, and it's sure not my fetish. Sir." She wanted to say, *go find a white girl to degrade*, but she had a lot of white friends, and some had already suffered from assholes like this. Sisters—no matter the color—needed to stand together.

His eyes turned mean. "You—" But he bit it back and waved her off.

Submissives weren't the only ones who had to be polite.

She walked away, head tall, wishing she could throw her tray at him. But he wasn't the first Dom who'd wanted race-play. It was simply another fetish, after all. The guy might well find a black submissive who was into that, just as some women enjoyed being called slut and whore. Consent was everything.

Still, it left her feeling icky and shaky inside.

When she reached the long oval bar in the center of the club-room, she set her serving tray on the glossy, mahogany bar top.

Rough-looking Master Nolan and his redheaded wife, Beth, were dispensing drinks, which meant Master Cullen was probably doing a scene with Andrea.

"I'll be right there, Zuri." Beth called from farther down the bar.

Zuri, hmm? Beth's youngest had shortened Uzuri to Zuri—and somehow the name was spreading through her friends. She was getting fond of the way it sounded.

Beth hurried up and took her tray. "Wow, I love your outfit. Only you could make white and cute look perfect in a BDSM club."

"Thank you." The gratifying compliment came from a woman who owned the nicest fetwear in the club. Tonight, the rich blue corset Beth wore made the most of her slender figure and brought out the color of her eyes. *Excellent attire.*

Beth took the drink orders and smiled. "I'm so glad Master Z went back to using our own members for the waitresses. It was weird having outsiders in the club."

"It was." Uzuri wrinkled her nose. When the trainee program ended, Master Z had tried hiring waitresses. The way they'd stared had been off-putting. "It's nice to get a cut in the membership dues, too."

"Clever Master Z. No wonder there are plenty of volunteers." Beth headed off to fill the orders.

Since Uzuri had been the last trainee left, Master Z told her she didn't have to pay, since 'no dues' had been part of the trainee deal. However, she didn't feel right taking and giving nothing back. Besides, she'd never been a typical trainee. All the rest had wanted to find permanent Doms. She'd only wanted a safe place to explore submission, gain some experience with men, and work through her fears.

In the initial interview, she'd expected Master Z to toss her out. Instead, he'd said the trainee program was flexible enough to accommodate her. But when he'd wanted to discuss *why* she was afraid, she'd flat out refused and told him her credo: *"My life started here, and I have no past."*

She still couldn't believe she'd told Master Z *no*.

He'd been so kind. He'd let her join with the proviso that if she didn't work through her problems, she'd tell the Masters about her past, let them help, and pay a penalty for stalling.

Hopefully, he'd forgotten. After all, she wasn't a trainee any longer.

And that was good—it was.

She shook her head. At one time, she'd dreamed of a career in fashion and a gorgeous husband—a Dom—who would adore her and care for her, just as she'd adore and care for him.

After Jarvis, her longing for that dream husband had frayed into nonexistence.

Although one bad garment on a rack didn't mean the entire designer line was off, and one crazy stalker didn't mean all males were evil, she wasn't willing to chance the risks. Being betrayed again was one thing, but having those she loved hurt? Never again.

"Here are the beers. And that's water for you because I know you forget to take care of yourself." Beth returned with a half-loaded tray. She waved at Master Nolan who was pouring rum in a glass. "He's handling the mixed drinks for you."

"Thank you." Gratefully, Uzuri drank and realized she'd been thirsty. "How are Grant and Connor doing these days?"

"They're great." The mention of her two soon-to-be-adopted youngsters brought a smile to Beth's face. "Connor already has his alphabet down; he'll be able to read before he gets out of kindergarten."

Uzuri smiled. "They're amazing. Do you need a babysitter this weekend? I could use some little boy time."

Bottle in hand, Master Nolan looked over. "You free Sunday afternoon from two to five? We need to do something without the boys."

"You bet, Sir. I'm your girl."

"All *right*." Beth grinned at Uzuri and her Master. "Shopping it is!" She danced a little in place, then hurried over to get a drink order from a Dom at the end of the bar.

"You do have to ask for something in return, pet. That's how it works." A corner of Master Nolan's mouth lifted in his version of a smile. Even having seen how sweet he was with the children, the Dom still scared her a bit. After setting the rum and Coke on her tray, he nodded at someone behind her.

Uzuri turned to see Master Z and Alastair's cousin, Max.

With a frown, Max lifted his chin at Nolan in a guy greeting and moved away.

"Z." Nolan picked up the vodka. "Been a while since you spent an entire evening down here. Are you escaping your miniature Domme?"

Uzuri giggled. Master Z's daughter was around seven months now—and adorably demanding.

"In a way. After a day with my in-laws, she and Jessica returned with a carload of presents. Every toy emits ear-splitting noises." The most powerful Dom in the Shadowlands—probably in the world—shook his head ruefully. "I hadn't realized my mother-in-law hated me that much."

Nolan's harsh laugh burst out. "So you escaped down here?"

"Precisely." Master Z set his hand on Uzuri's shoulder, warm and very firm. "I need to steal your barmaid, Nolan. Austin will fill in for the remainder of her shift."

Uzuri froze. "You want to talk to me?" *Oh no.*

He lifted an eyebrow in reproof.

What was *wrong* with her? She quickly reiterated, "You wish to talk to me, *Sir*?"

"Much better. Yes, I do need to speak with you."

When Uzuri didn't move, Master Z slid his hand behind her back and directed her straight toward his sanctum—although he called it his office. He didn't speak as they walked, and her glances up at his grave face offered no insight.

As the heavy wooden door swung shut behind them, the music and sounds of whips and floggers and groans faded to a low murmur. He pointed to the black leather couch and chairs in the center of the room. "Take a seat, please."

Nervously, she settled into a corner of the couch. Her strappy shoes sank so deep into the dark brown carpet that the strands brushed her toes.

At his antique desk on the far side of the room, Master Z flipped through some papers. Was that her file?

Pretending to study the prints of Titian's Italian Renaissance nudes that decorated the cream-colored walls, she watched him. He never got less intimidating, although she wasn't sure why. He was just a man, after all. Tall, leanly muscular, somewhere in his forties. Always in black. Like Alastair, he obviously shopped in Europe and favored impeccably tailored shirts and pants. Over the last couple of years, the silver in the black hair over his temples had widened. She'd blame Jessica, but in all reality, the bubbly blonde—and their new baby—probably kept him young.

Silently, he crossed the room and rested a hip against the arm of the couch.

When he crossed his arms over his chest, worry sent a cool breeze up her spine as if her back zipper had torn loose. Keeping a calm expression on her face, she gave him her attention. "Is there a problem, Sir?"

His lips curved slightly. "Is there a reason you want to hide your reactions from me?"

The breeze turned into a gale-force blast of anxiety. "Of course not, Sir. Am I in trouble, Sir?"

"No, you're not in trouble. But...your time is up, kitten. You've been here over two years. We agreed when you joined that if you didn't work through your problems, the Masters would step in."

"B-b-but—"

The slight tilt of his head invited her to protest further...at her peril. Because he was correct; she hadn't worked through anything. She bowed her head. "Yes, Sir."

His voice gentled. "For the Masters to help you overcome your wariness of men, what will have to occur first?"

Her breath caught in her throat. Oh, she knew the answer—and had avoided it. "I'll have to tell them what happened."

"I'm afraid so, little one. I told you there would be a penalty for the delay, did I not?"

Oh, no. Why did he have to have a good memory? At forty, shouldn't he be getting a little senile or something?

Gaze on her, he waited until she nodded her reluctant agreement.

"You have a choice. Either discuss everything with me now. Or —and this is your penalty—you can find a male Shadowlands Master and tell him."

Male? She couldn't use Mistress Anne or Olivia or Cat? "But...why?"

"You tell me."

She dropped her gaze, knowing the answer. "Because I need to be able to tell any Dom I play with what happened, and I play with male Doms, so that's who I need to talk with."

"Very good." Sympathy warmed his gray eyes. "The first time is the hardest, then it will grow easier. In the future, I expect you to confide in your play partners."

This evening was getting worse and worse. "Yes, Sir. So...all the Masters will know?"

"I'm sorry, little one, but yes. To help you, they have to know what caused the problem."

No way. She gritted her teeth. *I'm out of here.*

Only this was her...her home in a way. She didn't want to leave.

The couch cushion compressed as he sat down beside her. He took her hand in his firm grip. "Uzuri, we are worried about you. You aren't sleeping well. You're tense."

The concern in his deep voice made her eyes burn with tears.

"Whatever is wrong must be addressed before it becomes worse. If you prefer, you may see a counselor."

When she'd gone to one in Cincinnati, the therapy had helped everything except...this fear. She hadn't wanted to admit it, but Master Z was right; it was getting worse. And if she wanted help, the Masters would need to know why. They were all about avoiding triggers and traumas while helping with problems. "Here. I want to deal with it here."

"All right. Who do you want to talk with?"

Did he think she'd choose him? *No, no, no, not a chance.* There were rumors he could read minds, and even if he couldn't, he was a psychologist. He'd want to talk everything to death like the counselor she'd seen. She blurted out, "Not you."

To her relief, he didn't appear insulted. If anything, he looked amused. "Then?"

Holt. She could go dump all this on Holt. Of course, as more of a friend than a lover, Holt might not be...exactly...what Master Z would consider a "play partner". Perhaps it would be best not to mention her choice. "I'll...I'll find someone."

He considered her for a long moment. "All right. Tonight, Uzuri. No delays."

"Yes, Sir."

CHAPTER FOUR

A fter doing one full circuit of the club without finding Holt, Uzuri started to worry. Where was he? Earlier, he'd been dungeon monitoring in the main room. Although his time would be over, he wouldn't leave without doing a scene. Maybe he'd taken someone to the upstairs rooms? She scowled. Although the private rooms had tiny windows, she sure didn't want to go and peer into each room to find him.

Instead, she walked out to the foyer. "Hey, Ben."

The huge security guard looked up from a professional photography magazine and frowned. "Are you leaving already? Is there a problem?"

Mistress Anne often teased him about being a worrier...and he was. "No. I'm looking for Holt. He's still here, right?"

"Nope. He had a flight to catch and left right after his dungeon monitoring time. Z would've let him skip his shift, but Holt said he might as well work."

Master Z had known Holt would be gone. She should've known being sneaky wouldn't work with him. Anxiety shot through her. If Holt wasn't here, who could she talk with?

She swallowed hard. Most of the Masters were now in permanent relationships or had children, so they'd taken to rotating their nights at the club. "Which Masters are here tonight?"

"Not many still here." He ran his finger down the attendance record. "I got Dan, Nolan, and Sam here. Cullen and Andrea are gone. So are Sally and her crew. Jake and Rainie and Saxon left a while ago. Alastair and Max are here."

That's right. Master Z had announced Max was now a Master. "That's all?"

"Looks like you got a problem." He frowned at her. "Can I help?"

The giant had a teddy-bear heart. "I'm afraid not. It's a Master Z assignment."

"Ah. Good luck, then."

"Thanks, Ben." Head down, she walked back into the club-room, barely sidestepping a Domme leading her sub with a leash attached to clothespins on his balls.

Talk to a Master. But who? Master Dan? Oh, no. Although he was a good Dom, he was also awfully strict—probably because he was also a cop.

No cops.

Nolan was manning the bar for the rest of the night, so he wasn't available.

Master Sam? No way. Although he was nice, still, he was a *sadist.*

Lordy, this wasn't good. Alastair was out. She couldn't face him after she'd yelled at him in public. She doubted he'd have forgotten.

What about his cousin Max? Her spirits brightened. Since Max was a brand new Master, and she didn't know him hardly at all, he wouldn't push her to tell him more than she wanted.

She shivered. He was as harsh looking as Nolan and Dan—and they were very strict.

Yet...the one time they'd met, he'd been kind of nice. Even better, he didn't consider her a potential play partner. In fact, at

Beth's party, he'd said, *"Best you leave my bag alone, pet. I don't think we're in the same weight class."* She might have considered his word a challenge, but his detached expression had made it clear he wasn't attracted to her.

But his lack of interest would make it easier to talk with him. There would be no male-female awkwardness. Since he didn't particularly like her, he'd undoubtedly settle for a short—really short—explanation of her past, and she could make her escape.

As she walked through the room, she spotted him and Alastair easily enough. She grimaced. Why couldn't Master Z select some short Masters?

The cousins were watching a predicament bondage scene and exchanging quiet comments. As she moved to stand in front of them, her heart started pounding painfully.

"Uzuri." The resonance in Master Alastair's subterranean voice was smoother than velvet stroking her skin. "Is there a problem?"

Ben had asked her that, too. Her expression must look horrible. "Um, not exactly." She turned her gaze to Max. *Master* Max.

Silently, he regarded her with razor-sharp eyes.

"Could I talk to you, Sir? It, um, shouldn't take longer than five minutes."

His dark eyebrows lifted and then he nodded. "Whatever you need, darlin'." To her dismay, he held his hand out to her—something he'd done the first time they'd met.

When she put her hand in his, the stunning heat of his palm made her realize her fingers were cold. And trembling.

His eyes narrowed, but he simply closed his fingers around hers. "Lead on, princess. Back in a few, cuz."

Alastair gave her a slight smile before telling Max, "I'm through for tonight, so don't hurry on my account."

"See you at home then." Max turned back to Uzuri.

She led him to a secluded conversation area near the back where she could speak quietly.

He'd barely seated himself on the black leather couch when

she started talking, "When I joined the club, Master Z agreed that—"

"Uzuri," he interrupted in an even tone and motioned toward the floor.

Oh. Right. She knelt quickly and assumed the standard position with butt on heels, backs of hands to thighs, and head bowed.

"Better, but I want your eyes on me."

She lifted her gaze.

His eyes were a breathtaking cobalt blue. When he met her gaze, the pit of her stomach did a slow slide downward. He might be new to the title of Master, but he sure wasn't new to the lifestyle. His dominance showed in every move he made, in the power of his voice...and the controlled assessment in his gaze. Oh, she might have made a bad choice.

"That's better." His voice, less deep than Alastair's, held a dark roughness. "What did Master Z agree to?"

She swallowed. *Wrap this up in a few sentences.* "He agreed I didn't have to talk about my past if I worked things out on my own, but I didn't, so I need to tell you what happened to me, and then you need to tell the other Masters."

He frowned. "Tell the others? Isn't that an invasion of your privacy?"

His displeasure on her behalf was...was heartening. "Master Z says the Masters can't help me if they don't know the cause."

"Well, hell. He has a point." He studied her a second. "Okay. Tell me."

"Years ago, I broke off dating a guy, and he turned into a stalker for months and then beat me up. So I'm a little"—*a lot*—"scared of big men." She pulled in a breath. *There. Done.* "That's all."

He stared at her, muscles tense. His square jaw had turned to stone.

She jumped to her feet. "Thank—"

"Stop. Did I say you could rise?"

She froze in place.

"A stalker, huh?" After a second, he took a slow, audible breath. He pointed to the floor, then leaned back, arms outstretched along the back of the couch.

As she sank back to her knees, she realized his posture was that of a Dom settling in to spend some time. Her mouth went dry.

"What was the name of your stalker?"

"Jarvis."

He made a *keep-going* motion with his fingers until she added, "Jarvis Kassab."

"Now give me a description."

A description of Jarvis? He was so huge and heavy that he had blocked out all the light in the room as he stood over her. His shouting had hurt her ears as his dark face had contorted with rage. Waving the knife, he'd splattered her blood on the walls.

Her hands clenched. Iron bands of fear locked around her chest until she couldn't draw a breath.

"Whoa, baby, take it easy now." Slowly, Max sat forward. With carefully controlled strength, he gripped her arms and pulled her between his legs, then set her forearms on his thighs.

Shivering, she looked down, staring at the floor, still hearing the screams, the shouting.

"Look at me, darlin'."

When she managed to look up, the sharpness of his eyes sliced through her memories, cutting the ties to the past. He rested warm hands on her shoulders. "When you kneel before me, you are under my protection. Nothing and no one will hurt you. Do you understand that?"

The absolute certainty in his growling voice wrapped around her, swaddling her in safety. "Yes, Sir," she whispered.

"Good. Now describe this asshole, Jarvis Kassab." The low anger in his voice said he was on her side.

"You believe me?"

His chuckle was a rasping sound as he stroked a callused finger along her jawline. "You're a beauty, but you don't have the skills to lie to me. I believe you."

That was almost insulting, yet she flushed. He thought her beautiful?

"A description of Kassab, please."

"Your height, but wider. Heavier," she whispered. Alastair was like a sleekly muscled racehorse. Max was a Percheron, a draft horse—more muscular and still beautiful. Jarvis was a...a rhino—heavy and ungainly from top to bottom. "Black hair, black eyes. Skin about my shade only his undertone is more taupe than umber."

"What the hell is 'tope'?"

She looked into the confused, so very male expression. "T-A-U-P-E. Taupe. It's more grayish-brown than umber's golden-brown color."

"Of course." He gave her an easy-to-read look, as in why didn't she just say that before?

And somehow, she'd relaxed. *Okay, tell him about Jarvis.* "Jarvis and I are both biracial; that's why we started talking. He understood how it is to be in the middle. Not truly white. Never black *enough*."

Oh lord, what was she saying? This Dom was white, wouldn't have a clue.

However, he nodded. "Alastair ran into that—hell, he's not only West African and white but has some Japanese tossed in. Even so, he's not the type to let it bother him. England's more civilized, anyway." When he curled his fingers around her forearm, warmth seeped into her bones. "How did you and Jarvis start dating? Were you intimate?"

Intimate. Her instinctive retreat was cut short by his unyielding grip. Oh, talking with him was such a bad decision. Master Sam didn't like to talk. Even being a sadist, he wouldn't have been this...*difficult.*

"Answer me, Uzuri."

"I went to an all-girls high school and had only started dating and wasn't impressed by guys my age." She'd been so naïve and ignorant. "I met Jarvis, and he was older and always seemed to know what he was doing. He took me to my first BDSM play parties and clubs. I was, uh..."

"A new subbie." Max nodded. "Overwhelmed by the power dynamics and unable to separate the desire for submission from what you felt for the man?"

Her eyes opened wide. "Yes." That was exactly what had happened. Before Jarvis, she'd believed herself skilled at differentiating good people from bad people. Afterward, she no longer trusted herself at all. Only maybe she did have those skills and had merely been blinded by her fascination with BDSM. The realization eased a worry inside her.

"What happened?"

"He got serious and was calling me all the time, even at work, and insisted I spend all my time with him. I realized he wasn't quite right and refused to see him. And one night, he was waiting outside my apartment, and he yelled at me and backhanded me."

The hand resting on her forearm clenched, then relaxed. Max's voice held no expression. "What did you do?"

"I grabbed my phone and started to dial 911 while I yelled at him that he wasn't anything to me. He left when my neighbors came out."

"Good for you." The open approval in Max's voice was heartening. "But he didn't accept the breakup?"

"He kept following me and calling me. I changed my number and got an unlisted one twice, and he still managed to find out what it was. He broke into my place and destroyed things, and I'd see him...everywhere I went. Across the street, on the other side of a bar, standing outside my apartment. If I visited anyone, they got harassed, too." That had been horrible, realizing she'd caused them trouble.

"How long did this go on? Did you get the police involved?"

"Almost a year, and yes. However, there wasn't much they could do. He was...careful." Her friends had pulled away—and she had, too, to keep them safe. Feeling trapped, she'd begun to despair. "I was arranging to move—to escape him—and he found out and broke into my apartment in the middle of the night and...lost it."

"Lost it how?"

She stared down, seeing how Max had trapped her between his long legs.

He cupped her chin and forced her to look at him. "Uzuri. Tell me how badly he hurt you." A Dom's command.

"He sliced me up a bit. Dislocated my shoulder. Gave me cuts and bruises." In her nightmares, she'd hear herself begging and screaming. He'd kicked her—his boots had been... Not wanting to remember more, she breathed out, trying to relax her muscles.

His gaze didn't waver. He knew.

She bit her lips and finished. "He kicked me and broke my ribs and...my jaw." The horrible cracking sound, the rush of blood, hot and liquid, the sharp, burning pain. "And he had a knife." He'd sliced across her stomach. Lightly. Pressed harder. She shook her head, pushing away the memory, the despair, the knowledge he was going to kill her. "The neighbors called the police, and they broke down the door."

"Caught him dead to rights with a deadly weapon. Good." A muscle stood out in Max's cheek. "I assume he landed in prison?"

"He did." Uzuri let the silence hang before asking, "Can I go now?"

"Did this happen in Pinellas or Hillsborough County?"

"In Cincinnati." Staring at the ground, she trembled.

"Ohio?" His gaze was a palpable warmth on her skin. "He was in prison, but you moved all the way here. Why?"

"I couldn't...settle. I kept thinking I saw him somewhere, or

I'd hear him breaking in, or I'd think I saw him standing over my bed. Even knowing he was locked up didn't help."

"Makes sense. Memories are hardwired to your senses, so even a scent or sound would bring everything back." He sounded as if he knew that from personal experience. His easy understanding relaxed a knot in her belly. "So you moved here, settled down. And found the Shadowlands?"

"I'd hoped to join the club, but when Master Z tried to discuss my past, I, um, refused." She lifted her eyes. "You know him. He wanted to help. To talk about it. I wanted the door to the past kept closed." And locked.

"Yep, that's Z." A laugh line deepened beside Max's mouth. "Sounds as if that closed door isn't working for you." The words were a statement with no judgment.

"I *was* doing better."

He gave her a look.

With a huff of resignation, she added, "For a while."

"Okay. Tell me about the problems you're having now."

"What?" She stared at him. "Master Z said I had to tell you about my past. Not more."

His hand on her shoulder tightened as if he knew she wanted to scramble to her feet. "Uzuri, you take orders from Master Z. Unfortunately, since Z stuck that 'Master' title on my name, you also take orders from me." The five-o'clock shadow couldn't disguise the stern set of his jaw.

Stubborn, stupid, damn Dom. She tried to glare at him and... couldn't.

"When we met at Nolan and Beth's party, you were afraid of me. Are you scared of all men or just big men or just pushy men?"

"Big men." Well, Holt was tall, but she wasn't afraid of him. Wasn't that odd? But he never looked at her like...like... "Big men who see me as...um, as..."

As someone to fuck.

After a second, comprehension lit his face. "Men who have a sexual interest in you?"

She nodded.

He considered her for a moment. "I've seen you play here"—his lips twitched—"with short guys. Do you take them home?"

She shook her head.

"Date them?"

She shook her head.

"Date *anyone*?"

She shook her head.

"Baby, that's not good." He frowned. "Do you have other friends—girlfriends—who visit you at home and you hang out with?"

"Yes, I spend lots of time with my friends." Her voice came out stiff. She wasn't a recluse. But...she didn't date, and his reaction made her think. Guys asked her out often, but she shut them down. Every time. She'd thought she was doing fairly well and believed her problem was only with large males. Apparently, her past was affecting...everything.

"Okay." His uncomfortably acute gaze penetrated deep, past skin and muscle and down to her very core. "Are you getting more comfortable around men—or is it getting worse?"

Her spine stiffened.

"Worse, then." He tilted his head. "Is the perp still in prison?"

The chill in her center sent a shiver across her skin. "He got out last spring."

"Ah, I see." His gaze was too perceptive. "Has he tried to contact you? Or shown up here?"

"No. I know he's still working there. I told Mistress Anne I had an ex who worried me, so she checks now and then to make sure he's still in Cincinnati." The Mistress had promised not to share with anyone.

"Clever girl."

At his open approval, she relaxed—and realized he was

rubbing her arm reassuringly. The desire to stay sheltered between his legs was so very potent she knew she needed to leave immediately. "Can I go now?"

"Hmm." His assessing gaze swept over her like a soft breeze. "All right, darlin'. You've satisfied Z's order. I'll talk with him, and he'll take it from there."

When he opened his legs and lifted his hand, she clambered to her feet too quickly to be graceful. Taking a couple of steps back —as if that would escape a Master's voice—she fought for control and evened her voice. "Thank you, Master Max."

"Just Max. I don't hold much with titles." He lifted his chin. "Scoot now. Go have some fun and forget about working the rest of the night. I'll let Nolan know."

"Yes, Sir." Before he could change his mind, she scurried away. Halfway across the room, she slowed and frowned. *"He'll take it from there."* From the tone and the words, Max didn't plan to be involved. He'd hand over her problems to Master Z and step away.

That was good, wasn't it? She set a hand on her quivering stomach. She could still feel the warmth of his hand on her arm, the strength of his fingers when she'd tried to move away. He was...strong. Careful. In control and in command.

At one time, he'd have been the answer to all her dreams, the hero who saved the maiden from villains.

This hero had been awfully nice, but was going to let someone else do the rest of the saving. That was...all right. Really.

Although it kind of hurt.

Inside the screened-in area behind their house, Alastair settled into a chair and stretched out his legs with a sigh. *Bless, Beth.* When the landscape designer, a Shadowlands submissive, had renovated the grounds, she'd added a garden "room" with a small two-level pond on the right side of the patio.

Although he'd thought the idea was a bit odd, he'd come to appreciate the tranquility it offered. With a melodic burble, water from the upper tier trickled over rocks into the lower pond. Small solar lights were hidden in the dwarf cattails, iris, and cannas around the edge. In the dark water, the bright goldfish were golden flickers around the night-blooming water lilies.

As he sipped his Laphroaig, savoring the soft smoky taste of the whisky, he considered the evening. The scene they'd done with Alyssa had been pleasant, although shallow. A different submissive might have added depth and emotions to the session. With Alyssa, no bond had been created between the three of them.

And here he was at home—alone. With a sigh, he shook his head. How could he feel pleased at the quiet and yet lonely?

It was good to live with Max again. Although they'd managed brilliantly when rooming together at university, he'd been unsure if sharing a home again would work.

Of course, after summers of volunteering in third world countries and a year with Doctors Without Borders, he was accustomed to crowded conditions. In fact, this house had seemed far too empty at first.

Max's company was as enjoyable as ever, which wasn't surprising. His cousin had always been his best friend—and a blood brother, for that matter.

Alastair snorted. As lads, they'd done the entire wrist-cutting, blood-brother ceremony. An ugly scar on his wrist demonstrated that his first "surgical" cut had almost been his last. Considering the amount of blood spilled, they were definitely "brothers".

He had to admit, Max's absence had left a hole in his life. It was good to have him back.

A shadow blocked the light, and then Max set down a glass filled with dark beer, lowered himself into a chair, and stretched out his legs. Shirt off, feet bare, obviously home for the night. "Hey, Doc. You been out here all night?"

"No." Alastair took a sip of his whisky. "I called Mum first to wish her a happy birthday."

"Jesus, cuz. Isn't it the middle of the night in London?"

"It's around dawn—and the best time to catch her. I daresay someone will be showing her a good time tonight." His mother had a multitude of relationships going at any one time.

"No shit." Max grinned. "She's something. You know, if I weren't related to her, I might have made a pass. I could have been her boy toy."

"That would have lasted until the first time she gave you an order in the bedroom." Alastair grinned. His mother didn't have a submissive bone in her body, and as a neurosurgeon, she expected everyone to dance to her tune. Max could take orders or he wouldn't have lasted as a Marine, but he was completely a sexual Dominant.

And thinking of "mother" and "sex" at the same time was enough to make a bloke vomit. Alastair took a bigger drink and asked, "What did Uzuri want to see you about? Or is it private?"

"Not private, though I bet she'd prefer that. Her deal with Z was she'd tell a Master why she's so wary around men, and the information gets shared with all the Masters. Why the fuck she picked me, I don't know."

Alastair frowned. Max was as dominant and experienced as any Master there. *But...ah.* He saluted his cousin with his drink. "You're the new chap on the block. Maybe she thought you'd let her get away with evasion."

That couldn't have worked well for her. The homicide detective disliked secrets.

"Well, damn. Here I figured she'd picked me for my good looks." Dipping his toes in the pool, Max watched the goldfish surface to investigate. "She didn't get to evade shit—and gotta say, she's fun to listen to. When she gets nervous, all her sentences run together."

Alastair grinned. He'd noticed.

"Anyway," Max continued, "her story goes like this: She used to live in Cincinnati, but..."

As Max explained, Alastair's anger ignited. The little submissive had been stalked. Frightened. Hurt. Had been so traumatized she'd fled her own city. "If she's afraid of big men, why would she ask Sam to set up a scene with me last year?"

"She said she'd done better for a while." Max frowned. "Bet Kassab's release from prison set her back. I should have asked more about that."

Yes, someone needed to explore further. Alastair reined his protective instincts in. She hadn't asked to confide in *him*; she'd wanted Max. "You can do that next time you talk."

"There is no next time." Max yanked his foot out of the pond. "She's not mine. I'm not open to taking on a subbie with baggage, especially this kind. Or a woman who'd cry if a fingernail breaks or take hours to get ready to go out for lunch." The bitterness in his voice was a tale in itself.

Baggage, yes, but the rest didn't sound like Uzuri—more like someone else. What had happened to Max in Seattle? Alastair frowned. "I like a woman who takes care of herself. High heels and a tight skirt are a definite plus." He smiled. Even with high heels, Uzuri wouldn't come close to his height.

"Yeah, well... true." Max leaned back and eyed him carefully. "Speaking of that, I saw your expression when I told Z we weren't looking for permanent relationships. You didn't agree."

Here was one reason he enjoyed his cousin so much. Not much got past the cop.

Alastair took a sip of his drink and laid out his thoughts. "I've enjoyed sampling the various delights the world has to offer, but my cousin and brother, I'm ready to settle down. To find a woman to walk beside me"—he gave Max a direct look—"or beside *us*?"

"Been thinking on this a while, have you?" As Max's gaze stayed on the glittering surface of the garden pond, he murmured, "I understand about wanting someone to care for, to live with."

Alastair waited.

"Since college, I've had long-term relationships. Been married. Always seemed like something was missing." His gaze turned to Alastair. "Figured that missing piece might be you."

A pause.

"Nothing ever felt as right as when we lived together and shared our woman."

"For me as well," Alastair said softly.

In the moment of silence, the resident screech owl gave a quiet trill from the old gnarly live oak in the backyard.

"All right. We'll continue on from here." Max nodded. "We'll look for someone who might suit us both for longer than a scene or two."

"How about Uzuri? Would you be interested in doing a scene with her?"

"Seriously, cuz?" Max shook his head. "She's got troubles."

"I'm not sure you'll find anyone who doesn't have some baggage, a few problems—and you and I aren't exempt."

"Maybe. But there are problems, and there are *problems*." Max scowled. "Besides, she doesn't like dogs."

Alastair took a drink of his whisky, deliberated, and finally nodded. He enjoyed watching a woman primping, didn't mind working through problems, but he wouldn't spend time with a woman who lacked a heart.

CHAPTER FIVE

F inished with their pre-opening meeting in Z's third-floor living quarters, the Shadowlands Masters headed down the stairs to the first floor.

The main topic of discussion had been Uzuri.

As Holt followed the others across the clubroom, his gut felt as if he'd swallowed a keg of ground glass. Why hadn't Zuri told him about her past?

He could have helped. For God's sake, she'd been there for him often enough. Like when a building had collapsed during a fire, almost killing him. Another firefighter had died that day. His friend. And tenderhearted Zuri had moved in for two days while Holt recovered—and mourned.

As Holt entered the Masters' private locker room, Z walked over.

"What's up, Z?" Hand on his lock, Holt turned to face the older Dom. Around him, the room was filled with conversations, lockers banging, and laughter.

"About Uzuri. She would have told you. She looked for you." All in black, Z studied Holt for a moment. "I waited until you'd left before forcing her to talk with someone."

Holt stiffened at the sense of betrayal. "Why, Z? You know we're friends."

"Whether she admits it to herself or not, she wants someone to love. A Dom of her own. Until she faces her fears—and can discuss them with possible Doms—she won't move forward."

Anger fading, Holt leaned against the locker. He'd never known anyone more loving than Zuri, but the chemistry had never been there between them. After a while, they'd abandoned being casual lovers in preference to being close friends.

As a Dom, he'd never seen her as *his* submissive. *Hell.* He'd let her down. "I should have pushed her. Dug more into her past."

"No," Z said softly. "That wasn't your task. Isn't your task. We're going to leave that to others."

Holt eyed him. A psychologist and Dominant, Z had as much need to "help" as Holt did. If the owner of the club could step back, so could Holt. "All right."

It helped to know Uzuri had wanted to tell him. "Thanks for the info."

Z nodded and headed to the main room.

Unbuttoning his shirt with one hand, Holt unlocked the combination lock and opened his locker. To disaster.

A deluge of Styrofoam poured out of the high locker and onto his head and shoulders. "What the fuck!"

The laughter of the other Masters echoed off the walls.

A blond Ken doll in a football uniform sat on the bottom of the locker. A fucking doll. Holt looked down at the sea of colored Styrofoam balls around his feet. The tennis-ball-sized ones were orange and white, some with an orange and black-striped "B." For the Cincinnati Bengals.

The rest were gold-and-red with a black, red, and gold "SF" for the San Francisco 49ers. *His* team. Insultingly, those balls were golf-ball size. *Smaller.*

A growl escaped. "That little brat."

One hand on her pregnant belly, Anne shook her head. "I'd

take balls over rubber cockroaches any day." She was actually laughing as she left the locker room.

Holt frowned. Couldn't she see the fucking insult his team had been given? The Mistress must be lacking the sports gene.

"What's with the balls?" The newest Master, Max, walked in late followed by his cousin. As Alastair went to his locker, Max stopped to examine the mess. "You redecorating the place?"

"Hell, no."

"Very colorful." With his foot, Raoul nudged a stray ball back into the mess. "Who do you think? Rainie, Sally, or Uzuri? Or all three?"

"Uzuri did this," Holt told him. The doll was a dead give-away. "The Cincinnati Bengals are her team."

"Uzuri? Get real." Max snorted. "She hasn't got the balls."

The remaining Masters in the room laughed, more at Max's lack of understanding than the pun.

"My friend," Raoul said to Max as he turned to leave, "You are very mistaken."

Walking by, Cullen slapped Max across the back. "Don't piss her off, buddy. She keeps score."

"No shit." Holt grinned at Max. He'd bet money the little brat would eventually target the two new Masters.

"How'd you get on her bad side, Holt?" Vance's blue eyes were lit with amusement.

"Hell, we were meeting for dinner last week, but the game I was watching ran into overtime, and I was late." *Not that late. Damn.*

"Ah, and thus the hit to your balls." Vance grinned.

"My Gabi can be a brat"—Marcus shook his head in admiration at the mess—"but that li'l Uzuri has a pure talent for sneakiness."

"No shit," Holt muttered. How the hell had she opened the combination lock? Ignoring the pile of balls on the floor until later, he followed the others out of the room.

Still bemused by the insult a submissive had delivered to Holt, Max walked into the main clubroom with Holt behind him.

What caught his eye first was Uzuri on the other side of the dance floor. She saw Holt, and her face lit with mischief and laughter—a completely compelling mixture.

Unsettled, Max looked away, then blinked at the changes in the room. The St. Andrew's crosses, spanking benches, spider webs, cages, stockades—every piece of equipment had been pushed against the walls and thigh-high and calf-high ropes blockaded them off.

A series of runner carpets laid end-to-end circled the perimeter of the room like a racetrack.

The sitting areas with leather couches and chairs and coffee tables remained, but the empty floor spaces were now cushioned with mattresses, exercise mats, and blankets.

"I should've checked the Shadowlands newsletter before coming," he muttered to Alastair. Or managed to clear out his caseload so he could arrive in time for the Masters' meeting.

From Alastair's rueful nod, he hadn't read his email, either.

"Welcome to 'Lights Out in Rome'." Z strolled into the center of the room.

As everyone moved closer to hear, Max noticed people were wearing casual clothing instead of fetwear.

Z continued. "During the Masters' dinner last month, we got caught up in a discussion of two things: how the modern environment overloads our senses, forcing us to shutter our perceptions in self-defense, and how preconceptions influence how we respond to others.

That was pretty much a given, Max thought. Cities contained too much noise, odors, and visual stimuli.

Preconceptions? Hell, as a cop, it was a constant battle to avoid stereotyping the people he dealt with. In turn, the minute he said he was a cop, he'd get tagged as either a rescuer or a brutal asshole.

Z motioned to the room. "Tonight, we will eliminate sight and hearing. The room will be darkened with only mandatory exit and restroom signs lit—although they'll be dimmed. To prevent accidents, everyone will crawl. No walking. No standing."

He waited for the murmuring to die. "Silence will rule. No one may speak. Negotiating won't be possible, thus, sexual play is limited to fingers and mouths." He half-smiled. "No fucking, people. No toys. Penetration is only with fingers and tongues. This is sensory play. Light pain is permitted, but since you can't see, impact play is forbidden."

Max raised his eyebrows. *Interesting.*

"For those in an exclusive relationship, your submissive must wear ankle and wrist cuffs to indicate he or she is off the market and will wear a tag that will glow when in close proximity with yours. If you're a single Dom and find a subbie wearing ankle and wrist cuffs, let her go. You may only play with uncuffed submissives. A single Dom who catches a submissive can keep or release."

Two of the Masters, Vance and Galen, were handing out elastic bracelets with tags.

"Questions?" When Z received only silence, he continued. "Movement is regulated by drums and bells. If you play, continue until the bell sounds. When the bell rings, clean up the subbie and yourself. At the double bell, all unattached subbies return to the perimeter carpet and continue along it. A drum is the signal for the submissives to crawl toward the center of the room."

Max glanced around. So each Dom should set up somewhere. Reminded him of lions waiting to capture prey at a watering hole.

"Silence will be enforced," Z said. "As always, you may use club safeword *red* to stop all play. Any other sound will be noted and punished afterward."

Someone in the crowd cleared his throat. "What about using yellow to indicate a need to slow down?"

"No." The Shadowlands' owner crossed his arms over his

chest. "That means the Top needs to go carefully, to use all senses —especially touch—to read how the bottom is reacting."

Max nodded. Interesting lesson in paying attention. *Fun game.* He glanced at Alastair and raised his eyebrows to ask silently if this would be a team or solo night.

Alastair held up two fingers to say they'd top together.

"To quit before the end of the game, simply stand up and wait. A dungeon monitor will escort you to the door." Z nodded toward Marcus and Raoul who held armloads of white garments. "Doms, Tops, and Masters wear togas. Switches—wear a toga if you want to top."

Max almost laughed at the uneasy silence that fell. No submissive wanted to be the one to ask.

To his surprise, Uzuri spoke up. "Master Z? Wh-what do the submissives, bottoms, and slaves wear, Sir?" Her soft voice was tentative—but sweet. So fucking sweet.

Laughter glinted in Z's eyes. "I thought I'd make it easy for you tonight, pet. You're all going naked. If your hair is longer than three inches, braid it back. There are ties in the dressing rooms."

The bell rang through the clubroom.

Uzuri smothered her sigh of relief as the Dom who'd "caught" her released her breast with an annoyed grunt.

Thank goodness this session was over. All the previous periods in Master Z's crazy "game" had been fairly long; this one had begun only a few minutes before.

Then again, Master Z did like to mess with everyone's minds —and he had her gratitude.

Her first three Doms had been fun, but this guy was clueless about reading her body language—or he simply didn't care. Her nipples burned from his pinches, and a couple of times, she'd actually shoved his hands away. He sure didn't know the meaning of "light" pain.

He slapped some clean wipes in her palm and set her hand on his dick. So she could wash him?

Aren't I grateful. With some Doms, she'd do anything to please them; with others, she'd rather squeeze their balls into jelly.

Quickly, she cleaned him—although it wasn't needed—and had barely enough time to wipe his touch off of her skin before the two bells sounded.

After tossing the wipes in a service station, she crawled away as fast as she could. The faint glow from the wall baseboards was barely enough to guide her to the "road" around the room's perimeter. Feeling the velvety texture of the carpet under her hands, she headed toward her right—the correct flow of traffic. The soundtrack from *Gladiator* covered the sounds of breathing and knees thudding, and she bumped into the other submissives around her. The Doms stayed in place, waiting for new subbies to venture into their lairs.

Master Z sure came up with strange games.

The drums didn't sound, so she kept crawling and crawling.

Did Master Z have a reason for when he'd start and stop the sessions? He could see the room, after all, since he and the devious dungeon monitors had donned night-vision goggles. That was actually reassuring. Apparently the "no speaking" ruled didn't apply to the dungeon monitors since earlier, Master Raoul had reprimanded a Dom for being too rough, and Master Marcus told a slave to stop stalling and get off the road.

A roll of drums sounded. Time for the submissives to head toward the center of the room.

Uzuri hesitated. The last Dom had wiped out a lot of her enthusiasm. Her knees were getting sore, too. With a sigh, she crawled across the floor, ran into a mattress, and detoured around it. She brushed against someone and startled. They both stopped, but her shoulder was rubbing against a man's *bare* side, so he was another bottom.

Without speaking, she turned away at an angle and continued.

Her hand bumped another mattress, and she started to back away.

Fingers closed around her wrist, halting her. Like a predator lying in wait, a Dom had felt the thump and snagged her. His hand was big—huge—and her heart skipped a beat.

But in the dark, she couldn't see his height or size. Couldn't tell if he really was big. Some short men had large hands, right? And, although he guided her firmly onto the mattress, his grip was controlled—not painful or mean like the last Dom.

When she was in the center, he squeezed her wrist slightly, so she stopped crawling, remaining on hands and knees. Not releasing her wrist, he stroked down her back, slowly. Sensuously. His palm was hard and callused.

Fingers under her chin lifted her head. A hand cupped her face, and a slow thumb ran over her lips. This hand was smooth.

She froze, barely breathing. A hand on her back, a hand holding her wrist—and one on her face? There were *two* Doms here? She couldn't see them. Her heart rate sped up. As fear wedged a cold blade through her insides, she whimpered.

A warm breath brushed against her ear. "Shh-shh-shh." When he caressed her cheek reassuringly, she realized he was trying to help her avoid Master Z's punishment for making noise.

The other Dom's hand rested on her back as he waited for her to relax.

She slowly pulled in a breath. The two weren't trying to scare her. On the contrary. Her muscles relaxed, and she bowed her head. *All right.*

As if she'd spoken aloud, they started moving. Slowly, silently, they explored her body. One ran his hands over her face, her shoulders, and arms. The other rubbed her bare feet, stroking his rough palms up her calves. He was the one who gripped her hips and rolled her onto her back.

She gasped at the vulnerable position. Blind. She could feel them, their size and strength, looming over her. She tensed.

Again, they waited, hands on her, but unmoving. She fought her fear back down.

At some silent signal between them, they started again.

The Dom kneeling beside her upper arm moved warm, firm hands over her shoulders, across her collarbone. She lifted her hands to touch him—and he pressed her arms back to her sides in an obvious order—they would be the ones doing the touching.

And he did. His hands claimed her breasts, kneading and stroking. But when he rolled one abused nipple between his fingers, she winced.

He stilled.

Feeling vulnerable, she tried to sit up. Hand on her shoulder, he kept her in place. Then, a tongue ever so lightly swirled around her scraped left nipple as if to make it feel better.

With a lingering ache, her areola wakened and puckered, and he teased his tongue over the hard nub. As his hand cupped her other breast, she realized his hands were huge.

The Dom who'd captured her had large hands, too. How big *were* these two men? A warning shiver ran over her, but she couldn't *see* them, and the fear stayed at bay.

The one with callused hands knelt beside her right hip, and his soft tunic brushed against her bare skin. With both hands, he massaged her thighs, moving upward, stroking past her pussy to her waist and back down.

The other Dom remained beside her left shoulder. Releasing her breasts, he kissed her. His lips were soft, gentle, and ever so sensuous. He lightly teased her mouth and nibbled her lips until she opened. His tongue took possession as his long-fingered hand curved under her chin and along her jawline, letting him control the kiss.

When his face brushed hers, she felt a short, trimmed beard. Each breath brought her the fragrance of a spicy citrus and vetiver aftershave. Was his kiss familiar?

She tried to think, but being the focus of two Doms' attentions made her dizzy. In the complete darkness, she had four hands fondling her. She didn't know where they'd touch. What they'd do. The sense of having no control shook her. Heated her.

As her center unexpectedly warmed with arousal, she squirmed.

The hardened hands of the first Dom—the one who'd captured her—tightened on her thighs in an unspoken restraint, and she forced herself to hold still. When he kissed above her pelvis, his jaw held the rasp of a clean-shaven man with a day's stubble—harsh, rough, and ever so sexy. Her belly quivered, and his lips curved against her skin.

Hands on her hips, he leaned on her, pressing her backside into the mattress. And, somehow, the feeling of being held down wasn't frightening but totally intoxicating.

The bell...didn't ring, and the music continued as the two Doms played with her. Enjoying themselves.

Enjoying her.

Dom Beard nibbled on her ear and down her neck, and goosebumps rose on her arms. When he licked over her nipples, his tongue was hot. Wet.

Dark desire hummed straight to her pussy.

As if in response, Dom Captor kissed downward from her belly and over her mound, deliberately rasping his chin right over the cleft. He pushed her legs apart about a foot. Ever so slowly, his tongue traced the crease between her hip and thigh, then touched her outer folds.

She pulled in a startled breath. The waxing had left her skin highly sensitized. There were no post-shaving bumps or little hairs, nothing to offer resistance to his tongue or lips. Every nerve ending felt more exposed. She felt the slickness between her legs increase.

His tongue touched her inner labia.

Too intimate. With a will of their own, her legs pressed together.

He lightly nipped her thigh in a silent reprimand.

She froze, barely breathing, cringing as she waited for him to punish her.

The pain didn't come. Instead, he moved her legs apart again. His slow, warm breaths brushed over her mound, and then coolness washed it as he moved back. His powerful grip anchored her hip as his other hand cupped her pussy. Her jerk of surprise was halted before it even began.

And there were two Doms.

When she'd jolted, Dom Beard's hands had closed on her arms, restraining her upper half. He nipped her shoulder in warning.

Fighting the instinctive need to flee, she lay still, heart pounding, as an unsettling heat flushed her skin. The controlled power in the way they handled her was making everything inside her sink into an unfamiliar, wonderful submissive space.

Dom Captor slid a finger between her folds, and she gasped at the intimate exploration. As if unworried about being interrupted by the bell, he swept his slickened finger up and around the sides of her clit...never touching the actual nub. Holding her down, he teased the nub until it swelled, then cycled between her clit and entrance until her whole pussy tingled with a full, hot sensation, growing more and more sensitized.

Dom Beard held her upper arms firmly, increasing her feeling of being captured, as he nuzzled her breasts. Alternating from left to right, he licked the nipples and sucked—lightly—obviously remembering her tenderness.

Her breasts felt hot and swollen, the nipples hot and aching.

Gripping her right hip, Dom Captor continued to tease her pussy, even as he bent forward and kissed her mound.

When his lips moved lower, she caught her breath. Ever so slowly, his tongue teased the hood above her clit.

Omigod, the *sensation*.

She tried to move. Heard Dom Beard chuckle against her breast. His grip stayed firm.

Restrained. Pressed into the mattress. Helpless and at the mercy of *two* Doms. Somehow, her arousal grew and grew until she shook with need. Her thighs trembled as her hips lifted in an effort to get more.

She felt the huff of Dom Captor's breath in a silent laugh, but his hand tightened on her hip until she lay still again. The fabric of his tunic slid over her hip and right thigh as he moved closer. Unhurriedly, his mouth moved down...and his tongue brushed right on top of her aching clit.

Oooh. Fiery pleasure lanced through her system.

Even as it did, Dom Beard squeezed her left breast and sucked hard on her abused, right nipple.

Omigod. The flash of erotic pain shot straight to her clit, and she gasped.

When Dom Beard lifted up, his tunic grazed her lower breast and stomach.

Cool air wafted over her wet nipple and tightened it to an aching point.

Dom Beard shifted his hands, one on her right breast, the other holding her upper arm to keep her in place for whatever they wanted to do.

Shivers of excitement and anxiety shook her body.

Dom Captor circled his tongue around her clit. Holding her still, he slowly, determinedly, pressed two slick fingers between her folds and up inside her, filling her.

Her center clamped down on the ruthless intrusion. As Dom Captor thrust in and out and continued to lick her clit, the sensations were growing overwhelming. She heard herself whimper.

Dom Beard laughed almost silently. He closed his mouth over her nipple and sucked even as Dom Captor did the same with her clit. Both of them sucked in long, slow pulls. Hard pulls.

Oh, oh, oh. As the ruthless fingers inside her pumped in and out in a steady rhythm, the exquisite torment grew unbearable. She hit the precipice, teetering as the pressure built, yet she couldn't... couldn't...

His mouth enclosing her clit, the suction unrelenting, Dom Captor tongued the very top of the sensitive nub.

Oh God! The impossible, unstoppable pleasure detonated within her core, blasting outward in dazzling surges of sensation.

Dom Beard put his hand over her mouth, smothering her cry.

As her hips bucked with the orgasm, Dom Captor held her down, mercilessly working her clit and pussy to wring every last spasm of pleasure from her.

Slowly, the shudders eased.

Heart thumping crazily, lying on her back, limp with pleasure, she stared up into the darkness.

After a minute, she realized the Doms were...petting...her. The long, slow, gentle strokes of their big hands felt like they'd enjoyed themselves as much as she had. She'd never felt so cherished, and the feeling of closeness to them was disconcerting. She didn't even know who they were, but she wanted to crawl into their arms and hug them.

The bell rang, one chime for cleanup.

Uzuri struggled to sit up...and was pinned in place by Dom Captor.

Dom Beard tore open a cleanser packet and wiped her breasts, setting her nipples to burning.

Then, despite her squirming and occasional squeak, Dom Captor thoroughly cleaned her pussy. Finished, he helped her sit up, keeping one hand on her back to ensure she was steady.

Unexpectedly, her eyes filled with tears, and her breathing started to hitch. After the cruel Dom, she'd felt lost, as if she was stupid to be in a BDSM club. But...these two were everything she'd longed for when she'd first realized she was submissive. She unsuccessfully gulped back a sob.

"Shhh." Even though the warning was almost silent, she could hear how deep Dom Beard's voice was. His hand brushed over her face, reached her tear-dampened cheeks, and paused. With a low, comforting hmm, he sat behind her and drew her against him so her back was against his hard chest. His arms closed around her stomach in a firm, warm embrace that filled the empty feeling inside her.

After a few seconds, Dom Captor found her hand and set a wet wipe in it. When she hesitated, unsure of what to do, he gave her his left hand. *Got it.* She was to clean his hands.

Her heart lifted as if on wings, and she smiled. His dominance came through loud and clear, even without words, and everything in her responded. There was nothing more she wanted than to do his bidding. To feel useful and needed. To serve.

Happiness welled inside her as she concentrated on cleaning one hand, then the other. When finished, she pressed kisses to the backs of his hands.

A low hum of pleasure was her reward along with a devastatingly voracious kiss, one that left her feeling more possessed than having sex with someone else could do. The scent of his aftershave was like a walk through a springtime woods—and very, very masculine.

He drew back slowly, his hand gentle on her face. After pressing another wipe into her hands, he pulled her forward out from Dom Beard's embrace and then turned her.

Knowing what to do this time, she took Dom Beard's hands and cleaned them. He had fewer calluses than the other Dom, but his hands were bigger with long fingers like an artist. Heart full, she finished by kissing his fingers and rubbing her cheek against his palm.

As the two bells rang, he took her chin and gave her a leisurely, oh-so-sensual kiss that melted her insides. Slowly, he kissed down her neck to the top of her shoulder. There, he used his teeth in a surprisingly rough, sucking bite.

Chills ran over her skin, and her mind went blank.

When he stopped and kissed the curve between her neck and her shoulder, she pulled in a shaky breath.

He sat back, and a pat on her ass from Dom Captor sent her on her way.

Emotions unsettled, she crawled back to the carpet "road", wondering if she'd ever know who the two had been.

For long minutes, she traveled the perimeter with the other submissives, and then...the lights came on.

The game was over.

The game was over. Alastair rose and checked that the blasted toga was covering him. He was as exposed as he would have been in a kilt. Did the Scots like having cold drafts sweeping over their legs and genitals?

"We need to position ourselves near the exit to the ladies' loo," he told Max. As the people in the room stood, stretched, and chatted with others, he headed for the dressing room with his cousin beside him. Other members were moving toward the food and drink area where Galen and Vance were handing out bottled waters.

Carefully, Alastair scanned the room, trying to locate their last little subbie. The first four women they'd played with had been pleasant enough, but this last one...was something special. Sweetly responsive. And, although obviously timid, she'd kissed his hands and then him with all her heart and soul.

Her tears had tugged at his heart. When he'd realized she was crying, he'd touched Max with his wet fingers. His cousin had caught on. A second later, Max had tapped his leg. One slow tap, one quick, and then two slows. In the Morse code abbreviations they'd used as lads, "Y" indicated "yes." In this case, Max had meant *let's have a look at this one*.

Alastair studied the females that they passed. The one they wanted was medium height, nicely curvy with full breasts and a high, round ass. Like the others, her hair had been braided tightly back, but the braid hadn't quite reached her shoulders. Springy hair.

"Damn Z anyway," Max muttered.

As they crossed the empty dance floor, Alastair glanced at his cousin. "Why?"

"He was right. Again. I hadn't realized how much I rely on my eyes."

"Meaning you don't think you'll be able to find her."

"Exactly. How about you? You've been a member here longer. Did you recognize her?"

"No." Alastair smiled. "That's why I marked her."

"You *what*?"

"There should be a fine hickey at the top of her left shoulder."

"Way to go, Doc." When they reached the women's dressing area, Max glanced at the crowd milling around the food. "You want to scout or hold position?"

"I'll scout and bring you back some water."

Max leaned a shoulder against the wall on the left side of the door where departing members would have to walk past him. "Grab me a handful of chocolate chip cookies, too." He eyed the first two submissives.

They noticed his concentrated attention, stopped dead, and gave him nervous glances.

Alastair shook his head. When not smiling, his detective cousin could make even a stone-cold killer nervous. "Try not to terrify the subbies, Max."

When Max shot him an amused look, the two women relaxed and started moving again.

Leaving Max on guard, Alastair crossed the room to the munchie area. He studied each woman he passed, and even then, he almost missed her—because in the dim light of the Shadowlands, his hickey mark didn't contrast markedly against her brown skin.

Uzuri?

They'd played with Uzuri. Now there was a bloody surprise.

As always, upon spotting him, she detoured to avoid him. Apparently, she had no idea he and Max had been the Doms in her last session.

He turned, caught Max's attention, and indicated the little mixed race submissive.

Max followed his gaze, blinked in surprise, then his expression darkened. He shook his head. *No.*

Unsurprised, Alastair continued on his way to the food and drinks. *Uzuri*. The discovery that someone had hurt her had troubled him. Now he knew how passionate and emotionally sensitive she was. Now he was truly concerned.

Bloody hell. He wanted to help.

CHAPTER SIX

On Sunday afternoon, standing on Nolan King's doorstep, Max called himself a fool. This was his day off; why the hell was he playing cop?

Because he couldn't stop worrying about the two orphans being tended by a woman who didn't even like little dogs. Only last summer, their abusive, drug-addicted mother had died, and they didn't need any more traumas in their lives.

He wanted to ensure they were all right. That was all.

Max rang the King's doorbell, heard "The Yellow Rose of Texas" chime through the house, and snorted a laugh. Texans were insane bastards.

But... He considered and started to smile. He needed to find out who'd coded King's doorbell. Be worth money to see Alastair's expression if their doorbell played "God Save the Queen". The Brit'd go nuts.

Just for fun, Max punched the button again.

The thudding of small feet sounded, and the door was flung open.

"Hey. It's Max!" Grant, King's soon-to-be-adopted, seven-year-old, tried for a cool tone, although he couldn't conceal his grin.

"Max!" Pint-sized Connor hit Max's leg with all the weight of a skinny kindergartner and clung there, beaming at him. "I di'nt know you was coming."

"Got something I'm dropping off for Nolan." A couple of months ago, Alastair had interviewed the boys about their interactions with an incompetent social worker. Max had brought a copy of the unedited DVD that showed the boys playing with Alastair before and after. The Kings would enjoy watching, and it gave him an excuse for the visit. "Can you get him for me?"

Grant shook his head. "He's not here."

"He and Beff are having a growed-up date," Connor explained solemnly.

"Grant, Connor." The melodic voice came from the living room. "I know you've been told not to answer the door without an adult with you. What if someone bad is there?"

As the pretty submissive crossed the foyer, Max tried to forget how she'd trembled under his hands. His mouth. How she'd kissed his fingers.

"I checked first, Zuri." Grant pointed to a window next to the door through which a visitor would be visible. King had designed his house well. "It's Max."

Seeing Max, Uzuri stiffened and took a step back. "Good afternoon."

Sensitive to body language, Connor frowned. "Max isn't a bad person."

No, *he* wasn't. But what about *her*? If she didn't like pets, little energetic boys with loud voices were probably even lower on her list. Connor liked to hug—and usually had peanut butter, mud, or jelly on his hands. Wouldn't that be worse than fur? What would she do? "Afternoon. When is Nolan due back?"

She glanced at a clock. "Any time now."

"I have something for him. I'll wait." And make sure the kids were safe.

"But—" Her expression shouted her dismay. Unless she put on

a complete poker face, she wasn't difficult to read. Last night, even without lights, her body had telegraphed every emotion. Damn, he'd enjoyed that.

"It's okay, Zuri," Grant said. "Nolan lets him visit us. He works with Mr. Dan."

"You're a cop?" Her flush was cute. "I mean...in law enforcement?"

Max nodded. "Yep. Got a"—*not a homicide, Drago*—"stolen bike case you need solved?"

Connor took her hand easily, as if he'd done it often. Then again, Connor had that kind of personality. "Can we finish our story?"

"Uh..." Her glance at Max said she wanted him to leave.

"I'll stay out of your way."

"Please, Zuri?" Connor looked up.

Her sigh held resignation. "Oh, okay."

Max almost laughed. No one was immune to Connor's pleading brown eyes.

Grant took her other hand. Interesting that the reserved boy felt so comfortable with her. When she took a seat on the great room couch, Connor crawled right into her lap and Grant snuggled against her as easily as he did with Beth.

Max settled down in a chair across from them, smiling when he saw the book cover displayed a duck surrounded by ducklings.

She read a page to them and then Connor tugged on her shirt. "I want the funny voices. Like you read it before."

Although her brown face darkened with a flush, she kept her gaze firmly on the book. "All right." When she continued reading, each animal had a unique, purely hilarious voice.

When Mr. Mallard showed up with a New York accented, pseudo-baritone, Max huffed a laugh.

Grant threw him a grin, and Connor was already giggling.

Every now and then, Uzuri would stop and ask Connor to read

off the letters in a word, and Grant would sound it out. Then she'd resume, keeping the story moving.

The little subbie was a damn good reader and teacher. Max frowned. Aside from his presence, she was comfortable and enjoying the boys. She'd obviously read enough books to the children that they had their own routine. Her patience wasn't an act put on for Max's benefit.

She liked the boys. *His* boys. They might belong to the Kings, but he rather considered them his, as well.

In his mental tally, that gave a woman a slew of points.

He almost grinned as he realized he was keeping points like the women he'd overheard in a bar last month. *Jesus.* They'd rated men on shit he'd never considered important. Could give a guy a complex.

A burst of laughter drew his attention back to Uzuri—or *Zuri* as the children called her. Her appearance was different today. She'd put her kinky, black hair into a half-dozen twists fastened at her nape, probably so she could swim with the boys. She wore no makeup, and although she looked beautiful with makeup, he almost liked her more without. Her velvety, seal-brown eyes sure didn't need any enhancement, and her skin was like poured chocolate begging a man to take a lick. That won her several points in his mental tally.

Amused, he subtracted points for the crease in her shorts. Who the hell ironed denim shorts?

Rather than a T-shirt, she wore a button-up shirt, but he couldn't object to the tailoring that showed off her curvy shape. That one broke even.

She was barefooted though, and she had incredibly sexy feet. Having been married to a fashionista, he knew manicures and pedicures were a black hole for dollars, but...the pink polish on her delicate toes was as sexy as hell.

For all he knew, she might do them herself.

When Connor snuggled closer to her, Max knew he'd been

wrong with his worries about her babysitting. Apparently, even if she didn't like animals, she enjoyed children. The boys obviously adored her, and although most kids could be fooled, survivors of abusive or drug-laden households learned to pick up if someone was faking their friendship.

Still... Merely because she was one of the prettiest women he'd ever seen didn't mean he was going to change his mind about getting to know her. Hating animals was a deal-breaker. Sure, the way she unconsciously cuddled the boys against her was eroding his brain cells, but he wasn't about to let his hormones choose his actions.

He'd grown out of that right around his second year of college.

Okay, then. Mind cleared, he leaned back in his chair, relaxed, and enjoyed the story, right along with the kids.

Uzuri was reading the last paragraph when the sound of the garage door going up drifted into the house. Thank the heavens, Nolan and Beth were back.

Long legs stretched out, Max was still lounging in the chair across from her and the boys. His arms were crossed over his muscular chest so that the sleeves of his T-shirt strained around his biceps. In the clear light coming through the patio doors, his eyes were the mesmerizing color of ultramarine, as deep and changeable as the sea the color was named for. His face was weathered to a dark tan that made his eyes even more striking. Barely brushing his shoulders, his wavy, brown hair looked...soft. Touchable.

Had he been one of the Doms who played with her last night?

To keep from being identified, the longer-haired Doms had tied their hair back. Dom Captor's jaw had been rough. Although Max was clean-shaven, she'd bet he had serious stubble after a day's time. She looked at his hands to see if they were callused.

What would she do if they were?

Nothing.

She still couldn't believe she'd been touched by two Doms at once. She'd never, ever thought she'd like being with two men, yet it had been as exciting as it was scary. Whoever they were, they had been wonderfully patient. And sweet. She remembered the one Dom's low "*Shhh*" when she'd made a noise. A shiver ran through her.

"Uzuri?" Grant asked.

She jerked back to reality and met Max's perceptive gaze. He'd caught her *staring* at him. She felt herself flush—again—and could only be grateful that she didn't turn a revealing beet-red color like most of her friends. A girl of color enjoyed the few advantages the world gave her.

Hastily, she said, "Go meet your parents, guys."

Two sets of wide brown eyes focused on her.

"Parents. That's like a mother and father, right?" Grant's voice was timid.

"A mommy and daddy?" Connor whispered.

Oh, she'd stepped in it now. She knew Beth and Nolan hadn't talked with the boys about calling them anything other than Beth and Nolan. After all, their mother had just died last summer. But... Beth had said she wanted to be called Mom or Mommy, but was afraid to bring it up. Uzuri bit her lip, seeing the hope in Connor's eyes. Feeling the trembling of Grant's hand. *I think the time for slow is over.*

Uzuri smiled and said firmly, "Exactly like a mommy and daddy or mom and dad. When you're ready, you can call them that."

That was all it took.

The boys raced across the house toward the garage. Connor was yelling, "Mommy, Mommy!" Grant was right behind him with a, "Daaaad."

Imagining the look on Beth's face, Uzuri felt her eyes fill with tears.

The cushions beside her compressed as Max sat down and held out a tissue. "Good job, darlin'. I bet Beth is bawling her eyes out, too."

When she looked up...and up...at him, his sheer size stunned her, and she froze. After a second, she whispered, "Get back."

"Uzuri." His chiding tone drew her attention to his face and the sympathy in his eyes. "I know you're frightened, but am I sitting all that close to you?"

She checked the space between them. A polite couple of feet. The problem was...he was so menacingly *tall*. "Please move," she whispered.

"I will if you seriously need me to, but I'd rather you found your courage instead." His gaze stayed level. "Baby, I'm not going to haul off and wallop you." He snorted. "Actually, to get me to hit you, we'd have to negotiate first, and you might have to beg. I'm not much into hurting subbies."

Her mouth dropped open at how bluntly he brought up a subject that wasn't discussed in polite society.

He didn't move.

Then again, he never had, had he? He was still holding the tissue out, forcing her with silent pressure to shake off her paralysis and take the Kleenex.

She turned her head away.

"Don't be a rude little submissive," he said gently.

Rude? She stared at him in shock. She was never rude. Unable to endure the directness of his gaze, she looked down, trying not to hunch her shoulders. Yet he was correct. He'd politely brought her a tissue. He'd complimented her and said she'd done well. He hadn't sat too close.

She was acting as if he carried a disease.

"I'm sorry," she said to her hands. *Courage, girl.* Hauling in a breath, she straightened and plucked the tissue from his hand. Watching to make sure he didn't move, she wiped her eyes. "I'm sorry for being discourteous."

"No problem. I hear worse from my partner all day." His blue eyes narrowed to a painful intensity. "As you wanted, I told Z everything you said. Did you two talk?"

"He said he's going to let the Masters—and me—mull everything over. And see how things go. If he needs to, he'll step in."

Really, Max had been much easier to confide in, and wasn't that strange?

"It's good he won't let you coast forever. He shouldn't have waited so long to begin with." At her scowl, the laugh lines at the corners of Max's eyes deepened. "I know you didn't want to discuss your past. But fear has to be faced, baby, or it'll come back at awkward times."

"I don't—"

"Like when somebody offers you a Kleenex." His smile changed his entire face. From cold, controlled, and dangerous to sexy, fun, and charismatic.

She couldn't pull her gaze away, and heat wafted over her skin.

His eyebrows lifted, prompting her for a response.

"Um. Right. I'll get right on that, Sir." With the way he exuded dominance, she couldn't hold back the honorific, even though they weren't at the club. But, even when merely sitting and talking, he was so completely in charge that her stomach got all hot and melty.

"I'm serious, baby. You need to work on that fear of yours. You got any ideas on what might help get you past it?"

"I don't want to talk about this."

"Yeah? Sucks to be you, because it's what we're discussing. Answer my question."

The heat this time was purely from anger. How dare he push her? And what in the world was keeping Beth and Nolan? "I don't know what would help. I try not to think about it." She glared at him. "I've tried hard *not* to think about the past. Having it—"

Her explanation was interrupted when Connor and Grant darted into the room.

"Zuri, Beff—Mommy—is back," Connor shouted.

Grant bounced up and down in excitement. "Zuri, Nolanman got us *bikes*."

"Did he?" Uzuri rose and held out her hands. "Let's go see."

As they exited the room, she glanced over her shoulder. Max still sat on the couch, arms spread across the back, simply...watching...her.

A shiver, both hot and cold, ran down her spine.

CHAPTER SEVEN

In a dungeon monitor's gold-trimmed vest, Alastair strolled through the Shadowlands, inspecting the various scenes. He had a small pack clipped to his belt containing the necessary tools. The contents reminded him of a doctor's bag: bandage scissors, gauze pads, alcohol swabs, and latex gloves. A small flashlight was clipped to the outside. As usual, he tried to be prepared for anything. Saturday nights in the club tended to be quite busy.

He stopped at a St. Andrew's cross to help Olivia release her submissive. Still in subspace, the bottom couldn't support her own weight, so he scooped her up and laid her on a couch outside the roped-off area.

"Thank you, Alastair." In a black biker jacket and black leather pants, her honey-colored hair cut short and wickedly spiked with gel, the Mistress looked as if she'd be able to handle any problems that came her way.

"You're quite welcome."

"I haven't played with her before, and even with a light scene, she went deeper than I'd expected." Olivia's British accent was a pleasant hint of home.

"You'll be ready next time." With a nod, he continued on his rounds.

Over the next hour, he wandered the club.

He provided some gauze to a Top who'd flogged open a strip of skin on his partner.

Hearing a "red, *red*" from a scene area, Alastair headed there quickly, but the Dom had heeded the safeword. He was already releasing the terrified-looking young man from the stocks. From the looks of it, the submissive had panicked simply from being restrained.

That happened.

The Dom was caring for the submissive appropriately. Very good.

Alastair detoured to check on a needle play scene with an appallingly noisy submissive. She'd scream. When the Dom would stop, she'd apologize, "*I'm sorry, Sir. No, I'm fine, keep going.*" With the next insertion, she'd scream again.

Bloody hell, she would have driven him bonkers. Maybe he should advise her Dom that Masters could call off scenes as easily as submissives. However, the Dom was experienced. If he continued, he probably had a reason.

A glance at the clock told Alastair his stint of monitoring was over. As he moved toward the bar, he listened to the ethereal voices of Switchblade Symphony coming from the hidden speakers in the room. He'd forgotten how much he liked the *Serpentine* album.

"You had a nice busy shift, eh, buddy." Serving as the bartender, Cullen handed over a Tanqueray and tonic. "Olivia said to tell you thanks again."

"Did the submissive come out of it all right?" Alastair savored the drink.

"She did. Sounded like she went deeper than Olivia expected. But apparently, they'd already made plans for the subbie to spend the night with her. She'll be safe enough." Cullen frowned. "It'd be nice if Olivia kept someone more than a week rather than roving from girl to girl."

"Some Dominants prefer not to"—Alastair grinned—"be tied down."

"I felt that way right up until a sassy wench begged—*pleaded*, actually—for me to marry her and make her an honest woman." Cullen winked at Alastair.

Cullen had regaled the Masters with the herculean effort he'd made to get Andrea even to consider marriage. Alastair smothered a smile. "Begged you? Pitiful. Where was her sense of dignity?"

An affronted gasp came from the stunning Hispanic submissive who was drawing a beer. "I never begged." Her amber eyes sparked fire as she turned to her Dom. "You *cabrón*, you asked *me*. You tell him that you did." Although her voice never rose, the beer in the glass swirled in a threat.

Cullen's hearty roar of laughter brought grins from everyone around the bar. "Got you, love. No need to tell him. Alastair knows which one of us did the begging."

Andrea eyed her fiancé suspiciously. When she noticed Alastair's grin, her scowl increased. "*You*. Everyone thinks your cousin is the bad boy, but you, with your suit and solemn ways, you're worse."

"Thank you. That is indeed a compliment."

Eyes flashing, she growled and hefted the glass of beer, obviously still wanting to throw it.

"I wouldn't do that, sweetie," Cullen cautioned. "I haven't pounded on that gorgeous ass in far too long and..." He stopped. "It *has* been a long time. I'm a Dom; I don't need an excuse to treat myself."

Grabbing his wide-eyed woman by one wrist, he took his toy bag from the shelves behind the bar. Opening the lift-up bar top, he hauled Andrea after him. "Alastair, be a pal and babysit the bar. Jake'll be here to take over in a few."

Alastair took Cullen's place. When Andrea's hissing Spanish curses were abruptly cut off, he started laughing. The Dom had probably put a hand over her mouth. Or gagged her. The hot-blooded submissive had quite the vocabulary, and despite Cullen's easy-going personality, he was still a Dom. The two must have an interesting relationship.

Alastair filled the current drink orders, pleased he only had to pull up a drink recipe on his phone once.

"Hey, Alastair, I thought you were dungeon monitor, not bartender tonight." Jake ducked under the bar top without bothering to raise the lift-up.

"I was." Alastair motioned with his chin toward the scene area to the right of the bar. "Cullen had an impertinent submissive to reprimand."

"Last week, he asked Raoul about something she'd called him. It translated to something like 'drooling slug'." Jake laughed. "You gotta love the mouthy ones."

"I appreciate her versatility, as well as the way she delivers her insults so quietly." Spirit was good; noise wasn't. Perhaps he'd absorbed too much of his mum's British reserve. Even when he and Max had almost burned down the London house, she hadn't raised her voice.

And on the sprawling Drago ranch in Colorado, his uncle and father moderated their volume inside the house. Having had an abusive first husband, Aunt Gracie couldn't tolerate yelling. Despite that handicap, his aunt was no pushover.

Having had relationships with some strident women, Alastair had come to appreciate volume control.

Jake grinned. "There are days I think it's better not to know what my submissive calls me when she's annoyed."

"Where is she today?" Alastair asked. Rainie was always a delight.

"She took an orphaned litter of puppies home from the clinic." The veterinarian grinned. "Once they're weaned, she plans to give one to Nolan's kids in hopes it'll keep the boys from nagging them for a little sister. For a while." After playing with Z's little Sophia, the two boys had decided they needed a little sister.

As a pediatrician, Alastair approved of waiting. Nolan and Beth were excellent parents, but a family needed time to settle. "Brilliant plan."

Jake expertly filled a beer mug and slid it down the bar to a waiting collared slave. Holding it carefully, she trotted back to her Master. "You on the schedule for next weekend?"

"Not Friday. I'm on call for the clinic all day—and problems often last into the evening." Alastair stepped out from behind the bar. "Give Rainie my best."

"Will do."

Before he reached the exit, he was intercepted by Z. "If you have a minute, perhaps we could talk." Z gestured toward an empty seating area.

"Of course." Alastair sank into one of the comfortable leather chairs.

"Maximillian did a fine job with Uzuri." Z smiled slightly. "I'm impressed he was able to obtain as much information as he did."

"He's a skilled interrogator," Alastair said mildly. "And she did go to him, after all."

Z chuckled. "I daresay she'd hoped a newer Master wouldn't push her as vigorously as one of the others."

"Max has never let being new slow him down." Probably something he'd learned when serving as a US Marine.

Z steepled his fingers. "Uzuri agrees she needs to work through her fear of large men. I'm looking for experienced Doms —big ones—I can trust to work with her. Would you and your cousin be interested?"

That was a fine compliment, although the thought of the little submissive playing with other Doms was unpalatable—even more now than it had been in the past. Alastair studied Z. "What other...qualifications...are you looking for?"

"Ah, that's the tricky part. Uzuri admitted to Maximillian that she wasn't afraid of Holt because he wasn't interested in her sexually." Z shook his head. "I'd seen them interact and thought she was doing better. I completely missed that distinction."

"I don't think any of us realized." After a second, Alastair caught on to the "qualification" Z wanted, and he huffed a laugh. "Yes, Z. Both Max and I are interested in her sexually."

"Then you would be willing to work with her from time to time? Nothing permanent, I remember."

"Max will have to speak with you himself." After seeing her at Nolan's house last Sunday, Max had said he was torn. He didn't want to get involved with her, yet he was drawn to help her. "For my part, I'm interested."

"Excellent." Z glanced around, spotted a submissive, and raised his hand.

A second later, the slender brown-haired male hurried over and bowed his head. "Master Z, how may I serve you?"

"Austin, I believe Uzuri was watching a scene in the dungeon. Would you bring her here, please?"

"Yes, *Sir*." The young man trotted off, bursting with the pleasure of being asked to serve.

The sight warmed Alastair's heart.

Within a couple of minutes, Austin was back.

Uzuri trailed behind him, and at the sight of Alastair, she bit her full lower lip.

Alastair smothered a smile. Well, might as well start as he meant to go on. He held out his hand.

She stopped dead, glanced at Z, and got no help. She took a step closer.

Alastair waited. The Dom who had trained him and Max at university had been big on silent domination. Without a verbal command, a submissive had to make a decision. Taking a Dom's offered hand meant she'd lowered her first defenses.

She set her hand in his.

"Good girl." As he closed his grip on her slender hand, her fingers trembled...and although most submissives were wary of Z, Uzuri's gaze was on Alastair. She was afraid of him.

He knew her fear was illogical, wasn't personal, yet it still burned like acid. Acknowledging her unintentional insult, he pushed it away. A Dom had no use for hurt feelings.

Instead, still holding her hand, he nodded at the floor.

She sank gracefully to her knees and managed to tear her gaze from his to look at Z.

Z studied her. "Uzuri, have you decided if Alastair sees you as yourself—and isn't interested in you because of your race?"

Alastair pressed his lips together to keep from smiling.

In the dark sitting area, a flush on her skin wouldn't be visible, so he laid the backs of his fingers against her cheek. Quite toasty.

Her head bowed, and her voice was close to a whisper. "I wasn't...honest, Master Z. I know he's not like that."

Z gave him an amused glance. "I'm pleased to hear that, because I asked Master Alastair to be one of those who will work with you on getting you past your fear of larger men."

She didn't...quite...cringe. "Yes, Sir."

Alastair waited until she looked up at him. "Your task tonight is simple. I want you to bring two bottles of water from the bar and join me until we finish the water. That's all, pet."

She swallowed. "Thank you, Sir." She was gone before he could add anything else.

When Z rose, Alastair lifted a hand. "Last week, when the lights were off, and you wore night-vision goggles, were you... controlling...the timing when the submissives left the carpet?"

Z smiled slightly and tilted his head in acknowledgement of a hit. Then he grinned. "She'll probably avoid you next week, but stay with it. I'll know you're making progress when she sabotages your lockers."

Uzuri returned a few minutes later with two bottled waters. Her footsteps were slow. Reluctant.

"Thank you, pet." Alastair took one bottle, then patted his lap. "Sit here, please."

She stiffened, and he could almost hear her telling herself to obey. He wanted to reassure her, to tell her he didn't plan to do anything, but her overcoming her own fears was the point of the exercise.

After a minute, she perched on his thighs, holding herself stiffly upright.

"Good girl." After drinking some water, he put an arm around her tense little body and shifted her to a more comfortable position against his chest. Then, leaving his arm around her waist, he leaned back and relaxed.

Minute by minute, her body maintained the rigid—tiring— posture. His silence and obvious lack of interest slowly registered.

After about ten minutes, her weight came to rest on him more and more.

When a half hour was up, he opened his eyes and smiled at how she'd ended up snuggled against him. Good enough. That had been all he'd planned to accomplish today.

"Off you go, love. Our time is over."

She looked up at him. Such big brown eyes, dark and beautiful. And confused.

CHAPTER EIGHT

I n her office at Brendall's Department Store, Uzuri glanced at the clock and winced. She needed to get out of here if she was going to get to the Shadowlands in time for her Friday barmaid shift. Thank goodness, her orders were almost finished.

Once again, she considered her buying plan for the spring clothing line. The classic blazers she'd ordered would look fine on any figure, and the colors were rich and clear. They should sell well. Oh, and she needed more of the basic black. More North-easterners were moving to Florida, and they adored wearing black. When she visited New York, sometimes it felt as if everyone on the streets was heading for a funeral.

Sighing, she rotated her aching shoulders. Talk about a late day. She'd have been finished sooner if she could have kept her mind on the work this week.

She blamed Master Z for a good half of her inability to focus. She still couldn't believe how he'd handed her off to Master Alastair last weekend.

And the memories of Alastair himself didn't help. He hadn't pushed her for a scene or tried to paw her or anything. Instead, he'd had her sit on his lap. Not talking. Not moving. Her fears had slowly trickled away. Wasn't it amazing how she'd ended up leaning against him? Warmth pooled in her center as she remembered his masculine scent. She'd simply...snuggled...against him, enjoying the slow rise and fall of his chest and the strength in the arm around her waist.

She'd had dreams of being held like that. Not needing to do or say anything, simply being...with...a man. He had no idea of the gift he'd given her.

Would he be there tonight? Flutters rose in her stomach like a myriad of wings.

What about Max? What if they were together? What if—she shook her head. *Focus, girl. Numbers.*

She stared at the purchase list. What about these straight skirts? They probably wouldn't sell as well. That design of skirt required a certain build to look good. So less of those. She lowered that number.

Her head lifted when she heard a couple of the other buyers leaving. "Zuri, have a nice weekend." "See you Monday."

"Good night, you two." The people upstairs here in the marketing and buying departments were wonderful, and she was making some good friends.

That sure wasn't true any longer with the sales associates in the women's clothing section. The incident with Carole had festered into a nightmare. Carole and her friends—all older white women—were telling the sales force that Uzuri, young and with a new college degree, had no knowledge of retail and was causing trouble.

No knowledge of retail? Uzuri snorted. She'd started in sales at sixteen in Cincinnati. It was true that she was new to this location, but she'd worked as an assistant fashion buyer in the other Brendall's in St. Petersburg. She had worked her ass off, both in selling and in taking evening college classes, to climb the ladder to the position of buyer.

However, she could hardly explain that to each woman, could she?

Her stomach knotted. Somehow, she needed to solve this. The sales associates were on the front lines, hearing everything the customers said about the current merchandise, what people wished the store carried, and what they didn't like. A buyer needed to be able to talk with the salespeople. Uzuri had always enjoyed that part of the job.

And it...hurt...to be disliked. All her life, she'd worked to be nice. To be polite, no matter the provocation.

Shaking her head, she returned to studying the numbers.

Sometime later, the buzzing of her phone interrupted her. A text message from her friend Kayla showed on the screen. "**Help! Have interview for a human resource position. Which outfit?**" Two selfies were attached.

Smiling, Uzuri leaned back in her office chair and studied them. *Hmm.* For a human resource job, there was no need to look particularly creative. A dependable, honest, friendly image would be the best choice.

The first photo showed her tall friend in a light blue dress that was lovely with her brown skin, but showed off her curves a little too well and the hemline was too short. The second photo showed Kayla in a classically tailored charcoal gray suit. Much better. The pink, lacy blouse had to go, though, as did the three-inch heels. A blouse in blue would project sincerity. Black pumps were boring but more appropriate.

Uzuri texted back with recommendations, received more selfies, and finally approved one. "**Nailed it**."

As she put her cell phone away with a feeling of satisfaction, she realized her small office window was dark. A glance at the clock showed it was after eight o'clock.

What? Omigod, if she didn't hurry, she'd be late getting to the Shadowlands. She gathered her purse and briefcase and hurried out of her tiny office, waving a hand at the janitor on the way to the elevator.

A hard rain was falling as she stepped out the employee door and opened her umbrella. Glowing like small moons in the darkness, the antiqued parking lot lights were beautiful but cast very little light. Uzuri stumbled over the curb, almost falling.

Fool girl. She needed to set an alarm on her phone and leave the building before sunset. Glancing around for her car, she smiled. It wasn't a problem to find it at this hour.

There were only three vehicles in the whole lot.

At her car, she discovered her key ring flashlight was dead. Triple A batteries didn't last long, did they? Juggling her umbrella and keys, she fumbled with the lock, got the door open, and tossed her stuff in.

A gust of wind blew rain over her before she could get the umbrella closed and the door shut.

With an exasperated grunt, she started the car and drove toward the exit.

Why wasn't the wheel turning evenly? The car felt *wrong*. Still in the parking lot, she stopped—this time under a streetlight. Not bothering with the umbrella, she jumped out. Her assessment didn't take more than a second.

The driver's side tire was pancake flat.

Oh, fine. As the cold rain pattered on her head and soaked through her clothes, she scowled. Forget being polite. She glared at the tire. "*Pike twa!*" Glared at the rain. "And fuck you, too."

So much for making it to the Shadowlands on time—or at all. Master Z wasn't going to be pleased.

She stared at the tire. She could change it herself. In the dark, empty lot? In the rain? No way.

The good Lord had put service stations on the planet for a reason. Her cell was in her purse. She'd call a tow company to come and change the tire.

After a glance around the dark lot, she shook her head. Not out here. Uh-uh.

She grabbed her purse, opened her umbrella, and started for the building. Leaving the pool of light was like leaving the last trace of civilization. Parking lots were creepy after dark. Really, really creepy.

Especially since Jarvis. In Cincinnati, when out with friends, she'd leave a nightclub, and in a dark parking lot, see him standing a few cars down. Just...watching.

Goosebumps lifted on her arms at the memory, and she sped up.

Should she call for a tow truck or simply take a taxi home for now? She winced at the thought of the cost. However, the unsettled feeling in her stomach increased, and suddenly all she wanted was to be home.

Taxi.

The rain hammered noisily down on her umbrella, and she squinted through the blackness.

The area around her lit up—and was that the sound of a car? She glanced over her shoulder and was almost blinded by the bright headlights heading for her fast.

Too fast.

With a scream, she leaped to the right. The car's bumper smashed into her left thigh, throwing her forward. She hit the pavement hard on her right hip and skidded over the wet concrete. With a horrible crack, her head hit the unyielding asphalt.

And the parking lot—the *world*—turned dark.

In the emergency room, Alastair smiled at his pale ten-year-old patient before giving her parents a reassuring look. "She's going to stay overnight while we run the tests I told you about. Meantime, we'll get some fluids into her. One of you can spend the night with her, if you wish."

As he left the parents arguing over which would stay—delightfully, they both wanted to remain—he glanced at his watch and sighed at the late hour.

"Hey, Doc. Your little Brianna is quite the cutie." In pink scrubs, a nurse slowed on her way to the nurse's station. "Your orders are in, and the peds unit knows she's coming right away."

"Thank you, Madge."

"No problem."

As they walked toward the desk, he heard a voice from one of the curtained cubicles.

"Mmmm, fine. Sleepy." The woman's resonant voice was like warm honey...and familiar.

"Madge, who's in there?"

"Not one of your kids, Doc. A pedestrian who got hit by a car in a parking lot." Madge stopped with him.

Frowning, Alastair took the clipboard from the rack outside the cubicle and pulled it up far enough to check the name. *Uzuri Cheval.* Concern tightened his grip on the board. "How badly is she hurt?"

"She got off lightly. Mild concussion, road rash, a hefty hematoma on one thigh where the bumper got her, hell of a bruise on her shoulder and other hip where she hit the concrete."

"Is someone here with her?"

"That's the problem. She said she didn't have anyone to call, and she's not thinking clearly enough to discharge her on her own."

A Shadowlands submissive—a trainee, no less—thinking she didn't have anyone to call? The thought hurt. He dropped the clipboard in the rack and walked into the cubicle.

For a while, Uzuri had been wavering in and out of the darkness, rousing for pain and questions, before sliding back into the warm pool of night. Night was better.

"Uzuri."

Some men had such beautiful deep voices.

"Uzuri." This time, authority underscored the demand.

She managed to open her eyes and winced at the brightness of the room.

In a tailored button-down, sapphire shirt, Master Alastair stood over her. Why did his eyes have to be so stunning? Not perfectly horizontal, but angling up slightly. Not brown, but a smoky green in this light and framed with thick black eyelashes that didn't need mascara. Even his intense frown couldn't detract from his amazing good looks.

"You're so pretty." Her voice was a raspy whisper.

"Thank you." His sensual lips curved up and matched the smiles of the happy-faced dolphins on his tie.

She frowned. He was a children's doctor, not an emergency doc. "What are you doing here?"

"One of my patients is in the ER. I was getting her admitted when I heard your voice."

"Oh." She tried to sit up—and stopped immediately. Someone was playing with jackhammers inside her head. Her hips and shoulder felt like she'd been kicked. No. Actually, *everything* hurt.

"Let me see what damage you racked up." Ever so gently, he turned her head. "Look at me."

Light stabbed into her left eye, then the right, and her head exploded with fresh pain. When she moaned, he patted her hand. "Sorry, pet. I had to check."

She concentrated on breathing through the pain. Masochists were insane. Who would want to be hurt for fun?

Carefully, he pulled back at the thin blanket to check her shoulders, her hips, and her legs. "Lots of scrapes and bruises. You're going to be sore tomorrow."

"I know."

He smoothed down the ugly hospital gown she wore. What idiot designed those things anyway? "Uzuri, how did you get run down in a parking lot?"

"That was my question, as well." Max stalked into the cubicle.

She stiffened as the two men loomed over her, one on each side. However, when her gaze met Alastair's, she saw his worry. For her.

"Uzuri?" Max prompted. Although his eyes were sharp—hard, even—his concern for her was there, as well.

"A car ran into me." It sure had. Her whole body hurt. And so did her head. She half closed her eyes to try to cut down on the brightness.

Max moved closer.

Although his sport coat was a boring brown over a white button-up shirt, it didn't disguise how broad his shoulders were. Think of how many jackets he could sell. Maybe he'd agree to model coats in the men's department. "And Alastair can model suits and then—"

Max snorted. "The little subbie is in la la land."

She started to shake her head and, at the stab of pain, changed her mind quickly. She forced her eyes open. When had they shut? "Can I go home now? I want to go home."

"Easy, young miss." Alastair put a warm hand on her arm and some of her worries faded. He glanced at his cousin. "What are you doing here?"

"Dan and I came—"

"Did someone die?" Alastair asked.

"Nobody's dead." Dan Sawyer entered the cubicle.

Uzuri frowned. *Why was Master Dan here?* He was a Tampa cop. In homicide. She hadn't killed anyone, had she? No. And she was still alive.

Right?

Dan walked over to the cart. "One of the dispatchers is a club member, and she gave me a heads-up about Uzuri. Max and I came by to make sure our trainee was all right."

"Not a trainee." She frowned at how drunk she sounded.

"Sorry, Uzuri, but we all still think of you that way." Dan grinned. "In fact, I'm not sure you're allowed to ever resign that title."

Well, honestly.

Frowning, Max curled his strong hand around hers. His *very callused* hand—she knew the feel of it. Her gaze went to Alastair who was holding her left hand. Her gaze focused on his long fingers and his perfectly groomed beard. Beard. *Dom Captor* and *Dom Beard.*

"Uzuri." Max broke into her thoughts. "What happened?"

Happened? Oh, the parking lot. Her mind felt like tattered fabric, not doing the job at all. "I left work late and it was dark and my tire was flat and I was going back to the building to call a taxi but a car ran into me."

"Deliberately?" Max growled.

"Yes. No. I don't know. It was hard to see, all dark and raining hard and my dress is dark blue." She gestured at her clothing only she was in a hospital gown. Turning her head, she spotted the remnants of her clothes. *What?* "The nurses *ruined* my dress."

Max actually laughed. "That is a fucking cute pout, baby."

"Could be you weren't seen," Dan noted.

Max frowned. "But the driver should have felt the impact."

"Unless he—or they—was drunk. Or stoned. It's Friday night." Dan's mouth flattened into a disapproving line.

"Guess that's possible." Max turned back to her. "Can you identify the car or driver?"

"No." All she remembered were the two giant headlights bearing down on her and jumping and pain. Her brows drew together. "How did I get here, anyway?"

"One of the cleaning staff left early and almost ran over your purse. When he stopped to pick it up, he spotted you and called 911."

Bless him. "My purse is here?"

Max walked over to where the ruins of her dress lay. "It's here. Still has wallet and money and cards. Keys. Umbrella. You're good, baby."

Alastair squeezed her hand. "I'll take care of you. Max and Dan will deal with your car." He looked across the cart to his cousin, then Dan.

Max nodded. "Yeah, Doc. You handle the medical; we'll take care of the mechanical."

A forties-something, brunette nurse entered, frowned at Max and Dan, and walked over to Uzuri with a smile. "You look more awake. How's the pain?"

The nurse wore a mock wrap, fuchsia scrub top that set off her curvy figure nicely, and Uzuri gave her attire a nod of approval. "I feel better. Can I go home now?"

"We'll see." The nurse turned to Alastair. "Dr. Drago." Her lips quirked, and she winked at Uzuri. "Isn't Ms. Cheval a bit old to be one of your patients?"

Alastair chuckled. "Uzuri is a friend. Is she discharged, Madge?"

Despite the stab of pain, Uzuri tried to sit up and look healthy.

"Maybe." Madge frowned. "The radiologist said nothing interesting showed on the scan or x-rays. However, Dr. Benson says that since she took a thump to the head, she needs someone with her for the next twelve hours. If no one is available, we'll admit her overnight."

Oh no. "I'm fine," Uzuri whispered. "I don't need anyone to—"

"I'll be with her," Alastair said.

"What?" Uzuri's gaze flashed to his and dropped when he gave her a look. A Dom look.

The nurse nodded. "Excellent. I'll get the discharge forms."

"Sounds good," Max said. "Dan and I'll check on the vehicle, and I'll report when I get home. Or are we staying at her house?"

Uzuri stared at him. *We? Staying?* "B-b-but..."

"Our place," Alastair said.

"All right." Max's easy agreement stunned her. He leaned forward. "Be a good girl and don't give Alastair any trouble, princess." His voice lowered to a growling whisper. "Neither of us hits subbies, but Alastair enjoys spanking them."

At her quick inhalation, he laughed and kissed her cheek. "I'm glad you're not badly damaged, darlin'. I was worried." Straightening, he nodded to his cousin. "Take care of her, and I'll see you in an hour or two."

Alastair sat Uzuri on the closed toilet seat in the guest bath and smiled at her confused look.

The little miss was always polite, but she wasn't impossible to read, even when she tried to cover up her emotions. Months ago, during their scene, he'd easily picked up when she grew anxious, although he hadn't understood why at the time.

Now, however, she showed no fear of being alone with him—probably due to the medications she'd received in hospital. Perhaps someday the reason would be because she knew him and trusted him.

"You're heading for bed, but we shall get you cleaned up first," he said gently and wet a washcloth. To keep from setting off her fears, he went down on one knee beside her. A scrape on her cheekbone glistened with antibiotic ointment, and he carefully cleaned the dried blood streaks from her cheek and jaw.

"I can do it." She tried to take the washcloth.

"You can barely sit upright." He wiped the mud off her neck. The nurses had irrigated, debrided, and bandaged the abrasions and lacerations, but had only cleaned off enough of the other areas to ensure there were no other injuries.

He moved down. Since her clothes had been cut off in the ER, the staff had offered a set of scrubs. He'd dug out a spare shirt from his hospital locker instead. The shirt was far easier to slide on and off. He unbuttoned the first few buttons before she noticed.

"Sir. No."

"Pet, you're covered in mud and blood."

She looked down, saw the red stains on the fabric, and her stricken look wrenched his heart. "I've ruined your shirt."

"Blood washes out." When her unhappy expression didn't lighten, he touched her cheek and said lightly, "I'm a doctor; I should know. But we must wipe you down before you get in bed."

"I can do it."

"Sweetheart, you can barely move."

Her big eyes focused on his face as he unbuttoned the shirt and slid off only the right side, leaving her left side covered.

"No."

"Uzuri, I've not only seen your bare breasts, but I've played with them, too. Twice."

Startled, she stared up at him. "Oh. You really have. I'm being silly. But...twice?" Her forehead wrinkled. "We did one scene and then...it *was* you. You and Max. Last weekend. I *knew* it."

Interesting that she'd figured that out. "Yes. Tomorrow, we'll talk about the scenes we've done together, but for now, let's get you comfortable and into bed." Gently, he washed down over her collarbone. Her breasts—undoubtedly protected by a bra—were clean and uninjured. She had lovely breasts. Not too pendulous, but heavy enough to have some sag, to be a good weight in his hands when he cupped them. He did like to be able to fill his hands.

Nevertheless, this wasn't the time.

As he washed, he catalogued injuries. Her right shoulder had nonstick gauze on it. He checked beneath and found the extensive scrapes were well cleaned and glistened with antibiotic ointment. Still oozing. He'd change the pad later.

Her side and back were muddy, but undamaged. Her right hip was deeply scraped, swollen, and bruised. Her skimpy dress had offered no protection against concrete. "This is going to hurt, pet. Hold still for me now." Rinsing the washcloth frequently, he washed that side, and tweezed out a couple of fabric threads the nurses had missed.

Breathing through the pain, the brave girl silently endured the treatment, although tears filled her big eyes. When he finished, she studied her hip. "No wonder it hurts."

"I'm sure it does. Stay put for a minute." Max kept his clothes until threadbare, so the flannel shirt Alastair dug out of his dresser was worn soft as a tissue.

Trying to keep her at ease, he pulled the flannel shirt on over her cleansed right side before removing the bloodstained one on the left.

After he finished washing her torso, he checked her left thigh. Swollen, hot, black from bruising. She was lucky the bone hadn't fractured.

The driver of the car hadn't even stopped. What a fucking wanker.

Alastair tossed the washcloth into the sink. In the war-torn countries where he'd volunteered, mangled bodies were far too common. Yet seeing this little subbie covered in blood had shaken him. "All finished."

"Oh, good." Her smile could brighten any man's day.

He slid her left arm into the flannel shirt and buttoned it up, then grinned. She wasn't that small, but Max's huge shirt made her look like a child in a big brother's clothes. The sleeves ended inches below her fingertips.

After rolling up her sleeves, he rose. "You may use the facilities alone, if you promise to call when finished, so I can assist you out of the room."

"I can walk by myself." Her mouth set in a stubborn line.

Relief washed through him. She was starting to feel more herself. "That isn't an option I offered, now is it?"

After a second, she sighed. "All right."

Wasn't it amazing how a full bladder could hasten accord?

He helped her stand, put the toilet cover up, and left her to complete the rest herself. She'd be hurting, but that task she could accomplish.

And then he'd tuck her into bed. The thought of her sleeping peacefully under his roof was quite pleasing.

It was interesting his cousin had agreed so readily to give her shelter. Despite Max's protestations, he wasn't immune to the little submissive's appeal.

Yellow headlights came at her, straight for her, but Uzuri's feet stuck to the pavement as if someone had glued her pumps down. The car slammed into her. The *pain*. Screaming, she flew—

She woke, gasping for air.

Her hand was clutching something soft. A blanket. She wasn't on pavement, but was lying on something soft. A glow from her left revealed a bathroom with a nightlight.

Oh. She was at Alastair and Max's house. The crack in the curtains showed only darkness outside, and the bedside clock said it was eleven at night. When she rolled over, she had to stifle a moan. An hour had been long enough for every single bruise and sore spot to stiffen.

Gritting her teeth, she sat up. Her right shoulder and hip hurt, her left hip was even worse, and the scrape on her forehead burned. Her head felt as if someone was rhythmically wringing the brain tissues inside. But she needed to pee. Needed water.

Needed to move. Carefully, she eased out of bed and limped into the bathroom.

While she was washing her hands afterward, she discovered that someone—some saint of a person—had left a glass, an unopened toothbrush, and a travel-sized tube of toothpaste on the counter. As she painfully brushed her teeth, she wished he'd left her a massive bottle of aspirin, too.

She winced at the sight of herself in the mirror. Talk about a disaster. The side of her forehead was bruised black, her abraded cheekbone was swollen, and her complexion was a dismal muddy color.

Her eye makeup? Omigod. She saw where Alastair had wiped the streaks from her cheeks. Rather than a clown, she resembled a zombie. A slutty zombie.

That, at least, she could fix. Gingerly, she washed her face.

At a noise, she opened the bathroom door. Alastair stood in the bedroom.

As his gaze ran over her, she was suddenly too aware of the shortness of the flannel shirt and how her breasts wobbled against the thin material.

He smiled. "You do look better, although I'd hoped you'd sleep all night. Since you're awake, would you like to come downstairs for a bite of something—or should I bring it up here?"

Have a Shadowlands Master running up and down the stairs to serve her? The thought was an outrage. "I'd like to go downstairs. Please." If she could manage without breaking her neck. Her aching head felt as if her skull was stuffed with cotton batting. Her legs seemed to be attached to someone else. Or something else. Maybe a penguin.

How in the world was she going to drive home?

"Downstairs, it is." When she reached the door, he wrapped an arm around her waist. Rather than frightening her, his size and strength were comforting as she limped down the stairs.

He settled her in a buttery-soft leather recliner in what he called the television room and tucked a soft, beige-and-bisque-colored afghan over her bare legs. Bending, he put two fingers under her chin, lifted her head gently, and studied her face. "You appear to have a headache."

She nodded carefully.

"Then a pain tablet will come with the food."

"Oh, yes. Please."

"I'll be right back." After kissing her cheek, he disappeared into the kitchen.

She put her hand to her cheek where the warmth of his lips lingered. Why was he being so nice?

Head aching, she gazed around at the room. It was beautiful with a high ceiling, heavy crown moldings, and tall, arched windows. Beige Venetian plaster on the walls served as a backdrop for the rich brown couch and chairs. A dark red and brown area rug in a western design covered the gleaming hardwood floor. Elaborately carved bookcases ran the length of the far wall. A widescreen TV unabashedly took up the other wall with the furniture arranged to view it. This was a cozy room designed for movies and popcorn, sports games and beer, or even a good book and hot chocolate.

Alastair carried in a tray with wine, water, toast, and soup in a mug. He set everything but the wine on the end table beside her. "You get nothing fancy until we see how your stomach handles food. But you need to eat something before taking a pain med."

"Thank you, doctor." She'd tried for a wry tone of voice, but it came out sincere instead—because she truly was grateful. She picked up the heavy mug, sipped, and smiled at the familiar taste. With every heavy snowfall, Mama had made tomato soup. The memory was comforting, even as the soup's warmth melted away the last of the cold inside.

She sighed and tried the bread. The heavy grain toast was buttered and hot. Perfect. "This is a beautiful room."

"We like it." Picking up the glass of wine, Alastair sat on the couch to her right and stretched out his long legs. He'd changed into casual khaki pants and a short-sleeved, tan shirt. His feet were bare, and even his toes were long and elegant. "Combining two homes gave us plenty of options. This room has mostly Max's furniture."

"It looks like Max." The seams of the leather recliners and couch were studded with antiqued nail heads. Masculine to the nth degree.

Alastair grinned. "My furniture edges toward the Victorian period. Max's is more traditional western U.S. We've both traveled and returned with knick-knacks from everywhere. Merging everything has been interesting."

Western and British. Black and white. "Um. How did you and Max... I mean, you're black and Max is white. You're from England, and he's American."

Rather than being offended, Alastair looked amused. "My mother's black, British, and loves volunteering in poverty-stricken countries. She met my father—he's white—when he'd flown to the Philippines to provide disaster relief after an earthquake. They apparently clicked."

Uzuri nodded. Death and disaster. Perfect ingredients for a passionate affair. "But they didn't stay together?"

"No. When I made my presence known, they married, but Mum is a city girl, through and through. My father and Max's father own the Drago ranch in Colorado and are ranchers to the bone. The marriage simply didn't work."

As close as he and Max were, his father must have gotten custody. But, no. "If you grew up with Max in the States, why do you have an accent?"

"I spent a lot of time flying back and forth. I attended school in London and spent every summer vacation on the ranch." He smiled. "Mum used the childfree time for her volunteer work."

"Oh." She glanced around the room again. Max had only been in Tampa since summer, and she'd heard Alastair bought the house before that. Although it had been dark when she arrived, she'd seen that the cream-colored brick house was an Italianate style with a square center tower and probably well over a hundred years old. It was about as classic and conservative as a man could get. She'd bet the antique, beautifully carved bookcases were Alastair's—yet they were perfect in this room. "Confining yourself to all one style can be boring."

She didn't do that herself. Her business attire started with a stylishly classic suit or dress. Then she'd add a colorful scarf and shoes, signature necklace or belt to show her individuality within the confines of what was permissible in business. She did the same with her hair—restrained enough for business, natural enough to satisfy her own needs.

As Uzuri ate and looked around, Alastair quietly drank his wine. His silence was...undemanding, exerting no pressure to try to fill the quiet. The old house felt peaceful, too, as if it had seen its share of drama and not much ruffled it any longer.

There she went, getting all fanciful.

She swallowed the last bite of toast. "That was just what I needed. Thank you. And thank you for uh...breaking me out...of the hospital."

"It was our pleasure, pet."

"If you tell me where my car is, I'll get out of your hair."

"You're not in my hair. I enjoy your company."

That made her feel all warm and happy, even if she didn't believe him.

He tilted his head, listening to something. "For the answer in regard to your vehicle, I believe Max is home."

A door shut, and footsteps sounded in the foyer.

"In the TV room," Alastair called.

Max appeared. With his sport coat off, his pistol was on full display. He really was a police officer, wasn't he?

As his gaze ran over her, a smile lightened his harsh face. "Nice shirt, baby."

She looked down. The shirt she wore was an aged blue flannel —not Alastair's style at all. He'd given her one of Max's shirts. "I..."

"I like you in it, princess." He glanced at Alastair. "I need to shower and change. I'll be back shortly."

Before she could ask about her car, he disappeared. Alastair leaned forward and handed her an oblong white pill. "Before he returns, let's get that pain under control."

Ugh. She hated taking pills. However, she swallowed it dutifully. Anything to relieve the headache.

Within a few minutes, Max returned, clad in blue, cotton drawstring pants and a white, V-neck T-shirt. On him, the casual look was incredibly sexy.

Beer in hand, he took the other chair and leaned forward to study her. "How're you feeling?"

"Really, not too bad. I'm fine."

He glanced at Alastair and raised a brow. "Doc?"

"Fine might be overstating matters, but she suffered mostly bruising and road rash. The headache should ease by tomorrow. The limp might take longer. She's lucky not to have a broken femur."

"No shit." Max took a long pull of beer. "For your car... What with the rain and being a Friday night, the roadside assistance companies are backlogged. Dan and I would have changed the tire ourselves if you'd had a spare."

She winced. "I used it last month and...didn't get it replaced." When he frowned at her, she felt like a total loser.

"No worries. The tow company will bring a tire and change it out tomorrow afternoon."

"Tomorrow afternoon. B-b-but..." *Okay, think, girl.* She'd simply take a taxi home tonight. Then tomorrow—or even Monday— take one to the department store to pick up her car. "If you let me know the cost of the service and the tire, I'll bring the money to the Shadowlands next weekend."

"Don't worry about it, Zuri." Max's mouth tightened. "From the looks of your tires, they're all due to be replaced."

Yes, she knew. She picked up her glass, swirling the water. "I held off on the tires because I was going to get a newer car. I almost had the money, but I moved and had deposits and stuff." College tuition had eaten up her extra money for years. With her recent promotion, she'd now be able to pull ahead.

"I should be going before it gets much later." She rose.

"How exactly are you planning to get home?" Alastair asked softly.

"That's why taxis were invented." She needed her purse and phone...which were upstairs. At the thought of climbing those stairs, she felt her hip start to whine. She limped toward the door.

And was swept off her feet. As her head spun crazily, she was cradled against a rock-hard chest. "Hey!"

"You are not going anywhere." Max frowned down at her and gently set her back on the leather recliner.

"Excuse me. You can't...can't...." Unable even to think of the right words, she struggled to stand again.

"Do. Not. Move."

At Max's growled order, her muscles went on strike, and all she could do was stare. "B-b-but I need to go home."

"You can barely walk, let alone see straight." Max shook his head. "No."

She turned to Alastair who would surely see reason. During the drama, he hadn't even moved. No, he had; he'd put his feet up on the coffee table.

"When I did you the favor of"—his grin appeared and disappeared—"*breaking you out*, I took responsibility for you. Would you have me go back on my word to the ER doctor?"

She stared at him. The time in the emergency room was foggy, but she did remember they hadn't been willing to let her leave. Until Alastair had appeared. "I can't stay *here*."

"Why not?" Standing two feet in front of her, Max frowned down. "You don't like the bed? Don't like us?"

Omigod, she'd been rude. "I'm sorry. I didn't mean that. It's wonderful, and you've been wonderful and—"

"Max, now you've done it." Alastair's hazel eyes lit with amusement.

"I haven't even started." Max pinned her with a penetrating stare. A cop's stare.

She picked up the glass of water to have something to hold. "Is something...wrong?"

"Now, see, I'm trying to figure that out. The reason you had a flat was because someone cut off the valve stem."

The valve stem. Wasn't that the little rubber thing sticking out where a tire got air into it at the pump? "Cut it?" She shook her head, wishing her brain would kick into gear.

"Yep." He made a scissor-like gesture with his first two fingers. "It was deliberate."

No. As fear iced her bones, her hand went limp, and the glass dropped—only to be caught by Alastair in mid-air.

He set the glass down, rose, then gently lifted her and sat down in the recliner—with her in his lap.

"No, no. Let go." Panic swept through her and she struggled.

"Shh-shh-shh, sweetheart. You're safe here. Shhh." The deep, slow voice penetrated the fog of fear and swept it away.

She sucked in a breath. *Safe. Not alone.* Her fingers curled into his shirt pocket and gripped.

"There now. That's better." Alastair snuggled her closer, his left arm around her shoulders, and his right across her thighs.

The warmth of his body seeped into hers and eased the shaking that had started deep inside. With a sigh, she leaned her head on his shoulder.

After a minute or two, Alastair said quietly, "Go ahead with your questions, Max."

Max moved to sit on the arm of the couch and studied her.

"Way I see it, we have three choices for who flattened your tire. Your stalker, Kassab. Some asshole who wanted to trash a car—any car. Or someone who's mad at you."

A day's beard growth darkened his jaw. "The person who flattened your tire might be the same one who ran you down. Or not."

Someone had run her down. *Not Jarvis. Please, don't let Jarvis be here.* Her muscles tensed, making her head throb painfully.

"Easy, darlin'." Max's voice softened. "Anne looked up Kassab for me. In his factory, he does three to four ten hour shifts and hasn't missed any workdays. She checked—and I don't want to know how—but he didn't take a plane from Cincinnati. So unless he spent a whole day driving down here, which is possible but not likely, he's not your hit-and-run driver."

Uzuri let out a soft breath of relief.

A reassuring rumble sounded deep in Alastair's chest. To her relief, his arms stayed around her, a barrier against the world.

Max leaned forward. "Besides Kassab, is there anyone who'd want to cause you grief? Maybe someone at work?"

She got along with everyone in the offices. There wasn't anyone...except for Carole down in sales. Uzuri stiffened.

Max's keen eyes sharpened. "That's a yes. Who?"

"Although she's a little...angry...with me"—Uzuri shook her head—"I can't point a finger at her. She probably didn't—"

"We'd have trouble proving anything with no witnesses and you not seeing anything." Max took her hand. "But I'd like to keep an eye on things. Maybe talk with 'her' so she knows the police are taking an interest."

Send the police to talk with Carole? It would make everything worse. "I don't want—"

"Zuri. Give me her name, or I'll show up at Brendall's and interview everyone from the owner to the janitor." His tone held out no chance of compromise.

"You *wouldn't*." She stared at him.

"Tell him, love." Alastair's deeper voice was just as unyielding.

"Carole Fuller. She's a sales associate in women's clothing."

"Good enough." Max squeezed her fingers before releasing her hand.

"It's late, and she's exhausted." Alastair rose, lifting her as easily as if he were carrying a pillow. "Time for bed, pet."

Max also rose. He stepped close and cupped her cheek. "Night, princess." He lightly kissed her lips.

"But. My car. I need—"

Max shook his head. "Get a good night's rest, and we'll discuss it in the morning."

"But..."

"This is not up for discussion at this time," Alastair told her and steel underlay the soft tone. The Dom was fully as uncompromising as his cousin.

With a resigned sigh, she leaned her head on his chest and... and simply took in the sheer comfort of being carried. Being cared for.

Being protected.

CHAPTER NINE

Max entered the guest room midmorning and smiled. Zuri was still zonked out. He and Alastair had taken turns looking in on her last night, although he'd insisted that Alastair do the neuro checks. Shining lights in people's eyes and asking idiotic questions should be left to the sadists in the crowd.

Taking a moment to sit beside the bed, Max did a quick assessment. Her breathing was regular and even. Color was much better.

Damn, she was a pretty woman, all smooth skin and long eyelashes. Her lips were slightly bowed, her lower lip fuller. Bitable. Her delicate fingers were tipped with a sky blue polish. She couldn't afford tires...so did she do her own nails or spend the bucks at some salon?

She was on her back, one arm flung over her head, beautifully relaxed. Seemed like in his presence, she tensed up. Given her past, he understood why, but it eased his heart to know she trusted him and Alastair enough to be able to sleep like this.

The rest would come.

No. No, it wouldn't.

Jesus, what the fuck was he thinking? He had no future with

this little bundle of troubles. Look what'd happened to him with the last woman he'd tried to help.

Shaking his head, he walked out.

A couple of hours later, Max was enjoying a late cup of coffee on the patio when a noise caught his attention.

The French doors were open. Uzuri stood in the doorway, obviously not wanting to disturb him. Her eyelids were puffy with sleep, her hair pulled into a haphazard twist. She wore one of his old robes that he'd left on the foot of her bed. "Good morning?"

"It is. C'mon out, baby." He pointed to the chair on the other side of the patio table.

Moving stiffly, she settled on the edge of the chair.

"How do you feel?" he asked. "Did you find the pain pill and milk Alastair left on the nightstand?"

"I feel better, and yes, thank you." Her chin lifted slightly. "I appreciate the care you've taken of me. I'm going to call a taxi and get out of your hair now."

"Nope."

Fuck, he liked when she wasn't awake enough to conceal her emotions. Surprise was followed by a healthy bit of anger. She was damned cute.

"You can't keep me here."

"Well, no. That might be against the law"—he scratched his cheek—"I think. Though sometimes, the letter of the law does kind of escape me."

Her brows drew together, and she started to stand up.

"However, Z said to keep you for another night. In fact, he doesn't want to see any of us until next weekend."

She sank back into the chair. "Master Z?" She spoke the name as if the Shadowlands owner was God Himself.

Max smothered a laugh. Guess to the submissive members, that would hold true. "Alastair let him know you were hurt."

Her big brown eyes rounded. "Oh noooo, I was supposed to be a barmaid last night. I didn't call to say I wouldn't be in. How could I have forgotten?" Looking as if she'd be whipped to death, she slumped in the chair.

Max frowned. Had he missed seeing a sadistic streak in the Shadowlands Master? After a second, he carefully asked, "Will Z punish you physically?"

"Oh no, of course not. It's only...he's done so much for me. I hate to let him down."

She wasn't worried for herself, but couldn't stand disappointing Z. Here was a true submissive—one who wanted to serve more than take. *Huh.*

"But he said you had to put me up for another night? *Why?*" Her question came out almost a wail.

This time Max couldn't suppress his laugh. "Two reasons, baby. One: You're still moving badly, and he doesn't trust you not to overdo. Two: When the ER staff asked you if you had anyone to help you, you said no. According to Z, you have a whole crew of girlfriends who would drop everything to be there for you. Gotta say, if I was one of your buddies, I'd feel pretty hurt."

Max's words stabbed into Uzuri. Right into her heart. Despite the ache in her shoulder, she wrapped her arms around herself to contain the unexpected blow. She'd hurt her friends?

She swallowed hard. "I was trying not to be a bother. I didn't mean to-to hurt their feelings."

Warm hands closed on her shoulders. Alastair had walked up behind her chair. "It will be all right, Uzuri."

No. No, it wouldn't. Tears filled her eyes.

Max's face softened. "Why, baby? Why didn't you call them?"

She couldn't speak. She wasn't even sure of an answer.

Dressed in a white tank and khaki shorts that revealed muscular legs, Alastair sat beside her and took her hand. "I knew a service submissive who was overjoyed to give, but felt guilty if she needed help herself. Add to that the *strong black woman* image so prevalent in this country?"

"And a little subbie ends up in a trap." Max frowned. "Does that sound right, princess?"

Uzuri nodded. Needing help felt like failure. She was strong. Still...all her friends counted on each other. Called each other for help. She frowned. Why didn't she ever ask anyone, then? The answer welled up, dark and ugly. *Because I don't deserve—*

"Deserve?" Alastair's hand tightened on hers.

Omigod, she'd spoken aloud.

Max crouched in front of Uzuri, took her other hand, and asked in a rumbling croon, "Explain to me, darlin'. Don't you think you merit help?"

She shook her head no and then bit her lip. That wasn't right, was it?

"Why?" Alastair rubbed his thumb over the back of her hand. "Did your mother feel you weren't worthy?"

How could she feel trapped between the two Doms and yet... cared for? "Mama was wonderful. She was always proud of me. She even enrolled me in a private school so I'd get the best education possible."

"Your buddies at the school, maybe?" Max asked. "Did they make you feel unworthy of support?"

"A private school can be cruel," Alastair prompted.

Uzuri shook her head. Sure, a few snotty girls in her private Catholic school hadn't wanted the poor black girl to be in their classes. Others had become her friends, and her set had been the smart, fun ones. They'd helped each other with everything, including pulling tricks on the... *Oh.* "The teachers." Her brows drew together.

"What did the teachers do, Zuri?" Max asked.

"Some of them didn't think I should be there. They wouldn't answer my questions or help when I couldn't figure something out. It was like I didn't exist. I shouldn't exist." She realized her hands had fisted over the men's and wouldn't relax.

"Because they saw you as nothing but a black girl?" Max asked.

She blinked. The Dom was awfully blunt, wasn't he?

Max gave his cousin an amused look. "Shocked the subbie again, did I?"

When she looked up at Alastair to see his reaction, his attention was on her, not Max. "Was that the reason they didn't approve of you, Uzuri?"

"Maybe." She sighed. "Or because we weren't rich. My mama was a secretary and put in time at the school after hours to pay the tuition. It sure seemed to bother some people."

A small smile tipped the corners of Alastair's sensuous lips. "Ah. That's more the British way. If you're in the lower class, it doesn't matter if you're black or white."

Max snorted. "In that case, it's a good thing you were born with a silver spoon between your lips, cuz."

"Quite." Alastair studied Uzuri. "Do you feel as if you're less deserving of help than everyone else?"

"N-no. Not if I think about it. I do deserve help. I'm smart. And strong." She frowned. "I work hard and I'm honest and...and I'm a nice person."

The sun lines at the edges of Max's eyes crinkled. "Good to know. But it's not good that you got turned down so much when you were a kid."

"Probably in ways that hurt." Alastair's expression held an understanding she wasn't used to. "So much that now you instinctively avoid asking for help."

"Guess we'll have to work on that response, too." Max squeezed her hand and rose. "I'm going to watch some football. Come on in if you want to watch the Buffaloes kick Wildcat ass."

As Max disappeared into the house, Uzuri turned to Alastair. "Wh-what did he mean, work on my response?"

"We're Doms, pet. You're a submissive with a problem. What do you think?"

Oh no. "But Master Z asked you to help me learn to be around bigger men. Nothing else."

His lips quirked up. "No worries, little miss. We're quite flexible." Alastair tapped her chin. "While I get you some food, I want you to consider what we discussed and why you need to be able to ask for help like other people."

Quietly, he walked into the house, leaving her alone on the patio. With *homework*.

An hour later, Alastair opened the front door and smiled at Jake's woman, Rainie. In a bright blue sundress that showed off her colorful tattoos, the lushly curved submissive beamed at him. "Are you ready for the new member of your family?"

"We are, indeed." He looked down to see a dog hiding behind her. The way the pup watched with frightened dark brown eyes quite broke his heart.

"Hunter is a little timid," Rainie said. "I think he had a rough time of it after his owner died."

"I see." Alastair motioned her forward. "Come on in."

"Actually, I have a cat in hysterics." Rainie glanced back at the van she was driving. "Jessica said Uzuri was here?"

"She is."

"She knows Hunter and the adoption routine. She'll walk you through it."

"Why would Uzuri know—"

"Gotta go." Without waiting for him to finish, Rainie thrust the leash into Alastair's hand along with the folder she was carrying. "I'll be back as soon as I get the calico settled in her new home." She hurried back to her vehicle and opened the van door.

Alastair could hear the cat screeching. No wonder Rainie was in a rush.

"Well, Hunter." He looked down. First get the dog inside, then they could make friends. "Let's go see if Uzuri knows you." Although that did seem unlikely considering her distaste for animals.

The dog's nails clicked across the oak flooring as Alastair led him to the back and outside onto the wide, screened patio. Enclosing the swimming pool, the tables and chairs, and the garden pond, the huge screened-in patio overlooked the land-scaped backyard to the southwest. Although caging the pool as well as the patio had involved immense amounts of screen, he appreciated the insect-free-zone.

He looked toward the mini-pond to his right. The pretty submissive was curled up on a lounge chair in the shade of the live oak.

"Uzuri, Rainie bought Hunter by."

"Rainie?" She sat up and saw Hunter. "Puppy!"

With a yip of delight, the pointer tugged the leash out of Alastair's hands and charged across the concrete.

Alastair stared in surprise as the self-professed dog-hater slid out of her chair and onto the concrete. Despite her pained movements, she still pulled the dog into her lap as if he were the puppy she'd called him instead of around sixty-five pounds.

Squirming happily, Hunter covered her face and neck with frantic licks as if to say, *Rainie brought me here and left me with a stranger!*

Alastair simply watched. *Dog hater, hmm?*

Winces and grimaces showed Uzuri was hurting, but her focus was on comforting the dog. "You're okay, Hunter. You'll be fine. This is a good place, puppy." Her voice was a low murmur, much the way Alastair talked to terrified children, and within a couple of minutes, the dog was calm and ready to look around.

Uzuri bit her lip, looking up at Alastair. "Please don't be upset with him. His owner was old and lived alone. Hunter's had a lot to deal with in the last month."

"I understand."

For someone who hated pets, she appeared quite comfortable hugging one. Holding the dog against her, she ruffled his short hair.

Giving both the dog and girl some space, Alastair picked up the folder, settled down on the concrete, and leaned against a post.

Hunter and Uzuri both relaxed. Alastair smiled as Hunter's nose lifted in his direction, testing the scents now that he wasn't terrified.

"He's a beautiful dog," Alastair flipped open the folder. The forms were starred where signatures were needed, and a pen had been tucked in the pocket for convenience. Quite nicely organized. "Rainie said you knew your way around the adoption papers?"

"I help her out occasionally." Uzuri rubbed her cheek against the dog's, collected a few more licks, and giggled. "It gives me a chance to get my puppy and kitten fix met."

"Ah." As he pulled the papers out, he studied her more closely. The Shadowlands member records focused on BDSM preferences, adding medical and personal histories only when the information might affect scene play. Although Z received more information from the mandatory background check, he kept most of it confidential. "What exactly do you do at Brendall's?"

"I'm a fashion buyer."

"Are you now? No wonder you dress so beautifully."

Her face lit. "Thank you."

As he perused the papers, he smiled. Stylish wasn't the operating word today since she was wearing a huge robe of Max's and no makeup. Despite her outburst to Rainie about not liking dogs, she didn't appear concerned about getting fur on her only item of clothing. Alastair signed two papers about dog care before he noticed Hunter's brown nose next to his leg. *Progress.* He worked through another paper before holding out his hand, palm up.

Hunter sniffed his fingers, then dropped his head and lowered his gaze. Alastair stroked his short fur, suffering a pang of loss at the familiar feel. Even now, he missed Jeeves.

Hunter's hand-length docked tail started to wag.

"You're a good boy, aren't you," Alastair murmured. The wagging increased in speed.

After collecting more petting, the dog bounded back to Uzuri and right onto her lap, earning a soft "oof" of pain. Thinking of her injuries, Alastair started to call Hunter back, but the little submissive's arms closed around the pup.

Hunter gave her a sloppy lick across her chin.

Giggling, Uzuri kissed the top of his head.

"Well, look what arrived." Max's rough voice came from the door a second before he stepped out. He grinned and squatted. "Hey, pup."

Obviously feeling more at home, Hunter trotted over to sniff another set of fingers and collect some pats. Before long, he was making short forays across the patio before returning for approval and reassurance.

Max watched him. "Careful, isn't he?"

"But not afraid of being hurt. I'd say his world got overturned with his owner's death, and now he's wisely cautious with strange environments and people." Alastair smiled and held out his hand. "Hunter, come."

The dog ran back, tail wagging, obviously expecting praise and patting.

Alastair gave a hearty scratching. "That's a good dog. Good dog."

Wiggling all over with pleasure, the dog ran back to Uzuri to leap into her lap again and share his joy.

Laughing, she hugged him, collecting another lick.

Alastair glanced at Max, seeing the same confusion. Uzuri had been quite emphatic how she felt about animals, after all. "*I hate pets. I hate dogs. They shed and lick and...and ruin my clothes.*"

A few questions would be in order.

Leaving Max to make friends with the dog, Alastair went inside to scrounge up some American-style afternoon snacks—iced sweet tea and his favorite gingersnaps.

Back on the patio, he set the tray on a table and looked around.

Max had coaxed Hunter outside of the screen-enclosed area to explore the backyard lawn. Uzuri was still sitting on the cement. Probably was having trouble standing.

Alastair walked over and held his hand out. "Come, love. I'll help you up."

Startled, she cringed. A second later, she'd regained control and let him pull her to her feet.

Taking the chair beside her, Alastair set out the glasses of iced tea. "You weren't cringing from me when we did a scene together. Not until we were well into the session. Are you more frightened of men than you were last year?"

Obviously stalling, she sipped her drink. Her eyes finally met his. He'd heard of melting brown eyes, but this was the first time he'd ever thought such an over-blown description would apply to anyone. Beautiful.

"I was doing better. Until last spring." Her hands tightened on the glass. "Last year... I'm sorry I accused you of wanting me only because I'm not white."

"I will say your refusal—and anger—were a surprise."

Leaving Hunter to prowl the yard, Max silently stepped back onto the patio. With his years in special ops, he moved more quietly than a stalking cat. After an interested glance at Alastair, he stopped behind Uzuri, listening to the conversation. Sneaky bugger.

Her look of guilt was rather adorable. "Did Master Z...give you trouble?"

"No worries, pet. He has no problem with preferences. After all, he likes curvy women, Cullen prefers big submissives, and some Doms want quiet personalities. However, Z dislikes a Dom making choices out of laziness." Alastair took her hand. "I had to agree with him. Nonetheless, you knew full well that I asked you because I knew you and liked who you were."

Ruefully, she took a breath and met his gaze. "I'm sorry."

"An apology isn't enough. You owe me a scene, Uzuri."

Her mouth dropped open. He shouldn't enjoy upsetting her, but...by God, he did.

Behind her, Max shot him a grin. Without speaking, he walked back to the patio door and gave a shrill whistle through his teeth.

Hunter came running, paused to get his ears ruffled, and headed straight for Uzuri. He set one paw on her knee and panted in her face as if reporting to the boss.

She hugged him around the neck, "Did you have a good time, my man? Scare all those evil squirrels out of the garden?"

"He did." Max dropped into a chair on Uzuri's right...and pulled it closer to her.

Again, she stiffened.

When Max leaned back, obviously not planning to jump on her, she relaxed. Hunter still had his paw planted on her thigh as she stroked his head.

Max nodded toward the dog. "So, baby, why'd you tell Rainie you hate dogs?"

She froze before gently pushing Hunter down. "I don't hate dogs. I just didn't want a dog, and I had to come up with a good excuse. Rainie can be pushy."

Rainie was pushy. She was also reasonable, and Uzuri was quite articulate. Her panicked excuse meant she hadn't wanted to discuss the real reason. He was betting on something to do with her stalker. "Did something happen with a pet and the man who bothered you in the past?"

"Jarvis Kassab," Max growled, giving him the name.

Her face paled to almost gray. After a long moment, she spoke almost inaudibly. "He hurt my little dog." The tears in her soft brown eyes could break a man's heart. "I never thought he'd"—she pulled in a shuddering breath—"I had to give Hugo to my cousin, had to get him out of Cincinnati to make sure he'd be safe."

Alastair remembered the day Jeeves had busted a leg; his heart ached at merely the memory. How much worse would it be to have an ex deliberately hurt a pet—and feel at fault? How bloody helpless she must have felt to have given up her Hugo to keep him safe. They'd thought her unfeeling. Instead, she felt too much. Unable to help himself, Alastair plucked her from the chair and cradled her in his lap. "I'm sorry, love."

His cousin gave a muffled laugh.

Yes, seeing a child or a woman hurting or frightened wasn't something Alastair had ever been able to ignore. His first instinct was to offer shelter—as he had last night. At this rate, Uzuri would be in his lap quite a bit.

He had no problems with that. As her round body, soft in all the right places, slowly relaxed against him, his anger eased. Being able to give comfort in this way was…sweet. Satisfying. Filled a need he hadn't realized he had. When she leaned her head against his chest, he tightened his hold.

With a soft whine, Hunter pushed his nose under her elbow.

She reached down to rub his head. "It's okay, puppy. Nothing's wrong."

Actually, something was right.

Feeling like a complete prat, Alastair watched her comfort Hunter. He was an idiot. The woman had lied to Rainie about not liking dogs, and neither he nor Max had caught it. Yes, she took care with her appearance; however, her clothes took second place to a pup's need to sit on her lap. She had set aside her own worries and discomfort to reassure the dog.

She had a caring heart.

Alastair had lived long enough to know how precious a gift that could be. When bundled with a beautiful face and figure, intelligence, and a sense of humor? Amazing.

Where did Max stand? Alastair arched an eyebrow at him.

Max's gaze on Uzuri was troubled, and Alastair received neither a nod of agreement nor a shake of the head. Max wasn't ready to decide yet.

Apparently, his cousin was as bullheaded as the steers on the Drago ranch. It was fair that Max should get time to think... however, a judicious nudge or two might be advised.

What else were cousins for?

After a supper that Max and Alastair had put together, not letting Uzuri help with either the cooking or the cleanup, she'd gone back outside. The sun had set, and tiny lights around the small garden pond glowed in the increasing darkness. From inside the house came the clatter of dishes and the low murmur of the Dragos.

Not helping them seemed wrong and made her uneasy.

But Alastair had been adamant that she use this time to think of ways to overcome her problems. He and Max planned to discuss her goals and objectives with her later. There were times the Doctor Dom seemed like one of her college professors.

Nonetheless, she'd better come up with some goals and objectives.

She tipped her head back, enjoying the soft brine-scented breeze. Hillsborough Bay was only a block away. Max planned to jog with Hunter along Bayshore Boulevard in the morning. On the waterside. Happy dog.

The pointer had settled in more easily than she'd anticipated. Then again, he'd found himself a "pack" that had two dominant males to tell him what to do.

Very dominant males.

At one time, she'd have given up just about anything to have one of them for her own. Not now, though. She sighed and hugged her knees.

Getting involved with a guy was dangerous. After all, she'd thought Jarvis was wonderful. How wrong could a girl get? Even worse than beating her up, Jarvis had hurt her pet and the people she loved. He'd harassed and driven away her friends and any potential boyfriends.

She'd sent him to jail, yet he still controlled her life in too many ways. She was afraid of big men. She didn't date or let anyone get too close. She hadn't told even her besties about her past. She lived in fear in her own self-created prison.

Wouldn't Jarvis be delighted at how he'd ruined her life?

Yet, he wasn't the only one to have influenced her adversely. Frowning, she considered what the Dragos had said—that she didn't ask for help because of "habits" she'd developed in school. Because some teachers had considered her undeserving of assistance. Since Mama had been so pleased to get her admitted, Uzuri'd never mentioned the small cruelties. She'd simply struggled harder to prove she belonged there.

I don't think I'm undeserving. I don't.

Apparently something inside her did.

Her lips compressed as anger burned. Jarvis and those teachers—was she going to let them win? Let them rule her life?

No.

Her career was on track, but the rest of her life was a shambles. She needed to get over her fears and stop letting the past affect her behavior. If she ever wanted a lover, a Dom, a husband, she had to get her act together.

Number one: she had to manage to be around big men. A shiver ran through her. Easier said than done. Size did matter, and a man could easily overcome her. Then again, Mistress Anne wasn't a huge woman, but she could take down anyone, male or female.

Uzuri, however... A ten-year-old could probably kick her butt.

It was her own fault, too. Losing a bet with Holt had forced her into the Shadowkitten self-defense classes, but she hadn't... exactly...put her heart into learning anything. How stupid was that? Maybe she should practice what Anne taught in those classes.

Ideas dancing in her head, Uzuri rose. Time to get a notebook and make a list. Her life was going to change. It *would*.

When she stepped inside, Max was turning on the dishwasher.

Alastair smiled at her. "We've decided tonight is tequila night. How do you feel?"

"Pretty good." She shook her head cautiously, then more vigorously. "My headache is gone, and alcohol would help the other sore spots." In fact, she was totally ready for a drink.

Max pulled a bottle of Casa Dragones from the cupboard. "Do you prefer to sip your tequila?"

Ick. Or as Sally would say, "*Gag me.*" "No, thank you." She hesitated, and then offered, "I make good strawberry margaritas if you like those."

Max pulled out a blender. "I drink my tequila straight, but the doc prefers his mixed. Go to work, baby."

An evening drinking with two Doms. She'd wanted to get used to being around men; she sure hadn't planned to put the resolution into practice right away.

She was really going to need that drink. Chin up, she crossed the kitchen.

Sprawled on the couch, one leg up, the other foot on the floor, Max was as comfortable as a man could get. He set his empty glass—his fourth shot—on the end table and bit into a lime slice. He was enjoying the alcohol fuzzing his brain—although he'd regret it in the morning, which was why his over-indulgences were few and far between.

Hunter was sacked out at Alastair's feet.

Across the room, Uzuri poured more of the strawberry

margarita for Alastair before refilling her own glass. Alastair still looked sober, Uzuri less so. Max smiled at how much she'd relaxed.

After seeing her with Grant and Connor, he'd figured she'd be a fun drinking companion. She was far more than that. He'd never met anyone so funny and polite at the same time.

Yeah, it was a shame he and Alastair planned to destroy her equilibrium now. While cleaning the kitchen, they'd discussed their responsibility to this little sub and realized they didn't have much time in which to work. Right now, her defenses were down.

As she headed for her chair, Max glanced at Alastair and lifted an eyebrow.

His cousin nodded.

Time's up, baby. As Uzuri walked past the couch, Max snagged her wrist.

She froze for only a second before relaxing. *Improving. Good.*

"You spent some time thinking today, darlin'." Sprawled out, his back against the couch's side arm, he pulled her down to sit on his belly. Hopefully, if she had the high ground...so to speak...she wouldn't be too terrified. And she'd be close enough he could touch her and assess her reactions. "Did you arrive at any interesting conclusions?"

She sat as stiff as a cornered mouse, holding her glass in her left hand. Pulling in a slow breath, she nodded. "A few. Yes."

He curled his fingers around her right hand, pleased to feel only minor trembling.

"The correct answer is 'yes, Sir'." Alastair's correction let her know that they were proceeding as Doms, not friends.

Her voice grew even softer. "Yes, Sir."

Alastair took a leisurely drink of his margarita, drawing out the tension. "Excellent. Share with us."

If possible, she grew even stiffer. Her body language was as revealing as a shout.

Max bit his cheek to keep the laughter out of his voice. "Sometime today, princess."

She tugged at her lower lip before finding her courage—courage he no longer doubted she possessed—and met Alastair's gaze. "I realized how much my past has affected my life. How I've let my bad experiences and my fears put me in a cage."

"Good. What are you going to do about that?"

She huffed. "I was coming to get paper to make a list when I was hijacked into drinking."

Max squeezed her fingers. "We'll help you with brainstorming ideas. And Alastair never forgets anything, even if he's had a few."

"Ever?" She gave Alastair a worried frown. "For studying, a perfect memory would be great. For experiences... I heard you volunteered as a doctor in some bad places."

No shit. Max knew Alastair had as many ugly nightmares as he did. The only difference was that Max had wielded a weapon. And killed. Nevertheless, the aftermath of a battle was ugly, no matter what a man had done. Max was grateful that time was blurring his uglier experiences. Alastair's memories were undoubtedly still far too sharp.

"That's one of the reasons my volunteering in war zones is finished. Why I made changes in my life." Alastair moved his shoulders as if throwing off the past. "What are the changes you're planning?"

The little subbie looked as if she'd have hugged Alastair if she'd been standing. Softhearted, all right.

After a second, she took a sip of her drink. "I'm going to talk with my friends, let them know about Jarvis and the school, and try to explain why I never told them before." Her eyes grew damp. "I'm not sure how to go about it though, because they're going to be hurt I didn't share and that I shut them out."

"It hurts to be shut out," Alastair said mildly. His gaze met Max's. Showing the pain.

Oh. Fuck.

Max closed his eyes. Yeah, he'd been an idiot. Letting go of Uzuri's hand, he twisted enough to pour another shot into his glass and down it. He'd need the alcoholic spur because he wasn't leaving the room before unloading on Alastair. And Uzuri as well, since they actually had something in common. His nod told Alastair he'd won.

Alastair's nod said he knew. *Asshole.*

Max cleared his throat. "Good start, Zuri."

Her gaze had followed the silent interplay, but unlike the grand majority of people, she let it pass. That politeness of hers had something going for it.

Max continued. "You might have done better in Cincinnati if you'd had people there to support you. What else are you planning?"

"I'm scared of big men and sometimes I'm just scared. Like I'm...paranoid about stuff. I need to work harder to get over all that, only I'm not sure how."

That sounded like something he could help with. "Have you thought of taking self-defense classes?"

Her shoulders hunched slightly. "I do already, with the Shadowkittens. Andrea and Anne teach us."

Max frowned. "All women in the class?"

"Mmmhmm. It's nice with only women, and I'm not the only one who..." Her voice trailed off.

Who'd been attacked by some bastard? Yeah, Dan had filled him in on the slavery ring that'd targeted BDSM clubs. An all-women class would be easier on those survivors; however, comfort wasn't the point of self-defense classes. They needed to learn to fight against man-sized attackers—despite their fear.

"Simply being around bigger men will help, pet," Alastair pointed out. "You've gotten better already being around us."

"I have?" After thinking for a second or two, she lit up. "You're right. I have."

Damn, she was cute.

"Sharing with your friends should help put things into perspective." Max grimaced. *Man up, Drago.* "Let's see if it works." He looked straight at his cousin. "It's time to tell you what happened in Seattle."

Alastair set his drink down, stretched his legs out, and prepared to listen. Silently and without preconceptions. One of his cousin's finer traits.

Max glanced at Uzuri. "A year ago, I worked in the Seattle Police Department. The reason I moved is..." As he remembered the clusterfuck his life had become, his jaw tightened until he felt as if he'd crack his teeth.

Alastair's voice broke into his thoughts. "Uzuri, if you would, I think Max could use someone to hold onto."

Still perched on his belly, she looked down at him, and her eyes filled with sympathy. To his surprise, she set her glass on the floor and lay down on top of him. He didn't move.

Putting her head on his shoulder, she melted against him, giving of herself—the most beautiful of a submissive's gifts. She was soft, curvy, and warm. His arms went around her slowly, careful to keep her from feeling trapped. As she snuggled against him, he breathed in the fragrance of lavender and rose from the soap in the guest shower.

Nice. He wouldn't mind holding her for a year or two.

Alastair cleared his throat. "The reason you moved..."

Story. Right. "One night, I backed up some officers on a domestic violence case. The abuser was wealthy. Powerful. Quite a bit older than his wife who was in her thirties and also rich. He'd beaten the shit out of her off and on since they'd married a couple of months before. After he was jailed, her family rallied around her, but for some reason, she latched onto me. I tried to support her. Figured she needed the extra encouragement to testify. It takes courage to face an abuser in court."

He felt the tiny movement as Uzuri nodded. Yeah, she'd know.

Max stroked her back, wishing he'd been around to help when

she went up against her own stalker-abuser. "The husband was sentenced to prison. She obtained a divorce. All done. Or so I thought. But, when I wished her well after the trial, she had a fit. Cried. Said she couldn't live without me."

Alastair frowned. "A woman? This isn't what I'd imagined went wrong."

Max almost smiled. His cousin had probably figured Max had been in a shoot-out or something.

Still frowning, Alastair folded his arms. "I can't see a clingy woman driving you out of Seattle."

"Who knew?" Max said lightly. "Trouble was, no matter how often I told her that I had no intention of dating her—ever—her possessive behavior kept escalating. If I went out with someone, she'd show up and cause a scene. When I ignored her, she insisted someone was out to get her and made phone calls to my police station—even to 911—begging for *me* to protect her. She used her family's influence to try to have me appointed to be her bodyguard."

"Did you believe her?" Alastair asked.

"She showed us a half-dozen threatening notes. Damned if I knew what was the right tactic to take."

Uzuri lifted her head. "You're a cop. You knew she was probably making everything up to get to you, but if there was a chance she was truly in danger, you couldn't ignore it. Right?"

Max's arms tightened. Uzuri didn't really know him, and she already understood him. "Yeah."

Alastair tilted his head. "You investigated? Which meant being around her again?"

"Yeah. She lied and told my lieutenant that we'd been intimate, so he was pissed-off at me. Told me it was my mess to clean up and dumped the investigation on me." Max felt his jaw tighten. Fuck, he'd felt betrayed. He'd worked there for years and only his closest friends in the station had believed him.

"What happened?" Alastair asked.

"The threatening notes were always left on her bedroom pillow. Without telling her, I put a camera in there. The recording showed her writing the notes herself." Although the lieutenant had been forced to eat his words, most of the station still believed he'd done something to set her off.

Uzuri pressed her hand against his chest in a surprisingly comforting gesture. "Didn't she stop when everyone knew she was lying?"

"She felt justified. Felt it was the only way she could get my attention and make me see we should be together. She went back to putting on pressure."

"I never thought about men having stalkers," Uzuri whispered, almost to herself. One little hand patted his shoulder as if to comfort him.

Such a sweetie.

Max kissed the top of her head. "When Alastair settled here in Tampa and asked me to join him, it seemed like the right time." Seattle had no longer felt like his home.

And he'd missed his cousin. His blood brother.

Alastair's grim expression disappeared with his white grin. "In that case, perhaps I shall write her a letter of thanks."

"There are benefits to being chased out of the northwest, I guess." Max squeezed the warm body on top of him. "It got me a sweet subbie to snuggle with."

The curvy body went stiff, and he grinned before he whispered, "You forgot all about my size, didn't you?

A tiny growl came from her. "I remember now." She tried to push up.

He didn't loosen his hold and deepened his voice to a command. "Stay put, baby."

Damned if she didn't relax, although it took her a couple of seconds to put her head back down. But she did.

How fucking appealing could one woman be? He wouldn't forget how she'd put aside her fears in order to comfort him.

And she loved dogs.

Alastair lifted an eyebrow. *Well?*

After a glance at Uzuri, Max rocked his head slightly. *Explore, yes. No promises.*

Despite a snort to express his opinion of Max's wariness, Alastair raised his glass in agreement and rose. Stopping beside the couch, he ran the backs of his fingers over Uzuri's cheek and gave Max a slight smile. "I have early rounds at the hospital in the morning, so I'm calling it a night."

"Night, cuz," Max said.

"Good night," Uzuri said. When she started to sit up, Max tightened his arms around her.

Alastair motioned to Hunter, and the two headed out.

Alastair had Hunter; Max had Uzuri. Good deal.

Max ran his hands up and down her back. He remembered her shape from playing with her at the Shadowlands. Slender neck. Strong shoulders. Soft waist widening into curvy hips. Unable to resist, he spread one hand over her beautifully round ass and felt her shiver.

His cock thickened. Demanded.

Too bad. Tonight, his dick would just have to suffer.

Sure, Zuri had enjoyed Max's intimate attentions during the blackout game at the Shadowlands, and she knew him fairly well. Hell, he probably knew her better than a lot of her friends did.

However, neither of them was close to sober, and it had been an emotional evening. This wasn't the time to complicate matters with sex, especially when she was so fucking vulnerable. *All right.* He gripped her shoulders and pushed her up so she could see his face—and he could watch hers. "I'm going to kiss you, princess," he murmured. "And then we'll head for our own beds."

Although her lips held a trace of a pout, her body relaxed slightly. She wanted him and yet didn't.

Yeah, this was the right decision.

He boosted her higher on his body, enjoying the feel of her

full, firm breasts against his chest, then put a hand behind her neck and guided her to his lips. Just as at the Shadowlands, she had a generous mouth with soft, willing lips. The shiver that ran through her now wasn't from fear.

Long before he wanted to quit—hell, he wanted to bury himself inside her—he broke off the embrace and helped her to her feet. From the way she was moving, she was still pretty bruised up.

"C'mon, darlin'." He tucked an arm around her and guided her up the stairs, giving her another kiss before tucking her inside her own bedroom. *Alone.*

He was a fucking saint.

CHAPTER TEN

Tuesday, Max followed Detective Edith Umbers through the women's clothing section at Brendall's. When Max asked if he could tag along when she investigated the hit and run, the gray-haired, lean, and New England-terse detective had simply said, "Not a problem."

Brendall's was a high-end regional department store, Tampa's version of Nordstrom's. Max followed the detective past a perfume counter where exotic fragrances drifted in the air. The underwear section was next, and a mannequin wearing a sheer pink negligee caught his eye. Wouldn't Zuri look fantastic in that? Unfortunately, that led him into wondering if she already owned sexy nightwear...and what she normally wore to bed...and how much fun he'd have removing anything she wore. Even sweats and a T-shirt would be fun to yank off of her.

Aaand this wasn't the time to be playing out scenarios. Although he'd like to see how she'd react if Alastair joined them, and—

Get a grip, Drago.

A shame she'd gone home Sunday. Dammit, she'd only been

with them two nights, and he already missed seeing her in their home. Considering he wasn't sure he wanted anything more serious than brief scenes in the Shadowlands, he was being an idiot.

But that was why Alastair was taking the lead with the little submissive. Then they'd see what happened. Nonetheless, he couldn't help looking for her in the store even though she probably hadn't returned to work yet.

Regaining his focus, he joined the detective in the department manager's office.

After hearing about the flat tire and hit and run, the manager filled them in about Carole Fuller's animosity toward Uzuri and why. Apparently, Carole Fuller and a friend had left together that night.

Max leaned against the wall. Without a dead body, homicide wasn't involved. He couldn't help thinking that Uzuri could well have died in that parking lot—and ended up one of his murder cases. The idea was so god-awful, he felt like putting his fist through the wall.

The manager glanced at him and retreated a pace. "I'll fetch Carole and Retta Jean." She almost sprinted from the room.

Edith huffed a laugh. "Drago, if you scare the suspects too much, I won't get a word out of them. Lighten up."

"Sorry." He forced his muscles to relax...but a smile wasn't going to happen. "How about I play the silent, bad cop."

"I'd say you have that role down pat." She turned as the manager escorted two women into the office, and the tiny space grew crowded.

The manager motioned to the heavy-set woman whose brittle blonde hair was teased high and wide. "This is Carole Fuller." The other suspect, a late forties brunette, had the peeved expression of a discontented bulldog. "And this is Retta Jean Potter."

Edith displayed her ID badge. "Ladies, I'm Detective Umbers."

Both women took a step back and turned pale.

Yeah, they did it.

Ignoring the nervous glances at Max, Edith continued. "I have some questions about last Friday night. Why don't you tell me what you did on the way out of the parking lot?"

The bulldog glanced at Carole. "N-nothing. We didn't do anything. We just left."

"You didn't deliberately run your car into Uzuri Cheval and then drive away?" Edith gave them a cold look. "That's hit and run at a minimum. Possibly attempted murder."

"What?" Carole gasped, her hand going to her chest. "I never... We only gave her a fl—" Her mouth snapped shut.

"You cut the valve stem and flattened her tire. Is that correct?" Edith asked politely.

Carole didn't speak.

Time for bad cop. Max straightened, folded his arms over his chest, and narrowed his eyes.

Under the silent intimidation, timid Retta Jean wilted. "We did." The brunette swallowed. "I gave Carole my scissors, and she cut the tubing."

When Carole glared, the bulldog scowled back. "I knew we shouldn't do such a stupid thing. What is this—high school?" Her gaze flicked to Max before she spoke to Edith. "That's all we did. We both drove out of the parking lot at the same time. I didn't see Miss Cheval."

"What time was this? And did you go home after that?" Detective Umbers asked Carole.

Carole's shoulders slumped. "Around seven or seven thirty." She knew she was caught. "We ate at the buffet down the street. After that, I babysat my grandchildren while my daughter went out on a date."

"I, uh, went home." The bulldog flushed. "My father lives with me. He can tell you I was there."

Family would say anything to keep a loved one out of trouble, but Max wasn't hearing any lies. They'd vandalized Uzuri's car, but hadn't been the ones to run her down.

Question was...had the hit and run been an accident or something more deliberate?

CHAPTER ELEVEN

Uzuri stood in the door of the closet and stared at her arranged-by-color wardrobe. She had something—lots of somethings—for every occasion, so why was she angsting over what to wear on a Friday night date?

Well, duh. Because the date was with *Alastair*.

He'd called her midweek and invited her out to eat tonight. Normally, she'd be going to the Shadowlands, but Master Z had told her not to show up until she was moving easily.

She felt pretty good. After all, it'd been a whole week since she was knocked down by that car. However, she did still have a bit of a limp—enough of one that the exacting Master would send her home.

So instead of going to the Shadowlands tonight, she had a date. With a man.

A *Dom*.

It was the first objective on her list of ways to get out of her self-imposed, paranoid prison. *You go, girl.*

So...what in the world was she going to wear?

As she waited for inspiration to hit, tiny butterflies of anticipation danced in her stomach. She had a date with *Alastair*.

And last Saturday, she'd kissed Max. Oh, more than that—she'd made out with him. If he hadn't stopped, they'd have had sex right there in the TV room.

She put a hand over her lower belly, remembering how badly she'd wanted to continue and how completely aroused she'd been, as every long-repressed hormone in her body had flooded her system. His hands had been hard. Firm. He'd possessed her mouth in a way that made everything inside her melt.

She'd dreamed about him...and about Alastair. Both of them. That seemed so wrong.

Tonight she'd go out with Alastair. Oh, that man scared her spitless, although she'd sighed over him since the first time she saw him. In fact, she'd yearned over him so obviously that Master Sam had noticed and arranged for Alastair to top her. Only she'd ruined the whole scene by panicking.

But tonight, Alastair knew all about her fears...and he intended to deal with them. The butterflies in her stomach grew to Godzilla-size.

Her cell phone rang, and she retrieved it from the dresser. *Alastair* showed on the display.

"Hello, Sir. Um, Alastair." This was a date. What was she supposed to call him?

His chuckle was so deep and perfect that shivers ran over her skin. "We'll talk about terms of address sometime. For now..." "*For now.*" His tone sounded...off. Grim.

"Is something wrong?"

He paused, as if surprised. "Yes, and no, pet. I had the kind of a day that would make me bad company, and I fear I cannot tolerate a crowd tonight. Can we reschedule for tomorrow?"

Although disappointment surged up, her concern for Alastair rose above it. She'd never heard him sound so...unhappy. Whatever had happened, she knew—*knew*—he shouldn't be alone. Hesitating, she bit her lip. She was supposed to be learning to be brave. Why did it have to be so scary?

With an effort, she gripped the cell and made her tone very firm. "We can change the plans, yes, but not for tomorrow. Come here and I'll cook you supper."

The silence on the phone was frightening, but he didn't yell at her. Her fingers relaxed slightly.

Finally, he repeated, "You'll cook? For me?"

Her lips curved. "Yes, Sir. For you. Here." If he was reluctant, she shouldn't give him any decisions. "I'll expect you at seven."

Silence again. Then... "All right."

As she hit the END CALL, her insides felt as frothy as a storm-churned bay. With renewed anticipation, she turned back to the closet.

So...what should she wear for a quiet, Friday night date?

Alastair knocked on the door of Uzuri's duplex, wondering how he'd ended up agreeing not to cancel the date. For such a polite submissive, she had some smooth moves.

She opened the door, a sweet sight in a royal blue blouse and cropped khakis. Even her shoulder-length hair looked casual, parted on one side and combed out. She gave him a long, assessing look. "You look awful."

"That's not how my dates usually greet me." He tried to smile. "I'm sorry about tonight." He should have stayed home and not subjected her to his grieving.

"Oh, Alastair." She took his hand, tugged him in, closed the door, and wrapped her arms around him.

Surprised, he stood for a second before pulling her tighter against him. She was all female curves and quivers, and heart-warmingly alive. He hadn't realized it, but he needed that hug more than he could say.

Without speaking, she simply leaned into him and held him.

From inside, he could hear the music of Libera, their clear voices flowing into a soaring hymn.

Eventually, he managed to let her go. "Thank you, sweetheart. I needed that." He leaned down to kiss her forehead.

"Come." With surprising boldness for this little submissive, she took his hand and pulled him into her small living room.

The typical off-white walls and neutral beige carpet of a rental served as the backdrop to a dark green couch, green and blue upholstered chairs, and a random mix of brightly colored pillows. Two glasses of wine stood on the coffee table. The fragrance of olive oil and garlic drifted from the kitchen.

On one wall, framed prints from fashion shows were hung in an asymmetrical, yet balanced array over a hanging shelf holding... He tilted his head. *Barbie dolls?*

Indeed they were. In designer clothing, the dolls were lined up like the photographed models on the wall. "What are these?"

She followed his gaze. "Oh, I sometimes use the dolls when showing sales associates how to pull together a complete look. Although the computer is easier, some people like to play with their hands, and dressing the dolls works better for them."

At the end of the shelf was a doll that looked much like Andrea. It wore a wedding dress and stood next to a larger, male doll in a tux. Clean-shaven, shaggy brown hair, green eyes—a Cullen look-alike. The doll was holding a flogger behind its back. Alastair snorted. "Is this going on the wedding cake?"

Uzuri burst into laughter. "Can you imagine her grandmother's reaction? No, no, no. It's a little wedding present—a private one."

"You're quite good at this, pet. Have you been doing it long?"

She brightened at the compliment. "When I was little, I sewed clothes for my Barbies. Since they never looked like my African-American friends or me, I painted them and restyled their hair, too. Since Mama was proud of being Louisiana Creole —mostly Haitian—I learned to make ethnic clothing."

Creole. From Louisiana? He frowned. "I thought you were from Cincinnati."

"Daddy and Mama lived in New Orleans until he got stationed in Ohio. He was in the Air Force." Sadness shadowed her face. "He died in some training accident before I really knew him."

"I'm sorry, love." To erase the sorrow from her eyes, Alastair pointed to a doll that looked like Michael Jackson and raised his brows.

Uzuri laughed. "Some of my college tuition came from selling one-of-a-kind celebrity dolls on eBay."

Interesting. She had a wealth of creative talent, didn't she? And she positively glowed when talking about her hobby. "Should I ask if other Shadowlands Masters have dolls?"

"Don't you dare tell Master Sam. Don't you dare." She actually took a step back.

"Shhh." He cupped her cheek and watched her pupils dilate at his touch. "Your secrets—all your secrets—are safe with me, Uzuri."

Her lips parted.

Unable to resist, he bent and took her mouth, contenting himself with a gentle, far-too-short kiss.

When he released her, she stared at him, and pulled in an audible breath. After a moment, she took his hand again and pulled him over to sit beside her on the couch.

Brave little submissive.

She picked up a glass and handed it to him. "I didn't know what kind of wine you like, but we're having pasta, so you get Chianti."

He took a sip, smiled, and took another sip. "Very nice."

"Alastair... Um, Sir." She made a frustrated sound. "What am I supposed to call you?"

"Ah." Her question was a typical one. Submissives always wanted to please a Dominant by doing everything right. "Max and

I are easygoing about how we're addressed. We prefer Sir when we're in scene."

Her brows drew together. "Not Master? Or Master Alastair?"

He touched her cheek. "The title has ugly associations for some. Although I'm pleased to be awarded the status in the Shadowlands, and I don't mind being called Master, I'm not particularly fond of it." He grinned, remembering Max's face when Z called him Master Maximillian. "Max prefers Sir."

Uzuri nodded, then her forehead puckered again.

He traced a finger over the perfect, elegant curve of her eyebrows. "Another question?"

"A date isn't a scene. Or...is it?"

So many worries. She truly did pull at his heart. "You'll know when we're in a scene." He smiled slightly. "Also, since I'm a sexual Dominant, I want respectful address during those times as well."

"Oh."

He stroked her cheek and noted the increased warmth from her flush. "In everyday life, if you feel in a submissive mood, I never object to being called Sir."

Her worried expression faded as she took that in. In fact, she looked pleased. Yes, they were on the same wavelength. She picked up her glass and drank some wine.

Leaning back, he stretched out his legs and did the same.

After a minute or so, she turned to him. "Can you tell me what happened today to make you so"—her head tilted—"sad?"

Compassion. Seeing it in her eyes was like stumbling across a life-giving river in the desert. He was parched.

However, talking about the tragic aspects of his profession wasn't something he did. Over the years, he'd learned to absorb the losses, hide the pain, and get on with life. The trouble was, the longer he was a doctor, the more difficult it grew to bury everything. Rather than the calm woodland of youth, his mind had become a cemetery, studded with graves marking sorrow and anger and frustration. "Nothing to speak of, pet."

A small brown hand settled over his. "Tell me, Sir. Please." The most respectful demand he'd run into.

He sighed. "Uzuri, it's not something you want to know. It would only hurt you."

To his surprise, her chin lifted. "Perhaps. All the same...it also hurts to be shut out."

Those were his own words tossed back at him. He studied her. He'd seen her put aside her own fears to help Max.

And now him. She was stronger than he'd realized.

He turned his hand over and curled his fingers around hers. "I'm a pediatrician," he said softly. "I love it. Children are filled with energy and joy. They're open and loving and delightful."

She nodded. "I saw you with Grant and Connor last summer. They adore their 'Doctor Dragon'."

His smile at the name faded quickly. Beth's boys were orphans, had been through heartrending abuse and neglect, and somehow survived with their enthusiasm for living unabated. Although their past would undoubtedly return to haunt them, Beth and Nolan would be there for them.

Some children weren't as lucky.

"Alastair?" Uzuri squeezed his hand, bringing him back to the present.

"Even children get AIDS, you know."

She nodded, sadness in her gaze. "I know."

"I had a four-year-old. She'd had treatment and was doing well. Unfortunately..."

"What happened?"

His lips tightened. "Her grandmother is the caregiver; however, the woman is..." He sighed. "She can barely cope with her own life. She has some mental problems, abuses alcohol, and is on disability. She stopped giving the medications and didn't notice the signs of an increasing viral load." He wanted to yell. To kick something. To let out his anger that someone—anyone—

could be so blind. "It was too late when she brought the child in." Multiple organ failure.

"Were you still seeing the little girl?"

He shook his head. "Specialists had taken over her care, and many patients skip seeing their regular doctors when they're buried in specialists. Since she was still listed as my patient, the hospital notified me when she was admitted. She died a few hours ago."

Uzuri's eyes filled with the tears that Alastair could not shed. "I'm so sorry." She wrapped her arms around him again.

Sympathy and understanding, freely given. *Such precious gifts.*

Uzuri didn't know how to comfort a man. Oh, if he'd been one of her BFFs, she'd know. They'd talk everything out, over and over, and cry together and rage, and pull out the alcohol and talk some more. Maybe make chocolate chip cookies or brownies. Simple and straightforward.

However, her daddy had died when she was little. She had no brothers. She didn't know men.

Alastair bottled up his feelings even more than she did, and his story simply broke her heart. Pushing him to talk had felt right. Maybe submissives shouldn't nag at Doms, but he was a man, too. A wonderful man with an aching heart.

And hey, he and Max had forced her to discuss her problems, and their sympathy had helped.

Talking had helped Alastair, too. As she held him, his arms tightened around her. His breathing changed and deepened, as if he'd only been taking small breaths...like those she'd taken when her ribs were bruised.

His heart was bruised.

Arms around him, she rubbed her cheek against his soft green button-down shirt, breathing in his clean, masculine scent. Despite the strength of his arms, she felt no fear that he'd hurt her. He was always incredibly controlled. Always polite. Always reserved. He was the pediatrician for the children of many club members, including Master Z's daughter, so he must be superb. He'd volunteered with Doctors Without Borders, which said to her he was a good person. She hadn't realized how deeply he cared about his patients.

Eventually, his arms loosened.

When he kissed the top of her head, she realized she'd forgotten all about him being a man. She hadn't even been nervous about hugging him.

"Thank you, sweetheart." He straightened, his reserved manner back in place, and picked up his glass of wine. He considered her for a long moment. "You look better. Have you returned to work?"

She almost smiled. This wasn't a man who would stay vulnerable long. In fact, she felt as if she'd been given a gift, that he'd let her see a piece of his soul. "Today. It's been a week, after all."

"Ah. Was the person who flattened your tire at work?"

"No." Uzuri moved her shoulders uncomfortably. "Carole and another sales associate were fired Tuesday. There are rumors going around about the reason."

"Why do I have the feeling you haven't set anyone straight?" With a thumb and forefinger, he stroked his beard as he watched her.

She looked down.

"Are you going to press charges?"

"No. They lost their jobs. That's enough." Why she felt guilty about them didn't make any sense, but she did.

"You have a soft heart, pet. I'm not quite so forgiving. I'll need to see how well you're healing before I decide."

She moved her arms. "I'm moving fine. See? All healed up."

"Mmmhmm." Sliding closer to her on the couch, he ran his hands down her arms and set her skin to tingling. Then he started to unbutton her blouse.

"Hey!"

His gaze met hers. "Is anything on the stove going to burn?"

She swallowed. The pasta wasn't on yet. The sauce was in a slow cooker and could stay there for hours. She shook her head.

"Excellent." He undid another button. He'd done the same thing in the bathroom at his house, only that time, his eyes hadn't been filled with heat.

Her heart crammed into her throat. "Sir. Please." She covered his hand with hers, making him stop.

"Uzuri," he said softly. He lifted her chin with his fingers. His eyes were level. Controlled. "Are you seriously objecting? Or is this from habit?"

"Um..." Which was it? The warmth shimmering across her skin certainly wasn't fear. Nevertheless, to want him so much? Oh, it did make her anxious.

Yet, she'd promised herself she'd strive for courage. *Okay. Okay.* She managed to uncurl her fingers from his hand. "Habit. I'm... nervous. I'm sorry, Sir."

His sensuous lips curved in a smile of approval. "Nervous is fine, especially since I'm going to push you a bit. If there's anything you don't enjoy, you tell me. Is that clear?" Without waiting for her answer, he resumed unbuttoning her blouse.

She had to swallow before she could answer. "Yes, Sir."

He pushed her shirt off her shoulders, and the cooler air wafted over her bared skin.

With a hum of appreciation, he trailed his fingertips over the top curve of her breast above her lacy blue bra. "I like your under-wear...and how you fill it out."

Like a newly lit sparkler, sweet tingles danced outward from his touch.

He undid the front catch of her bra, pushed it off, and lifted her to her feet. Still seated on the couch, he pinned her between his long legs as he undid her khakis and tugged them to the floor, leaving her dressed only in her blue thong. It too dropped past her knees to tangle around her ankles.

She'd stripped in the Shadowlands. Often.

This felt entirely different.

As she stood there, stark naked, he leaned back and looked her over in a Dom's assessment. After a slow perusal, he twirled his finger for her to turn.

As she shuffled in a circle, an embarrassed flush rolled upward into her face. With each second that passed, her pussy was dampening, her heart rate increasing, her breasts tingling.

"You're healing well. Good."

He'd only wanted to check her bruising? Disappointment coursed through her. She was getting aroused, and he wasn't interested in her that way at all. Humiliation held the sting of a thousand bees. Her voice snapped out. "Well, I'm so happy you approve." Bending, she grabbed her khakis.

When he set a foot on top of her pants to prevent her from pulling them up, she glared. "Damn you, let go!"

"I'm not sure why you're angry, pet, but you know you can't speak to me that way." His British accent added a measured formality to the mildly disapproving tone. "Perhaps it's well we get this out of the way so you can stop fearing what I'll do if you annoy me."

Leaning forward, he gripped her arm, moved a leg to her left —and yanked her face down over his knees.

"What are you doing!" Her kicking feet got tangled in her pants.

"The Masters discussed you, you know." As his ruthless palm between her shoulder blades pinned her down, he massaged her bottom. "When you joined the Shadowlands, Z said you weren't to be pushed—which meant you've never received more than a few easy swats. Any bondage was very light. Your reprieve ended last week, little miss."

"What?" Uzuri couldn't believe how the evening was going. First, she'd been rude to him—which she almost never was. Now, he planned to punish her? For that?

His hand smacked her bottom lightly, a forewarning of things to come.

"Wait. No." She got one foot free of the tangled clothing.

"You've told everyone you don't like any pain." His voice stayed easy as he smacked her slightly harder. "But no Master has assessed your boundaries. We'll make a start on that tonight. You may use *red* as your safeword if you need it."

Although she tensed in anticipation of the drowning, horrendous panic, it never arrived...because he'd given her a safeword.

With a steady hand, he pressed down on her back, forcefully enough she couldn't escape. Not cruelly. His palm smacked her bottom, slowly and regularly, each blow as precisely measured as a surgeon's, each impact carefully calculated to sting and fade before the next.

The burn spread and began to *hurt*. As she squirmed helplessly, her world, everything around her, quaked. He wasn't going to stop. She had no control over what was happening. He was totally in charge.

Her fingers dug into the carpet as the unfamiliar feelings ran through her.

"Spread your legs, Uzuri." The command was quiet.

Gulping back pleas, she parted her knees.

"More, pet."

"Please. I don't like this." She inched her legs apart. Her bottom burned.

"Shhh." His long fingers slid between her thighs, stroking over her wet—very wet—pussy, and the jolt of heat that shot through her was like nothing she'd felt before.

He made a low sound of pleasure before circling her clit with one finger. She could feel the nub swelling, tightening.

Then he removed his hand and resumed spanking her. Harder, much harder. *Smack, smack, smack.*

"You will speak to Doms politely, Uzuri." His quiet, resonant voice held a note of steel. "Or you will be punished like this."

Under his hard hand, fiery pain spread over her bottom, and she was gasping and kicking and squirming.

Yet, somehow, the heat flared elsewhere, as well. Her pussy throbbed and tingled.

When he stopped to slide his fingers through her drenched folds, a delicious thrill flared to life. He pressed one finger inside her, igniting a storm of excitement, and her urgent moan was humiliating.

"It appears someone should have pushed you before." He deliberately rubbed over her clit, firmly, far too expertly.

When she squirmed, he simply pressed harder on her shoulders, and continued to stroke, driving her up and up and up.

Everything inside her coiled into a hard knot, every sense focused on those expert fingers. Her legs trembled as she hovered on the edge of orgasm and could only whimper.

"Oh, you're a definite pleasure." Moving his hand, he smacked her three more times, shockingly hard, before his finger returned to glide right over the top of her clit. Once. Twice.

She *came*.

Overwhelming, terrifying pleasure broke over her and shook her like a doll. When he thrust two hard fingers inside her, she fell into an ocean of sensation, tumbling over and over.

With his merciless touch, he drew out every iota of her orgasm until she lay over his thighs as limp as a rain-soaked shirt.

Even his hand rubbing over her tender bottom only elicited a whispered whine.

"Up you come, sweetheart." When he lifted her and arranged her on his lap, she buried her face against his neck. Each breath brought her his aftershave, a clean scent like walking through a summer meadow. When he tangled his fingers in her hair, tugging at the ends, she sighed happily, pleased she'd worn it in a style he could play with.

Eventually, reality slid back into focus, and she stiffened.

"What's bothering you, love?"

She lifted her head and met his gaze. His eyes were amazing. Never the same color twice. The tawny golden brown around the pupil somehow transformed into a wide dark green rim.

"Uzuri?"

"Oh. Um." What had she been worried about? "It's that I..."

When he rubbed her back, she realized she was completely naked and sitting on his lap. He was still dressed.

His full lips twitched with his amusement. "Go on."

"How could you get me off? You spanked me, and it hurt, but it felt...exciting, too. No one ever..." When Jarvis had hit her, all she'd felt was pain. What she'd felt with other Doms had been a far cry from this.

"Ah." He tucked her head back against his chest, and she cuddled into him. The sense of safety was like being wrapped in a soft, sun-warmed blanket. "I can only guess, pet."

She smiled against his shirt. Such a careful doctor. No wild guesses for him.

"I doubt that you're a masochist who enjoys pain for pain's sake. However, if you are already aroused, that can be a different matter. Pain often adds to erotic sensations, feeding into what's already going on. In other instances, possibly you weren't excited. Or..."

When he paused, she frowned. "Or what?"

"Possibly you didn't trust the other Doms enough to let yourself enjoy anything?"

"Um. Maybe." She trusted Holt, but he didn't make her all hot and bothered. He felt too much like the brother she'd never had. With other Doms, many had been sexy, but she hadn't truly trusted them.

When talking, when being punished, when coming—and afterward, the little submissive was simply delightful. Alastair rubbed his cheek on her springy mass of black hair. He never knew how she'd wear it from one day to the next, and he was learning the style might offer a clue as to her mood. Tonight, she'd felt free enough to wear it loose.

The confusion in her voice when she asked him why she'd come after receiving a spanking had been interesting. She had no idea of the splendid compliment she'd given him. What Dom wouldn't rejoice in knowing a submissive was both aroused and trusting?

Time to continue with the lesson. No reason that learning had to be only from a book, eh? He rose with her in his arms and chuckled when she grabbed his shirt with both hands. "Relax, pet. I won't drop you."

Her lovely eyes were huge. Tempted beyond his will, Alastair bent his head and took her lips. So sweet.

When he looked around, he spotted the door to her bedroom and headed that way.

In subdued blues and creams, her feminine bedroom was a serene retreat. The ruffled blue bed skirt, elaborate Florentine Baroque mirror, and Venetian headboard said she was a romantic at heart. As a doctor, he did enjoy how she kept her world so tidy.

After laying her on the floral bedspread, he smiled when she struggled to sit up. "No, little miss. On your back. Hands over your head. Legs spread.

A shiver ran through her, making her full breasts jiggle nicely. The dark nipples were bunched into tight peaks that begged for his mouth.

For her comfort, he lit the candles on the dresser and turned off the overhead light. Her skin glowed in the soft candlelight, her curves creating tantalizing shadows. The soft music from the living room drifted in.

Taking his time, he stripped completely and sheathed himself. The spanking and watching her orgasm had left him incredibly hard.

On the bed, she watched his every move with big eyes, and he realized she'd never seen him unclothed. During their scene together in the Shadowlands, he had cut the session short due to her anxiety.

The growing heat in her eyes pleased him, although she was also biting her lip nervously as she regarded his cock.

Monitoring her for any increase in fear, he moved onto the bed and knelt between her open thighs. Leaning forward, he cradled her face and enjoyed a deep, wet kiss, one slow enough to let her know there would be no rushing tonight.

Her muscles relaxed, her mouth softened. He took—and she gave, generously. Beautifully. Even nicer, she'd been good and kept her arms over her head.

"You are such a good girl," he murmured and enjoyed the way her eyes brightened. Could there be anything more appealing than a submissive's need to please?

Sitting back, he used his palms and fingertips to explore her neck, the hollow at the base, her sternum, her soft belly. Spreading his hands apart, he moved up, over her ribs, and took possession of her breasts. Warm and soft, heavy in his palms as he pressed them together. *Lovely.* Unable to resist, he bent and tongued a tight, hard nipple.

Her chest lifted with her sudden inhalation, and he smiled.

What male didn't like a reaction like that? "Do you know how beautiful you are, woman?"

The stunned pleasure in her eyes said she didn't.

Her hands remained over her head, and as he licked around her nipple, he laid his palm over her right upper arm to monitor her response. Carefully, he closed his teeth on the areola, bearing down slowly until, under his hand, her muscles tightened in protest.

There. "Easy, sweetheart." Lifting his head, he licked over the tender nipple.

She was panting for breath.

He reached down to fondle her pussy and smiled at the

increased slickness. For his own pleasure, he inserted a finger as he bent to her other breast.

He licked, nibbled, and teased until her breast swelled, then he bit that nipple gently. Before reaching her pain limit, he stopped.

Her cunt had tightened around his finger like a vise.

"It seems you like that. Don't you?"

She shook her head.

Still not being completely honest with herself, was she? He merely smiled as he studied her face. Her eyes were glazed with passion, lips and cheeks darkly flushed.

To increase her sense of surrender, he pinned her wrists above her head with one hand and teased her breasts with the other. It didn't take much to have her squirming in need.

It seemed that with Uzuri, arousal mixed with the right amount of pain would drive her to the edge of orgasm. By God, she was perfect.

When she was whimpering, he released her wrists and kissed his way down her body. Slowly. Savoring every inch. Her belly was softly rounded, her ribs nicely padded. Her pussy was bare, the dark outer labia sweetly plump. Her scent was rich and womanly, the taste appealing.

It didn't take much time at all to have her glistening clit engorged and poking out from the hood.

"Please," she whispered. "Oh, please... I want you inside me." Her hands were on his head, and she was straining her hips upward despite the forearm he'd put across her pelvis.

"All right, sweetheart." In serious discomfort and need himself, he rose up on his knees and fitted himself to her slick entrance.

Definitely tight. As her fingernails dug into his shoulders, he slowly worked his way into her wet sheath. Her eyes widened as he continued in by increments, trying to let her adjust as he went. Although the heat engulfing him was shaking his control, he didn't let himself hurry. He'd take the time she needed.

"There, pet. All in."

Her sigh was equal parts relief and pleasure.

Slowly, he eased out and back in. Stretching out on top of her, he planted a forearm beside her head—and continued to monitor her responses. Her eyes were still worried, her mouth still slightly tight. Her palms were on his shoulders, not...quite...pushing him away.

"Shhh, baby. It will be all right now."

In, out. In, out.

When her hips started to lift to his, and her lips parted with pleasure, he smiled and increased his speed. Her arms slid around his neck. She was a joy to fuck—and he was looking forward to sandwiching her between him and Max and driving her past everything she'd ever known.

He kept his movements slow until she started to tremble and clutch his shoulders. A fine sheen of sweat appeared on her skin. When her pussy tightened around him, he bent to kiss her—and changed his angle so his pelvis rubbed over her clit.

As if plugged into an electric socket, her whole body tensed under him. "Omigod." Her voice was low, throaty. Beautiful.

Chuckling, he continued, plunging forcefully while nailing her clit with every stroke. Her core tightened around his cock. Lifting her trembling legs around his waist, he drove deeper.

Her tiny breaths bathed the base of his neck—and stopped. Her fingernails dug into his shoulders even as her cunt fisted around him.

As her neck arched, her lovely keening echoed in the room. Her core spasmed around him hard, over and over, and he groaned in pleasure.

Abandoning his control, he thrust short and fast, feeling everything inside him draw up. With a low groan, he plunged in to the hilt and came so hard he could swear he heard the angels sing.

When the choir finished and he'd recovered enough to locate

a few working brain cells, he gathered her close and rolled with her in his arms. "Thank you, pet, for not allowing me to cancel tonight."

Her husky gurgle of a laugh made him grin. "You're very welcome, Sir." With a happy sigh, she snuggled against him, cheek against his chest, and one leg over his thighs. Soft and warm and loving.

Breathing in her sultry, rich scent, Alastair ran his hand up and down her back, feeling the sweetness of the moment. He'd never found it difficult to find intelligent women to date—or to bed. But to find an intelligent, independent submissive who was also devastatingly compassionate and generous?

The universe didn't hand them out in large numbers.

He kissed the top of her head and smiled. "Sleep, love. While you can."

CHAPTER TWELVE

I n the small coffee shop across from the karate studio, Uzuri listened as her friends did a catch-up of the past week. There were only seven of them this week: Jessica, Sally, Beth, Gabi, Andrea, Kim, and Uzuri.

Kim was talking about a recent firefighter benefit dinner where she and her Master had run into Holt and his date. Raoul apparently hadn't been impressed with the redhead, which was a concern.

Uzuri frowned. Hopefully, Holt wasn't serious about this one.

When Kim finished up, Jessica asked, "Who's next?"

Stalling, Uzuri drank her coffee. Where would she even begin? So much had happened since she'd seen them two weeks ago.

Like...she'd had sex with Alastair last Friday. Omigod, she'd never felt so overwhelmed in her entire life. He'd been so in control and careful and...

Had she actually thought Max was the scary one?

Alastair had hurt her—deliberately—and she still didn't know exactly when the pain had turned into a hot, roiling pleasure. Everything he'd done had become more and more intense until her whole world had...blown apart. And afterward, when she was shaking in his arms, he'd held her and murmured to her in that deep accented voice.

They'd gotten up eventually to eat the neglected dinner. Afterward, he'd taken her back to bed and held her all night long. She'd never slept so well. Ever.

At dawn, she'd barely woken up when he had rolled her onto her belly and taken her hard and fast. Honestly, she'd always hated morning sex, but he'd found her clit with those magic fingers, and she'd been coming before she was even fully awake.

"Very nice, sweetheart," he'd said, patted her ass, grabbed a slow, tender kiss, and tucked the covers around her. He'd been gone before she could even offer him breakfast.

He was amazing.

She sighed and realized Sally was watching her, her brow puckered with concern. "Zuri?"

Uzuri wasn't ready to talk. She turned. "How are the wedding plans going, 'Drea?"

Andrea closed her eyes and shook her head. "*Dios*, I need a few drinks before talking about it."

Gabi frowned. "Why? What's wrong?"

"*Everything*. The reception gets bigger and bigger because mi *abuelita* and *tía* keep inviting more people, and Cullen's father and stepmother do the same, even though they're flying here from Chicago. When my aunt called yesterday, I started crying.

Uzuri gasped. Andrea wasn't the sort to cry. She wasn't.

Jessica took her hand. "What can we do to help?"

"*Nada*. Really." Andrea gave a wry smile. "At this point, I don't care what the reception looks like. I simply want it over. Cullen feels the same. It'll be all right."

Maybe. But a reception wasn't enough to make Andrea this unhappy. "Is something else wrong?"

Gabi flicked her a look of agreement. "Tell us what's bothering you, girlfriend."

Andrea's golden eyes filled with tears. "It's stupid."

Beth snorted. "My Master told me that"—she lowered her voice to imitate Master Nolan's harsh voice—" 'feelings are feelings. They don't have dumb or smart labels.' "

"So true." Gabi smiled. "Tell us, 'Drea."

"I miss Papa." Andrea wiped away a tear. "You know how you dream about when you'll get married? In my dream, my papa always walked me down the aisle, and he'd be all proud of me and everything." She half-laughed. "That's what's silly. He's been gone for years and years, and before he died, he was...drinking and got...mean. Still"—her breathing hitched—"I guess I feel l-lonely or something."

Uzuri was the first to jump up to hug and hold her, and the others immediately followed.

Within the huddle of females, Andrea shed a few tears and then laughed. "Thank you." She took a deep breath. "I didn't realize what was bothering me so much. Maybe I can let it go now."

Maybe she could, but Uzuri couldn't. Surely, there was a way she could help.

As they resumed their chairs, Andrea frowned at Uzuri. "It's your turn, now. Sure, you called us about your parking lot battle—Zuri versus car; car wins—but I can see there's more. Don't think we haven't noticed."

On the spot. Woman up. "I want to tell you about...about...why I moved to Florida." Uzuri took her own deep breath and stepped through the door she'd cracked open with Max. "It's like this..."

Master Z had been right. It was easier the second time.

As Uzuri shared, she stared at the tabletop to avoid seeing what would surely be reproach in her friends' eyes. Halfway through, Sally took her hand on one side, Kim on the other. "...And then I managed to tell Max everything, and he told Master Z, and so all the Masters know, and I wanted you to know, too."

She stared at the maroon napkins, really a poor choice of hue in the coffee shop's orange color scheme. "It's not that I didn't trust you—I do—but I didn't want to ever think about the past. I'd left it behind."

"Uh-huh." A snort from Jessica made her look up. "I thought it was something like that."

Beth nodded, "We knew you'd tell us someday. I'd thought you had an abusive husband or boyfriend. A stalker is a whole different ball of nastiness, but you'd already dumped his ass before he hit you. I'm proud of you."

Proud. "You're not mad?" She looked around the table at her friends and saw sympathy on every face.

"Why would we be mad? Although we'd like to have kicked his ass." Looking like a Hispanic Wonder Woman, Andrea gave her a fierce look, then smiled. "No, *chica*. We're friends whether we share all of our pasts or not."

"Speak for yourself. Me? I expect to get all the dirt." Sally's eyes narrowed. "No wonder you avoid big guys. Or retreat if a Dom comes on too strong."

"Or she pranks them." Andrea grinned at Uzuri. "Cullen still talks about the doll you tied to his bar for a 'bar ornament'."

In her soft Georgia drawl, Kim said, "That explains why you're crazy fun at our all-women parties, but get quiet when there're guys around."

"Actually, Jarvis can't take all the blame for me being more comfortable with women than men." Uzuri grimaced. "My mother is the one who sent me to a Catholic all-girls school."

Having been raised Catholic herself, Andrea burst out laughing.

"Seriously? They still have all-girls schools around?" California-raised Beth stared. "But what does that have to do with your reaction to men?"

"Girl, I didn't even know about male anatomy until I got out of high school. First kiss? I was twenty. You probably flirted and dated from kindergarten on, right?"

Jessica tilted her head. "Pretty much, yeah."

"I missed all that. In high school, I worked part-time in a department store and after graduation, I went full-time. Mama got sick then, so I took care of her in any spare time." Uzuri shook her head. "Even now, there aren't many men around in my section of the store. Guys still seem like strange creatures."

Kim rolled her eyes. "Honey, men *are* strange creatures. No *seems* about it."

"For pranks, well..." Uzuri grinned. "My set of friends raised pranking the priests and nuns to a fine art, so when I get mad, I fall back on that—with the Masters I like."

"Wow." Gabi stared. "I can't imagine getting a priest mad at me. Scary."

Uzuri huffed a laugh. "Actually, the nuns were a lot meaner. Think Mistress Anne with a ruler instead of a cane."

"Talk about a world of hurt," Kim muttered.

Uzuri's smile faded. "But...I need to work on standing up for myself with guys instead of going behind their backs."

"Damn right." The man's voice came from behind her.

Eyes widening, Andrea stared at something past Uzuri's shoulder.

Uzuri twisted around.

Holding a takeout cup, Max was standing on the other side of a plant-topped divider.

He'd been listening? "How long have you been eavesdropping on us?"

He had a thoroughly devastating—and wicked—grin. "Not long." He took a sip of his coffee. "But it explains a bit."

Uzuri flushed, then frowned. "Aren't you supposed to be at work, making the streets safe for all mankind?"

"Actually, I'm here to do exactly that—for womankind." He glanced at his watch, finished his coffee in two big swallows, and rose. "I'm assisting with your self-defense class today. Don't be late."

Mouth open, Uzuri watched him walk out. *Omigod.*

The birth of a prankster. That did explain a lot. Max was still smiling as he crossed the street to the martial arts studio. She'd filled Holt's locker with football-team-colored balls because the Dom had annoyed her—and because she was comfortable with him.

Hmm. Max frowned. He and Alastair had annoyed her a few times when she had stayed with them. She hadn't done anything mischievous.

Apparently, she still wasn't comfortable with them. The thought was a tad disappointing. With luck, her comfort level would rise now. Last Friday, Alastair had thoroughly enjoyed his time with her. Even better, he'd looked more like himself than he had in a while. More relaxed. Less stressed.

The little prankster was good for him.

Max rubbed his chin. Maybe he should step away so Alastair could have her to himself.

The thought grated his nerves like sandpaper.

Yet, even if they decided to share her, she might not work out. He and his cousin had strong personalities. Unless a submissive could hold her own, a ménage might flatten her completely.

Shaking his head, he entered the studio. Anne, a Shadowlands Mistress, stood at the far end of the mirror-walled room, and he headed that way. "Hey, Anne."

"Max, thank you for volunteering." The pregnant brunette smiled at him. "I like your idea about having male opponents."

"Good. And looks like the *opponents* are right on time." Max held up his hand to get the attention of the three detectives entering the dojo. Although they were big guys, he'd chosen men who would be gentle with inexperienced fighters. "How careful do we need to be?"

"Well... The women have been meeting for quite a while, learning from Andrea and me—and Sensei when he has time.

They have some solid skills, although Uzuri only joined them recently. She's still catching up." Anne rubbed her belly unconsciously. "The problem is that most have a history of abuse or violence in their past. I'm not sure how they'll react to male opponents."

The Shadowkittens from the coffee shop headed across the studio.

Anne frowned. "A woman with an abusive past often freezes when confronted by a man. Uzuri certainly did last spring."

"Her stalker was here?" Max stiffened.

"No, this was something else." Anne motioned him away from where the women were stowing their gear into storage cubbies outside the mat-covered area. "An abusive bastard and friends showed up at my house to get the location of the domestic violence shelter. There was an altercation."

"I hope you beat the shit out of him."

Her satisfied grin reminded him that she'd served in the Marines as well as law enforcement. "We did. However, Uzuri froze. She wouldn't share why at the time."

Max nodded. That fucking stalker.

"This summer, she joined our classes, but her heart isn't in it. And although she's come a long way, I doubt she'll fight back if her opponent is male."

Exactly his concern. "That's what the guys and I are here for." However, the thought of scaring women, especially one little submissive with big brown eyes, made his gut twist.

Anne gave him an understanding look before she lifted her voice. "Ladies, we have volunteer instructors with us today."

Eyes went wide when the women saw the wall of over-sized men they'd be facing. It broke Max's heart to see little Zuri take a step back.

An hour later, after giving Sally, his current "victim", a rest break, Max surveyed the room. Damned if he wasn't enjoying himself. Aside from Anne, all the women were submissive, but...as any Dom quickly learned, submissives weren't cowards or weaklings. When they decided to fight, they could be downright effective. In addition, fists that were smaller could fucking hurt. It was like being hit with a broomstick instead of a flat paddle.

Marcus' Gabi had gotten in a couple of good punches, and despite the padding, he'd probably have a bruise or two.

Kim did well, too. Raoul had obviously worked with his brunette slave. She fought with a mixture of karate and street fighting.

However, as he'd feared, most of the women were momentarily freezing when attacked. They'd need work to get past that reaction...but then they'd do well enough in a real fight. He knew Beth would, since he'd seen the bruises on the bastard who'd attacked her kids last August.

Uzuri, though, was a whole different story. When one of his detective volunteers had "attacked", she'd panicked. After trying one more time, she'd given up and retreated to the sidelines. Seeing her fear sent all of Max's protective instincts into overdrive. Damned if he hadn't wanted to punch the detective for scaring her.

He'd also wanted to rip the detective a new one for flirting with her—and that was jealousy, pure and simple.

When was the last time he'd been jealous? Tuning out the shouts and grunts of battle around him, he considered. Not since high school when the love of his life had dumped him for a basketball player. Two weeks later, Max's affections had moved to a skinny, blonde swimmer.

He'd had his fair share of lovers since, but no one had roused his territorial instincts like Uzuri. What the hell was he going to do about this?

After sending Sally to work out with a different partner, Max crossed the mats to Uzuri. Fuck, she was pretty. Her hair was twisted flat against her scalp from the crown to the back of her head, before billowing out into gleaming corkscrews. Tight leggings showed her toned legs. She wore a loose shirt over a tank top that was probably supposed to conceal her assets—and it did hide her cleavage. However, she had no idea of how the hem kept riding up over her gorgeous round ass in an erotic hide 'n' seek.

He hated fighting when half-erect.

Ignoring the discomfort, he turned his focus to his current task. Teach her to fight, even though the poor baby was so nervous she was wringing her hands.

Her unfamiliarity with any kind of violence added to the problem. When he'd questioned the students about their pasts, he learned Sally had worked in a police station for a while. As teens, Gabi and Andrea had spent time on the street. Kim had grown up around the docks. Violence, in general, wouldn't shock most of them into immobility.

Uzuri, though... Catholic girls' schools didn't have many fist-fights. Her occupation kept her in nice quiet department stores, although...those Black Friday sales? Scary shit. Cincinnati had rough sectors, but her mama had been ill during the times when a girl might run wild. Uzuri probably hadn't even seen bloodshed, not until that asshole beat the hell out of her.

No wonder she'd retreated to the sidelines today. She wasn't mentally ready to defend against a strange male. So for this lesson, he'd work with her himself. At least she knew him somewhat.

"Time to go play, princess." He held out his hand.

"I'm fine right here," she said in a small voice.

"No attacking right now. We'll work on a block-punch combination." Then...maybe...he'd step it up.

"You won't attack me?" Her big brown eyes met his with a punch all their own. "You didn't do combinations with the others. Why..."

Focus, Drago. "They've taken enough classes that their reactions are close to instinctive. You haven't reached that level." Hell, it was obvious she could barely bring herself to hit a person.

"I'm not brave," she whispered.

"You survived, Zuri. Courage doesn't mean not being scared. In the Marines, we'd say, 'Courage is endurance for one moment more.'"

She stared at him, her lips repeating silently, "One moment more."

"That's it." Moving slowly, he gripped her wrist and ignored her flinch. "Make a fist."

When she did, he nodded. "You got that part down. Now punch me in the gut."

"What?"

He slapped the heavy padding covering his chest and belly. "You won't hurt me."

She still hesitated. The women were accustomed to pulling their punches upon contact with an opponent's clothing. That wouldn't do. He and his volunteers had donned padding, and expected full contact.

He hardened his voice. "C'mon, little wimp. You're not here to stare at me."

She hit him. Lightly.

"Sorry, baby. That wouldn't scare anything bigger than a poodle. Do you have any muscles at all?"

She gave him a pitiful look.

"Uzuri, look at Kim." Face sweaty, the brunette was smacking her fists into the handheld pads one detective held. A grunt accompanied each punch. "I want that kind of effort from you."

Her eyes held so many warring emotions. A submissive's desire to do what a Dom requested. Her fear of hurting him. Her abhorrence of violence.

"This is what you're here for. Make it worth both our whiles." He waited her out and saw resolve appear on her face.

The next punch had a bit of spirit behind it.

"Better." He gripped her arm and moved her fist to where it would strike below his sternum. "Aim here next time." He released her and stepped back. "Again."

The next punch was dead-on and even harder. She'd brought the energy from below and rotated her hips into the punch. "Good. Now use both arms and give me a one-two-three set of punches."

With only a second's hesitation, she complied. The three fast punches to his solar plexus were hard enough he almost winced. The smack of her fists against the padding was beautiful.

Laughing, he gripped her shoulders, giving her a light squeeze to shake the worry from her gaze. "Perfect. That was perfect."

"You mean it?" The wonder in her big eyes made his chest tighten. Fuck, she was adorable.

Stepping back, he motioned. "Again. And harder."

Uzuri could still feel the strength of his hands on her shoulders. Pushing that aside, she narrowed her focus and put her body into the right space in the way Anne had taught her, used her hips to add power, and pretended her fist would go right through the... the target. Not the body—the target.

Pow, pow, pow.

Her knuckles burned. Oh, she'd hit him so hard.

Yet, even as she stepped back, she heard his pleased chuckle. "That's a good girl." His far-too-devastating grin made dimples in his cheeks.

Her insides quivered in a way that had nothing to do with fear.

He saw—the Dom saw everything—and his blue eyes sharpened. Heated.

A second later, he was just her teacher. "I'm going to reach for you. I want you to block my arm and punch me. It's a one-two move; block, then punch."

Her heart was already racing at being so close to him, at hitting him, at the sounds of all the aggression. When he tried to grab her, she skittered back.

"Nope," he said. "Try again." He reached.

She hesitated too long, fighting her need to retreat, and he slapped her shoulder lightly. "Nope. You lost that one. Try again."

He reached.

Her block was sloppy and weak, but he kindly let her forearm knock his arm away. Her punch didn't get close to connecting.

"Better. Look here, Zuri." He held her arm out right beside his. "I'm a guy and have long arms. You'll have to step closer to punch me."

She shook her head. "You'll hit me."

"Maybe. It happens."

"*What?*"

"Going into a fight, you know you might get hurt, but baby, I want you fucking determined that you'll be the only one standing at the end." His blue gaze burned into her, driving his words home. After a second, he moved back. "Once more."

They did it again and again and again until she didn't fear him...she *hated* him.

"Again."

He attacked, she blocked and punched with an arm that felt like overcooked spaghetti. Nonetheless it made a solid smack against the padding, and the sound of his grunt was wonderful.

Grinning, he leaned down and planted a swift kiss on her lips. "That's the girl I want facing down an attacker. Good job."

His approval lit a happy warmth inside her.

He straightened. "Anne, we're due back at work. See you this time next week." His other detectives joined him.

Uzuri stared as he walked toward the exit. He had a deceptively lazy stroll that almost hid all that lethal power and watchful menace.

Because of his size and anger, Jarvis was scary.

Max was terrifying.

Before he walked out the door, he glanced back, caught her gaze, and held it. Held it. The mat she stood on seemed to drop a foot.

And then he smiled and was gone.

CHAPTER THIRTEEN

"Turn." Kneeling on the floor in the Catholic Church basement on Thursday evening, Uzuri picked up another pin and smiled at the teenager who was holding herself so straight.

The entire room was filled with women who were also hemming dresses or fitting necklines, sleeves, and waistlines for the underprivileged teenagers. Homecoming proms were coming up.

Others were helping teens find accessories—from jewelry to shoes to purses. Makeup lessons continued in another corner.

After watching the wonderful influence that Master Marcus—and the other Masters—had with a group of teenage boys, Uzuri had realized there were teenage girls in need of attention, too. With a couple of churchwomen, she'd organized something similar.

"This is a stunning color on you, Makayla." Uzuri put in the last pin and shifted her position with a smothered moan of pain. Every single muscle in her body hurt. It was obvious that going all out in self-defense would surely slay her faster than any serial killer.

Uzuri looked up at the girl. "Do you have a date for the dance or are you going with friends?"

The glow on the girl's face brightened the entire room. "Joshua asked me. I can't believe he asked me."

Uzuri bit back words of caution. "That's wonderful. Is...is he a good kid?"

"He is. He's smart. And nice. Not one of the jock bullies. Suzi went out with him, and he wasn't all hands or anything."

"Good. That's very good." Reassured, Uzuri picked up the box of pins and rose. Later tonight, one of the mothers planned a talk about dating safety...as well as how to say no politely and assertively. That would probably suffice. "Go change, and I'll show you how to hem your dress. We'll do it together."

Makayla bounced on her toes slightly, and Uzuri knew it was from not only the joy of receiving a beautiful gown, but also learning a new skill. The girl's mama was in prison. Makayla's father worked two poorly paying jobs, leaving little time to parent the girl and her two brothers.

A girl could get support from her besties, but...there was nothing like the anchoring effect of a mother or adult woman's help, advice, and care. That's what this group was all about.

Uzuri loved teaching the girls all the secrets her mama had shared. Probably one of the most important was that the world usually judged a person first by her appearance and only later by her competence and character. *I'm not saying it's fair, child. This is reality.*

Mama would tell her that a smart woman would don her "armor" before setting forth. *"Dress for respect, Uzuri."* "Armor" was more than mere clothing, and included hair and makeup and posture and speech.

The tools of preparing for a dance could also be used for preparing for a job. The organization would be working on job preparation next month and whenever needed.

"Lanna, your makeup is beautiful," Uzuri told a pretty blonde who'd been over by the mirrors. "Very understated."

"That's because this is my 'business face'. Juliet said I should come next week and learn how to do a 'date night face'." Lanna wrinkled her nose. "When I try to look sexy, I always end up more like a cheap hooker."

Uzuri smiled. "It's a skill like anything else. Once you learn the tricks, you'll do fine."

As the girl sped across the room to show off to her friends, Uzuri settled into a quiet spot beside her sewing box. Who would have thought volunteer work could be so much fun? Then again, matching clothes to people and occasions had drawn her...forever. Before she could even spell, she'd sewn clothes for her dolls. Then she'd graduated to dressing her friends. Even now, her BFFs begged her to shop with them.

She threaded the needle and smiled. Wedding dress hunting was the best. Andrea was going to be simply gorgeous in hers.

As her phone reminder went off, Uzuri silenced it and shook her head. *Absentminded, much?* After she, Kim, Gabi, and Rainie had gone on their self-assigned "mission" last night, she'd planned to call Jessica—and had forgotten.

Thankfully, her waxing appointment with Sally and Andrea had reminded her and she'd set the alarm on her phone. She grinned, thinking of the flurry of Spanish curses. Master Cullen had better appreciate the torture his submissive had endured to enhance their honeymoon.

Glancing around the room, Uzuri saw Lanna was still with her friends. Time to make the call. She punched in the number to Jessica's cell.

"Uzuri." Rather than Jessica's bubbly voice, she heard Master Z's deep, sophisticated voice.

"Uh..." She stared at the phone. Hadn't she called Jessica?

"Jessica is giving Sophia a bath. How are you doing?"

Oh, awkward. "I'm fine. I should be back tomorrow."

"Indeed. However, I gave all of Andrea's friends this weekend off. I know you are all buried in wedding duties."

"Really?" Uzuri sighed in relief. "That will help."

"Very good. Did you wish to leave a message for Jessica?"

"Yes. No."

Under the weight of his silence, Uzuri closed her eyes. How could he exert a Dom's pressure when he didn't even speak? "Sir. I actually wanted to ask *you* for advice...or something."

"Go on."

"It's Andrea. Um, she's missing her father and the wedding is coming..." Awkwardly, Uzuri spilled out what Andrea had said and how she'd cried.

When Uzuri finished, she sighed. Would she lose her girl card now for revealing secrets?

"I understand," Master Z said softly. "Thank you, little one. You did well to tell me."

The constriction in Uzuri's chest relaxed, letting her pull in a breath. "Okay. Good. Um, bye."

Even as she tucked the phone back in her purse, she had to shake her head at how totally inept she'd been. Unfortunately, that was how she was. In professional settings, she did fine. With women, she was smooth and confident. With dating or with Doms? She was a total fluster-face.

It didn't matter, though, did it? She'd survive feeling gauche if it meant Master Z would talk with Master Cullen about Andrea.

Then Andrea would be happy.

Uzuri smiled. Andrea would be such a beautiful bride. Master Cullen was going to totally light up when he saw his woman coming down the aisle. He loved her so much.

Uzuri rubbed at the knot of envy located right under her breastbone. It would be nice to have someone look at her that way.

Although, Alastair had given her a warm smile when he'd

come to her apartment. Really warm. More than an *I-want-to-fuck-you* look. That had been an *I-like-you* smile.

Yesterday, during the self-defense class, she'd caught Max checking out her ass. Only, he'd not been all leering and ugly about it, but more like an *oooh-shiny* moment, and then he'd caught himself and gotten back to business. He hadn't made her feel cheap, but pretty.

It was a good feeling.

If a bit confusing. Since she'd gone to bed with Alastair, shouldn't Max back away? Only, the Drago Doms did sometimes top together at the club. Did they share a girlfriend, as well?

Only, she wasn't a girlfriend. Not in reality. Merely someone Alastair had taken to bed. Of course, he *had* called afterward, so she was more than a one-night stand, right? Really, if she hadn't been out of town for a fashion show until two days ago, maybe he'd have asked her out.

Or not. He was so polite. That might be why he'd called. What if she hadn't been that interesting or good in bed?

She snorted. *Insecure, much?* She was. There were times she regretted her lack of experience—and the only one she had to blame for the recent lack was herself.

Seeing Makayla approach, Uzuri patted the bench. "Sit and we'll get—"

Her phone buzzed, and she pulled it out. Alastair. She should wait. Let it go to voice mail.

Not a chance.

"Hello?"

"Good evening, love. Are you back in town?"

"Um. Hi. Yes. Yes, I am." Oh, didn't she sound intelligent.

"Excellent. You see, Max's schedule got rearranged, which means we're both off tomorrow night. I know you're busy with Andrea's wedding, but if you can fit us in, we're having a few friends over for dinner. We'd like you to come." She could hear

CHERISE SINCLAIR

the smile in his voice when he added, "Hunter misses you—and so do I."

Her first instinctive response was to start thinking of excuses. She recognized her cowardice—*oh, how pitiful, girl*. She lifted her chin. *Courage*. She had it; she *did*. "I'd love to come."

"Good girl." The approval in his deep voice warmed her like being bathed in sunlight. "Around seven. And bring an overnight bag, pet."

Before she could respond to his outrageous assumption, he'd already disconnected.

"Oh-Em-Gee, that voice!" Makayla stood right next to Uzuri's chair and fanned herself. "All British and deep and... Oh-Em-Gee, he sounds like the Arrow's super hunky, cool stepfather."

Uzuri managed to stay sitting, but inside, she was spinning and singing, *"Omigod, he called, he called, he called. Alastair called me."*

With an effort, she said calmly, "He does sound like Walter Steele, doesn't he?" Oh, he truly did. Total voice-porn. *Yummy*.

Behave, girl. She pushed the sewing box toward the girl. "Let's get started on hemming your dress. Do you know how to thread a needle?"

CHAPTER FOURTEEN

On Friday night, Max opened the front door and smiled down at Uzuri. Now here was one beautiful woman. This was a totally different image from two weeks ago when she'd been schlepping around their house in his flannel shirt, hair in fat twists, and wearing no makeup.

Today... Her shiny black hair was pulled up and twisted back on the top and sides, then left to fall in in springy coils down to her shoulders. Made his fingers itch to play. She wore makeup—enough to make her eyes enormous and her lips glossy. That plump lower lip of hers could undo a man. Her crisp sundress was the color of a deep red rose, and her earrings, lipstick, and nails matched the color.

As a guy, he couldn't help wanting to untie that perky bow behind her neck—the one that held the halter-top up.

"Did I get the wrong time?" she asked. "You're frowning."

Yeah, he was. And erect, too. As he regained control of himself, he gave her another slow look. "You know, you really are stunning."

She blinked at his compliment before giving him a delighted smile. "Thank you."

"Only the truth." Taking her hand, he pulled her into the house and then into his arms. If she had to reapply her lipstick, too bad.

As he molded her against him, he took her generous mouth in a dark, deep kiss. To his pleasure, she kissed him back. Yeah, he hadn't forgotten how wholeheartedly she kissed.

When he lifted his head, he licked his lips. "You taste like strawberries."

"I nibbled on some while I was getting dressed."

Because they hadn't given her much time between leaving work and coming here. He frowned. "I should get you something to eat. It'll be a while before dinner is ready."

"Sally's right. Doms *are* overprotective." Delighting him, she went up on tiptoes to press a light kiss on his lips. "I'm fine."

"All right, then." He'd tell Alastair to serve the appetizers early. "C'mon. Hunter wants to see you."

If enthusiasm was a gauge, Hunter had definitely missed the little submissive. The minute they stepped outside, Hunter let out a bark and charged across the patio. Uzuri dropped down to her knees, bestowing hugs and pats. "Pretty puppy. Such a pretty puppy."

Stubby tail wagging frantically, the dog wiggled and squirmed in circles, getting in quick licks everywhere he could reach. Uzuri only laughed.

Grinning, Max stepped back, partly to avoid being bowled over. Yeah, she was a real dog-hater, all right.

Galen and Vance joined him. "That's a pretty sight," Galen said.

"It is, isn't it?" Max added, half under his breath, "I'd like those hands on *me*, dammit."

Vance punched his shoulder. "'Bout time someone wised up and made a move on her. I was beginning to think every Dom in the club was blind."

"Can't blame *them*. She wasn't about to let any man get close," Max said.

Galen blew out a disgusted breath. "A submissive's anxieties shouldn't deter a determined Dom...not if she is attracted to him. Or them."

Galen probably spoke from experience. From the gossip, Sally had put up a battle before her two Masters had won her.

But even if they got Uzuri past her fears, Max doubted she'd be comfortable with two men at once. Apparently, she'd been with only one Dom at a time.

However, when he'd talked with Alastair and offered to back off, his cousin had vetoed the idea. Alastair wanted a D/s V-triad —two Doms sharing one submissive. Period. Max shook his head. The doc wasn't nearly as hard-ass as Max, but he could be incredibly stubborn.

Which was a relief, because Max was getting pulled in far faster than he liked.

He glanced at the two Doms. "Any advice?"

Vance frowned. "Go slow, but don't give her a chance to let her anxieties overcome her courage."

"We found it was easier living together rather than trying to date. The interactions are more natural. You're not forced to try to interact together all the time." Galen leaned against the wall. "Lotta dynamics going on with a ménage. You each have a unique relationship with your woman, then you have your relationship with your co-Dom, and then there's another dynamic when it's all three of you."

"True. Living together is more relaxed. There's more down time." Vance glanced at him. "She was here for a couple of days. You probably each had alone time with her without thinking about it."

Interesting observation. "That's true. Well, we'll see where it goes."

Galen's gaze turned to Max. "She really is a sweetheart, you know."

"So I'm learning." Max grinned as Uzuri hugged Hunter, managing to hold him still long enough to plant a kiss on the furry head.

Sweet she definitely was. All the same, was she strong enough for a relationship with him and Alastair? For two Doms?

Uzuri rubbed her chin on top of Hunter's head, smiling at the feel of the soft fur. Oh, she'd missed him as much as she'd missed the two Doms. "You're such a sweetie."

He wiggled his agreement.

"Okay, honey, I have to get up now."

He didn't budge. Seventy or so pounds of dog was sprawled across her lap...and, since she was wearing a dress, scrambling out from under him wasn't going to work. Not unless she flashed everyone on the patio.

"Might you need some help?" Alastair asked from behind her.

"Yes, please, Sir." The Sir somehow slipped out. How did he do that to her?

"Hunter, come." He snapped his fingers, and the dog jumped off her lap to sit at the Dom's feet. "Good boy."

After tossing Hunter a treat, Alastair held out his hand for Uzuri. Even though he loomed over her, she looked into his steady dark eyes and relaxed. His hand closed around hers, and he lifted her easily to her feet.

"Thank you."

"Woman, this is how you thank a Dom." As he pulled her closer, he ran his fingers up into her hair—and gripped. The firm pull sent so many tingles through her that her body seemed to chime.

"I do like when your hair is loose and curly," he murmured. "I like being able to touch."

Oh boy, he could touch all he wanted. She might never use extensions again. As he tugged her head back and took her lips, her insides went into one super-gooey, meltdown. How could a man's lips be so soft and yet so firm? She could feel his perfectly trimmed beard, a different roughness from the adjacent clean-shaven skin. Each breath brought her the tantalizingly sunny citrus scent of his aftershave.

With a low hum of enjoyment, he ran his free hand down her back, flattening her against him. Although she'd wrapped her arms around his neck, he controlled her movements as he explored her lips, her mouth, and her jaw, slowly and thoroughly, until she felt as if he knew her better from one kiss than anyone had known her before. Wave after wave of heat moved through her until her skin felt as if it were radiating.

When he finally lifted his head, her legs had gone weak.

The muscles in his arm hardened to iron as he took her weight and smiled down at her. "Hunter isn't the only one who missed you, pet."

"I..." She was always polite and couldn't think of a thing to say. Could only stare up at him.

Laughter lightened his eyes to green. He picked up a glass of wine from the nearby patio table and handed it to her. "I brought this out for you. Come and join the others."

At a table near the garden pond, Sally, Rainie, and Jake had obviously enjoyed the show. Vance and Galen strolled over—also grinning—and sat on each side of Sally. Near the door into the house, Max smiled at her.

Oh, honestly. Hadn't anyone ever seen a kiss before? As Uzuri's cheeks heated, she smoothed her dress and walked over to the table. "It's good to see you all. Isn't this wonderful weather we're having?"

Vance's lips twitched. "It is, although perhaps overly humid. You look flushed."

She didn't glare at him, but if he said anything else, she'd turn all his whips and floggers into macramé hangings.

With his usual impeccable manners, Alastair seated her. "Would you like a Negroni as an aperitif or something else?"

"The Negroni sounds wonderful. Thank you."

When he left, Max stepped behind Uzuri. As he talked with Galen and Vance about the joys of adopting a dog, his callused palms rested on the bare skin of her shoulders.

All she could think was that a halter-top might have been a bad idea. Yet she didn't want him to move. Ever.

"We could get a pup since we're home more now," Galen mused. "At least Sally and I are."

"An adult dog might be a wiser choice." Vance shook his head. "Glock would consider a puppy a fine high protein snack."

"Glock?" Max asked.

Uzuri tipped her head back and smiled at him. "They have a big gray cat who rules the house."

"He's death on rodents," Vance added. "And has every dog in the neighborhood cowed."

"That's a hell of a name." Max snorted a laugh. "Next year, keep us in mind for a kitten, Rainie—one that looks like a Colt."

"A Glock'll take a Colt any day," Galen said.

Enjoying the quiet conversation, Uzuri realized Max was perfectly comfortable with everyone. Although he had a face as hard and deadly as Master Nolan's, he didn't have Nolan's taciturn nature at all. He liked people and liked talking with them.

And as he idly massaged her shoulders, she relaxed. Jarvis had been overly familiar, squeezing her ass or trying to fondle her breasts in public. Max's hands never left her shoulders.

When Alastair joined them, he settled on the other side of Uzuri, took her hand, and laced their fingers together.

They were treating her in the way a man might treat his date. His lover. His wife. Possessively.

Both of them.

Later that evening, Uzuri stood in the powder room and checked her hair and makeup. Everything looked good. Better than good, actually. She was glowing.

Being the focus of two very dominant men made her feel... incredible. Sexy and pretty. *Wanted.*

There had rarely been a moment when Max or Alastair wasn't touching her. An arm around her waist, a hand pressed to the hollow of her spine, or fingers laced with hers.

At first, she'd worried their public display of affection was merely to work on her fear of men. Only...maybe not.

Alastair liked her. Yes, she honestly believed he did.

Max did, too. His kiss had been hot. And branding.

But both of them? Talk about confusing.

Right now, she didn't care. She was having fun.

Besides, telling the Dragos that she was feeling a little anxious with their attentions would simply ensure they touched her even more. Doms liked to push the boundaries like that.

Aside from her worries, the evening had been marvelous. The food—Cornish game hens served over wild rice with a shitake mushroom sauce—had been superb, the conversation dynamic and filled with laughter. They'd invited her best of best friends, and she doubted the guest list had been by chance.

Although Alastair was more reserved than Max, he was articulate and interesting. He'd lived and traveled all over the world. He and Jake were a lot alike. Galen and Vance had been in law enforcement and spoke Max's language. Rainie and Sally were not only brilliant, but irrepressible. Truly a fun evening.

After a noisy thunderstorm drove them into the formal living room, Alastair'd brought out a late harvest Zinfandel he'd bought in France and an assortment of fruit and cheesecake tarts for dessert.

Uzuri shook her head at herself. The Zinfandel was probably the reason she felt so mellow. That last glass had been one too many.

As she returned to the living room, she heard the doorbell chime. Were the Dragos expecting more guests?

On his way to the front door, Alastair stopped to touch her cheek gently, leaving tingling warmth behind.

How could he get all her senses stirred up so easily?

Unsettled again, she took her seat and smiled at how the TV room and the living room differed. The TV room furniture was mostly Max's, and the room was all about comfort.

The more dignified living room was designed for entertaining. Against the pale gray walls, Alastair's European furniture ruled—a white camel back sofa with carved legs and several burgundy wingback chairs. The lights in the crystal hanging candelabra lent a soft glow to the room; the hand-carved limestone fireplace mantel simply cried out for real candles.

As she picked up her drink, she remembered something she'd wanted to ask. "Whatever happened to the pond's water lilies? Weren't there more of them last week?"

"The pup happened." Max nodded at the dog who'd fallen asleep at Rainie's feet. "We were eating breakfast out there yesterday. Hunter noticed the goldfish...and decided to go fishing."

Jake, the veterinarian, snorted. "German shorthaired pointers and water. You can't keep them apart."

"Oh, no." Uzuri could just imagine.

"I think the goldfish are still sulking." Max looked up as Alastair entered the room.

Alastair's gaze was unreadable. "Max, you have a visitor, I'm afraid."

Uzuri blinked. That was an awfully negative way to announce a visitor.

"Yeah?" Max rose.

A blonde stepped into the room, saw Max, and flung herself at him. "Oh, darling, I've missed you so much." She wrapped her arms around his neck and buried her head in his shoulder.

The odd sensation in the pit of Uzuri's stomach was...dread. With an effort, she blanked her expression.

The two looked as if they belonged together. The tall, slender blonde was extraordinarily beautiful with refined features and thick, wavy hair that fell perfectly into place. Her turquoise silk dress set off blue eyes that were swimming with happy tears.

Max had a girlfriend.

Why did I think he was interested in me? Feeling as if she was intruding on an intimate reunion, Uzuri glanced at the other guests. "Perhaps it's time to call it a night and leave them alone."

"I don't think he'd agree." Gazing at the couple, Rainie frowned. "That man is one unhappy camper."

"What?" Uzuri looked over her shoulder, and her jaw went slack.

Face dark with anger, Max yanked the woman's arms from his neck and took a step away.

"*Max.*" Hurt filled the blonde's face. "How can you treat me like this?"

"Maybe because I don't want to see you, hear you, or speak to you?" His voice was raw and rasping. "I've told you enough fucking times—there is nothing between us. Why the hell do you think I moved here?"

"Oh, my darling." After a glance at the people in the room, she put her hand on his chest. "Let's go somewhere private and talk. I'm sure—"

"No, Hayley." His icy gaze met Uzuri's. "See, darlin'? Men have stalkers, too."

Uzuri blinked. Omigod, this was his stalker? The woman who'd driven him from Seattle?

Max sighed. "Sorry, people. This isn't what we invited you for." He nodded to Hayley. "All right. Let's go in another room."

No. Just no. Getting Max alone was the woman's ploy. Jarvis had done the same, setting up situations where Uzuri would capitulate to avoid a scene.

When Hayley latched onto Max's arm, swift, hot anger flooded Uzuri's veins. That female needed to learn how nasty a "spectacle" could turn.

Jaw set, Uzuri stalked across the room, pushed between Hayley and Max, and used a hip to knock the woman back. Riding her anger, Uzuri snuggled up to Max and wrapped her arms around him as if she belonged there.

To her surprise, he pulled her even closer—and she couldn't help but notice the sheer power and strength of his body.

Unwilling to face his undoubtedly appalled expression, she rested her cheek against his chest and asked loudly, "Is this that horrid bitch you told me about, Max?"

"What?" Hayley looked as if she'd been slapped.

Uzuri felt a moment of sympathy, then it disappeared. Stalkers deserved to be embarrassed.

Behind Hayley, Alastair nodded at Uzuri and soundlessly voiced, "Go on."

All right, then. She frowned at Hayley. "You weren't invited to our party and never will be. Get a clue, girl. Go away and don't bother us again." Each pronoun implied Max and Uzuri were a couple. *Our* party. *Us.*

After a small flinch, Hayley narrowed her eyes.

Uzuri activated Rainie with a lifted eyebrow. Her longtime partner in prankster play leaped into the fray. "It seems they don't teach manners on the West Coast. Is everyone in Seattle this skanky?"

Uzuri sniffed. "I certainly hope not. Max wants us to visit there next spring."

Sally said to Vance in a loud whisper, "I can't believe the way that woman came on to Uzuri's man. That's so *trashy*."

Hayley scowled at Sally and Rainie, and her glare could have clawed the clothes from Uzuri's back.

When she turned to Max, her smile and voice were sweet

enough to rot teeth. "Darling, you can't possibly prefer that... person...to me."

Max's arm felt like iron around Uzuri's waist and didn't loosen. His gaze on Uzuri, he brushed her cheek with his knuckles and said softly, "In every way I can think of, I prefer Zuri to you."

Of course, he only said that to shake Hayley, and still Uzuri felt his declaration right down to the tips of her toes. She couldn't look away from the possessive heat in his gaze.

His eyes filled her world.

Somewhere, Hayley was protesting. Whining. "No. Max...but we... Max."

Max's lips touched Uzuri's. Firm, yet tender. Demanding, yet gentle. Overwhelming. When the ground under her feet disappeared, all she could do was hold on. To him.

Sometime later, he lifted his head and kissed her lightly. "Mmm." After a second, he looked up.

Uzuri glanced over her shoulder.

Hayley had a hand over her mouth. Her expression was one of utter shock.

Behind her, Alastair lifted an amused eyebrow at Max, before setting his hand on the blonde's shoulder. "You are unwelcome here. I will show you to the door."

Hayley resisted, her gaze flickering between Uzuri and Max, then her shoulders slumped in complete and utter defeat. Without a sound, she followed Alastair out of the room.

Max stared after the woman who had made his life hell in Seattle.

He couldn't believe she'd simply walked out. How many times had she intruded on his nights out and embarrassed his date? She'd never abandoned the field...until now.

The resignation in her face indicated this time she was actually gone for good.

Then again, no woman had stepped into the war as Uzuri had.

No woman had ever openly taken on Hayley, not only battling her, but also humiliating her.

And when Hayley had asked him how he felt, no one could have missed the ring of truth in his voice.

In his arms, Uzuri squirmed slightly and pushed against his chest.

Max grinned. Nope, he wasn't going to let her get away—not unless she seriously wanted to escape. A Dom shouldn't make assumptions.

Alastair walked back into the room, his dark face set in the frown he usually wore for incurable illnesses, tough crossword puzzles, and people he hadn't figured out. When their gazes met, Max looked down at the little submissive. He tightened his arms and nodded.

Alastair's frown disappeared. Slowly, he smiled.

Message received.

To hell with seeing where things would go. Things would go as they ordered—*forward*.

We're keeping this one...if she wants to be kept.

"Okay, beat this. Sneezing while putting on mascara." As Max's laugh rang out into the quiet night, Uzuri frowned. *Quiet* night? She looked around the dark patio. Where had everyone gone?

After Hayley had left, people had abandoned the living room for the kitchen and patio. More wine had been opened as the others shared various ways dates had gone sour.

Then, somehow, she and Max had started comparing notes on their most traumatic teenage moments. Omigod, she'd thought getting the dreaded red spot from a heavy flow was humiliating—not that she'd shared that experience. He'd totally won with his account of acting in a Shakespearean play and getting a boner. In tights.

But—she scowled. How had she missed noticing she was the last remaining guest? She vaguely remembered Rainie and Jake had said goodbye. When had Sally and her Masters left? Where was Alastair?

Uzuri frowned at the bottle on the table. How much had she had?

"Something wrong, princess?"

"Everyone else has left." She sat up on the long lounge chair. "Although I implied to Hayley that I live here, I don't, and I need to get home."

"Uh-uh." Max grinned. "You need to stay so you didn't actually lie. Isn't that considered a sin or something?"

"I'll risk it."

His voice held a Dom's edge. "You were told to bring an overnight bag. Did you?"

"Yes, Sir." How had she forgotten that she'd planned to stay? Then again, it wasn't Max who'd told her to pack a bag. "Where's Alastair?"

"The doc got tired. He was up early this morning for rounds at the hospital so he took Hunter and went to bed."

"He's gone?" Uzuri stiffened.

The tiny solar lights in the foliage and the three-quarter moon overhead lent enough light to see Max's amusement. "Yep. There's only the two of us left. Scared, baby?"

When he rose, tall and powerful, his broad shoulders blotted out the moon.

Too big.

But under his even, steady gaze, her fear slid away. Instead, a shiver of excitement ran through her and increased when he sat on the lounge recliner beside her. The sound of water splashing into the lower pond blended sweetly with Celtic Women's lilting music from inside the house.

Leaning down, Max slowly lifted her arms around his neck and then captured her lips. Oh, the way he kissed. Not soft or teasing, but out and out possession.

If she could have merged into his body, she would. His thick hair teased her arms, and she reached up to run her fingers through the cool silkiness. Pulling him closer, she let her tongue dance against his—and he took more.

When he lifted his head, his breathing was faster. "Fuck, you can kiss, princess." He traced a finger over her upper lip and down to her lower. "I've had carnal dreams about this mouth of yours."

Even as a flush washed over her skin, she imagined taking his cock in her mouth, sucking on it, teasing it. Heat pooled in her core.

"And ever since you showed up tonight, I've wanted to do this." With one swift pull, he undid the halter ties at her neck and bared her from the waist up. The breeze from the bay wafted over her exposed breasts, and she gasped.

When she tried to cover herself, he shook his head. "No, little subbie." He bracketed her wrists with one big hand and secured them over her head.

"Max, you—"

"Who?"

Oh, heavens, she recognized that look. That tone. He'd slid into Dom mode.

Every bone in her body went limp in utter surrender. "Sir," she whispered. What had she planned to say?

"Mmm. These are as pretty as I imagined." Casually, as if he had the right, he fondled one breast, lifting it in a warm, callused palm as if to weigh it. His thumb circled the peak. Slowly. Gaze on her, he smiled as if he could see the way her body was heating.

Her nipples peaked with a tightening, aching feeling.

"Look at you," he said softly. He leaned forward and took her lips in a lazy, drugging kiss, sensually exploring her mouth, even as he gently rolled her nipples, first one and then the other.

A slow pulse wakened between her legs, and she rubbed her

thighs together. *No.* She shouldn't be feeling like this. As guilt swept over her, a sound of protest escaped.

He eased back, his gaze intent. After a long perusal, he said softly, "You look torn, darlin'. Tell me what's wrong."

"This isn't... I was with Alastair this week. I can't—this isn't right."

"Of course. I understand, princess." He released her wrists and sat up, his hip against her thigh. "I thought this might happen. A lot of women don't want a relationship with more than one man. How about I take you upstairs to Alastair—or, if you'd rather, I'll drive you home."

He held her hand gently, and his thumb stroked soothingly over the back. His entire body language had changed, his intense sexuality buried. He meant what he said.

"I didn't want two men," she said.

"It's all right, Zuri." He started to rise and she pulled him back down.

"I'm not done." Her voice held a snap, and she pulled in a breath. "Sorry, Sir."

An eyebrow went up. "Actually, I like knowing you can hold your own. Good for you. Go on."

"I misspoke. I meant that—in the past—I had never considered being with two men." Hadn't that been somewhat short-sighted? "At this point, I'm not sure of...anything. I don't even know how this works." She should have asked Sally some questions.

"How what works?" Max asked gently.

"Well, Alastair was with me. By himself. Now you're here and he's gone." She motioned between the two of them. "This isn't a... a threesome, right?"

His chuckle was dry. "Gotcha. What you have to remember is that every polyamorous relationship works differently."

"Um. Okay. Have you done—had—this before. Outside of the club?" The words certainly weren't falling easily from her lips.

"Actually, yes."

Her eyes went wide, and he snorted.

When had he done a...whatever this was called? "I thought you and Alastair hadn't been together since college."

"That's right. College was where we discovered BDSM and sharing. In our senior year, we rented a house, and our submissive lived with us. Although we enjoyed our time together, none of us was serious. We all went in different directions after graduation."

"Oh."

He traced a finger down her cheek. "In the service, I was married for a short while."

He'd been married? The thought was oddly annoying. Of course, someone as sexy as he was wouldn't stay single.

Only he wasn't married now. "What happened?"

"Nothing earth-shaking. Shallow as it sounds, I fell for her beauty, but didn't know her. Most of our marriage, I was overseas fighting while she pursued her career in business. We ended up with nothing in common. She's a good woman. The trouble was—the things she considered important were nuisances to me. To be fair, she considered me to be on the overly rigid side."

Overly rigid? A Marine—and a cop? *Well, duh.* Uzuri's attempt to muffle her giggle was ineffective. As for his wife... "She was high maintenance?"

His grin was quick and white in the night. "Fucking unbelievably high maintenance."

Uzuri stiffened. So was she.

"No, darlin', you're not like her. Her makeup went on before she'd even leave the bedroom. She'd never hug a dog or let one lick her chin. Ever."

"Oh." The warmth in his gaze washed over Uzuri, erasing the hurt she'd felt.

"Your appearance is important to you—I get that." His hand caressed her face. "But pups and people rank higher on your priority scale."

Well, of course. However, she understood what he meant. Actually, she'd met men who were as self-absorbed.

He continued, "Even when I was first married and happy, I still missed what Alastair could have brought to the relationship. Unfortunately, my wife wasn't open to polyamory. Actually, she was disgusted when she found out Alastair and I had shared a woman."

Being shared by two men. Why had she ruled it out completely when Sally had mentioned it before? Right now, thinking of being with both Alastair and Max was a little anxiety provoking, but not disgusting or terrifying. "So, um, how does it work?"

"Depends on the needs and desires of everyone involved."

Oh, that didn't tell her much. Did everyone share equally? "So, are you and Alastair bi?"

Rather than take offense, Max laughed. "Nope. Would've been easier, actually, but our hormones don't bounce that way." He lifted her hand and nibbled on her fingers, sending tingles upward. When she shivered, his lips curved. "We like living together, like threesomes with a submissive, and like one-on-ones with her, as well." A dimple showed in his cheek. "Alternating works fairly well."

Her mouth opened at his blunt explanation. And excitement bubbled inside her at the thought of herself being the submissive on a bondage table at the mercy of these very experienced, very focused Doms. Or she'd be with Max one night and Alastair the next. Her jutting nipples ached, demanding to be touched again.

Max put his fingers under her chin and held her gaze. "So, princess. Should I take you home now? Or upstairs to Alastair? Or do you want to stay here?"

Her voice emerged in a whisper. "Stay." Her muscles tensed. Oh, what had she done?

"Relax, Zuri." His eyes crinkled. "Tonight—or anytime with

Alastair or me—you're expected to tell us if something isn't working for you, whether it's a position, a man, or a relationship."

The worry inside her relaxed. "Okay."

"Good. In case you need it tonight, your safeword is red."

"Safeword?" Like in a scene?

"Yeah, princess. A safeword." A second later, he'd pulled her arms over her head and secured her wrists to the top bar of the recliner.

Max watched the little submissive's eyes widen as she tugged ineffectually on her wrists. After a second, she asked in adorable outrage, "What kind of people have Velcro straps attached to their lounge chairs?"

"Doms, baby. Doms." He was enjoying how the arms-overhead position put her beautiful breasts on display. Smiling, he palmed both. How did her breasts manage to be so firm and so soft at the same time? He tugged at one nipple and watched it bunch into a tighter, smaller circle until the peak jutted out.

"Beautiful Zuri." He leaned forward and took her mouth, hard and thorough. As he deepened the kiss, he felt her stiffen again. He sat back and studied her. Her shoulders and arm muscles weren't tight. She wasn't pulling at the restraints. It wasn't the bondage making her fretful. "Talk to me, baby."

"I—" Her gaze was averted. Hmm. Her nipples were still erect, her color slightly deeper, darker. She was aroused. He wasn't scaring her, and the bondage definitely turned her on.

Wait. She *was* turned on—and by Max, after having been with Alastair last week. An intellectual discussion about ménage and threesomes was all very good, but possibly having another man's hands on her might be getting too real. Only one way to find out. "Are you bothered at getting this excited with me after having been with Alastair?"

She bit her lip—that gorgeous puffy lip—and nodded.

"Do you feel disloyal? Or maybe like a...slut?"

Another nod. Her velvety brown eyes showed her worry.

Damned if he didn't like her all the more for her conscience. His wife had taught him beauty truly *was* only skin-deep. Pretty was nice; character was what a real relationship was built upon. "I do understand, darlin'. Let me put it like this: If you had children, would you pick one to love and ignore the rest?"

Shocked, she shook her head. "Of course not."

"So you can love more than one person at a time?"

She got where he was going and gave him a disgruntled look. "Yes."

"Guess what, princess? You can get excited by more than one, too." He leaned in for a hard, close-mouthed kiss. "Alastair and I learned to share before we learned to walk, so we don't get jealous of each other. That said, if we're together and you chase after another guy, I'd get a tad peeved."

Her beautifully arched brows drew together. "You two don't get jealous of each other?"

"Nope." He stroked her cheek, pleased when she didn't pull away. "If things get unbalanced, then the unhappy party pipes up." As kids, there had been some noteworthy battles until they'd learned to talk to each other. "It helps that we're both into being "fair."

"Oh." She let out a little sigh. "This did feel like I was betraying him. You're sure he's comfortable with me being here with you?"

"Baby, why do you think he went up to bed early—and took Hunter with him?"

The way her eyes rounded was too cute.

He bent down and closed his lips around one velvety nipple. Her gasp was even cuter. He worked her, fondling, pressing, and squeezing her breasts, licking and sucking her nipples, until he could hear her arms straining at the Velcro straps. Perfect.

Oh, heavens. Her breasts felt as if they'd grown too swollen for her skin, and her nipples were so tight they ached.

Max rested his palms over her breasts and studied her for a long moment before smiling. "What's your safeword, baby?"

Safeword. Safeword. Right. "Red. Sir. It's red." Why was he asking...?

"Good." He reached under her dress and stripped her boy briefs down and off. "By the way, Zuri. The next time you wear underpants in our house, either Alastair or I will cut them off."

"What?"

Not answering, he gripped her left leg and lifted it over the lounge chair's armrest, letting her lower leg dangle outside. A Velcro band went around her ankle, the strap only tight enough to ensure her leg would remain over the armrest. With ruthless hands, he did the same on her right leg.

"Max!" She yanked at the wrist restraints, then the ankle ones.

"It's a pretty sturdy lounge. I don't think you can bust it that way." His grin flashed and disappeared as he trailed a finger from her breast, slowly down her stomach, then along the top of the fabric bunched at her waist.

Her muscles quivered under his touch.

"Let's see what you have under here now." He tucked the skirt of her dress up and out of his way, then simply studied her for a long minute.

A long, tantalizing minute.

He brushed his knuckles over her mound, and his lips curved up. "I remember this plump little pussy. So fucking smooth."

"Uuuh." The entire world heated until each breath of the humid night air felt thick and heavy in her throat.

Unhurriedly, he traced his fingers around her entrance and spread the wetness around her clit. Just...playing. "I like you wide open like this," he said. "It's like getting an after-dinner treat."

She tried to glare, but what he was doing with his fingers was...was...

He slid one finger inside, and she heard herself gasp at the electrifying pleasure.

"Fucking nice." His rumbling voice was easy. "Bear down, princess."

She tightened her muscles around him.

"Perfect. Keep your cunt like that...or everything stops."

What did he mean?

A second later, he slid down to kneel at the end of the lounge chair. He was so tall that when he bent forward, he could kiss the crease between her pussy and her leg. His warm lips teased over the sensitive skin, and she shivered.

"You know, I forgot to shave before company came." He deliberately rubbed his scratchy jaw on her inner thigh in an erotically rough caress that somehow woke her skin from her toes to her pussy.

Slowly, he pressed a finger inside her again and glanced at her in silent command.

She tightened her muscles around him.

"That-a-girl." His finger was still inside her as he tongued a circle around her clit.

"Oh, God," she breathed.

He chuckled and lifted his head. "Never heard you swear before, princess."

"Not polite," she gasped.

But when he circled his finger around her entrance and back inside with a head spinning thrust, she didn't know if she was swearing or not. Or maybe it was a prayer.

Lips curved, he lowered his head and licked her clit, teasing the top and sides with sizzling flicks. As he closed his lips around her and sucked, her senses reeled with stunned pleasure.

Heat gathered, seeping like hot lava into her core. Oh, *oh*, she was going to come. Her thighs trembled with the hunger. She opened her eyes, seeing the moonglow all around, feeling only the wet tongue tracing exquisite circles down there and the slow penetrating in-and-out.

He stopped.

Her voice came out a hoarse whisper. "Noooo."

"Tighten up, darlin'." Inside her, his finger moved in a blatantly carnal reminder of his order.

She clamped her muscles down, feeling the heavy surge of need move through her.

"Good girl." He nuzzled her stomach. "This is what I expect from you when I'm inside you. Right now is practice." His look of darkly erotic promise made her tighten involuntarily around him again.

He laughed and closed his mouth around her clit. The drawing sensation as he sucked whipped through her system. His finger—two fingers—thrust in and out in a heady rhythm, swiftly driving her right up.

Everything inside her clenched around his thrusting fingers as the pressure inside her increased. Sweat broke out over her body. When his tongue danced over her clit, her hips tried to rise to his mouth.

He set his free hand on her mound to flatten her down. Using those fingers, he pulled her labia open, exposing the exquisitely sensitive nub completely.

Arms over her head, legs spread...pussy held open. The sense of helplessness and vulnerability shuddered through her and rocked her to the core.

His tongue tapped right on top of her clit repeatedly, and the nub swelled further, becoming impossibly sensitive.

Her breathing slowed from panting to not breathing as muscle by muscle grew tense.

Flick, flick flick. Each touch careened straight to her center. *Flick, flick flick.*

The orgasm grew inside her, unbearably heavy, just waiting, like the fateful pause between the lightning strike and the crash of thunder.

Flick, flick—

Her release exploded, rolling through her in wave after wave of excruciating pleasure. His hand on her pelvis held her down. His fingers inside her felt huge as her sheath battered at them, the contractions going on and on until even the world seemed to shake.

With a last lick of his tongue, he lifted his head and withdrew his fingers, sending another wave of sensation crashing through her. Despite the roaring in her head, his "*mmmm*" of enjoyment was clear.

She heard a zipper. A crinkling sound.

"The restraints." She pulled at them, trying to move. "Please."

"You are where I want you, baby. And nice and open and wet." His palm pressed on her exposed pussy, firm and almost hot, putting pressure on the sensitive nub.

Another slow contraction rolled through her, making her shudder.

He moved, and the lounge chair creaked as his knees came down between her legs. Palming her breast with one hand, he leaned forward, bracing himself with an arm beside her shoulder. His firm lips touched hers. His tongue teased and demanded. His weight pressed her down.

As the lounge chair seemed to sink, the heady sea of arousal was pulling her under.

"Zuri, look at me."

She opened her eyes. He'd removed his shirt. Moonlight gleamed on the rippling muscles of his shoulders and arms in a superb play of light and shadow. His chest hair made a dark inverted triangle over his solidly muscled pectorals. "You're so beautiful," she murmured.

"Thank you." As she sank again, he chuckled. "No, baby. Eyes on mine, and keep them there."

Even as she looked into his eyes, she felt the head of his cock at her entrance. He was...big. Really, really thick. Too thick.

Max saw her eyes widen then tighten from discomfort, and he paused for her to adjust. Although his dick wasn't much above average in length, the girth could be a problem for some. He'd learned to go damned slow with new lovers. "Easy, baby. I'm in no hurry."

He smiled into her eyes and added a Dom's warning. "But you're going to take all of me."

The surrender in her trusting eyes pulled at his heart.

After a second, he pressed in again, and she stretched around him. She was damned tight, squeezing his shaft like a cranked-down vise. As he eased farther in, he monitored her face and eyes for when he needed to stop.

Pause. Press. Pause.

She was panting, and her eyes were slightly wild when he was finally seated to the hilt, as intimate as a man could get with a woman.

Possessing her—and being possessed, in turn. God had a hell of a sense of balance.

With one hand, he reached up and yanked the Velcro free from her wrists. "You can touch, Zuri."

With a small sound of satisfaction, she put her hands on his shoulders.

He smiled down at her, taking in the gentle angle of her cheek, the soft curve of her chin. All female. "Comfortable now?"

She nodded.

"Good. Then I'm going to take you hard."

A spark lit in her eyes, and damned if she didn't smile and wrap her arms around his neck. Could she get any better? She enjoyed bondage, being dominated...and liked her sex a bit on the rough side.

His cock hardened even more, and he withdrew and slid into her heat more firmly. Testing.

Her low moan of pleasure was enough to speed him up. Damn, she felt good. Her breasts were soft and full against his chest. Her forehead was against his neck as she turned her head to bite over his collarbone.

Fuck yes. He released his iron grip on his control and hammered into her.

Her fingers gripped his hair, trying to pull him closer. Despite the ankle restraints, her hips tried to rise to his.

The heat in his lower half grew, the pressure increasing even as he felt her core tighten around him.

Her brows drew together with her concentration...as she did what he'd asked of her. *"Tighten up, darlin'."*

She wanted to please him.

Nothing was sweeter to a Dom. With each thrust, he twisted his hips to slide his pelvis over her clit as he buried himself deep. She felt slick and silky and fucking amazing. He thrust faster. Harder. Pressure grew, a hot, heavy weight at the base of his spine.

Her panting breaths were hot on his neck; her fingernails dug into his shoulders. And then she gave a high cry, her neck arched, and he felt the rhythmic clenching of her cunt in another release.

Good girl. And he let himself go. Fiery pleasure blazed inside his balls and seared outward through his cock in mind-bending jerks as her spasming cunt did its best to squeeze him dry.

When he released her legs, staying deep inside her for a few extra minutes, she buried her face against his shoulder. Was he supposed to have heard the tiny whispered *thank you*?

Sometime later, when he figured his legs might bear weight again, he finished removing her dress, scooped her up, and carried her through the house to his room. To his bed.

With a sigh of pleasure, he pulled her into his arms, her back against his chest, her arse against his groin. Half-asleep already, she laid her head on his upper arm and cuddled his hand between her breasts like a teddy bear.

He'd thought she was hardhearted.

He needed glasses.

CHAPTER FIFTEEN

In the morning, after a quick shower, Uzuri walked into the kitchen. The early morning sun gleamed into the airy Tuscan style kitchen with dark brown quartz countertops, golden brown maple and glass-front cabinets, and a pale travertine tile backsplash.

Hunter was sprawled beside the square center island. The men were side-by-side at the stove. Alastair looked scrumptious in khaki shorts, a white polo shirt, and boat shoes.

Max was equally delectable in his own rugged way. He hadn't bothered to shave and his jaw showed a dark beard shadow. His collar-length, brown hair was still wet from a shower. His black shirt showed a zombie facing a sword-fighter and captioned: FENCING – A POST-APOCALYPTIC SURVIVAL SKILL.

She so totally had to learn how to use a sword, well, once she got good at the hand-to-hand stuff. Who knew when the zombies might invade the US?

Smiling, Uzuri breathed in the aroma of frying bacon. Why did everything that was unhealthy have to smell so good? Then again, she'd had enough aerobic exercise last night to justify eating an entire package.

Wasn't it odd to feel a lack of sleep—and like she was glowing? Unfortunately, she might also be walking bow-legged. The man had far too much stamina.

He'd roused her at some ungodly dawn hour, saying he was going jogging, and she needed to give him a send-off in case he got hit by a car. Seriously, what kind of line was that?

She'd tried to roll over and go back to sleep.

The devil Dom had cheated. The merciless bastard had pinned her on her back and held a vibrator to her clit. When she was moaning and almost coming, he'd rolled her over and taken her from behind. And set the vibrator back on her clit. The combination was...deadly.

She felt her cheeks flush, remembering her wailing orgasm. Even though Max's bedroom was downstairs and his cousin's upstairs, she'd probably woken Alastair up.

At least Max had let her go back to sleep and hadn't insisted that she join him and Hunter in their run. *Gag.*

"Looks like our little sleeping beauty is up." Max's gaze ran over her, making her aware that her makeup wasn't on, her feet were bare, and her hair pulled back with no styling at all. He smiled. "I like the casual look, princess."

When Alastair didn't speak, a trickle of unease ran through her. Max had said they liked sharing, but what if he were wrong? What if Alastair was upset? She'd never have made love with Max if it would hurt Alastair.

Alastair's gaze swept over her, and her nerves jangled. Then he gifted her with his heartwarming smile.

Oh, thank heavens, he wasn't angry.

Stepping away from the stove, he silently held out a hand.

When she reached him, he pulled her against him for a languorous kiss, wet and hot. By the time he finished, she knew he wasn't upset in the least. He lifted his head. "You look as if you and Max had a good time last night. I'm pleased."

She frowned. "He said you deliberately went to bed, leaving us down here together."

The flash of his white grin said it all. He *had*.

He ran a finger around her obviously swollen lips. "Since you look quite well-satisfied, you should thank me rather than yell at me."

As if she'd ever yell.

Max leaned against the counter, arms crossed over his chest. "I agree. Tell Alastair, 'Thank you, Sir, for sharing me with your cousin.'"

But... That felt so wrong.

When Alastair was amused, his eyes turned more green than brown. Lighter. They were very green now. "Are you going to be disobedient, little miss?"

"I-I..."

"Hope so." Max grinned. "I'll put you on your back there." He nodded at the table in the breakfast nook. "I'll hold your legs up in the air with your feet over your head—to make sure the doc has a good field of fire. While he paddles your ass, I'll play with your clit."

At the wave of heat that roared through her, her knees actually wobbled.

"Sit down before you fall, Uzuri." Laughing, Alastair guided her to sit at the table.

Before she got into something she wasn't sure she was ready for, she rushed out, "Thank you, Alastair. Sir. Thank you for sharing me with your cousin."

"Very nice, love."

As Max carried a stack of pancakes into the nook, he told Alastair, "Pity. I was hoping she'd stay silent."

"There will be another time." Alastair's eyes were still on her and held enough heat to set the ocean on fire.

As she arranged the dishes on the table, the two Doms

brought out scrambled eggs and bacon, a pitcher of orange juice, and a pot of coffee. An antique teapot already sat on the table.

Max took the chair to her right.

Following the food, Hunter disappeared under the table. Before she'd taken even a bite, his paw came to rest on her bare foot as if to remind her she had bacon...and a forlorn puppy was wasting away to fur and bones because of her neglect.

After putting butter and syrup on the table, Alastair sat to her left. "What do you two have planned for today?"

"I'm helping Andrea's family with some last minute stuff for the reception." Uzuri couldn't explain further since she'd been sworn to silence.

Max glanced at the kitchen clock. "This afternoon, I'm picking up some relatives of Cullen's from the airport. Apparently, they decided at the last minute to attend the wedding. Then I'll spend some time at the gun range."

The thought of why Max needed to be a good shot sent concern shivering through Uzuri. Appetite gone, she stared at him. "This isn't a good time to be a cop. People hate you."

"Some do, some don't." Max's sharp blue eyes softened. "It's a simple fact: Our country has a shitload of racial problems." He took her hand.

"Quite so." Alastair sighed. "All humans are hard-wired to belong to a tribe of some kind. Perhaps someday our tribe will be all of Earth rather than a country, race, or religion."

Yes. That would be a goal to strive for. Every day. Her fingers curled around Max's. "Still. Your job is dangerous."

"Darlin'." He moved his shoulders. "I'm a detective, not out on patrol."

Alastair pointed to Max's plate, filled with bacon. "He's in more danger from what he eats than from someone shooting at him. There's also—"

Max snorted. "Thanks, Doc. That'll do."

"—the stress," Alastair continued as if he hadn't been interrupted. "He needs to learn to lighten up."

"I see." Uzuri nodded at Alastair who, in her opinion, had just given her a physician's prescription. Kind of. She knew all sorts of ways to get a Dom to lighten up.

Smiling, she glanced at Max before studying Alastair. Doctors were under stress, too, weren't they? She'd seen that already. All right then. As she nibbled on a piece of bacon, a paw tapped the top of her foot. At the reminder, she broke off a piece to hold under the table.

Max gave her a stern look. "We have rules about feeding him, baby. Don't get yourself in trouble."

"I would never dream of getting into trouble." She blinked innocent eyes at the big, bad Dom as, under the cover of the table, Hunter gently took the bacon from her fingers.

Alastair took a sip of coffee. "Uzuri, I didn't get a chance to catch up with how you're doing these days. What is happening with the people at Brendall's?"

That wasn't such a pleasant thought. "Fine in the marketing and buying departments. In the actual store, it's not going as well. The sales associates who were Carole's friends have been spreading nasty rumors about why she was fired. And me. It might all blow over. If it doesn't, then..."

"Then you'll handle it," Max stated firmly.

"Yes, you will." Alastair's gaze held only confidence—wonderful, ego-raising confidence.

She pulled in a breath. "Yes. I will."

Uzuri had left—after helping with clean up—and Alastair poured another cup of tea and climbed the tower stairs to the third floor. He stepped through the sliding glass doors onto the rooftop terrace and took a deep breath. Florida in the fall had the finest weather in the world. The brisk morning air held a briny tang. Down near the Bayshore walk, seagulls were calling to the tourists and joggers.

Settled on one of the four terrace couches, Max had his bare feet up on the low center table with the dog stretched out beneath his legs. "Hey, cuz. Time to talk about Zuri?"

Max knew him well. In turn, Alastair knew his cousin well. Today, Max was relaxed in a way Alastair hadn't seen since his cousin had joined the Marines. More than physical satiety, Max radiated a soul-deep contentment. Uzuri was good for him.

Being with her was...life affirming.

And more. He'd never met anyone who called to him so deeply. Although she was quiet, she gave all of herself with no holding back. Generously. Sweetly. And held within that quiet personality was a wellspring of humor that bubbled to the surface in adorable ways. She had a mesmerizing mixture of traits—all of which appealed to him.

Whether logical or not, his emotions were already engaged. "Yes. I want more."

Max snorted. "Here I thought I was the impulsive one."

"Actually, no," Alastair said judiciously. "You're the paranoid one."

His cousin barked a laugh. "True. But hell, I can't stay paranoid about her. There's no meanness in that little subbie. Now that we've learned what she was concealing, she doesn't have any hidden corners. What you see is what you get. I like that."

"And?"

"Fuck, I feel the same way. She fits with us in a way no one ever has. I'm in."

"We could continue as we are," Alastair said in an effort to present all sides of the argument. "Dating, having her over."

"Nah. With our work schedules, we'd see her only a couple of times a month."

Alastair winced. Uzuri worked long hours, often leaving the

city for trade shows. Max's schedule was erratic at best, depending on homicides. With rotating on-call times, Alastair's was probably the worst. "You have a point."

"I've been thinking..." Max reached down to tug at Hunter's ears. "Even though Anne says Zuri's stalker is in Cincinnati, I'd say Uzuri half expects him to show up here. She'd sleep better in our house."

Lifting his cup to his lips, Alastair paused. He had noticed her quiet nervousness, how her tension never seemed to disappear. He'd attributed it to her fear of him. Of men. On the other hand...she'd been far more relaxed here than at her duplex. "I wonder how much of her troubles have been because she rarely feels completely safe."

Max's determined gaze met his. "We can fix that."

"We can." The need to do so was as strong as anything he'd ever felt.

"So...let's talk her into moving in with us." Max grinned. "Sunday would be perfect."

Andrea and Cullen's wedding was Sunday. Women and weddings.

Alastair chuckled. "That is almost Machiavellian."

CHAPTER SIXTEEN

On Sunday, Uzuri paid off the taxi driver and hurried up the sidewalk toward the Catholic Church. Entering, she paused to dip her fingers in the font and crossed herself before walking across the vestibule. Enjoying how the tall arched stained glass windows glowed in the late afternoon sun, she took a slow breath. Older cathedrals had their own fragrance—candles and incense and flowers and perhaps even the perfume of generations of prayers.

As she crossed the room, Holt spotted her and walked over, bending down to kiss her cheek. "You're late, sweetie."

This wasn't the time to explain. "You know, you look great." All of the Shadowlands Masters who weren't groomsmen were ushering and doing anything else needed—and they'd dressed for the duty. She certainly wasn't going to complain. "You should wear a tux more often."

His "I don't think so," was accompanied by a no-way-in-hell expression. "But you look fantastic."

"Thank you." With a pleased smile, she smoothed her tea-length, sleeveless pale blue dress. A lacy shrug covered her bare arms and cleavage-displaying scoop neck so she could wear it in church. With a resigned sigh, she'd passed over her fuck-me stilettoes for more modestly heeled blue and beige sandals. She did look good—and her dress was perfect for the reception to come.

"C'mon, let's get you seated before it's too late." Holt tucked her hand in his elbow and escorted her down the aisle.

An amazing number of people were in the nave. Despite the immense size of the church, Andrea and Cullen's families and friends had managed to fill the place.

To her surprise, Holt walked right to the second row on the bride's side before motioning her in. "Andrea reserved these two rows for you guys."

The pew was filled with all Uzuri's friends, and she felt the sting of tears with the quiet cheering at her appearance.

After a second, she realized the second and third rows were mostly Shadowlands people. The bridesmaids, Jessica, Kari, Beth, and Sally weren't there, of course, as they were up dressing the bride along with a wealth of Andrea's relatives.

Andrea had a huge Hispanic family; Cullen a huge Chicago-Irish one. After much discussion of how to choose between brothers, cousins, and best friends, the two had selected their bridesmaids and groomsmen from the Shadowlands members who had helped bring them together. Or, as Cullen said with his booming laugh, had helped bring them *back* together again.

Smiling, Uzuri gave a general wave to everyone. Gabi and Kim, Linda, Rainie, Dara, Austin, Maxie, Cat. Andrea's buddy, Antonio, was sitting with his boyfriend. Mistress Anne was with Ben. Olivia had brought her newest interest. So many people.

As Holt headed back down the aisle, Kim took Uzuri's hand and pulled her in. "Where have you been? We've all been calling you."

"I'm sorry about not answering the messages. There was a... problem." Uzuri sat, belatedly realizing her tone had come out too unhappy.

"What do you mean a problem?" Kim grabbed her shoulders. "What happened? Are you all right?"

On Kim's other side, Gabi and Linda leaned forward with worried frowns.

"It's not that—" Uzuri broke off when Kim gave her an impatient shake. *Okay, right.* She was learning to share. *Right.* "Somebody threw a rock through my front window. It shattered glass all over the place, and I had to call the rental management company. They found a handyman to board the window up until the glass company can replace it tomorrow."

"Oh my God. You can't stay there," Kim interrupted. "You should come home with—"

"Tonight you're with us," Gabi interrupted. "Marcus and I have a spare bedro—"

"You come home with me tonight," Linda interrupted Gabi. "You'll let Sam and me take care of you."

For the second time in five minutes, Uzuri felt tears fill her eyes. "Thank you." She squeezed Kim's hand and smiled at the other two. "I'm sure it's merely stupid teenagers. But—thank you."

To her relief, the priest entered, and Uzuri let herself fall into the comfort of the familiar ceremony.

Kim never let go of her hand.

By the time Cullen and his groomsmen appeared, Uzuri was relaxed and enjoying herself. And didn't Cullen look fine, just fine. Not nervous at all. Completely happy. However... Uzuri's eyes narrowed. At the front stood Masters Dan, Nolan, and Raoul. Three, not four groomsmen?

The priest smiled benevolently at everyone and spoke into the mic. "The bride requests that everyone remain seated."

Uzuri's gaze turned toward the ancient woman who sat in the mother-of-the-bride's spot. Andrea's beloved *abuelita*. Although the "little grandmother" had a will of iron, standing and walking hurt her aged joints.

Andrea had told the priest that tradition could be tossed out the window if it made her grandmother hurt. And everyone would stay seated so her grandmother could see.

Cullen had said once that his woman was beautiful, but it was Andrea's loving heart that had truly captured him.

The music changed to Pachelbel's "Canon in D", and people craned their necks to see the procession.

In a teal bridesmaid's dress, Jessica walked up the aisle. She was so beautiful with her blonde hair in curls that bounced slightly. Then Kari. The schoolteacher was walking carefully as if counting each step. Beth was next and the dress was almost the same shade as her eyes. She didn't like being the center of attention, but she'd do anything for Andrea. Finally, Sally appeared, and her smile was so wide it was contagious. By the time she reached the front, everyone in the church was smiling.

Uzuri was grinning too. Trust Sally to brighten up even a traditional church wedding.

Holding her bouquet of gold and ivory roses, Andrea appeared at the back of the church behind the flower girl. Her strapless A-line, wedding gown showed off her beautiful shoulders, and the champagne-ivory color was perfect with her golden-brown skin. Crystal beading on the floor-length gown added sparkle.

Perfect.

Then Uzuri frowned. The bride should be glowing. Instead, she looked...sad.

Andrea's heart ached as she watched her tiny cousin start her walk toward the front of the church. So cute. Missy was dutifully scattering flower petals every which way—and occasionally throwing them over her head and giggling.

My turn. Andrea pulled in a breath, willing herself to take the first step.

The church was filled with her family and friends. Her aunt and *abuelita* and so many relatives were crowded into the front pew. Her friends in the second and third row were beaming at her.

And there was her beloved *Señor* waiting for her at the front. She'd never known her heart could hold so much love—and feel so hollow.

Even knowing the reason she hurt didn't help. Not now.

Why aren't you here, Papa? He'd been a mess, and yet he'd loved her and she'd loved him and now...she missed him. Wasn't that completely stupid? She had an entire church filled with her friends and family. How could she be so silly to want someone who'd died years ago?

Why did the aisle to her *Señor* have to look so long and lonely?

Firm hands closed over her shoulders and turned her, and she looked up into silver-gray eyes.

"Master Z?" Wasn't the best man supposed to be standing next to Cullen?

He smiled down at her. "Come, little one. I don't think your Master is willing to wait much longer before he claims you." He tucked her hand into his elbow.

"You're...you're going to give me away?" She hadn't wanted anyone to do that, had she?

He bent and said very softly, "A submissive may think she knows what she wants. It's a Master's job to see she gets what she needs. It is my great honor to step in now since your father cannot be here.

Oh. Oh, she hadn't realized how much she'd wanted *all* of the tradition. Her eyes filled, her throat closed, and all she could do was nod.

"Good girl." He kissed her cheek, turned, and nodded. The resplendent chords of "The Prince of Denmark's March" filled the church.

She hadn't ordered that, either.

It was like the fairytale dream of her childhood. She could hear the music and the murmurs around her.

"She's beautiful."

"Lovely."

Her gown swished as she walked.

Without Master Z's guiding hand, she might have walked into a pew...because suddenly, the tears were gone and all she could see was Cullen's face. So strong. So filled with love. Her gaze never left his as she simply floated down the aisle.

How funny that she'd worried all through the practice that she'd trip. Master Z would never let her trip.

And as she continued on life's journey, now she'd have her Cullen beside her. Hand in hand. They'd walk the path together and help each other over the hard parts. She'd scold him in Spanish. He'd laugh his big laugh that made the entire world brighter.

They'd grow old...together.

When Master Z gave her hand to *Señor*, Andrea was so filled with happiness that she wrapped her arms around Cullen and hugged him with all her might.

The priest stammered to a halt.

Never at a loss, Cullen gathered her in even closer, kissed her long and hard, and then his booming laugh filled the church.

Dios, how she loved him.

Uzuri let out a happy sigh. When she'd called Master Z, she hadn't been sure he understood about Andrea. He had.

Andrea had beamed as she walked down the aisle on his arm.

And she'd positively glowed as she caught Cullen up in a happy hug.

An unexpected, long-lost hope struck Uzuri deep inside. Someday, maybe, perhaps, *she'd* be the one walking down the aisle. Since Jarvis, she'd put those ideas far, far away, but now...maybe she'd find someone who would look at her like Cullen was looking at Andrea. Would laugh and hug her as if he'd never seen anyone so breathtaking in his whole life.

I want that.

Of course, she'd have Andrea's dilemma if she ever did get married. Uzuri had no mother. No father to walk her down the aisle. Not any close relatives. She was alone in the world. An ache set up residence in her chest.

She watched Master Z take his place beside Cullen. After shaking his head at his teary-eyed Jessica in the line of brides-maids, he glanced at the audience...and spotted Uzuri. He nodded as if to say she was a good girl.

Then his eyes narrowed. A second later, he shook his head reprovingly, and his faint smile said for her not to be a foolish submissive.

He would be there for her, too.

The tightness in Uzuri's ribcage loosened. She wasn't alone, was she? How odd that she could have that feeling while surrounded by her friends. Her besties—and any Shadowlands Masters—would step in to help her, if she could only bring herself to ask.

From farther down the pew, Rainie leaned forward and met her eyes before motioning, "*I heart you*," followed by a thumbs-up. She'd figured out who'd told Master Z about Andrea.

With a happy smile, Uzuri sat back and simply enjoyed the rest of the lovely wedding ceremony, marking the highlights to remember and sigh over later.

Like the way Andrea gazed into Cullen's eyes as they said their vows. Her softly accented voice was clear and strong and completely sure. Just the way it should be.

After they exchanged rings, Cullen stopped the normal proceedings to announce, "During Z and Jessica's wedding, he gifted her with something that symbolized their journey together. I liked the idea."

Smiling down at his bride, he cupped her cheek in his hand while tangling his fingers in her darkly golden hair. "When I first saw you, I thought you seemed like an Amazon, and in the time we've been together, my opinion hasn't changed. You've overcome every trial life has set before you and only become stronger. You truly are a Wonder Woman. I know you forget that sometimes, and I want you to realize you don't have to face your battles alone. Ever." His lips quirked. "If I tried to get you to wear a superhero breast plate and cute little skirt to work, you'd probably deck me, so I abandoned that idea."

When Andrea sputtered, laughter rippled through the church.

"I settled for this in hopes it would remind you every day of your courage and your strength—and that you have a mate to fight beside you."

Nolan leaned forward and handed over something.

Cullen held up a gold filigreed cuff-bracelet glittering with diamonds, then fastened it around Andrea's wrist.

"Wow," Kim murmured.

"It's beautiful." Uzuri gave another happy sigh. A bracelet that wide would overwhelm her small wrists, but the size was perfect for Andrea, and the gold was lovely against her golden-bronze skin. Even better, the cuff was a classic that Andrea could wear with anything, from jeans to formalwear. Like fairy dust, it would add sparkling beauty to her day.

Cullen lifted Andrea's chin and stared into her eyes, his other hand circling the cuff. His low voice reached the first few rows. "You. Are. *Mine*."

She melted against him.

Uzuri smiled. Only Master Cullen would give a wedding present like this—after all, Wonder Woman's cuffs *were* named the "Bracelets of Submission."

A sniffle came from beside Uzuri. Kim had her hand on her day collar, her fingers fondling the small heart-shaped padlock. She was looking down and blinking hard.

In the row of groomsmen, Raoul was watching her, his dark, dark eyes soft.

Standing with the bridesmaids, Jessica was running one finger over her own necklace and smiling at her husband and Master.

His gaze on her, Master Z's expression was filled with love.

Uzuri looked down and bit her lip. She had never wanted

anything called a "slave" collar. All the same, she did envy Andrea the cuff that both concealed and displayed her submission and her Dom's love for her.

Would she ever find someone like that?

When the wedding ceremony came to an end, Uzuri waited for her pew's turn to file out and felt reality setting in. After watching all her friends and their Doms, she was feeling awfully single. Maybe she'd only stay a short time at the reception.

She'd hoped to hear from Alastair or Max last night, but neither had called. And she was being silly to think they might, since she knew full well they'd been incredibly busy with both work and the wedding stuff. And they knew they'd see her today.

Yet...they'd had sex with her, and it was the way of the world that scoring often wiped out a man's interest. If the Dragos were...were distantly polite to her at the reception, she wasn't sure she could take it. Not today.

Kim nudged her. "Time to go, girlfriend."

"Right." Uzuri rose—and was startled when a man gripped her arm and guided her out of the way of the others filing out of the row. She looked up.

Alastair's concerned hazel eyes met hers. "Where have you been, pet? We were looking for you." With her chin in his palm, he frowned and kissed her damp cheek. "You've been crying."

"Well, yes." A breath brought her his seductively masculine scent, and quivers started up in her low belly.

"Women and weddings." The exasperated rough voice was Max who was ushering the other side of the aisle. "Hang onto her, cuz. If she disappears, I'll have to beat on her."

Alastair snorted. "We will all watch in awe." As Kim started down the aisle, he snagged her arm with his free hand, still gripping Uzuri, as well. "Stay here, please, Kim. Since Raoul has to be present for the formal wedding pictures, he asked us to escort you to the reception."

"Oh. Okay."

Once the rest of the row had left, Alastair seated Uzuri and Kim. "After we usher out the rest of the guests, we'll drive you both to the reception."

Uzuri shook her head. "I can take a—"

"*Both* of you." Alastair's gaze was that of a Dom. One who somehow knew she was considering a retreat.

"But..." The strength to argue with him wasn't there.

Kim took her hand. "I'm glad we're going together." She leaned forward and whispered, "But don't tell Raoul I was crying, okay?"

And, just like that, Uzuri's mood changed.

She put her hand over her mouth to keep from giggling. "Too late. He was watching everything you did."

As the limousine headed to the hotel for the reception, Andrea smiled at her *Señor*. Her husband. *Mi esposo*. His black tuxedo fit perfectly over his broad shoulders. His usually tousled brown hair was neatly trimmed. Yet, nothing could make his powerful frame and hard-hewn face look civilized. And she wouldn't have it any other way.

She still couldn't believe they were married. Oh, it was nice to be alone with him for this little space of time. "I wish we could simply run off now."

He chuckled, pulling her closer. "Aye, love. It'll be hard to sit down at a fancy formal reception and pretend any interest in food when all I want to do is get you naked."

Heat shimmied over her skin. How did he do that? They'd been living together for months now, having sex...often...and he could still drop the ground out from under her with a look. A statement.

Tenderness filled his green eyes. "Thank you, little sub."

She frowned. "For what?"

"For trusting me. For loving me. For marrying me."

"I trust you, *mi Señor*, and I love you so very much," she whispered and smiled at him. "We're going to have a good marriage."

"Be nice if we could start it right now." He leaned down and kissed her with such devastating skill that all she could think about was the night to come.

Eventually, she realized the limousine had halted, and the driver was getting out. *Dios.* Andrea straightened her hair, laughed, and wiped a smear of her lip-gloss from Cullen's chin.

The chauffeur opened the door and offered his hand.

Gathering her gown, Andrea stepped out—and stared. "Where are we?"

This wasn't the stuffy hotel where the reception dinner was to be held. After a second of shock, she recognized the location.

She turned to Cullen who'd stepped beside her. "This is *mi abuelita's* street."

It was almost unrecognizable. Decorated sawhorses and barriers closed the street to traffic. At the far end were chairs and teal linen-covered round tables. The near end boasted a massive speaker system. Teal and gold streamers and balloons festooned houses, streetlights, and trees. Pagodas and booths dotted front lawns.

Andrea's aunt and *abuelita* stood with Cullen's father and stepmother at the entrance, all beaming.

Andrea gestured helplessly. "This is not..."

"It is different, no?" Aunt Rosa smiled. "We saw you getting unhappier as the size of the wedding grew. As things became more formal." She exchanged glances with Andrea's grandmother. "We didn't care about the...how you call it...venue, just that all the people who love you could be part of your happiness."

"*Mija*," her grandmother said. "We didn't realize we'd made you sad until your *amigas* visited us."

Andrea stared. "My bridesmaids came here?"

"No." Her *abuelita* looked embarrassed. "I think I had already told them no too many times. Your other friends visited me."

Her aunt got teary-eyed. "You have many good friends. I love that." She counted off her fingers. "It was Kim and Gabi and Uzuri and Rainie. And Linda who is a mother herself who said a girl should have the wedding *she* wants, not what her family wants."

Cullen's father took up the story. "Rosa called, and we discussed alternatives. Cullen, when you and Andrea got engaged, you'd both said you'd prefer a street party to some fancy affair. We decided to give you one."

"A street party?" To keep from screaming aloud, Andrea put her hands over her mouth. People in the street saw the limousine and were turning—and they were all relatives and friends. Cheering began at one end and went in a wave down the entire street.

Aunt Rosa patted Cullen's arm. "Dancing is at this end. The DJ was delighted to set up here rather than the hotel. There is a buffet and drinks at the far end—no fancy sit-down meal. Your best man—is his name really Zee?—and the groomsmen have the program and will round you up whenever you have to do something, like cutting the cake."

Cullen's dad snorted. "Your groomsman named Dan said he'd arrest anyone going over two minutes for the toasts, and I noticed he has a stopwatch and a weapon."

Cullen was beginning to grin.

"Thank you." Andrea had shrunk from the thought of a formal dinner and having to be oh-so-polite. Now, her dread was wiped away like grit and mildew, making way for the sparkling joy filling her. "Oh, *thank* you."

Past the barriers decorated in her wedding colors of gold, teal, and champagne waited the Shadowkittens.

As the music changed to Bruno Mars' "Just the Way You Are," Master Cullen escorted Andrea out onto the "dance floor."

With a bounce of pleasure, Uzuri sat up higher to watch.

Beside her at the round table, Alastair held her hand. On her left, Max had his arm across the back of her chair. She was sitting between some seriously fine man candy.

Intimidatingly confident, Alastair wore his black tuxedo as casually as if he were in jeans. It set off his long, lean body. His short sculpted beard outlined his squared-off chin and strong jawline.

In contrast to his cousin, Max wore his tux like a uniform—and his military bearing made her stomach all quivery. The excellent tailoring showed off his rock-hard body, flat stomach, and shoulders that seemed to go on forever. His swept-back, rich brown hair had been trimmed and now curled right at the collar.

Mustn't play with his hair, she told herself firmly, or, being Max, he'd play with hers.

Across the table, Rainie held hands with Jake, and Sally was between her two husbands. Everyone turned to watch the bride and groom's dance.

After a minute, Rainie grinned. "Cullen's singing the words to her."

"He doesn't have a shy bone in his body, does he?" Uzuri exchanged smiles with the other women. In everything he did and said, Master Cullen showed how much Andrea meant to him.

When Uzuri's lips started to quiver, she turned her gaze away to safer targets. Considering that every table was filled, she had plenty of people to watch. Who knew that a wedding reception could be so much fun? When Uzuri and the others had talked with Andrea's grandmother about how upset Andrea was, well, she hadn't expected the family to go *crazy*.

And at the last minute, no less. She'd been appalled. Nevertheless, everyone—including the entire neighborhood—had pitched in to make the new venue both fun and beautiful.

The sun was setting, bathing the newlyweds in a soft golden glow. Andrea's cousins were turning the strings of tiny gold and teal bulbs. Wrapped around each lamp pole, tree, and booth, the lights turned the street into a fairyland.

"The kittens did well." Alastair squeezed her hand.

On her other side, Max was running his finger over her bare arm, sending tingles across her skin. "You did. I don't think either the bride or groom has stopped smiling."

"That's all we wanted." Uzuri watched the couple dancing. When she'd helped Andrea shop for her wedding dress, she'd advised her to get one with a detachable skirt. Although she'd been thinking of dancing in a hotel, it was even better here. The floor-length underskirt was gone, leaving an angled lacy hem that was knee-length in front, ankle-length in back. Perfect for partying in the street.

Across the table, Jake leaned forward. "Hey, Dragos. Did Uzuri mention that someone threw a rock through her front window?"

Rainie sent Uzuri a guilty look.

"*What?*" Max's growl made the hair stand up on Uzuri's arms. He turned and pinned her in place with simply the power of his gaze.

Alastair's hand tightened on hers to the point of pain. "Have we missed discussing your apparent inability to communicate?" His resonant voice held an edge of steel that sent quivers through her stomach.

She tried to smile. "Dudes, this is a wedding. Not the place to talk about...ugly stuff."

With fine timing, the song finished, and Cullen kissed his bride to rousing cheers that, thankfully, drowned out Max's response.

Another song started. Uzuri knew Andrea had told the DJ to skip the customary Father-Daughter dance. "This should be Cullen's dance with his stepmom." A few months past, Cullen's father had married an old family friend. Cullen had mentioned

MISCHIEF AND THE MASTERS

she was a sweetie and that his father was happier than he'd been in a long time.

"Actually, Cullen will have to wait his turn." Alastair rose. His gaze was disquieting. "Stay here, pet. We have '*stuff*' to discuss."

Max stood and set a hand on her shoulder. "You be good. If we have to search for you, you won't enjoy the consequences."

Her mouth dropped open. A threat? Alastair was ordering her and Max was threatening her as if they were her Doms or something. "You...you can't say that to me."

"Baby." Max gave her a firm, close-mouthed kiss before whispering, "I just did."

Following Alastair, he prowled toward the bandstand, so big and threatening that people stepped out of his path instinctively.

Uzuri leaned back in her chair. Her heart was racing as if she'd been the one dancing. Well, honestly. Alastair and Max weren't her Doms. Not truly. Sure, she'd been to bed with them, but a smidgeon of sex didn't put them in charge of her. Did it?

She tried to muster up annoyance...and couldn't. Because the sensation of being cared for and growled at and ordered around was amazing. Wonderful. She realized she was staring after them. *Close your mouth, fool.*

Across the table, Sally and Rainie were having a giggle-fest at her expense. The two looked up in surprise as their Doms rose.

In fact, all the Shadowlands Masters were moving toward the dance floor. Meantime, Master Z was escorting Andrea out to the center of the dance area. The music changed to...

Uzuri frowned. Wasn't that the music from some Disney movie? "Is that from *Sleeping Beauty*?"

"That's it. It's Tchaikovsky's "Sleeping Beauty Waltz". Disney used it." Rainie grinned. "Might have figured Master Z wouldn't dance to country-western."

As Master Z and Andrea waltzed to the lushly romantic music, sighs came from every table. Andrea was smiling—and crying—and then Master Z twirled her out and into Master Dan's arms.

Master Dan turned with her, not missing a step, and said something that made her laugh as they danced. Halfway around the floor, he spun her out...and there was Master Nolan.

Uzuri's mouth rounded.

Smoothly, wonderfully, each Master took his turn with the submissive who had once been a Shadowlands trainee. Raoul, then Sam. Vance, Galen, Jake, Holt, Alastair, Saxon, and Max.

Rainie's gaze met Uzuri's. Growing up without fathers, they'd had to endure the Father-Daughter dances at school.

But their friend had gotten to be a princess for a night with a dance she'd never forget.

When the music ended, Cullen guided his stepmama out to the dance area—pausing to kiss his bride on the way.

Max was escorting Andrea toward the table, but they stopped to talk with Madeline Grayson. Uzuri watched, admiring how the woman's charcoal gray dress matched her eyes, and how her dark purple and blue scarf enhanced her coloring. Mrs. Grayson was always elegantly attired and always perfectly composed.

Master Z was a lot like his mama, wasn't he?

A pang of loss ran through Uzuri. Did a girl ever get over missing her mother? Her sociable mama would have loved how Andrea's wedding turned out. She'd have been proud of Uzuri for making it happen.

Miss you, Mama.

With a sigh, she let her gaze drift. So many people. Shadowlands members were everywhere, along with a ton of firefighters from where Cullen—and Holt—worked. Andrea owned a cleaning business, and her crews and clients had come. From Chicago, Cullen's hefty, blond and redheaded relatives were scoping out Andrea's Hispanic cousins. There would be some interesting pair-offs this evening.

Unlike some fancy wedding receptions, the guests here ranged in age from newborns to seniors. In the gathering twilight, three preschoolers were playing tag, weaving in and out of the people dancing. As one laughingly irate mama shooed them off, Uzuri's gaze snagged on a huge...hulking...figure on the other side of the street. Standing perfectly still. The lights from a booth gleamed off his shaved, dark scalp.

His head was turned toward her—and she could almost feel his gaze.

A chill ran up her spine, and she half rose from her chair.

"Uzuri, did you want something to drink?" Rainie asked.

"What?" Startled, Uzuri glanced at her friend, then jerked her attention back to the man.

He had disappeared.

Slowly, she sat back down, trying not to shiver. She was being silly. Paranoid. Jarvis was in Cincinnati. Even if not, he couldn't have gotten into the party. There were people checking invitations at the entrance to the blocked-off street. Not that that would stop a determined person.

And someone had thrown a rock through her window. The apprehension deep in her center didn't dissipate as she shook her head at Rainie. "No drink, but thank you."

"Hey, you guys." Accompanied by Max, Andrea approached and gave Uzuri, then Sally and Rainie hard hugs before dropping into a chair in typical Andrea-fashion. She pulled in a long breath and swiped a finger beneath her eyes. "*Dios*, I'm so glad you gave me my wedding present early, Zuri, or I'd have black streaks all down my face. Am I still presentable?"

As Max took his seat again, Uzuri tipped her friend's face up for a quick scrutiny. The waterproof makeup she'd given Andrea had held up to the task. No smears. "You look beautiful. Perfect."

"The 'new bride' glow doesn't hurt either." Rainie poured a glass of sweet iced tea and handed it over.

"I think part of that glow is from the heat." Andrea drank half of the tea in one breath. "Next time I get married, I'm choosing Alaska."

Approaching with Holt, Cullen heard and set his hand on her shoulder. "There will be no next time, love. I have you ringed and cuffed. You're mine."

Andrea rubbed her cheek against the back of his hand. "*Sí, Señor.*"

As the music changed to "Hotel Nacional", the dance area filled with the younger crowd. Holt pulled out an empty chair and sat down across from Uzuri. "Great job with the decorations, sweetie. It all looks great."

Andrea heard him. "This was your work, Zuri?"

Uzuri waved a hand. "Your family did all the hard work. I only helped with the planning."

"I might have known. You're the only one I know who could manage to make a street party look classy and fun, as well." Andrea tilted her head up and grinned at her husband. "Want to make the rounds and say hi to anyone we missed?"

"Aye." After helping her stand, Cullen gave a disparaging glance at the pitcher on the table. "I suppose that's tea?"

"Yes, *mi amor*." She patted his hand. "I'm sorry."

Approaching, Alastair overheard. "We stocked Guinness in the drinks booth for you."

Cullen's face lit. He patted Uzuri's shoulder. "Keep this Dom, pet. He's a good one." After a glance at Max, he amended, "Actually, love, you should keep them both."

Before she could respond, Cullen ushered his bride in a direct line toward the well-marked drinks booth.

With his low rumbling laugh, Alastair settled down beside Uzuri and appropriated her hand as casually as if...well, as if he had a right. "Speaking of keeping," he said, "Max and I have spoken about your broken window as well as your goals."

She stiffened. Talking about her duplex was one thing. Goals, however, were private, not something to discuss at a party.

"We decided you should stay with us for two or three weeks. Your window will be repaired. And we can help you with those goals."

"Whaaaat?" Some weather phenomenon had sucked all the air right out of Tampa. Struggling for her next breath, she stared at Alastair's darkly elegant face. "I can't do that."

Yet, a tiny whisper inside urged her to say yes. She'd never felt as safe as when she was with them. Well...safe in one respect.

"Sure, you can," Max said. "You've already stayed with us once." His arm was across the back of her chair again, and his powerful hand curved over her shoulder.

"That was because I was hurt. There's no reason now." Her heart was speeding as if she'd run from one end of Brendall's to the other. They wanted her?

Oh, she longed to say yes, she really did.

"You need to learn to ask for help," Max pointed out. "We can work on that."

"But—"

"You need to move past being afraid of men," Alastair added. "Living with two Doms would help."

Doms. That made it clear what kind of a stay it would be, didn't it? Did they feel taking her in was their duty?

She didn't want to be a duty.

Because...she could so easily fall for them. After a second, she had her voice under control. Her heart—perhaps not. "I don't think those are good enough reasons."

As smoothly as any British lord, Alastair kissed the back of her hand, and his resonant voice shivered across her skin. "Allow me to offer an additional reason. We *want* you to stay with us."

The action and the statement left her speechless. *Oh, Blessed Mother.* They wanted her.

Alastair waited, calm and patient.

And Max? His silence was as loud as a shout.

She turned to look at him.

His compelling gaze was an incandescent blue like the hottest center of a flame. "Say yes."

"Let me toss this in." Holt was watching with amusement. "My landlord is remodeling the apartment entry, and the construction noise keeps me awake. I could use a place to stay."

Uzuri frowned. "You want to move in with Max and Alastair?"

"No, sweetie. I don't swing that way." Holt grinned. "But, if *you* move in with them, I can stay in your duplex. I'll even clean up the broken glass for you."

"Oh."

Max turned her face toward him and repeated, "Say yes." In his carved face, only his eyes showed his desire.

She looked at Alastair and saw the same demand. They wanted her.

But two to three weeks? This wouldn't be the same as last time. She'd had sex with them. They'd want to continue.

Excitement and anxiety shivered up her spine, because she wanted to continue, too. She wanted to make love—have sex—with them. To wake up held in strong arms. To sleep knowing she was perfectly safe. To hear the low grumbling sound of a man's voice in the morning.

Could her life get any more confusing? She'd never felt this way about anyone—and now she was sliding right into...caring... for two men. Two Doms.

No. No, this was insane. She couldn't do this.

As the music changed to a romantic slow tune, the dance floor cleared and then several couples walked out. Cullen's grandparents. Gerald and Martha from the Shadowlands. Two men who were both gray-haired. A few more. All of them were seniors. "What's going on?"

Alastair stroked a finger down her cheek. "This dance is for those who've been together longer than forty years."

"Wow. They managed to stay together through...everything." What would it be like to walk beside someone for—for longer than she'd been alive? To outlast all the obstacles—the newlywed battles and mix-ups, the boredom and temptation and stresses in the middle, and somehow reach the final stretch looking... content. Still in love.

Max kissed her cheek and whispered. "Yes, they'd stayed together, but Zuri, they're also the ones who were brave enough to take the first step. Say yes, darlin'."

As in the dojo, he was challenging her to find her courage. There was no answer but one.

She pulled in a breath and looked at him and then Alastair. "Yes."

CHAPTER SEVENTEEN

O n Monday evening after work, Alastair carried Uzuri's suitcase up the stairs, feeling immense satisfaction at having the little submissive here in their home. Although she'd spent last night after the reception, this was better. Now she'd stay for weeks.

If not longer...

When she headed for the small guest room, he shook his head. "We prepared a different room for you."

"But why?"

Without answering, he led her down the hall to one of the house's three giant suites and stepped to one side.

Holding her market-sized basket containing sewing materials, paints, and some unclothed dolls, she walked in, and her mouth dropped open. "Seriously? I get to stay in here?"

"Yes, pet." He and Max had worked their arses off Saturday and most of Sunday to clean and prepare the empty suite for her. It still held the light scent of paint.

Pleased with her delight, Alastair looked around. As in the other master bedrooms, the bed was an extra-long, king-size—

large enough for all of them. The white iron canopy bed had delicate scrollwork on the head and footboards and filmy gauze draperies.

It also had ample anchor points in case they wanted to play.

Having seen her duplex bedroom, he and Max had used her color scheme of whites, creams, and blues. Pale blue floral drapes coordinated with the upholstered blue chairs and cream-colored sofa. A blue Oriental rug softened the dark hardwood floor. It was obviously not a room for a man—although Max had insisted the furniture be both comfortable and sturdy. *"After all, we'll be in that room. Hopefully often."*

His cousin was a smart man.

As Uzuri wandered through the room, Alastair waited patiently. Max had left the orientation to him, pointing out Alastair would be less blunt. Indeed, any discussion about sex would require tact, considering their subbie's shyness.

She returned from her survey to stand in front of him. "This is a beautiful room. Thank you."

"You are quite welcome. Now, I want to speak with you." Taking her around the waist, he sat down in a curvy wingback chair and tugged her onto his lap.

It was bloody wonderful when she snuggled into him. "Okay, I'm ready."

"Being with two Doms is new to you and might feel awkward at first. What we want you to remember is that there is no 'one true way'. If something doesn't work, we need you to tell us. Honestly."

Speaking up would be difficult for her. She was too polite, too submissive. They'd have to watch her carefully and prompt her.

Her brow was furrowed, but she nodded.

He continued. "For sleeping arrangements, Max and I hope that you'll alternate nights with us. Occasionally there might be a time when someone wants to be alone—this includes you, too, pet. In which case, the person simply says so."

"I can sleep alone if I want to?" Her voice was almost a whisper.

"You can. But if you prefer to sleep alone often, that indicates something is wrong—and we'll expect to discuss it." He tipped her head up. "Goals or no goals, we wouldn't have asked you to move in if we didn't want to be with you, Uzuri."

She seemed to be scarcely breathing. "Really?"

Ah, she could steal a Dom's heart. "Really." He nuzzled her ear and felt her shiver.

She leaned into him, her hand sliding up his nape into his short hair.

"Often, we'll want to be with you at the same time."

She tensed. "I haven't done that before."

Her records at the Shadowlands hadn't shown any threesomes. Considering her limited sexual experience, he wasn't surprised. "We'll go slow, sweetheart."

Gently, he kissed her, trying to reassure her through touch. Considering her heartbreaking courage, he understood why Z had let her into the Shadowlands. Why the Master had wanted to watch over her as she moved past her trauma.

Now Alastair and Max would take up that charge.

"Let's move on to the awkward subjects. Have you been with anyone besides me and Max since the quarterly blood test was done at the Shadowlands?"

She shook her head.

"Excellent. We haven't, either. Actually, neither Max nor I have had a woman without using protection in years. Since we're all clean and you're living here, would you be comfortable going without protection? Are you on the pill?"

"I'm on the pill." She hesitated. "I've never... Um, yes?"

Her willingness to try things despite her uncertainty was charming. "In that case, we'll consider ourselves fluid bonded. Polyfidelitous, actually."

"Meaning no messing around with anyone but you or Max?"

"Exactly. And the same applies to us."

"Sure." She actually looked pleased, and wasn't that lovely?

"Good." He rose and set her on her feet. "Go ahead and unpack. Then put on workout clothing—preferably nothing loose —and come downstairs. You know where our weight room is?"

"Yes, but...workout clothing?" She stared at him with an almost horrified expression.

"Yes." Alastair gave her a smile and walked out, closing the door behind him.

He stood outside the door until he heard her suitcase being opened. Good. She was moving forward, and he'd managed to put her off-balance without frightening her. Excellent beginning.

At least she'd packed "workout" clothing, although she'd had in mind a nice walk along the nearby Bayshore Boulevard, not a home gym. Wearing geometrically patterned Spandex capris and a black sports bra under a bright fuchsia racer tank top, Uzuri stepped inside the Dragos' weight room. She looked around, wondering if the huge, high-ceilinged space had been a ballroom in the original house.

The hardwood floor was sealed and polished to a high gleam. Across from the door, the creamy white wall displayed swords of all kinds, from thin and pointy to a massive one that looked like something carried in *Braveheart*. The right end of the room had mirrors on the walls and dark blue mats on the floor. She guessed it was the karate space.

Max spotted her and walked over. His hair was carelessly yanked back into a stubby tail with a black elastic band. His black tank top was damp with sweat and clung to his wide, muscular chest. His biceps and pectorals were so pumped up that the skin was taut, and veins stood out on his thickly muscled forearms. Black shorts showed off heavily muscled legs.

Her mouth went dry. No man should be allowed to be so sexy. There should be a law.

He held his hand out. "Zuri. Let me give you the two cent tour."

She gave him her hand, feeling the careful strength as he closed his fingers around hers.

He pointed toward the mat and mirror area. "Over there is where we'll work on your self-defense skills. It's also where Alastair and I fence when we're in the mood."

The quiver that ran through her had nothing to do with fear. Imagine the most masculine guys she'd ever seen fighting each other. With swords.

"I'd like to see that." Forget calling the mat and mirror area the karate space—it'd be the erogenous zone.

"Be a good girl, and we'll give you fencing lessons, too."

"Thanks, but I'd rather watch."

On the other side of the room were racks of dumbbells and iron plates. In a white tank top and track pants, Alastair straddled a bench at a cable machine that looked as if it belonged to some medieval torturer.

She didn't want to get anywhere near that device. "I, uh, take it that I'll be working out?"

"Oh, baby, you have no idea." Laughing, Max took her lips in a long slow kiss. He was hot from exercising, and his lips tasted of salt.

"Before that happens"—Max tossed a mat on the floor and pointed to it—"I need to see what kind of shape you're in. Do as many sit-ups as you can within a minute."

Sit-ups? Was he a crazy-pants? She stared at him. "I don't think so. I'll just walk on a treadmill." With a good audiobook, she could do that for hours.

She looked around. No treadmill.

A clank drew her attention back to the cable machine where Alastair was pulling down on a bar to lift a huge stack of weights.

The steely muscles in his back rippled and bunched in a way that kept her mesmerized.

Her fingers curled with the need to touch.

After easing the bar into place, Alastair turned. "Sweetheart, learning to fight isn't helpful if you lack muscle to put behind the punch. Or if you get winded within a few feet."

"Exactly." Max nodded. "Forget the treadmill. You'll jog with me and Hunter."

Jogging? He really was certifiable. "Are you off your meds?"

Oh, rude.

Before she could apologize, Max grinned. "Not all three miles...at first. I'll let you start slow."

"I thought you said you weren't a sadist."

"No more than any other drill sergeant." He pointed to the mat. "Sit."

As she sat on the mat, he added, "I'll make you up a workout schedule. We expect you to put in the gym time, even if no one is here to watch you. Bear in mind, if you slack off, Alastair will spank your little round ass. And then fuck you."

Mouth open, she glanced at Alastair.

The slow smile he gave her sent tremors through her center.

"And me?" Max nailed her with his sharp blue eyes. "I'll have you doing push-ups and squats until your muscles give out...and when you're lying there unable to move, I'll fuck you."

"But"—her entire core was going into a meltdown—"but I'll be all sweaty then."

"Oh, yeah." The heat in his eyes actually increased. "I'll get to peel all those tight clothes right off of you—at least enough to get access to what I want."

Alastair chuckled. "You keep talking, and she won't get the kind of workout we want her to have."

"I hate it when you're right." Max glanced at the clock on the wall. "Sit-ups, Zuri. Start...now."

After fifteen, her abdominal muscles were burning in a nasty way.

When Alastair walked to a cupboard in the corner and opened the door, she tipped her head to see.

Wow, the shelves held BDSM toys. "You keep that stuff in your workout room?"

"Keep going," Max growled. "And yes. This is a fun room to play in."

BDSM in a weight room? Well, it sure had enough benches.

Twenty sit-ups. Twenty-one. She got halfway up through the next, got stuck, and then flopped back ungracefully.

"Not bad, but not good," Max said. "We'll plan on you adding another ten to that before two weeks."

Uh-uh. Not going to happen.

Hearing a *snick*, she looked over her shoulder.

Alastair had put a padlock on one of the two toy bags on the top shelf. He smiled at her, padlocked the other bag, and added the key to his key ring. "We heard you have a problem with staying out of toy bags."

She was so going to get in there. "A vile and foul rumor."

Max snorted. "There are a lot of rumors about you and your girl gang, darlin'. We saw what you did to Holt."

A giggle escaped her. Holt's expression when he'd left the locker room had been awesome. *Total score.*

"We're not your Catholic schoolgirls, princess." Max's baritone lowered to an ominous growl. "Don't get yourself in more trouble than you can handle. Stay out of our toy bags. Seriously."

A frisson of fear ran through her...and disappeared. He and Alastair were good Doms. She might get in trouble, but they'd never truly hurt her. She knew that. And the knowledge was simply amazing. And freeing.

She rounded her eyes. "I would never do anything bad."

Behind her, she heard a huff of a laugh from Alastair.

She couldn't wait to mess with them.

However, when Max frowned at her, she had second thoughts. What if he punished her with sit-ups?

CHAPTER EIGHTEEN

That Friday after work, Uzuri had lined up her male dolls on the TV room's coffee table. A long-time buyer for her customized dolls wanted a Khal Drogo from *Game of Thrones*.

Wouldn't that be fun? Uzuri grinned. She picked up an African-American Ken doll and studied it. Not the right coloring for Khal. Actually, this one looked more like Alastair. The doll even had light-colored brown eyes. She could add some green. Its hair needed to be shorter, too.

Chortling, she got out her paints and tools.

Doll time was thinking time, and a good time to go over the past five days. Talk about a roller coaster.

Every day, she was a businesswoman—creative, assertive, and professional.

Every night, she was a submissive. Talk about a role reversal. And yet, in the presence of either Max or Alastair, she slid right into surrendering.

Actually, the mere thought of them—she set her hand over her stomach—made her insides feel all quivery.

But, as they'd pointed out, she was…mostly…a sexual submissive, not a slave or servant. Although the guys had added her to

243

the cooking rotation, they hired a weekly housekeeping service to clean, do laundry, and stock the refrigerator. Spoiled Doms. Then again, they did both work long, hard hours.

Unfortunately, they also believed in exercise. Omigod, they had her sweating like a pig.

She frowned. Did pigs sweat? Was she maligning little porcines?

Anyway, she'd never exercised like this in her life. She'd gone jogging twice with Max and Hunter. Kind of jogging. Okay, mostly walked.

On alternate evenings, she joined Alastair to swim laps in the pool. That was more fun—although the sadist wouldn't let her stop until her muscles were so exhausted she was in danger of drowning.

She didn't even want to think about how they made her work in the weight room. Scowling, she held out her arm, trying to see if she had achieved a visible biceps.

No.

But...aside from the Dragos' unfortunate affinity for exercise, she'd had a wonderful time.

Most evenings, they'd all gather in the TV room to watch television or read. She never sat alone though. Alastair insisted snuggling with them would help her conquer her fears—but Max had laughingly said, *"Actually, we only want to cop a feel."*

They were so fun. Max and Alastair would bicker about what shows to view, since Max was a sports junkie and Alastair liked documentaries. After a couple of days, she'd jumped into the battles, and they'd had to give her equal viewing time. They sure hadn't liked watching *Fashion Police*, but *Scandal* was a different story.

Watching all that sexing on the TV had led to very interesting activity afterward. They said they'd watch *Scandal* with her anytime she wanted.

The Doms kept surprising her with their kindnesses. One

night, when she'd come home complaining that her new shoes hurt her feet, Alastair had given her a foot rub...and after she was a happy, limp heap on the couch, he'd worked his way up her body. She gave a little sigh. That Dom had magical hands, no matter where he put them on her body.

Coming into the TV room, Max had only laughed and closed the door behind him as he left. She shook her head in amazement. The Dragos really weren't jealous of each other.

Finishing the Alastair doll, she picked up a different Ken doll. More heavily muscled. Blue eyes. Yes, this would do.

The Dragos weren't all about sex all the time, which was also nice.

One night, when Alastair was called to the hospital, she and Max had played a strange board game called *Pandemic* about combatting viruses like the plague and Ebola. Omigod, talk about insane. Before they'd found the cure to one disease, all of Asia had been wiped out.

She'd felt so guilty—and Max had laughed his ass off at her.

Yes, they were amazing.

Each night, one of them would join her in her bed.

As she worked on the Alastair doll's sculpted beard, she smiled. In bed, perhaps the only thing they had in common was how generous they were. She always got off at least once—if not more times. Just thinking of their skills sent a little wave of heat through her.

Max loved using toys—and he was a blatantly bossy Dominant.

Alastair was a more subtle Dom, but she was never confused about who was in charge. *Whew.* He liked to drive her right to the edge—of pain, of orgasms—and it was scary how well he could read her.

Most of the time, they treated her like a roommate. Then, without warning, they'd slide into Dom mode. Like when they'd watched the movie, *Set It Off,* which had a sexy scene with oil and massage. The way Blair had dragged the chain down Jada's back... She'd gotten all hot simply watching.

"You look a bit warm, darlin'." Oh, Max had picked up on her arousal immediately. *"I think she has a chain fetish,"* Alastair had said. *"We'll have to remember that."*

She'd found their conversation more than a little scary.

On the coffee table had been the long strand of pearls she'd worn as a chunky bracelet to work. Without even talking about it, they'd lain her on the coffee table and played with her. And the pearls. Teasing her breasts, her pussy. Around her neck. And she'd come. And come. And come. Alastair had smiled at her afterward. *"Since you can't stand up, you might as well be on your knees."* He'd ordered her to give Max a blowjob—then to do him.

Even now, she got all excited thinking about it. The Dragos— her Dragon Doms—were simply too sexy to be real.

At the sound of the front door and two sets of footsteps, she looked up, her heart starting to dance.

Then, she realized what she was working on and froze. *Oh, no.* She grabbed the basket to hide the dolls. Too late.

"Uzuri, would you—" Alastair spotted the doll she'd made up to look like him.

The beard was perfect. Hair nearly so. Eyes the exact shade. The doll had on a white lab coat, and she'd even used a fabric printed with tiny kittens to give the pediatrician a kid-pleasing tie.

Alastair busted out laughing.

"What's up?" Max appeared in the doorway and saw his doll look-alike. Brown hair swept back, not quite touching its shoulders. A dark shadow of beard stubble along its jaw. Intense blue eyes. Jeans and a T-shirt with a pistol holstered at its waist...and a pair of tiny handcuffs dangling from its back pocket.

Max didn't laugh. Didn't smile. Didn't even enter the room.

Uzuri frowned. In fact, he hadn't even said hi. This wasn't like him at all. When he turned to leave, she called, "Max, are you all right?"

"Fine. Bad day." Expression closed-off, he headed toward the tower room stairs.

Uzuri turned to Alastair. "Is he mad?"

"No, love." Alastair shook his head. "He gets like this at times. He has a difficult job."

She couldn't even imagine the horrible things a homicide detective must see. Dead bodies, day after day. When Sally had tried law enforcement, it'd only taken a couple of brutal murders and she'd switched careers. Max was dealing with horrors day after day.

Would he feel better by suppertime?

Oh, no. This was *her* day to prepare supper. She should have started already. Since the Doms were scheduled for the Shadowlands tomorrow, everyone would be home tonight.

She jumped up. "I need to get supper started." She'd picked up the fixings for Mama's favorite gumbo, but that would take too long. Okay, then, a jambalaya would only take an hour or so.

"Don't worry, sweetheart," Alastair said. "We don't have a set time to eat."

Maybe not, but Max was already upset. Only...he didn't look like he'd have an appetite.

Abandoning her kitchen prep, she poured a shot of Casa Dragones. The hike up the stairs to the third floor made her puff...although less than before. Maybe jogging and swimming were paying off.

She stepped out onto the rooftop terrace.

Max was sitting on one of the dark red couches, his gaze focused on the darkening waters of Hillsborough Bay and Davis Island's skyline. Although he was always aware of his surroundings—and she'd made noise coming up the stairs—he didn't acknowledge her presence at all.

She walked closer. "Supper will be ready in an hour."

He nodded.

She set his tequila on the coffee table, hesitated, and then sat beside him. "I'm sorry you had a bad day."

He eyed her and looked back out to the water.

Okay, that didn't work. Maybe she should smack him on top of his head. That's what her mama had done when Uzuri was being a butthead.

Hitting a Dom—especially one like Max—would be a bad idea.

Maybe he was dim-witted today and didn't understand she was there to help. "I listen well, you know."

"Nothing to talk about." After a frown, he picked up the drink and took a sip with a grudging, "Thanks."

She steeled up her nerve. He wouldn't hurt her for being pushy. Jarvis would have; Max wouldn't. "You said that sharing with friends helps put things into perspective. Talk to me. Let me help."

His voice came out in a rasp. "Listen, princess. I don't want your help; I want to be left alone. Go play with your dolls."

She couldn't suppress a flinch, although he hadn't made a motion toward her. He hadn't hurt her—so why did she feel like crying? She rose. "I'm sorry I bothered you, Sir."

When she reached the doorway, Alastair was there. Watching. His expression darkened. "He didn't strike you. Max wouldn't—"

"No, he wouldn't hit me." She glanced back at the still figure on the couch. *That might have hurt less.*

The dismay in Alastair's eyes made her realize she'd spoken aloud. "I'm sorry. I didn't mean that."

"Yes, you did." He held his hand out. "Uzuri, let's—"

She stepped around him and ran down the stairs, hoping he didn't follow. Hoping he wouldn't say anything to Max. It would be awful if she caused trouble between the cousins.

She couldn't do anything right, could she?

Moreover, since it was her night to cook, she couldn't even

leave and go hide somewhere. Part of her wanted to let Max starve, but...that wouldn't be right. He hadn't been horrible; he'd simply pushed her away. She'd done the same to them before, and they hadn't gotten all...all butt-hurt.

Get over it.

At the foot of the stairs, Hunter was waiting. *He* loved her. Down on one knee, she put her arms around him and pressed her face against his furry neck.

Max felt the cushions compress and sighed inside. Persistent, wasn't she? Undoubtedly, if he ignored her long enough, she'd go away.

She *needed* to leave him alone. Everything inside him felt raw, cut open, like flayed meat. What he'd seen, what that family had endured, shouldn't—

"Max."

Not Uzuri, but Alastair. With a sigh, Max turned.

In white shirt and tan pants, Alastair hadn't changed yet. A Transformers tie hung loosely around his neck.

"Problem?" Max asked, hoping against hope not. He was in no good place to help. "Need me for something?"

Alastair gave him a level look. "I need you to stop burying your problems and let others help. Specifically me...and the woman we share."

"No." Max shook his head as nausea swept through him. "This was gruesome. I can't—"

"You can't continue to bury your emotions. Either you'll break or turn to harmful methods of coping." Alastair half-smiled. "We're alike, you know. Sharing pain isn't what we do."

"Exactly."

"Yet, when Uzuri managed to coax me into talking about a child who'd died"—a flash of pain crossed his face—"it helped. More than I'd realized it would."

"You don't know the shit I deal with, cuz. Neither of you can handle—"

Alastair's bitter laugh cut him off. "I spent years repairing the damage to bodies from IEDs, shellings, and machine guns." Alastair met his gaze. "And my patients were usually women and children."

Fuck. "Sorry. I was out of line."

Alastair never held grudges. He nodded, and then his gaze hardened. "I believe Uzuri would prefer the ugly *"shit"* to you shoving her away. She didn't mean for me to hear, but she said getting hit might be easier."

Hearing that was a goddamned gut punch. "Hell. I didn't... I was trying to fucking *protect* her."

"I do know that, but she doesn't. Or if she does, she sees that you don't believe her to be strong enough to pull her own weight, let alone help someone else."

"She's..." Max stopped before saying she wasn't strong enough, because it wasn't true. She'd survived a hell of a lot, and rather than holing up in Cincinnati in fear, she'd packed, moved, and started a new life. She had a satisfying career, good friends—and was working to overcome the last few problems. She sure as hell wasn't weak. "She's probably braver than I am."

Max tossed back the tequila she'd brought, squeezed Alastair's shoulder in thanks, and headed down to try to make amends.

She wasn't in her bedroom.

She wasn't in the TV room. He paused there and frowned, then realized why the room looked different. She must have found the storage room upstairs. The dark red and white Turkish pillows that he'd bought at the military mall in Baghdad were piled on the leather couch. Looked...homey. Nice.

She wasn't in the living room.

Finally, he found her. In the kitchen, she stood by the stove, stirring something that smelled damned good.

He sat at the island, and as she determinedly ignored him, his mood lightened moment by moment. Fuck, she was cute when she was pissed-off.

Her lips were pressed together, gaze anywhere but on him. She'd obviously been home a while since she was in classy shorts and a sleeveless blouse that was somewhere between pink and purple. Weird color, but it made her brown skin glow.

Hunter walked over to rest his head on Max's thigh.

Silently, Max stroked the dog and tugged on his flopped over ears. "Uzuri."

She stiffened. After a long moment, she looked at him.

"I'm sorry." He searched for words to explain why he'd been rude

"Think nothing of it." She turned away from him to add the cooked chicken, rice, and tomatoes to the vegetables in a heavy pot. After covering the pot, she reduced the heat to a simmer.

He checked her cooking preparations. His mother had taught him that heavy conversations shouldn't be conducted when the cook was busy. But she had nothing out, and the pot was on simmer. Good enough.

He rose and walked across the kitchen. "Zuri." Gripping her shoulders gently, he turned her around and backed her against a counter. "Let me finish groveling, please."

"No need."

"Darlin', there's every need. I was rude when you were only trying to help. That's not acceptable." He put his forehead against hers. "You know, every day, I deal with assholes, people shooting at me"—he felt her stiffen, but soldiered on—"my boss yelling at me. I don't get upset often, but when I do..."

As she finally met his gaze, he knew he'd gotten through.

"What happened today, Max?" she asked gently.

He swallowed. Even knowing he'd volunteered to share, it fucking wasn't easy. "I'm a homicide detective. Death is never pretty, baby, but some...some are..." There were no words. *Find the words.* "A teenager decided his friends were laughing at him, and he found his daddy's AR-15. Why a civilian needs to own an assault rifle, I have no fucking clue. The kid went after his buddies and hosed them down." God, it had been ugly.

Uzuri's hand curled around his.

Max continued. "Trouble is, unless a bullet hits something, it goes a long ways. Lotta bullets. He got other people on the street.

"A young woman who was pregnant." She'd been even younger than Zuri, dammit.

"The owner of the craft store." He'd recently retired and bought the place. His elderly wife said that all his life he'd dreamed of sharing his joy in crafts.

"A taxi driver." A younger man with three children who was working long hours so he could buy a house. The American dream. Shot to hell and gone.

Max's voice came out husky. "One weapon and so fucking many people shattered and dead."

"Oh, no. N-no." With a choked-off sob, Uzuri pressed against him, head on his chest, arms tight around his waist. Her tears were wetting his shirt. "How can you s-stand it?"

With her tears, her acknowledgment of the same horror he'd felt, and her distress—for him—his edgy, off-balance feeling started to ease. The world wobbled and tilted back level again.

And damn, after he'd snapped at her like an asshole, she was hugging him and trying to make him feel better. Of the two of them, he was probably the weaker one.

He sighed. "I've never been good about talking about shit— feels like I'm bringing all that violence home. Like I'm not protecting you."

She made a tiny, snorting sound. "You brought your mood home. What's the difference? I'd prefer to know why you're upset." She squeezed him harder. "I can take it, Max. And I'd rather you get things off your chest. So...you can stew for a bit, but then you share."

Bossy, wasn't she? "I'll try to do better."

Her head came up in surprise. "You will?"

"Yeah." He kissed her soft lips. "I'm sorry I made you feel bad, baby."

She hugged him hard, and the corners of her mouth tilted up. "Don't worry. I'll make you pay for it."

"Sure you will." Softhearted subbie.

A couple of hours later, after a long, hot shower, a fantastic spicy meal, and a long walk with Hunter, Max felt almost back to normal. Although he still felt guilty about being rude to their little submissive. He should be horsewhipped.

As he walked out onto the patio with Hunter, he saw Alastair doing laps in the pool. For some strange reason, the doc preferred evening swimming to sunrise jogging.

As usual, Hunter started to run in circles around the pool. *Water tag with the human, oh joy!* Max figured about thirty seconds before the dog jumped in to play.

Alastair saw Hunter, then Max, and halted. He smiled. "You look better."

"Yeah. So, do you or Zuri have plans to watch anything on television tonight?"

"I don't, and Uzuri went out with her girls," Alastair said. "The room is all yours."

"Great." Leaving Hunter outside to annoy his cousin, Max swung by the kitchen for a beer. In the TV room, he dropped onto the couch, and hell, he was already missing Zuri's company.

She was...warm. Thoughtful. Adorably funny. Observant. Quietly confident. Seemed as if many women—including his ex— were like the gusty breezes before a storm, noisy, veering directions, knocking shit around.

Zuri was more like the soft wind off the Gulf on a sunny day.

Unless she had some tequila in her. Max grinned. Nothing like a quirky streak to keep life interesting.

But she wasn't here tonight. Time for sports.

Leaning forward, he reached for the remote, but it wasn't on the coffee table. Or the side table. He rose and checked the floor, then under the couch cushions.

On one of the recliners, maybe? The right recliner was empty. The left one...

He stared. One of Zuri's dolls—a male one—was seated on the chair. Brown hair, blue eyes, square chin, muscular. It wore jeans with a torn right knee and a black T-shirt with the sleeves ripped off. Max glanced down at his own clothes—jeans with a torn knee, black T-shirt with the sleeves ripped off.

Well, damn. He grinned. She was damned talented—that was far too close a resemblance for comfort.

Good thing the plastic bastards weren't anatomically correct.

After a second, he noticed his miniature replica had a rolled-up paper in its hand.

All right, I'll bite. He tugged the paper loose and unrolled it. *"Stressed is desserts spelled backward."* What the fuck did that mean?

Remote missing. Little subbie missing. Suspicion began to raise its ugly head. He glanced at the doll and could have sworn it smirked at him.

Max growled. *Okay, subbie, the lack of a remote is definitely stressing me out.* Then again, the note said *desserts*. Like something sweet? That had potential.

In the kitchen, he checked the refrigerator. Nothing interesting there, although he damned well planned to hijack the jambalaya leftovers before bed.

Cupboards? *Bingo.* The third one had an Alastair replica sitting on a covered cake pan. *Cake?*

He pushed Alastair off the goodies—"Sorry, cuz"—picked up the pan, and opened the lid.

Carrot cake with thick cream cheese frosting.

Oh, yeah. One bite and he had no stress molecules left in his body. Damn but the princess could cook.

After his first—and second—helping was gone, he licked the frosting off his fingers and studied the doll. Beard. Stethoscope. Lab coat. "Cute tie, cuz. Now, why don't you tell me where she hid my remote?"

Yep, there was another rolled up paper. *"The earth has music for those who listen."* –William Shakespeare

Right. There was a little subbie who needed her ass paddled. Yet his annoyance was sadly missing. Frosting—the fastest tranquilizer in the world.

He frowned at the note again. He *could* watch the television without a remote. Nah, they'd kick him out of the League of Manly Men.

"The earth has music for those who listen." The "earth" wouldn't be inside the house. Outside on the patio, he looked around. Nothing here. Alastair had already left.

Max stepped out of the screened patio.

Tail wagging, Hunter abandoned the doghouse and trotted over to say hi.

"Hey, buddy. Want to help me search the grounds?" Grabbing a rubber ball, he pitched the ball across the wide lawn. With a yip of glee, Hunter gave chase.

Max followed more slowly, inspecting the various plantings.

Ah-hah.

The bird feeder in the maple tree had acquired a new occupant. On the wide platform, a brown-skinned Barbie doll leaned back on her arms, face raised to the sun. Its legs were propped up on his missing remote.

That little brat.

Chuckling, Max grabbed the remote and the doll. Maybe he should be more upset, but her prank had been too fucking cute. Besides, his rudeness had earned him some harassment.

And she'd given him cake.

Yeah, he'd let her off the hook for messing with her Dom.

Settling down onto the couch with Hunter at his feet, Max flipped to a sports broadcast.

Spanish? The sportscast shouldn't be in Spanish. In growing disbelief, he found their usual news channel. *Spanish.*

Zuri had messed with his *television*.

"Okay, baby," he growled. "Game *on*."

CHAPTER NINETEEN

U zuri walked into the house that night. With luck, the Doms had gone to bed. Hopefully, at least *Max* had gone to bed. Over the past few hours, she'd grown increasingly nervous.

Rainie and Sally had bid her farewell as if unsure they'd ever see her again. Friends really were a comfort. *Not.*

She closed the door ever so quietly, removed her shoes, and tiptoed toward the stairs. From the TV room came the sound of a movie. In English, not Spanish. A snicker almost escaped her.

When she was halfway to the second floor, Hunter appeared and dashed up the stairs. His *oo-oo-oo* greeting made her cringe.

"Shhh, boo," she whispered. "I love you, but *shhh*."

"No need to be quiet, subbie." The rasp in the deep voice was all too familiar.

Busted. She straightened slowly.

Max was leaning against the bottom stair post. Muscular arms crossed. Hard face unreadable.

"Um. Good evening." She swallowed. "Sir."

"It's a good evening now, yes." He gave her a mean look. "Although I wasted a chunk of it trying to reset the TV default language to one I happen to speak."

She clapped her hands over her mouth, but her snicker was definitely audible.

He didn't react, but said far too quietly, "Television room. Now."

Her mouth went dry, and her feet froze to the stairs. A nervous flutter took up residence in her chest. If she said anything, it would come out a fearful whine...with giggles. Oh, she was so in trouble.

As she walked toward the room, Max snapped his fingers and said, "Hunter. Time for you to go out."

He was putting the dog outside. There would be no four-footed rescue for her.

On the couch, Alastair looked up as she entered. The corners of his mouth tipped up slightly. "I fear messing with his television might have been one step too far, pet."

She was totally getting that impression.

To think she'd been scared when Mistress Anne discovered who'd sabotaged her locker with rubber cockroaches.

This was a whole new level of fear.

"Seems you had a good time playing earlier," Max walked up behind her and firmly pushed her farther into the room. "Since we take turns in this relationship, guess that makes it our turn to play."

"*Our?*" Her gaze flew to Alastair. "I didn't do anything to you."

"Max and I share." Alastair raised an eyebrow. "Our house, our food, our submissive. Our problems."

Max set a foot on the coffee table and rested his thick forearms on his thigh. "You used dolls to guide me to the remote. Alastair and I did the same for you." He pointed. On the coffee table next to his open toy bag were the three dolls.

They were the same dolls she'd used for his treasure hunt: Detective Dragon, Dr. Dragon, and Zuri-doll, only now Zuri-doll was naked and arranged across Dr. Dragon's lap, ass in the air.

Detective Dragon was on one knee...his hand between Zuri-doll's plastic legs.

"Get naked, subbie," Max said, ever so softly.

"But—"

He lifted his chin. And waited.

But, but, but... Fingers trembling slightly, she stripped off her clothes and folded them in a neat pile on the coffee table.

The Doms she trusted—*she did...mostly*—were silent as she straightened, put her arms behind her back, and lowered her gaze.

"You really are beautiful, little miss." Alastair's words set up a glow inside her.

"Little miss? More like little *mischief*." Max glowered. "Why did I think the tales about you were exaggerated?"

Don't *laugh.* She kept her eyes lowered.

"Look at her. She's trying not to laugh." Max made a disgusted sound.

Oh, God, she couldn't *stand* it.

She exploded into giggles—and couldn't stop. Even putting her hands over her mouth didn't help.

When she looked up, Alastair was laughing, as well.

"You bastard, you're not helping." Max's exasperation set her off again.

She stopped...finally...although her cheeks hurt, and her stomach hurt, and she had to wipe the tears from her face.

"Never heard her laugh like that before. Have you?" Max said.

"A time or two when she was with the Shadowkittens," Alastair said.

Huh, she never did lose it like this around men. How odd to be in trouble and still go into a giggle-fest.

Max frowned at her. "All right, darlin'. Because I started my movie so late—"

Late because he couldn't find the remote. Ignoring the sound that escaped her, she forced her face into serious lines.

He pointed at her. "Do *not* start laughing again. The movie isn't finished, and Alastair and I want to see the end. You may sit quietly and not bother us."

"Of course, Sir."

"Good. We've also talked about getting you ready for anal."

It took her a second to make the leap in subjects. Anal what? Omigod, anal sex. They'd mentioned it a couple of times and asked if she wanted to try it.

Although it'd been on her limits list in the Shadowlands, she hadn't told the Dragos no. Sally said it was fun.

Sally was a smidge on the certifiably crazy side.

"I-I... Now?" Her voice squeaked like a mouse that'd had its tail bitten off.

Alastair beckoned to her. "A small plug today. Over a few days, they'll get larger until you're ready for a cock. Turn around and bend over, sweetheart."

When his smooth baritone dropped into a Dom's command, her willpower disappeared. She turned. Heat rising into her face, she bent, closed her eyes, and curled her fingers around her knees in a death grip. Shockingly cool lubricant drizzled between her buttocks.

Alastair pressed the smooth anal plug against her back hole.

Ew. Her involuntary jump and attempt to straighten was blocked. Max's ruthless hand on her nape kept her bent over.

Alastair didn't waste time. Slowly—mercilessly—he pressed in the thick head of the plug. Her anal muscles closed around the thinner portion.

Something inside her *there* felt *strange*. Dirty and wrong...and intensely erotic.

"Up you come." Max helped her straighten. "As long as we're decorating our plaything, we'll do it right." He removed nipple clamps from his toy bag, tossed them to Alastair, and turned her to face them both. "Hold still, princess."

He pulled and rolled her nipples between his fingers. Pleasure zinged through her as he continued until he had jutting peaks. "That should do it."

While Max pulled on the tip of one, Alastair applied the rubber-tipped clamp and tightened the screw slowly.

The pinch grew and grew, and she whined a protest.

He stopped, finally, having gone a lot further than any Dom before. The thing felt as if it was biting her nipple. *Hard*.

Without waiting, they did the other breast.

The burning pain in both nipples froze her in place. *Ow, ow, ow*.

"Uzuri." Alastair captured her face in his big hands and forced her to look at him. His steady, perceptive gaze held hers. "Inhale. Deeper. Exhale. Again."

She clung to his gaze like a lifeline, and after a few seconds, the pain from the clamps eased to a constant, low throbbing, somehow matching the uncomfortable feeling in her ass. The bare skin over her whole body felt hot and sensitized. Under her feet, the hardwood floor was cold. Alastair's hands felt cool against her flushed face.

"Good girl." He smiled at her and stepped back.

"Now this, little mischief." Max squeezed her shoulder reassuringly before attaching a thin yard-long chain between the clamps. The cool metal bounced against her bare stomach. The small painful tugs on her nipples coursed straight to her ever-dampening pussy.

Uncomfortably, she shifted her weight—and stilled as she saw both Doms were watching her. And smiling.

"One last thing," Max said. He took a pink U-shaped sex toy from his bag. A wire ran to a controller. "Spread your legs, Zuri."

Her legs were extremely reluctant to move apart, and it seemed to take forever before he smiled his satisfaction.

"Since you don't get to watch the movie, I didn't want you to get bored. This should help." Reaching between her legs, he slid one end of the U into her vagina. When he stopped, the other end rested directly on her clit.

Holding the toy in place, Max looked up at her. "Close your legs."

She pulled her legs together, feeling the foreign intrusion inside her. Two foreign intrusions.

Naked. Penetrated. And in trouble. Oh, this wasn't good.

"Alastair and I discussed your behavior." Max paused. "We like your sense of humor, Zuri. Normally, something like hiding the remote wouldn't get you into trouble, especially if you're doing it to prod me out of a bad mood."

Alastair continued. "The problem is when you're out for revenge."

Uzuri frowned. "I don't understand."

"Max snapped at you," Alastair said, "but I believe he apologized?"

She nodded. He had. He'd been sweet about it, too, in a way she rarely saw.

"The way you hid the remote was funny." Max smiled. "Adding in the carrot cake..."

"That was brilliant," Alastair said.

"I was in a great mood by the time I got to the remote." Max shook his head. "I might have had fun with you when you got back, but punishment sure wouldn't have been involved."

Uzuri felt a warm glow inside.

"However..." Max's smile faded.

She stiffened.

"When you changed the language on the television, I'm thinking that wasn't to help your Dom or to be cute." He pinned her with a chilly look. "That was payback and not in a nice way."

"How did you feel when you were setting everything up? Do you see the difference?" Alastair asked quietly.

Her shoulders slumped. Actually, she did. When she'd been

creating the treasure hunt, everything she'd done was to make Max laugh. To make him feel better.

But then she'd started thinking about how he'd snapped at her and how mean he'd sounded, and the television stunt had been... not for Max, but for her. For revenge. Even though he'd apologized, and she'd forgiven him, but apparently, she hadn't. Not down deep. How petty was that? "You're right," she whispered. "I'm sorry, Sir."

When she dared to look up, Max's stern expression had disappeared. He ran his finger down her cheek so very gently. "We're all learning to work together, darlin'. And we'll undoubtedly fuck up."

Alastair added. "If we make a mistake or disagree, we discuss the problem. Honestly. And try to mend matters. There is no need for vengeful actions—and such actions will get punished."

She nodded. But...she liked playing. For fun. She bit her lip. "What if..."

"Ah." Alastair smiled. "Fun mischief will get you 'funishment'."

Fake punishment that everyone enjoyed. When Gabi had talked about what she "earned" from Marcus, Uzuri hadn't seen the appeal. Now, actually, with the Dragon Doms, she thought she might like some. "Um. So...what is tonight?"

"A little of both," Max said.

"Starting with punishment," Alastair sat down on the couch next to where she stood. "Ending with fun. At least for us."

Wait... That didn't sound exactly good.

"Remember the doll's position, princess?" With hard hands, Max turned her, then bent her over Alastair's thighs.

Gripping her arm, Alastair pulled her all the way down, adjusting her so her ass was high in the air. His thighs were like iron beneath her belly and pelvis. As Uzuri braced herself with her palms on the floor, she felt...humiliated. It had been embarrassing enough when Alastair'd spanked her and they'd been alone. With two of them? Somehow, it was much worse.

For a silent minute, Alastair simply massaged her bottom with one hand. His other hand was on her back, holding her in place, pressing hard enough to let her *know* she couldn't escape.

Pulling on her tender nipples, the chain from the clamps dangled to the floor. Alastair set his bare foot on the end. "I recommend you don't move from this position, pet."

"Yes, Sir." Anchored under his foot, the chain still had enough slack she could take a breath, but any real movement would pull on her sensitive nipples. *Don't move.*

Alastair patted her bottom lightly. "I believe a spanking feels different with a plug in."

She stiffened, realized what he meant—and he started slapping her ass.

Whap, whap, whap.

Each quick light smack jarred the anal plug slightly and made her squirm. The sting of the blows wasn't bad, not at first.

But he hit her harder, and the burn grew. And grew. Tears filled her eyes. She wiggled, tried to rise up, and the nipple chains pulled painfully. Pain in her breasts, pain in her bottom. It all rushed over her, terrifying her. "*Yellow.*"

Alastair stopped immediately.

Max squatted in front of her and lifted her head slightly. "Talk to us, baby."

When she sniffled, he wiped her damp face with a tissue Alastair handed him.

"It hurts," she told him.

"I know." Max's face was tight, his blue eyes dark and unhappy. "This is punishment and isn't meant to be fun. But we won't go past what you can bear, darlin'. Did it reach that point?"

As his warm hand cupped her chin, she felt Alastair stroking her back, soothing her. Her bottom burned, her breasts throbbed, but...not unbearably. Not really. Not now that she had a moment to think. "I guess I got scared." She took a breath.

They'd stopped right away when she got overwhelmed. And

had talked to her. She knew she deserved the punishment, but they wouldn't continue if she couldn't take it. The thin thread of trust in her two Doms grew stronger. "I'm okay."

"All right." Alastair smoothed his hand over her burning ass cheeks. "Enough for the moment. We'll continue at the commercial break."

"What?" Her indignant cry won her a smack on her tender bottom.

"And next time, remember to breathe through the discomfort, love."

She choked. Only a doctor would call mean, nasty spanking "discomfort." If she'd had a syringe handy, she would have stabbed it into his leg. Instead, she pulled in a slow breath and managed to relax. A little.

"Good girl." As she lay across Alastair's legs, he petted her like a kitten.

Max walked around her feet and sat down on the couch, moving closer to Alastair until he could stroke her thighs. "Hang on, mischief."

The U-shaped sex toy between her legs came to life. The vibration was both inside her and over her clit, pulsing in a wave-like pattern. *Br, brr, brrr, brrrr, BRRR.*

Omigod.

Alastair patted her butt. "We didn't want you to be bored during the movie." The television clicked on.

Seriously? Seriously? With Alastair's foot on the chain and his hand pressing down on her back, all she could do was lie still as the vibrator buzzed on her clit and inside her, going up and down in slow arousing waves that lasted...never long enough.

She tried rubbing her thighs together and received a smack on her thigh. "Ow!" Max's hand could rival the hardness of an oak paddle.

"Lie still, little mischief."

With a feeling of despair, she heard the sound of a car commercial.

"All right, pet." Alastair slapped her ass. Hard and even and merciless. The burning blossomed and grew. Pain filled her and, although she had her teeth clenched, she sobbed.

He stopped. "Tell me why you're being punished, Uzuri."

Stall...stall. The longer she took to answer, the—

Smack. "I require an answer today, love."

A whimper escaped her. "Because my motivation wasn't to help my Dom, but to get revenge."

"Precisely." Alastair paused. "Do you see the difference?"

"Yes, Sir."

"Excellent. I believe you can fast-forward through the commercial, Max."

Her second of gratitude disappeared when he resumed spanking her.

At least the commercial break was a lot shorter this way.

As the movie's closing credits scrolled up the screen, Alastair relaxed against the back of the couch with Uzuri still lying across his thighs. He fondled her beautifully round ass, feeling the heated skin. His own palm stung.

He sighed. Although he'd appreciated the way the vibrator had set Uzuri to squirming, he hadn't enjoyed the two spanking periods.

Neither had Max. Because of his mother's history of abuse, Max didn't like to deal out physical punishment.

Alastair...well, he had enough sadism in his soul that spanking a little submissive was rather fun. He'd prefer more erotic pain, however.

Unfortunately, Uzuri needed this lesson. Vengeful pranks didn't belong in a D/s relationship.

Other pranks? Well, some submissives simply had mischievous natures. He liked that side of Uzuri's personality as much as Max did. They were both in high stress and high stakes professions.

With her warmth, generosity, and adorable sense of humor, Uzuri had brought balance back to their lives.

In all reality, he could see that she'd needed them as much. Over the week, her tension had disappeared. She was less jumpy, more relaxed, laughed more often. And those giggles. He smiled. Simply beautiful.

Therefore, they'd finish her "punishment" now with something far more pleasant.

On his lap, Uzuri had started to squirm. Alastair glanced at Max. His cousin was playing with the remote, undoubtedly raising and lowering the vibrations. From the sounds and wiggles, Max had found a good setting for her—enough to excite, not enough to climax.

Max saw him looking, nodded, and shut off the vibrator. Time to move on.

Alastair took his foot off the chain, lifted Uzuri up, and sat her on his lap.

She winced as her sore buttocks made contact with his jeans and squirmed at the increased pressure from the anal plug.

He grinned. It was the little things...Putting his right arm behind her back, he studied her.

Sweat and tears had streaked her face and smeared her eye makeup. Her lips and cheeks had darkened with arousal. Her lovely brown eyes were slightly glazed, her expression confused. Helpless. She didn't know what to expect.

The chain from the nipple clamps brushed his left hand. He glanced at Max. "Restrain or remove?"

Max eyed Uzuri and smiled slowly. "Oh, I'll restrain." He rose, put her wrists together behind her neck, and held them there in one hand.

She looked confused. "I wasn't moving."

Max laughed and used his free hand to hold her left nipple clamp steady.

"Remember to breathe, sweetheart." Alastair unscrewed the clamp and pulled it off.

As the blood rushed back into her tender, abused areola, Uzuri's eyes went wide. "Ow, ow, *owwwww*." She pulled at her arms.

Max didn't release her wrists. "Only one more to go, baby." He bent to anchor the right nipple clamp.

"You...you..." She glared at him. "And you say you're not sadistic."

Alastair choked on a laugh. She started to struggle as he unscrewed the clamp. He removed it.

A second later, a high-pitched shriek sounded even though her mouth was tightly shut.

"I can almost see why you enjoy torturing little subbies so much." Chuckling and still holding her wrists behind her neck, Max glanced at Alastair.

"This part is even more fun." With his hand under her left breast, Alastair tipped her back enough that he could close his lips over one exquisitely sensitive nipple.

Her squeaking noises were gratifying. He circled the velvety areola with his tongue, knowing to her the sensation would be sensuous—and painful. Both. He sucked lightly and made her gasp. After blowing air on the distended peak to cool the burning, he licked again before moving to the other breast.

As Max's hand on her straining wrists held her immobile for his cousin, Uzuri felt the world blur around her. Alastair's tongue swirled around her nipple ever so softly, yet every circle burned across the tender spots where the clamps had dug in. The areola pebbled and started to bunch with a tingling throb.

And thick, hot pleasure poured in a molten stream from her breasts to her pussy.

As Alastair straightened, he kept his right arm behind her back, pulling her closer to him. "I think she's ready for you, Max."

"Ready for what?" Half dizzy, Uzuri bit her lip.

"Ready for more." After releasing her wrists, Max bent and kissed her so deeply that the world slid sideways. "Pretty Zuri."

"Now for those arms." He studied her for a second and then folded her arms so they pressed upward on her breasts. "Stay like this, baby. Alastair will enjoy it."

Alastair chuckled. "I will indeed." His right arm was behind her back, supporting her. After tipping her back slightly, he closed his left hand over one plumped-up breast and she squeaked.

As Alastair played, her breasts swelled even more, throbbing and aching and sending hot zings downward to her pussy.

She heard Max speak. She heard the words, but the meaning felt out of reach for a good second or two, and she opened her eyes and lifted her head.

He was kneeling between her legs, pushing her knees apart. "What?"

His eyes crinkled. "Open. Your. Legs."

Oh. Legs. She moved them apart.

As Max pulled the vibrator from her pussy, it dragged over her sensitive clit. She gave a jerk and tried to sit up.

"Easy, love." Alastair's arm high around her waist tightened, and his hand on her breast pressed down, the actions forcing her to stay half-reclined. She was completely under his control.

Heart beating faster, she looked down her body.

Max had moved between her knees. His eyes were intensely blue as he studied her a second. He bent down and ran his tongue down her mound straight to her still-swollen clit with unerring precision.

Pleasure shot through her, leaving sheer throbbing need in its wake. "Omigod, oooh."

Max pushed a finger, then two inside her vagina, penetrating her slowly, and the stretching became a tingling heat. As her pussy clamped down, he murmured. "Very nice."

His smoldering gaze trapped her, held hers as his fingers did a slow in and out. And then, with his other hand, he wiggled the anal plug.

"Aaah!" Her hips jolted upward as every nerve back there shot to life. The feeling was incredible.

When Max bent his head and licked over her clit, the nub swelled with each long stroke of pleasure.

She sagged back against Alastair's arm.

"Uzuri, look at me." Alastair's hand cupped one breast. As his thumb circled her nipple, the sensations above and below were growing overwhelming.

She looked up.

Hazel eyes, mostly green, pierced through her.

He held her gaze as Max teased her clit with his hot, flickering tongue. His fingers thrust relentlessly in and out of her swollen, slick pussy even as he wiggled the anal plug. Her entire lower half grew acutely sensitive, every brush and touch and movement exquisite. The hot, molten pressure grew, even as her insides tightened around the plug and his impaling fingers.

Her muscles tensed, her fingernails digging into her own skin. Shudders ran through her.

Alastair gave a rumbling sound of approval. "Now."

Unexpectedly, she was leaned farther back, and Alastair's lips closed around her nipple, and he sucked. Hard. In slow, deep pulls.

At the same time, heat engulfed her clit—and Max sucked. Hard. In slow, deep pulls.

Everything inside her coalesced into a rigid ball, and deep in her core, the spasms began like the first ripplings of an earthquake. Pleasure shuddered through her, growing and growing, shaking her body, ripping apart boundaries and defenses, changing the terrain of her entire world. So much pleasure.

Another quake shook through her and another.

Slowly, the earth settled, shudders to minor quakes, to tiny tremors.

Her heart was still banging inside her rib cage when she felt Max move back and slide the anal plug out, leaving her empty inside. As he moved away, her inner thighs felt cold where his warmth had been.

As Alastair sat her up, the world shuddered back into place around her, and she felt...alone. Strange and shaken. She'd been punished. Hard.

She'd deserved it.

When Alastair had spanked her, she'd been angry. Hurting. Not truly remorseful.

But now...the guilt swelled inside her. She'd been bad and had disappointed them and let them down. She hadn't been a good submissive. Tears welled in her eyes.

She'd been nasty to Max and rather than being nasty back, they'd disciplined her—even though they didn't want to—and had given her pleasure. So much pleasure.

They hadn't taken any for themselves.

Max was standing beside her. She looked up at him, eyes blurry. "I...I'm sorry. I didn't mean to be bad."

The steel in his eyes turned soft. "We know, baby."

She turned and met Alastair's green gaze. Her chest felt tight, her words thick and hard to get out. "I'm sorry, Sir. Don't be mad at me."

"Sweetheart, we never were. Come here, love." Shifting her closer on his lap, he pulled her against his chest. Wrapping his arms around her, he tenderly, firmly, guided her head to his hard shoulder.

With a hitched sob, she pressed her face against him.

And she cried.

She didn't even know why, but every emotion inside her came out in a waterfall of tears and sobbing. As she clung to him, his arms were safety and strength.

With one big hand, he rubbed her back, making soothing sounds.

Eventually, her crying slowed.

"There we go." Alastair's deep voice rumbled in his chest, his British accent somehow soothing. "Take her to bed. You can finish making up."

"Not going to object to that." Max bent and scooped her up. Thicker chest, harder arms, a different scent, rougher voice—and yet, the sense of safety was the same.

She started crying again, and rather than complain, he tightened his arms around her. He was even rocking her slightly, like a baby, with his cheek against the top of her head. "Shhh, shhh, shhh."

He took her to his bed, tucked her in, and held her as she fell asleep.

When he woke her in the middle of the night, said it was time to finish "making up," and fucked her back into total limpness, she could only giggle.

CHAPTER TWENTY

"Max."

On Monday evening, Max looked up from the news to see Zuri. "Hey, princess. Going to watch the day's disasters with me?" Pleased, he patted the cushion beside him. In the week she'd lived with them, he'd discovered the joys of watching the news with her. The insane world didn't seem nearly as out of balance with her soft body snuggled against him and her logical, but kinder view of humanity.

"No, no news today."

Catching the trouble in her tone, he clicked off the television and turned to study her.

Posture stiff, soft lips compressed into a determined line.

"Spit it out, baby. I'm listening."

Her nod of approval was so much like his mother's that he almost smiled. She handed him the frosty glass of beer she was carrying. "Can you go to the roof terrace?"

The way she tensed in worry over his answer made his response a no-brainer. "Of course, princess." He rose and cupped her chin so he could watch her eyes. "Problem?"

"Not exactly." She rubbed her cheek against his palm. "I... Please?"

Well, she'd undoubtedly explain when she was ready. "I'll see you up there, then."

Her relieved breath puffed against his wrist. After a quick kiss, he headed up to the third floor. If something were stressing her out, he'd do what he could to fix it.

Hell, there wasn't much he wouldn't do to smooth her path and make her happy.

Up on the rooftop terrace, Max put his bare feet up on the coffee table, sipped the cold Fat Tire—excellent bribe—and settled in to wait.

Shortly, she appeared with his cousin.

Carrying whisky in a tulip-shaped glass, Alastair sat down on the opposite couch. Not leaning back. Not relaxing. Grim lines bracketed his mouth, and his eyes were empty. The doc was in a piss poor mood.

Frowning, Max straightened.

Before he could speak, Zuri shook her head. She sat beside Alastair, leaning against him despite his stiff frame.

That wouldn't work, Max wanted to tell her.

But she didn't do more than snuggle against his cousin and sip her own drink. "I had a crummy day today." Her voice was softer, the lilt suppressed. "Although the sales for the entire store are adequate, the numbers for the women's clothing section are down."

After a second, Alastair gave her a puzzled look.

Max knew why. The little submissive rarely talked about her troubles. She usually had to be pushed...something he and Alastair had realized and started doing.

Casually, she slid her hand down Alastair's arm and tangled her fingers with his—something else she rarely did.

All right. He'd play along until he figured out the game. "Why is the women's section worse?"

She sighed. "The morale is crummy. There are rumors that I had Carole fired because I didn't like her. The bosses haven't revealed her part in how I got hurt."

Alastair seemed to wake up slightly. "What are you planning to do, pet?"

"I have a few ideas. As soon as I have a cohesive plan, I'd like to run it past you guys for fine-tuning."

"Of course," Alastair agreed.

Zuri took a sip of her drink. "Max, what was your day like?"

He'd caught another homicide. Before he could side-step the question, he saw the plea in her soft brown eyes, and her scheme came clear. She talked. Max talked. Then Alastair would have to talk. *Clever, subbie.* He gave her a nod. *I'm in.*

A sip of beer helped to prime the pump. "The day started off like hell. Had a murder in an alley in Ybor. But it turned out to be a straightforward drug deal gone bad. The dealer'd miscalculated how desperate his customer was."

When Zuri shivered, Alastair frowned and put an arm around her. "Pet, Max's job isn't a good one for conversation."

Heh, bad move, cuz.

Zuri's chin came up, and once again, she reminded him of his mother—that was the disapproving stare Mom'd get when Max fucked up by the numbers.

Good news was the little subbie's stare was directed at Alastair, as were her words. "Max has a scary, gritty job, but he needs to be able to share it and give some of the pain to people who can carry it. I am one of those people, and so are you. That's part of *our* job."

When Alastair reacted as if she'd smacked him upside the head, Max barely smothered a laugh.

Zuri glanced over and gave a royal wave—*continue*—so Max dutifully related the rest of his day, editing out the worst of the gory details.

The hug and kiss he received were a gratifying reward. Oddly enough, he felt better, too—as relaxed as if he'd downed a couple of shots.

When Zuri settled back against Alastair's side and smiled at Max, he recognized his next cue. "Your turn, cuz. Tell us about your day."

The way Alastair stiffened showed his day had been fucked-up. The way his gaze narrowed on the beautiful subbie nestled against his side said he realized he'd been set up.

But after all the shit they'd given Zuri about sharing her problems, the doc was screwed, and he knew it.

With a sigh, he laid it out. Bright little kid. Dirt bike. Accident. Coma. The doc wasn't a neurologist, so he wasn't the lead on the case or whatever medical people called it, but, being Alastair, he'd still gone by to see the kid in the hospital. To make sure the family was holding up.

It'd hurt him. Hell, it would upset anyone to see a kid laid low, but the doc had a fucking tender heart. He'd already gotten cut up from working war-torn hellholes all those years.

"That was my day," Alastair finished. He stared at his hands, turning them over as if somehow they'd let him down.

Uzuri slid onto his lap and pulled his arms around her. With a slow sigh, Alastair rested his cheek on top of her head. In a gentle voice, she told him, "You can't fix it all, Sir. The last time I looked, even a Master isn't God."

Max snorted. "Baby, are you *trying* to depress him? You're supposed to think we walk on water."

When Alastair chuckled, Uzuri's shoulders lifted with her breath of relief.

"Is that what I was supposed to think?" She turned her head far enough to grin at Max. "No wonder no Dom wants me."

Actually smiling now, Alastair leaned back and put his feet on the coffee table. His arm stayed firmly around her waist, keeping her planted in his lap. "Wrong, pet. *We* want you."

When Alastair picked up his drink, Max did the same.

Meeting Uzuri's eyes, Max lifted his glass in a quiet toast to their big-hearted mischief-maker.

CHAPTER TWENTY-ONE

Ouch, ouch, ouch. Uzuri dropped the comb back in her lap. The instrument of torture might be seamless and wide toothed, but this Tuesday evening, her hair wasn't in the mood to cooperate—and neither were her muscles. Sitting on the floor in the television room, she stared blindly at her taped Project Runway show...and she stewed.

Exercising sucked. Seriously.

Weightlifting? So not fun. Her legs and butt felt as if someone had pounded on her muscles with a big stick. Max insisted he wasn't a sadist, but who else would have assigned an exercise called "squats".

And sit-ups? Oh Lord in heaven. Her stomach muscles hurt every time she moved.

But to top off the misery that was her life, Max had decided yesterday she needed more "upper body strength."

Bench presses and military presses and incline presses. When she'd told Max she was tired of all the "presses," suddenly she was doing "pulls." Pull-downs and pull-ups. And rowing sans any boat.

He was a mean person. Period.

Blessed Mother, even the muscles beneath her breasts were sore. That was just wrong.

Her Dragon Doms were trying to kill her.

Every other morning, Max would drag her out of bed to jog with him. Around *dawn*. Who could be enthusiastic about getting all sweaty before the day even started? Although... She smiled. Sweat looked really fine on Master Maximillian. His tank would darken in a line between his pectorals and cling beautifully to his washboard abs. *Yummilicious.*

But to do all that sweating herself? Thank you, no.

On alternate days, she'd swim in the evenings with Alastair—and the eye-candy was just as fine. Smooth rippling muscles beneath wet, dark skin. When those finely sculpted muscles pumped up, she had a burning need to trace every perfect definition. With her tongue.

But the swimming stuff as it applied to her? Did they not realize what chlorine did to hair? The Brillo pad look was so not a good one on her.

This had been swimming day. Not being an idiot, she'd wetted and conditioned her hair beforehand, then washed and conditioned afterward. Once mostly dry, she'd applied a leave-in conditioner and sealed it in with hair butter.

She should buy stock in the conditioner companies.

Now she had to comb her hair out. Only...her arms felt as if they weighed at least fifty pounds—each—and were growing heavier by the second.

Just do it. Gritting her teeth, she sectioned off her hair and started combing.

Max was in the kitchen now. He'd cheated on his cooking day by bringing home a ready-made pizza to bake. At least there would be a salad, too, since Alastair insisted on a minimum of healthy food with the evening meals.

Neither of them would have thought to make sure there was chocolate, though.

Stupid men.

She heard the thump of footsteps. Boots. Max. Continuing her combing, she ignored him. The couch behind her groaned as he sat down. She felt like groaning herself.

Hunter had followed him in and happily curled up beside her.

Max put his beer on the coffee table and picked up her jar of hair butter. After a second, he set it down.

Finished with one section of hair, she took a break...and considered screaming. Five more sections to go. Her arms might fall off. She'd been so proud of getting her hair from the big chop to almost shoulder-length...but if she stayed here another week, a TWA was looking good. There was a lot to be said for a teeny-weeny Afro.

"I love your hair when it's all shiny and springy like this." Max started to play with the hair she'd combed out.

"Hey." Without thinking, she slapped his arm away. "I'm not some dog you can pat without permission."

Oh. Omigod.

She felt the weight of Max's silence behind her. And spotted Alastair in the door, his expression grave.

With a merciless hand, Max gripped her hair and firmly pulled her head back.

Helplessly, she stared up into intense blue eyes.

"Want to explain what the fuck that was about?" He didn't bother to say that, as her Dom, temporary or not, he could touch her. Anywhere he wanted. Anytime he wanted.

Silently, Alastair took a chair.

"I'm sorry." Uzuri tried to look down, but Max didn't release her.

"I'm sure you are. I'd rather hear why you reacted that way." He paused. "You mad at me about something I don't know?"

Shame filled her. All he'd done was give her a compliment. And touch. "Even if I explain, you won't understand."

"And if you don't explain, I won't understand for sure."

Releasing her hair, he gripped her waist, lifted her up, and sat her on the couch. As he turned to face her, the steel in his eyes softened. "Talk to me, darlin'."

"I...I had a bad day, and I took it out on you."

"Mmm. That you did. What made this a bad day?"

He wasn't going to let it go, was he? The effort not to glare probably skyrocketed her blood pressure into the danger zone. *Okay, fine.* He wanted to hear about her day? "I wanted to be super feminine today, so I'd pulled my hair to one side and made corkscrew curls on one side."

"I remember. It looked great." He always noticed her hair. Liked her hair.

"Well, I was at a design show, and this white woman comes up and tells me my hair is so cool and starts fingering the coils. Handling my *hair*. And she yells to her friend, 'You should feel her hair. It's all soft and kinky.'"

"And that pisses you off."

"Honestly, how would they like it if I walked up and fingered their 'do." She forced the swear words back. "My hair is *mine*. My body; my hair. I'm not a pet dog everybody gets to touch."

Beside her on the couch, Max regarded her quietly, obviously thinking about her words. His nod was...a relief. "All right, baby, I see why that'd piss you off. Touching someone against her wish is a form of assault."

"Exactly."

He offered her his hand, palm up, and waited until she gave him her fingers. "Zuri, I don't think of you as an animal to be disrespected. Nonetheless, I do think you're our submissive, and touching without permission falls under the Dom rules. Unless you want to negotiate otherwise."

She shook her head, feeling like an idiot. "I don't. I reacted before I thought about it."

"Because you were angry," Alastair said.

She sighed and confessed. "I've been kind of mad all day."

Expression thoughtful, Alastair set down his whisky and looked at his cousin. "The beauty of home is that we can, hopefully, set aside the racial stress and relax. There are days, especially in the States, when being a person of color can leave a person full of anger...and sometimes that relaxation takes time to achieve."

Uzuri saw Max's brows come together. "I'm white. Can't get around that detail." His gaze came to her. "Do I make things worse?"

She bit her lip. How many people did she know who would drag everything out in the open? These two were amazing. "No, not worse..."

"Some would consider her a traitor to her race for being with you." Alastair's lips quirked. "Of course, that means my mother—and Uzuri's—were also traitors for having sex with white males. As mixed-race children, we're considered damaged goods in a way."

Max snorted. "Not if you listen to Sam. He's not much for purebreds in any species. Told me he prefers hybrids—and that Uzuri was a shining example of the beauty of crossing races."

Her mouth dropped open. "Master Sam said that?" The sadistic rancher-farmer never said anything he didn't mean.

"Yeah. But... Zuri, we asked you here to help you. And because we wanted to see how we'd do together. Not to make life more difficult for you." His hand opened, letting hers go." If being with a white man is—"

"No." She wrapped her fingers around his. "It's true that, in some ways, it's easier to be with another person of color. There's a shared history and pain and acceptance." She thought about it. "But I don't think that keeping races separated is best for the human race as a whole."

He nodded. And waited. He and Alastair had an ability to... listen...that she found incredibly compelling.

"But it's hard," she confessed. "And sometimes, I want to go out and slap stupid people."

"I've felt the same," Alastair admitted. "That anger isn't confined to our race, though." He motioned to Max with his glass. "Our cop here is driven by a need for fairness and justice—which means, every summer in Colorado, he fought more battles over prejudice than I did."

Max snorted. "Never did see how you could be so fucking laid back about that shit." The growl in his voice was...sweet.

Uzuri squeezed his fingers. "I spent a couple of years enraged all the time, seeing injustice and putdowns and micro-aggressions everywhere. One day, on the subway, this blonde kept glancing at me as if she thought I planned to steal her purse or attack her or something. I got madder and madder."

Max frowned. "Being a cop, I hope you ignored her. Personally, I hope you punched her one."

His annoyance on her behalf came through loud and clear. Uzuri laughed. "When I walked past her to get off at my stop, she stood up—and said she'd fallen in love with my suit. Would I tell her where I bought it?"

Max stared at her, and then his lips curved up. "Didn't see that coming."

In Alastair's gaze was the miles-deep understanding of what she was saying. She squeezed Max's hand. "The way people of color are treated isn't fair. Yet, the expectation of hostility was ruining my life. Now, I try to judge each person and each interaction without preconceptions."

Alastair nodded. "Pick the battles and speak out when you can make a difference."

"Although it's too slow, we make progress each generation." Her grandmother would never have been able to work as a fashion buyer. All of Mama's friends had been black; Uzuri's came in all colors. "The next generation will do even better."

Max nodded.

"So, I don't choose my friends or lovers or Dominants by race. Other things are more important." At one time, she'd made a list

—and hadn't consulted it. The Dragon Doms had walked into her life, and she'd simply said yes. "The answer to your question is that you don't make things worse. But sometimes I will have an *I'm-black-and-I'm-angry* day."

"All right. Then, if that's settled..." Max smiled and pulled her onto his lap.

She squeaked—a sound she hated.

Ruthlessly, he held her in place with a powerful grip on her wrists. Typical Dom. The air was cleared, now he'd remind her she was the submissive.

She *was* the submissive. And there was nothing she wanted more than to be held right now.

"I love this robe." Releasing her wrists, he pulled her closer. "Your silky ones are sexy as hell, but this one makes me feel as if I'm cuddling a kitten."

A kitten. She could only smile. After being mad enough to claw him like an angry alley cat, now she wanted to purr. Apparently, she hated being touched without permission or feeling like a pet—unless Alastair or Max did it.

Life was crazy. Or maybe she was.

He ran his hand under her hair, down her shoulder—and she tensed when his fingers hit her sore muscles. He stilled, huffed a laugh, and pressed harder.

"*Ow.*" He *was* a sadist. She tried to pull away and got nowhere.

"You're not used to all this exercise—especially weight training." He glanced at Alastair. "You like hurting little subbies. Why don't you give her a massage before bed?"

"Excellent idea." Alastair smiled slowly. "Are her pectorals sore?"

Ignoring her struggles, Max tightened his arm around her waist, set his other hand between her breasts, and dug into the muscles on each side of her sternum.

Her shriek made Hunter jump. "*Owww!*"

Mercilessly, Max continued, stroking firmly down her ribs, over incredibly painful muscles.

Her whining escalated until it sounded as if she was being murdered. "*Pauvre con*, stop!"

He did.

She sagged against him.

"Yep, you'll have fun with her, cuz." Max tipped her face up. "Speaking from experience, any massage the doc gives will hurt like hell, but when he's finished, you'll feel a lot better."

"Uh, that's not necessary. I'll finish my hair and go to bed early. I'm sure a good night's sleep will fix my muscles." That sounded like a much less painful plan to her.

Alastair's low laugh rumbled in a way that reminded her it was her night to sleep with him. And how massage might lead to other things.

She licked her lips.

When he smiled at her, she knew she'd be getting a massage... and everything else. Well, okay.

"If her shoulders are sore, a comb out might be difficult," Alastair said.

"Huh. Good point." To her shock, Max set her on the floor and picked up the wide-toothed comb. "I'll help with your hair."

"No, you will not." She held out her hand for the comb.

"I've been well trained, baby." To her surprise, he easily finger-combed out the next section.

"You had a black girlfriend?"

"A few. More importantly, I have a black aunt who loves having someone else mess with her hair." He gently started at the ends with the comb. "She's a neurosurgeon, and her hands are tired by the end of the day."

Alastair's mother was a neurosurgeon. Why was that no real surprise?

Stretching his legs out, Alastair enjoyed their little mischief's bemused expression. She wasn't used to being pampered—especially by men.

She was indeed a sweetheart, and one who'd survived everything thrown at her. It was good to see her in a temper, even better to watch her identify the cause of her anger. She had apologized sweetly.

As he sipped his whisky, contentment welled up inside him. The better he knew her, the more he liked her.

With a low hum, his cell phone vibrated. He pulled it out. "Drago."

The voice was low. "Holt here. You out of Zuri's hearing?"

"Please wait a moment." He stepped into the quiet foyer. "Go ahead."

"This isn't especially good news," Holt said. "Sometime last night—at the duplex—my Harley got tipped over, and my Forerunner got keyed."

Alastair's hand tightened on the phone. "Do you suspect Uzuri's stalker?"

"The neighborhood kids are a pretty nice bunch, and I'm not inclined to point a finger at them. Still...there are a bunch of teens here."

"Teens are unpredictable." However, if the vandalism wasn't caused by locals, then possibly Kassab was in Tampa. Alastair hadn't forgotten that Zuri's window had been broken on the day of the wedding.

"I called Anne. The asshole works long factory shifts several days in a row, then gets three days off. He wasn't working yesterday or the day before. However, he didn't buy any plane or bus ticket. Didn't use his credit card...anywhere...for those days."

"Which gives us nothing. He might be here or might not."

"Yeah." Holt sighed. "Just in case, keep an eye on her?"

"Oh, we shall do that." Anger tightened his voice. Uzuri was trying to recover from the past. The stalker's mere presence would set her back. Jaw tight, Alastair swiped the phone off. For

Kassab, he'd make an exception to his rule of not beating a person into bloody mincemeat.

When he returned, Uzuri gave him a worried look. "Are you all right?"

"I am, thank you." He glanced at Max.

His cousin caught his grim mood, and his eyes chilled before he nodded. Yes, they'd have a conversation later.

But for now, Alastair introduced a new topic. "We didn't have a chance to do our day's catching up, and I miss it. However, this was a quiet day for me, mostly sniffles and coughs. How about you, Max?"

Max worked the comb through Uzuri's hair. "Quiet, too. This close to Halloween, there are more drunks and vandals than murders. I spent most of the day in court and the rest doing paperwork."

"That's a nice change." Uzuri's expression was relieved.

Max kissed the top of her head. "And you, baby?"

"Everything in the office is going well." Her mouth turned down. "But..."

When she didn't continue, Max gave her a gentle shake, as if to rattle the information out of her.

"Stop that." She glared over her shoulder at him, then at Alastair for laughing.

"Fair's fair, pet. Sharing is what we do," Alastair said. "How is it going with those rumors?"

"Not good. Sales are still down because of the poor morale, and administration is angry."

Max stiffened. "At you? If they think that—"

"No, no, no. The sales staff is in trouble." She frowned. "Management is considering replacing a lot of the sales associates, but some of those women have worked there almost their entire lives. That would be horrible."

"Damn, baby," Max said. "You're more tenderhearted than is good for you."

She was, indeed.

At the sweet words, Uzuri took a long happy breath. They liked her and worried about her—and Max was combing out her hair. Happiness was a warm glow inside her, despite the subject of their conversation.

"Is there an alternative?" Alastair asked.

"Well, maybe. I suggested they meet with the sale associates and explain the problem. I even told them I'd talk to the staff and explain what had happened with Carole."

Max's cynical expression resembled her boss's.

Management had said no, but she'd persisted. "They eventually agreed, but said I was in charge of it all. The meeting. The threats. The explanations. Everything."

"Ah." Amusement lit Alastair's eyes. "Are you feeling like a sacrificial lamb?"

"Kind of," she muttered. "I'm not sure I can get the sales staff to understand how their behavior affects the entire store. Everyone. The future."

"Show them? Graphs and all that?" Max asked.

"They're not people to be influenced by graphs." She shook her head. "Maybe I can show them that people aren't always the way they see them, and that a person they neglect today might turn into a person they'd make a huge commission on in the future. There's no doubt that if a customer feels neglected, she'll never return to Brendall's."

As Max worked on her hair with small tugs, she simply enjoyed the feeling. When he turned her head to get to a new section of hair, she noticed her three dolls on the fireplace mantle. The Zuri-doll held a pot. The Detective Dragon had a scrub brush. Apparently, it was her turn to cook tomorrow with Max doing kitchen cleanup.

The *dolls*. She'd used them at work in the past to demonstrate mix-and-match outfits. Of course, dolls wouldn't sit well with the staff in this mood. But...maybe real people would.

She straightened, getting a reprimanding tug from Max. "If I had a line-up of real people of various economic levels and different ethnicities, maybe I could show the sales force that rich doesn't always look rich."

"Sounds like a plan," Max said.

"But the meeting is Monday. How in the world am I going to find examples? I mean—you can't hire people like that."

Alastair snorted and asked softly, "Do you have any friends, Uzuri?"

"Of course I do." She stopped. "Oh. I do."

"You appear to forget their existence far too often." Alastair looked at Max in one of their unspoken exchanges.

A very ominous exchange. She shivered.

CHAPTER TWENTY-TWO

Home from work the next evening, Uzuri walked outside to the patio. She'd expected to find Alastair swimming laps. Instead, he stood out in the backyard beside a patio table. His polo shirt clung to his wide shoulders and hard contoured pectoral muscles, even as the emerald color brought out the green in his hazel eyes.

At his feet, two king-sized sheets of rubber were spread on the grass. Intrigued, she left the patio to join him. "What are you doing? What is that?"

"We decided to play an active game this evening." He poured something out of a jar onto the rubber. "You need a day off from working out, but the self-defense lessons will continue."

Was that why Max had let her sleep in this morning? And no weight lifting? "A day off sounds great."

Catching a summery fragrance, she saw a tub of coconut oil on the table next to a squirt bottle and MP3 player. Wariness sparked to life. The Doms had interesting ideas of what might constitute a game. "Does this game have a name?"

His dark beard framed his white smile. "I don't think so. You may begin by stripping down. All the way."

She stared at him. "We're outside."

"Indeed. However, the privacy fence was built for a reason."

When she didn't move, his warm hazel eyes cooled. "Now, little mischief."

Uh-oh. Alastair had more patience than Max, but the amount wasn't inexhaustible. "Yes, Sir. Sorry." She unbuttoned her red, silk crepe drape blouse, laid it to one side, and continued with her black pencil skirt and undergarments until the sultry breeze wafted over her entire body.

He smiled. "You are one beautiful woman, Uzuri. Come here."

Standing next to him, she felt dwarfed by his size.

Wearing only cut-offs, Max sauntered out, carrying one of Alastair's canes. His gaze moved over Uzuri, and hunger darkened his blue eyes. "I think I'm going to like this game." He tossed the cane in the grass beside the sheeting.

A cane? She turned to Alastair. "I don't like pain."

"We know, pet." He pulled off his shirt and unzipped his shorts. "That's why it makes an excellent incentive. Step onto the sheeting, please."

An incentive? That didn't sound good at all. Her fingers dug into her palms as she backed onto the rubber square, avoiding the two-foot wide puddle of oil in the center.

On the other side of the sheeting, Max had also stripped. The inverted triangle of brown chest hair couldn't conceal his thick pectoral muscles. A tantalizing line arrowed over a hard six-pack and down to his thick and fully erect cock.

Omigod. Sex outside and during the full light of day? Was that even legal?

It took an effort to pull her gaze away. Did the sunlight make an erection look bigger—or was he growing?

Alastair was now naked—and erect—as well. With a slight smile, he touched the MP3 player attached to the small speaker box, and the music from the game *Call of Duty* filled the air with its martial strains.

Was that supposed to be sexy?

Without a word, Alastair picked up the tall bottle from the table and squirted the contents over her breasts.

"Sir!" She swiped at the oil running down her body. "What are you *doing*."

"Getting you ready." He tossed the bottle to Max who sprayed her back and legs.

Oh. My. God. They were insane. She crossed her arms over her oily breasts and glared. "White boy, *you* may need a tan, but I don't."

Max snorted and ignored her. "This is a type of role-play. The sheeting is your 'bedroom'—and where you'll be when you're attacked by an intruder."

"What?" Role-playing a helpless female versus an intruder didn't sound like fun at all.

Alastair tapped his foot on a wide green line on the rubber sheeting. "Green marks the door, which is the only exit."

Was she allowed to refuse this game? She pursed her lips. "What about windows? All bedrooms have windows."

He ignored her. "You have to escape the bedroom within three minutes." He pointed to a kitchen timer, which lay in the grass. "If you fail, the intruder will give you at least five strokes with the cane, although if he's in a bad mood, he might keep going. After caning you, he'll enjoy himself anyway he wants before the clock starts again."

Despite the humid evening air, a chill crept over her skin. "But—"

He held up his hand to keep her silent. "You, however, have a friend." Alastair smiled slowly. "Friends can be useful. If the pain —after five swats—is too much, you can call on your friend for help."

Max's arms came around her from behind, giving her a momentary sense of security. Until he said, "Do you understand, Zuri? You don't like pain, so ask for help from your friend. And darlin', fight hard. No eyeball gouging or biting, but use your fists. Bruises and black eyes are acceptable."

Her mouth felt dry, and a shiver ran over her.

Alastair continued. "If you should need something else"—in his dark face, his eyes lightened with amusement—"ask your friend for that, as well. Whatever happens, whatever you need, ask your friend."

She swallowed. "Who's my friend?"

Alastair crossed his arms over his chest. Considering he was naked in his backyard, he should look foolish. Instead, he looked lethally powerful, like a legendary African warrior. "For this first round, Max is the intruder, and I am your friend. Then we'll switch roles."

She was positive that switching roles didn't mean she'd ever get to be the friend or intruder.

Max released her and pointed to the pool of oil in the center of the sheeting. "Kneel there, princess."

"Princesses don't kneel."

Her sass earned her a raised chin and a sinking feeling in her belly. Moving to the center, she dropped to her knees. At least the coarse St. Augustine grass under the sheeting made a nice padding. She should be grateful the game wasn't on the cement patio.

To her surprise, Max went down on one knee on the edge of the clear oil. She'd have a fair chance to escape.

"Ready?" Alastair picked up the kitchen timer and hit the start button. "Go."

Before Uzuri could move, Max lunged for her. Grabbing her, he pulled her through the lake of oil, laughing as he swatted her ass.

With a shocked shriek, she shoved him away.

He yanked her back—and smacked her thigh. Harder. "Fight me, bitch." His words were an ugly low rasp. "Or else."

Fear swamped her, totally swamped her, and she froze.

"Uh-uh, Zuri." Max's deep voice washed over her. Familiar and safe. "Use your fear. Hit me, princess."

She looked up into his concerned blue eyes, hearing his words from their training sessions: *Going into a fight, you know you might get hurt, but baby, I want you fucking determined that you'll be the only one standing at the end.*

As the paralysis faded, she shoved at him. Weakly.

"Wuss." He batted her hand aside with a growl of annoyance. "Hit me like you mean it."

She tried to scramble away, and he yanked her onto her back. And then he dragged her by one arm to the center of the sheeting. Her head was in the puddle of oil. Her *hair*!

With a yell of outrage, she rolled up onto her knees and punched him in the shoulder. Hard.

"That-a-girl!" He blocked the next punch and rolled her onto her back again. His palm slapped her thigh, making the skin sting.

"You-you-you!" She kicked him in the gut, rolled over, and scrambled toward the exit. But her feet slid right out from under her, and he pulled her back by one ankle. His hands slipped on her slick skin, and she yanked her foot away and tried to escape again.

Ding-ding-ding. The timer went off noisily.

"Now there's a pity. You lose. Looks like I get to beat on you," Max said.

Despite his light tone, she could hear misery mixed with determination. He didn't want to hit her.

But he did.

Flattening her on her belly, Max put a knee in the center of her back, picked up the cane, and gave her five fast strokes.

She sucked it up, breathing through the pain, although tears filled her eyes. That was five. She tried to push up, expecting him to be done.

His weight stayed on her. After a couple of seconds, he hit her again. Paused. Again.

She screeched a protest. "What are you *doing*? It was only supposed to be five."

"Five minimum." His voice was rough. Tight. "I continue until I get tired or until someone makes me quit." He hit her again, harder.

She'd have bruises. Tears ran down her cheeks. He wasn't going to stop. Panic unfurled ungainly wings.

A pause. He hit her again. He'd go and go...*"Until someone makes me quit."*

Someone. Alastair had said, *"Whatever you need, ask your friend."* She turned her head.

Alastair stood at the edge of the sheeting. Worry and concern and determination were in his eyes.

She tried to say something. Couldn't.

With another slap of the cane, more burning pain streaked across her bottom.

"Please. Please help," she whispered. "Alastair, help."

His expression didn't change, but approval radiated from him. "Intruder, halt. No more caning."

The knee moved off her back, and she pulled in a breath.

"Aw, hell, I was starting to have fun."

Max was such a liar. His expression was tight. Unhappy. Then he tossed the cane into the grass—and flipped her onto her back.

She stared up into his intense blue eyes, seeing them lighten.

"Now, subbie." He fondled her slick breast and teased the nipple. "Open your legs as wide as you can."

"What?" At the look she got, she amended hastily, "Yes, Sir." Honestly, she'd been a trainee. Why was she having so much trouble doing as they said?

She inched her legs open, feeling the breeze hit her damp pussy, feeling the sun's warmth. Well, that explained it. She was having trouble because she was outside—not in a properly designated scene area in the Shadowlands.

She looked at the set of his jaw and opened her legs wider.

The other reason she was anxious was because of these Doms. At the Shadowlands, other Doms had been careful with her. Hadn't pushed her. These two utterly confident Masters deliberately made her nervous, shoving her out of her so-carefully arranged comfort zones.

If she hadn't been the one to ask them to help her, well, she might have hated them a little.

"That'll do." Max lay down between her open legs...and simply started licking her pussy. With each slow slide and wiggle of his tongue, a zinging pulse of electricity zapped through her. The increasing throb of need ramped up until she was squirming.

Chuckling, he stopped, leaving her right on the edge of an orgasm. The second the need faded, he drove her back there with a lick and rub over her clit.

For long, long minutes, he kept her on the pinnacle, past enjoyment to where arousal became pain, to where her desire turned into desperation and anger.

The sound she made through her gritted teeth was ugly.

"Have a problem, baby?" He swirled his tongue over her clit again. And stopped.

"I need..." Tears sprang to her eyes. How could he do this to her? She'd thought he liked her.

"What do most people do when they need something and can't get it themselves?"

She looked at him blankly. Then...ohhhh. "*Ask your friend,*" they'd said.

Turning her head, she saw Alastair. His arms were crossed on his chest. He lifted one eyebrow.

"Please, Sir, I..."

"What, Uzuri?" he asked softly.

Why was asking for help so difficult? What if he said no? What if he didn't think she was good enough? Omigod, how insane were those thoughts? She clenched her hands. "I...I...I want to come. Can—will you..."

But what could Alastair do?

"Good enough." Alastair tilted his head toward Max. "She's been a good girl. Get her off, please."

Max slanted her a look. "You're lucky you have good friends, Zuri." His gaze held hers as he let her absorb his comment. She had good friends.

Actually, she did. And she shouldn't have such trouble asking them for anything. Sneaky Doms with their *game* to teach her to fight *and* ask for help.

His lips curved. "You're catching on. Well, your friend wants you to be rewarded." His head lowered, and his lips closed over her clit, and his tongue went to work, lashing across the trapped, swollen nub. Hot and wet and irresistible.

With uncanny skill, he pulled her away from the precipice, drove her farther up the mountain toward a climax—and shoved her off.

Devastating pleasure ripped through her like a massive ball of lightning, expanding in sizzling eruptions of sensation. "Aaaaah, ah, ah, ah."

When his hand holding her hip slipped, his forearm came down on her pelvis, pinning her to the ground as he sadistically wrung every last spasm from her.

She lay on the sheeting, sweaty, oily, and exhausted.

Max held out a hand. "Time for round two."

"What?" Her hand felt limp in his strong one as he pulled her to a sitting position.

"I get to be your buddy this time." He rose and walked off the rubber.

If he was her "friend," did that mean Alastair would be the so-called "intruder"?

In answer, Alastair walked forward and went down on one knee in front of her. "Kneel, mischief. Remember, you have only three minutes to escape."

Seriously? She shook her head. "But—" Her bottom still hurt

from Max's caning—and *Alastair* was the sadistic Drago. And he'd have a cane. Her heart hammered as he pointed to her spot on the rubber sheeting.

With a low whine, she knelt in position.

Max started the timer. "Begin."

This time she totally lunged toward the marked "exit," and almost, almost made it.

With a laugh, Alastair dove forward and seized her ankle. Slick with oil, it slid from his grasp, and she gained another few inches. Her fingertips were on the green line when he landed on top of her like a ton of bricks.

Flattened, she yelled in anger, and the minute his weight was off of her, she tried to run again. And got nowhere.

"Jesus, hit him, Zuri." Max's voice came from the side.

At the pointed command, she threw a punch.

Alastair gave a grunt as her fist impacted his stomach. "No help from the sidelines unless she asks."

She got in one more punch.

"Bloody hell." he grunted. "Good job." He blocked the next and grabbed her, putting her belly-down on the sheeting.

Ding-ding-ding. The timer went off.

He shoved her legs apart and knelt between them, actually putting a knee on the back of her thigh to pin her down.

Instinctively, she strained against his hold. She was helpless. "*Koulangèt!*"

"That one of those Creole words?" Max tossed Alastair the cane.

The damn sadist whacked her five times right over the place she'd been hit before.

Okay, she shouldn't take the name of Christ in vain, but still...*ow, ow, ow.*

He didn't even pause before administering a sixth smack across the backs of her thighs.

"*Pike twa!*"

"I don't know what you said, young miss, but it didn't sound polite." He swatted her again.

Fuck you in English wouldn't sound better.

Wait. Max waited right over there. A *friend*.

"Help!" She lifted her head and begged. "Help me?"

"Anytime you ask, darlin'," he said. The sincerity in his voice pushed his words deep. "Sorry, cuz. Stop hurting her."

Alastair gave a hum of approval. "You were faster at asking this time, pet. Good." Still kneeling between her legs, he yanked her up onto her hands and knees. His grip tightened, and she quivered in his grasp as she felt his shaft press against her pussy.

That was all the warning she had before his cock drove in, penetrating her completely in one hard thrust.

She gasped. As he pulled back and thrust in again, she groaned at the slick, wonderful feeling.

Burying his hand in her hair, he tugged her head back even as he hammered into her.

"Toy, please," he called, and Max tossed him something. Suddenly, a vibrator was pressed against her clit, ramping her up and up, and...

He pulled it away before she could come. His cock slowed inside her, barely moving, keeping her on the edge. *Again. Damn them.*

In increasing frustration, she slammed back against him and forward, doing the work herself.

Laughing, he yanked on her hair, holding her head back until she couldn't budge—and then worked his hips so his cock moved in circles inside her. God, that felt good. With his other hand, he pressed the vibe against her clit for one second. Two.

And removed it again.

"*Cochon!*"

"That one I recognize, cuz. I think it's French for pig." Max was laughing. "She did mention her mother was Creole."

"I'll have to look up the other words," Alastair said like a fucking professor. As his cock slid in and out, ever so slowly, the vibrator touched her clit again.

Oh, ohhh. Her excitement built again, the heavy pressure inside her increasing quickly. She tilted her hips, trying for more. Just a little more. She needed to come so badly.

He moved the vibrator.

Damn him. She moaned. Her tight, swollen clit ached for relief.

Max—would Max help her? He was her friend. She tried to turn her head to see, to assess his face, but Alastair wouldn't release her hair.

A groan broke from her, low and pitiful. "M-Max. Sir. Please."

"Yes?"

He wasn't going to help her. A tear spilled down her cheek.

"Ask him, Uzuri." Alastair said in a low voice.

"Please. I hurt. Can I come?"

"You only had to ask, baby." Max's voice was gentle. "Make her happy, Doc."

"With pleasure." Alastair's deep laugh rang out, and suddenly he was hammering her hard—and the vibrator was pressed firmly against her clit.

The sensations burst across her nerves like a whirlwind of electricity. She went up and up and up. Everything inside her clamped down until her vagina was so tight around Alastair's cock that she could feel every ridge and vein. And then the pressure released all at once, contracting and convulsing. Pleasure lit her up like fireworks, exploding in a dazzling burst of sensation.

A second later, she felt Alastair pulsing inside her, and each hard jerk of his climax sent fresh pleasure through her.

He moved back into a kneeling position. With a hard arm around her waist, he pulled her backward onto his thighs, embedding himself even deeper. With his other hand, he rolled her nipples between his strong fingers.

Swamped by the sensations of being overpowered and impaled, she went over again, squirming helplessly in his arms.

When she finally went limp, the sadist laughed, pulled out, and laid her down on the rubber sheeting.

She lay where he'd put her, gasping for air.

"My turn." Max strolled onto the sheeting, and his eyebrow quirked up. "Doesn't look as if she's got much fight left."

"Her arse is getting sore enough, she might surprise you." Alastair patted her right on the swollen area they'd caned.

"Ow!" She rolled over and sat up, getting her tender backside out of his reach. Her head spun for a second, and she breathed deep, still feeling the internal quaking of the magnificent orgasm she'd had.

Alastair rose to his feet, easily, and walked over to the table, returning with a bottle of water, already uncapped. "Drink this, love."

She sucked it down, feeling her parched tissues reviving.

When she finished, Max took the bottle and tossed it out onto the grass. "Ready?"

"No."

"There's a shame." He went down on one knee and smiled at her. The glint in his eyes said he planned to take her this time and take her hard.

A shiver of anticipation grew inside her. But not enough to eliminate her determination to escape the caning this time.

She failed.

By the end of the battle, five more painful stripes lined her upper thigh, but this time she'd quickly asked Alastair to intervene. She'd had only five swats.

Max rolled Zuri onto her back and smiled down at her as he stroked his hands over her full breasts. The slickness was delightful.

So was the way she squirmed. He chuckled. She'd gotten off twice already. Apparently getting lightly caned—because they'd gone easy on her—and restrained was something she enjoyed. He caught Alastair's gaze and saw his cousin's slow smile.

Yeah, she could definitely keep up with two Doms...and he'd say she was ready to take them both at once.

Not today. Her first time in a threesome should be more romantic.

Right now, he wanted to be inside her. After all this playtime, he wasn't going to last long once he got there. "Toss me that new one, cuz."

Alastair picked up the second toy they'd prepared, the one that looked like a sexy beetle.

Uzuri frowned as he sat back and placed the round section over her clit, then tucked the soft, slender "arms" inside her puffy outer labia to keep it in place. "What's that?"

He pressed the button on top of the vibe to hit the highest setting and grinned as she gasped. Taking her hand, he pressed her palm over the device. "That's fun times, princess. Hold it there for me."

After pulling her legs around his waist, he leaned forward with a forearm beside her head. Slowly, he slid inside her very slick, hot cunt. *Oh yeah.*

Without being asked, she crossed her ankles above his ass.

He smiled at the feeling of her soft inner thighs pressing against his waist. "Perfect, baby. Now you can put your arms around my shoulders."

"We're having vanilla sex? Seriously?" As she looked up at him with liquid brown eyes, her grin was adorable.

"In a way." He settled into the saddle, as it were, and as his weight pressed the soft, buzzing vibrator against her clit, her eyes widened. When her cunt clenched around him, he laughed.

Then he got down to business, because damn, she felt good, especially with her arms and legs around him. As he thrust into her, hard and fast, he felt surrounded in heat and softness. The wet sound of his cock thrusting into her pussy was accompanied by the noise of the vibrator. The buzzing was softer when his weight came down on her, louder when he pulled back.

Within a minute, she was panting. Her fingernails digging into his shoulders reminded him of his job.

This is a lesson. Stay in control, Drago. He pulled back, keeping his cock inside by an inch, as he lifted his weight off the vibrator.

She let out a wail of frustrated disbelief. This time, there was no hesitation. Her head turned one way, then the other, as she looked for his cousin. She spotted him. "Sir. Please, please, please, Sir. Be my friend. I want to come. Please."

Alastair's laugh held his delight. "Yes, we're friends, pet. Give her what she needs, Max."

"Be my pleasure." Max dropped his weight back on her and drove in, angling to hit the G-spot with each hard thrust. *Might as well do it right.*

It took less than a minute.

Her little body went rigid; her fingers turned into claws, and her cunt clamped down like a vise before spasming hard around his shaft. *Oh, yeah.* As she came apart under him, he couldn't stop grinning. Fuck, she was gorgeous when she came.

He tossed the buzzing vibe to one side. Putting his elbows under her knees, he lifted up her legs, raising her pussy in the air, letting him go deeper as he pistoned into her.

The pressure built up at the base of his spine. Her cunt was still giving little contractions when his balls tightened up against his groin. Heat rushed downward, through his cock, and out in mind-blowingly pleasurable spasms.

When he let her knees go so he could come down on her, instead of objecting to his weight, she wrapped her legs around him again. His cock was deep inside her, her arms and legs were around him, and he lay there, savoring the most intimate embrace possible.

A tug deep in his chest cavity said he was falling for her. Falling hard and fast.

Uzuri had totally limp-noodle limbs as they yanked her up onto her hands and knees for the next round. With Alastair. Her butt and thighs still burned from the other canings—and she might cry if she got more.

She whined under her breath. She'd gotten off, each and every time, and all she wanted right now was a nap.

Alastair lined up behind her.

Max said, "Go."

Without waiting, Uzuri punched Alastair hard in the belly. Spinning around, she kicked him in the same place, used the impetus to shove her toward the exit—and over.

Shocked, she knelt there as the coarse St. Augustine grass prickled her knees and hands. She looked over her shoulder. Alastair sat on the sheeting, holding his stomach, and grinning.

"I escaped?" She rose to her feet and yelled, "I did it!" The victory dance came out of nowhere.

Even as she spun and boogied and giggled, she heard a cowboy *yeehaw* from Max. Alastair was clapping and laughing. Both were as pleased as she was that she'd conquered her fears. Had fought back. And won.

God, she loved them.

CHAPTER TWENTY-THREE

The next day was Thursday, and Uzuri swung by her duplex to get more clothes. Holt's Harley was in the driveway, still pinging slightly. He must have recently gotten home.

Apparently, he'd heard her car since he waited in the open door. "Hey, sweetie." He tugged her into his arms for a long, warm embrace. The Dom had hugging down to an art, and the day's irritations drained right out of her.

With a sigh of happiness, she squeezed him back. Holt was one of her favorite people in the whole world. Like every woman in the Shadowlands, she'd lusted after him. At first. But as she'd come to know him, he'd reminded her more and more of Nicky.

She'd met Nicky when she wrecked her skateboard and sat bawling on the sidewalk. Taking pity on her, the big teenager had bandaged her knees and walked her home to her apartment. The tough blond lived a flight up and turned into the big brother she'd never had. Nicky'd protected her from mean dogs, bullies, and perverts, teased her about doll costumes, and shoplifted new fabrics for her. When he and his father moved away, she'd mourned him like family.

Like Nicky, Holt had turned into family. She grinned up at him. "I've missed you."

"Me, too, you."

She stepped back. "How's life? Are you getting caught up on your sleep now you're somewhere quiet?"

"Yep." Taking her hand, he pulled her into the house. "I'd forgotten what non-apartment life is like. Sure, I can hear Mrs. Avery sometimes, but since she's—what eighty?—she's not into wall-banging sex, horror flicks, or playing grunge rock so loud the dishes rattle. And duplexes share only one wall with someone else. Not four walls and the ceiling and floor, too."

She laughed. In her last apartment, she'd always known when the construction worker upstairs was home. *Thump, thump, thump.* "I like this better. In an apartment, when the neighbor's children screamed, I'd get irritated. Here, when the kids are playing outside, it feels...nice. Like a home."

"Yeah. That's it exactly." He led the way to the kitchen. "Beer? Coke?"

"If there's diet."

"Considering the six-pack is one you left, yes, there's diet Coke." He handed her a can from the fridge and pulled out a beer for himself. "Gotta admit, I didn't expect to see you. Did you have a fight with your Doms and want your place back? Or are you here to see if I've destroyed the place? Or maybe to pick up some girly shit?"

Giggling, she leaned against the counter. "Answer C. I didn't pack much since I thought I'd be back here within a couple of days."

"Yet, you're still there." Holt sat at the table, rested a boot on the chair next to him, and studied her. Like Max, his eyes were blue, but Max's were an intense Caribbean blue, deep enough to drown in. Holt's gray-blue eyes were like the sky on a windy winter's day.

"I am. But..."

"But?" Holt crossed his arms over his chest, his tattooed biceps stretching the faded black System of a Down T-shirt. "How is it going with your two Masters?"

"I'm not sure." Uzuri smoothed her dark red, linen skirt. "They treat me like...like Jake treats Rainie. Like Galen and Vance treat Sally."

"Like you're their submissive?"

She nodded as confusion welled inside her again. "And like they...care."

Holt's brows drew together. "We all care about you, Zuri."

"I know." Well, maybe she hadn't truly realized it before. Now she did. "Only they're acting"—she frowned—"possessive? Different somehow."

At the Shadowlands on Saturday, they hadn't played. She'd had a barmaid shift, and they'd been dungeon monitoring, but they'd constantly checked on her and made it clear to everyone that she was under their protection. That she was...theirs.

"Right." With a finger, Holt rubbed his mouth as if to wipe a smile away. "I did get the impression they see you as...hmm... perhaps, more permanent than you realize."

The happiness swelling inside her was disconcerting. Nevertheless, those were the words she'd wanted to hear, because she was starting to see them as more than temporary Masters. As if they were hers. As if she could have a...a relationship with them. "They do?"

"Yeah, sweetheart. But how do *you* feel?"

She dropped into a chair across from him at the table and let her despair show. "Oh, Holt, I think I'm falling in love."

Taking her hand, he rubbed the back with his thumb. "Looks like it to me. Why's that a problem? Don't you want to love anyone?"

"I do." She traced a water stain on the tabletop. "I grew up hearing stories about my wonderful daddy and all the sweet things he'd do for my mama. I don't remember him well, but they were completely in love. She never got over losing him."

His voice darkened. "I'm glad you had a start to life like that."

"I'm sorry you didn't, boo." She studied the strong, lean hand holding hers. When she'd first met him, she'd labeled him California beach boy. All tan and muscled, with streaky blond hair and chiseled features. He looked a lot like the actor who played Thor in the movies. In fact, in college, he'd picked up extra money modeling.

However, he was much more than merely gorgeous. Considering the ugly start he'd had in life, he could have been a brutal, vicious killer rather than one of the finest people she knew.

With a shrug, he squeezed her fingers. "I'm glad you haven't given up on love. That you got past the asshole stalker."

"Finally." Her lips tightened. "I'm doing my best to forget he ever existed."

"Atta-girl." Dimples showed in his cheeks when he smiled.

"Bro, you really are too good-looking for words."

His laugh was like the smoky whisky Alastair liked so much. One Shadowlands submissive said she could come just from hearing him laugh. "Tell me, did you fall for one of the Drago cousins or both of them?"

"Both." Uzuri shook her head. "Which is strange considering how different they are." Max with his cop sternness, more openly friendly, yet far less trusting than Alastair who, despite that British reserve, still believed in the basic goodness in people. Max had a huge heart, especially for anyone weaker. Alastair's heart was as big, but...the doc edged disconcertingly close to sadism with how he loved pushing her right to the boundary between pain and pleasure.

Complicated guys. She truly did love them both.

"You tell them how you feel?"

"Are you a crazy-pants?"

He busted out laughing. "Want me to share how you feel with your Masters? Seems like something a friend should do."

Could she slaughter her so-called best friend and stuff his body in the closet? No, that would be rude. She settled for a dirty look.

"Yeah, I'm scared now." He pretended to shiver.

Forget politeness. Which closet should she use?

Then again, killing him would leave her carpets blood-stained, and his body would be awfully heavy to drag around. Instead, she tried out the puppy-dog look that Hunter managed so well. "You wouldn't tell...would you?"

"No, sweetie." A glint in his eyes said he knew she was playing him. Then his expression turned grave. "However, I want to know why *you* aren't sharing how you feel with them."

She sighed. "They signed on to help me—for a set time period —not to get some wimpy subbie thinking their help means hearts and flowers and forever."

"Yeah?" Holt shook his head. "I figured the time period was more to reassure you than to put limits on *them*. Nonetheless, I doubt you'll stay uncertain for long. Not with those two."

Hope leapt up and...crashed down again. After his experience with bitch Hayley, Max wouldn't want to get involved with another woman for a long time. She made her lips curve up. "I need to get my stuff and get moving. It's my turn to cook tonight."

As she headed out of the kitchen, Holt gave a pitiful sigh. "I could use some homemade meals."

"Oh, please. You could get any woman you wanted over here to cook for you." After packing her nail polish and mani-pedi kit, she gathered clothing. Opening a dresser drawer, she stared at the underwear that wasn't hers. "You're a cross-dresser, now, dude?"

"I'm a *what*?" He appeared in the doorway, saw the drawer, and chuckled. "I told Nadia she could leave some spare clothes here."

"Is she the blonde lawyer or the redheaded broker?"

"Redhead."

Uzuri grimaced. Master Raoul didn't like that woman.

Holt always juggled his multiple women with such skill, charm, and honesty that none felt misused. None had ever been allowed to leave clothes in his place. Until now. "Are you serious about her?"

"Well..." The uncomfortable way he moved his shoulders was a dead giveaway.

"You are!" Although the redhead wasn't who Uzuri would choose for him, at least he'd found someone to care about. "Good for you. Have you told her?" She waggled her head at his silence. "Want me to share how you feel? Seems like something a friend should do."

He scowled, displeased at getting his own threat back. "Remind me to tell your new Masters about some of your dislikes. Like having your toes played with."

She narrowed her eyes at him. "I have more Styrofoam balls, you know."

Unfazed, he only laughed and left her to her packing.

A few minutes later, Holt lugged her oversized tote out to her car for her. "Come on by next week and tell me what happens. Besides, you'll need more clothes by then." He grinned.

Truth was truth. She would definitely need more clothes. "Okay. Just in case, be prepared to move out."

"Right."

She threw her arms around him and gave him a hearty hug. "It was good to see you again."

"It was." He dropped a kiss on her forehead. "Be a good subbie and don't get in too much trouble, okay?"

"Pffft. Those Dragon Doms need something to shake them up a bit, don't you think?"

"Yeah. You could tell them you love them."

That kept her silent all the way home.

CHAPTER TWENTY-FOUR

At the Shadowlands that weekend, Uzuri tried the door. As expected this early in the evening, it was locked. She pushed the dragon doorbell on the side panel.

After a few seconds, Ben opened the heavy oak door and smiled down at her. The muscular security guard was huge, at least a couple of inches taller than her Dragon Doms. "C'mon in, Zuri."

Uzuri followed him into the entry, shaking her head at his faded Willie Nelson T-shirt and jeans. Apparently, Master Z's Halloween theme night of heroes and villains didn't apply to him.

As he walked behind his desk, he grinned. "Are you Wonder Woman?"

Uzuri glanced down at her metallic-appearing breastplate, short golden skirt of leather flaps, and long, golden wrist gauntlets. Her costume—and Andrea's—had taken forever to construct. "No, Andrea is Wonder Woman. I'm Philippus who was occasionally Queen of the Amazons as well as Diana's trainer."

Perched on Ben's desk in a Supergirl outfit, Jessica grinned. She'd also perused Sally's stash of comic books last week for inspiration. "I remember her. She was black and tough and hot. You look perfect."

"Thank you." Uzuri flexed her arm and eyed her biceps dubiously. She might have failed on the *tough* part of the assignment. "Where's Sophia? Who's with her?"

"She's in bed already." Jessica held up a baby monitor. "I'll hear her if she wakes up."

"Nice that you can run up and down from the third floor," Ben said. "When our baby comes, Anne and I will be juggling schedules."

"Actually, Z's considering hiring a manager for the club and letting him or her have our place. He wants Sophia to grow up in a quiet, safe neighborhood where there are other children around. Above a BDSM club? Uh-uh."

Uzuri glanced at the inner door, thinking of the paddles and floggers adorning the walls. The chains dangling from the ceiling beams. "I'd worry, too. I sure snooped into everything when I was little."

"Me, too. At least we're safe until Sophia starts to walk." Jessica grinned. "And as long as I'm here, I can help with Shadowkitten shenanigans."

"Shenanigans, huh? Whatcha up to this time?" Ben asked Uzuri. "You already know how to open a combination lock. Hell, you're faster than I am."

"I needed to be." After he'd shown her the trick, she practiced constantly. Sneaking into the Masters' locker room was as foolhardy as a mouse checking out a bowl of cat food.

"Today, I need help with this." From her tote bag, she pulled out the padlock she'd bought.

He took it from her. "Why? Z uses only combination locks on the lockers."

"I know. Would you believe Alastair and Max padlocked their *toy bags*?" She gave him a disgusted frown. "Somebody warned them."

Ben's hearty laugh made the walls echo. "Probably every Dom in the club warned them." He tossed the lock in the air and caught it. "No worries, sweetie. These are even easier than combination locks. Got a bobby pin?"

"I do." Jessica pulled one out of her hair and handed it over.

"First we make our tools." He pulled the rubber off the bobby pin and bent the end. "Bobby pins work well. Or there are alternatives." He held up a pen. After removing the metal pocket clip, he bent the tip and inserted it into the keyhole.

"Keep pressure on the lever." He picked up the bobby pin. "Then put in the rake and wiggle it until you feel a release."

The tiny sound was almost inaudible. He yanked up the curved padlock top. "Open."

"Wow." Wiggling with anticipation, Uzuri tossed back her cape and held out her hand. "May I try?"

As she carefully followed his instructions, he watched closely, giving further directions on how to adjust for different locks.

Keeping tension on the pen part as she raked the bobby pin over the keyhole innards, she felt something give. She grinned. "*There.*"

"Perfect," Ben said. "Now, keep turning the lever upward, yeah?"

The lock opened.

"That was fun!" Snapping the padlock shut, she bent to do it again.

Fifteen minutes later, tools firmly in hand, she followed Jessica to the Masters' locker-room.

Tossing her blonde hair out of the way, Jessica punched a code into the keypad outside the door.

Nervously, Uzuri glanced behind her at the silent main club-room. "Does Master Z know that you help us?" It was one thing messing with her Doms—or even the regular Masters—but Master Z was a whole different category of threat.

Jessica held open the door. "I'm pretty sure he suspects.

Thankfully, he prefers not to interfere in interactions between other Doms and their submissives. If I actually...did...anything to annoy a Master, I might get in trouble, but hey, I'm simply holding open a door, right?"

Uzuri snorted. "Don't try that excuse with an officer of the law."

"Cops are a special breed. Thank goodness Dan married a sweetie like Kari rather than sneaky females like us." Laughing, Jessica poked her in the shoulder. "You, however, might have chosen the wrong Doms. Max looks like he's as strict as Dan."

"You have no idea."

"Is that why the raid on their bags?"

"Totally. You should've seen how mean they were to me this morning. Three separate punishments." The paddling was bad. Having to wear a giant anal plug was worse. She'd walked like a duck for two hours. And the third...

Walking down the row of lockers, Uzuri spotted her Doms' names. The inscribed metal tags Master Z used were very helpful, not that she'd mention that to him.

"How come the punishments?" Jessica asked.

"Oh..." Uzuri opened her bag and removed the cutout from a soda can. "I didn't do a weight workout for a couple of days. Sometimes I don't feel like getting all sweaty, you know?"

"I hear you." Jessica grimaced. "Z decided I wasn't getting enough exercise, and now I have to walk all the paths in the garden every morning, even when it's raining. What were the other things?"

"There was—" Uzuri's cheeks heated. She hadn't put in the butt plug for two days. Because... well, having a Dom insert it was okay. Kind of dirty, and yet sexy. But shoving something in there herself was too gross. *Eww.*

And telling Jessica that would be TMI.

Jessica sat on the bench and looked up expectantly. "Was what?"

"Um. Nothing much." Flustered, Uzuri skipped to her third punishment. "The third was the worst." Alastair'd asked if she'd called anyone for Monday's conference at Brendall's. Her evasions hadn't worked—and he'd pointed out she'd had over two days to act. "They cuffed my hands behind my back and my legs together for three hours, and I had to beg them for food or water, to scratch an itch, to use a Kleenex, or even for help in the bathroom, and omigod, it was so humiliating. All because I didn't call my friends to ask them for help. I can't believe they—"

"Wait... What kind of help?" Jessica's eyes narrowed. "Aren't I your friend?" She waved her hand at the locker-room. "We break-and-enter together, right? Why didn't you call me?"

"I..." Unable to bear Jessica's displeasure, Uzuri concentrated on the combination locks on the Dragon Doms' lockers. It only took a minute or two to get both locks open using the cutout. *Thank you, Ben.* She and Sally had made good use of the skill more than once.

A girl had to wonder about what other tricks those Special Ops soldiers knew.

"*Uzuri...*" Jessica tapped her foot.

"Girl, you've got Master Z's tone down pat." With a resigned sigh, Uzuri faced one of the nicest, bestest friends a woman could have. "Helping with Shadowlands pranks is one thing. I know you like getting involved. But this is something not related to the Shadowlands, and getting you—everybody—to show up on a Monday morning would mean you'd have to make baby arrangements and go out of your way and—"

"Oh, my God, Zuri, just *ask* me."

Uzuri felt like pounding her head on a wall. *I did it again.* Talk about being dense. And slow. She needed to get over this hang-up. After a breath, she launched into the explanation. "There's a problem where I work. I saw this sales associate catering to the rich people and—"

"Carole? The one who let the air out of your tire?"

At this evidence of how closely Jessica had listened, Uzuri blinked. "Um. Yes. And since then, the morale in sales for that department has gone downhill, and so sales are…"

As Uzuri gave Jessica the story, she set Alastair's toy bag on the bench. After inserting the "lock pick" from the pen clip into the padlock, she manipulated the bent bobby pin.

Click. She pulled the lock open and bounced on her toes in victory.

"Good job. And I'll be there on Monday." Jessica hesitated. "I'm not going to contact the rest of the gang. Your Doms are right; you need to learn to ask for help."

Finishing with her exchanges, Uzuri put the padlock back on and set the bag in his locker. Finally, she looked up to meet Jessica's eyes. "I understand. I'm sorry I didn't ask you earlier. It's…hard."

"Hey, Andrea has almost the same problem. And you did ask me—finally." Jessica frowned. "You're always helping everyone else, Zuri. Babysitting, giving fashion advice—even critiquing swimsuit selfies which is way above and beyond friendship limits—and being there when one of us has guy problems. You do margarita therapy. You have to let us help *you* sometimes or the balance feels off."

"Oh." Uzuri hadn't looked at it like that. Friendship should go both ways.

"But this is your warning. If I don't see a bunch of our friends on Monday, I'll tell everybody you were afraid to ask for help. Can you imagine the grief you'll get?"

Uzuri looked at her in horror. "You—you're evil."

"Cool threat, huh? Comes from living with Z." Grinning, Jessica rose. "I wish I could help here, but I have to be able to say I've never touched anything inside the Masters' room. With luck, he'll never ask about the keypad outside."

"If I had Master Z for a Dom, I sure wouldn't be touching any keypads." Uzuri pulled Max's bag out and almost dropped it. What did he have in there—lead weights?

Almost at the door, Jessica glanced at the wall clock. "You'd better hurry. The Masters' meeting won't last much longer."

"I will. Thank you." Uzuri started to rummage through Max's bag and realized she didn't have time to snoop. Instead, she switched out the various items and pulled the Max doll from her own bag. "Ready for action, Detective Dragon? You totally look *up* to the job."

Jessica glanced over her shoulder and sputtered. "Oh my God, Max's going have a fit!"

"Mmmhmm." Snickering, Uzuri laid Detective Dragon in the bag, zipped it up, and relocked the bag and lockers.

As she slipped out of the room, she heard the Masters coming downstairs and through Master Z's private entrance. Cullen's booming voice echoed in the hallway.

When Alastair's deep laugh and Max's rougher chuckle followed, her heart did a slow somersault of happiness in her chest. No, more than happiness, it was *love*. She loved them. *Loved. Them.*

Then she thought of the sabotaged toy bags and froze. Oh, no. Oh, *no*, what had she done? Sure, the dolls were funny, and if her Masters spotted them at home, they'd laugh their fool heads off.

But here? In public? And with the rest of the stuff she'd done?

Dread shook her, and she ran back to the locker room. She had to get that stuff out.

Only the door was locked and Jessica was gone.

———

Toy bag over his shoulder and with Alastair beside him, Max led their little submissive across the clubroom toward the scene area they'd chosen to use.

Hell of a place tonight, he had to say. It seemed the Shadow-lands' membership got into costume nights, especially a Halloween theme. The submissives were all in brightly colored superhero costumes. He passed a "little" in a PowerGirl costume and two gay slaves wearing Batman and Robin outfits. Raoul's Kim was dressed as Aquagirl.

Master Z had decreed that "good" would suffer tonight which meant Dominants, Masters, and Tops were all villains.

Max glanced down at their own little superhero. He hadn't seen her costume before, since she'd changed at Andrea and Cullen's. Shoulder guards were held in place by several gold chains. He ran a finger over the guards and realized they were made of gold foil and matched the arm and shin gauntlets. Some-how, she'd transformed a bustier into what looked like a gold metal breastplate. Her ass was covered by golden leather lappets; the strips of leather hung to mid-thigh like a gladiator kilt. A dark red cape finished off the look.

She was incredibly sexy.

Her hair was cornrowed tightly to her scalp, which suited a warrior queen. Her brows were darker. Gold eye shadow and thick black liner made her eyes huge.

Those eyes were turned to the floor rather than taking in all the other costumes around. He frowned. "You're awfully quiet, princess. Are you still angry about this morning's punishments?"

Silently, she shook her head no.

A fizzle of concern made him study her more closely. Tense shoulders. Walking farther from him than normal. Head bowed. Eyes lowered.

If she'd been a suspect, he'd reckon her guilty.

He alerted Alastair with a glance. His cousin turned his atten-tion to their pretty woman. An eyebrow went up.

"You been up to something that we should know about?" Max asked.

The slight hesitation in her stride and the tiny hunch of her shoulders shouted the answer. "I'm female. I'm always up to things."

"Of course you are." Alastair pointed to a clear space inside the roped-off scene area. "Kneel there."

As she sank to her knees, eyes still down, Max frowned. Every muscle in her body was tense.

Well, whatever she'd done, they'd figure it out and deal. "Good thing we lock our bags," he told Alastair in a low voice. He pulled his keys out of his pocket. "Want to use your leather cuffs tonight? They fit her better than mine do."

"Agreed." Alastair unlocked his bag and rummaged through it. His hand stilled. "Bloody *hell*."

Max stared down into his own bag. "Seriously?"

A glance at Uzuri showed she hadn't moved. Gaze down. The hands on her thighs were clenched. Little mischief was worried. As she should be.

Spotting a cluster of Shadowkittens, he said quietly, "We got company, cuz." Some Doms were gathering as well. *Well, hell.*

He looked at his bag again. His sturdy leather cuffs had been swapped with a cutesy pink set. With rhinestones.

Alastair lifted his exchange—blue with silvery paisley patterns.

Max's ropes looked like an artistic macramé job.

Alastair pulled out his flogger. Same artist.

Beneath the ropes, Max found the grand prize. "His" brown-haired, beard-shadowed doll wore jeans, a white button-up shirt, boots, and a police belt complete with holstered pistol and night-stick. The jeans were open and pulled down far enough to accommodate the doll's balls and giant—erect—dick. The cock and testicles were lashed together in a genitorture device made of tiny chains that would impress even sadistic Mistress Anne.

He could swear he felt his balls shriveling, and a chuckle escaped him.

Alastair's deep laugh rang out as he motioned to his bearded replica in the bag. The doll wore a lab coat—and nothing else. A tiny stethoscope was knotted around the big black erection.

Max eyed the dolls' cocks. She'd even gotten the proportions correct. His thicker; Alastair's longer. "Jesus. Show and tell time?"

"Might as well. So they understand her crime." Still grinning, Alastair held up the two dolls.

Laughter swept the entire area.

"Gotta say, we were warned," Max muttered.

Alastair set the doll back into his bag. "By more than a few. I thought we'd taken adequate precautions. You checked your bag before we left, didn't you?"

"Oh yeah. The sabotage was performed here." Max picked up the lock. "How did a Catholic schoolgirl learn to pick locks?"

Their little submissive looked as if she was shrinking. She knew she was in trouble.

Understanding grins came from the other Shadowlands Masters. Yeah, many of them had also been on the receiving end of the brats' pranks.

Standing on the other side of the scene rope, Z glanced at the padlock in Max's hand and nodded toward the exit. "*Ben.*"

Ben? Right. The security guard had served as an Army Ranger. Although pranks weren't his style, the guy wouldn't balk at "helping out" if a cutie-pie like Uzuri asked. Max smiled wryly. "Good to know."

Z tilted his head in acknowledgment, then reached out an arm, and casually snagged Jessica...by her long blonde hair. "I believe it's time we discussed keypads, kitten." Ignoring her worried squeaks, he led her away. Toward the back.

"Well." Alastair lifted his eyebrows. "Apparently our girl had no trouble asking for help to sabotage toy bags."

"So it seems." Now what to do about it?

Somehow, he and Alastair had to teach their subbie where the limits lay...without breaking her spirit, since, hell, he'd laughed. If a subbie heard her Dom laugh, he'd already lost the high ground.

He moved closer to Alastair. "I'll give her points for originality and cuteness. The dolls would've been fine if we'd been at home. But I wish she hadn't busted into our bags."

"As do I. The first day, you quite clearly told her to stay out of our bags—and direct disobedience goes a step too far." Alastair's tone was grim as he frowned at Zuri.

She looked so little. So helpless. Neither of them liked punishing her, dammit, and she'd already been spanked this morning. Max shook his head. "Cuz, we can't hurt her again. It's gotta be something else."

"Agreed." Alastair considered. "We have disobedience along with embarrassing her Doms. What are appropriate consequences?"

"Embarrassment goes both ways." Max smiled slowly. "I could take offense to having chains wrapped around my dick."

Alastair's gaze met his. "Chains?"

Max grinned. "I've been carrying some since you teased her about it."

"Public consequences and the chains. Medical room or bondage table or..." Alastair looked toward the center of the room. "Cullen mentioned the recent lack of bar ornaments."

Max had watched a submissive be tied to the bar soon after he'd joined. Couldn't get more public than that. "Well hell, we'd best do something before Cullen gets cranky."

Alastair shook his head. "Do you want to bring her or shall I?"

"Cuz, you know you like scaring little subbies, especially since, normally, you come across as so fucking reassuring."

"So little they know." Alastair headed for Uzuri.

After slinging both toy bags over his shoulder, Max moved out, passing the audience they'd gathered. Standing beside Sam and Anne, Nolan grinned and stepped out of his way.

Near the three Shadowlands Masters, a newer member said to his friend, "I'm thinking Uzuri doesn't much respect those so-called Masters of hers."

"Obviously." His friend puffed up. "She sure never tried stupid tricks when I topped her."

Brows together, Sam turned. "That little girl only plays tricks on Doms she trusts. She got me good once. Nolan, too. And Anne." The sadist's sandpaper voice was harsh enough to scour the hide from the two pups. "You sayin' she doesn't respect *us*?"

Both Doms took several hasty steps back.

Ignoring them completely, the silver-haired rancher gave Max an approving nod. "I worried when she moved in with you two, but you got past her defenses and earned her trust."

"Good job." Nolan slapped Max's back. "A warning, though. Don't let her fuck with your beer."

Beer, too? Hell. "Thanks for the heads-up."

"Max." Anne had a dangerous glint in her eyes. "I heard Z. You know, when rubber cockroaches infested my locker, I didn't consider how the subbies had gotten in." The Mistress glanced toward the entry. "Ben and I will have a...chat...about his helpful ways. Tell Uzuri her doll's excellent modeling of cock and ball torture won't go to waste."

As she stalked toward the exit, Max glanced at the other two Masters. "I think my balls just tried to climb into my belly."

"Ben's fucked. Even an Army Ranger can't win against a pissed-off Mistress." Nolan shook his head. "Especially a pregnant one."

Sam snorted. "The boy's gonna be walking bowlegged for a while."

"Yeah." Feeling almost sorry for the poor bastard, Max continued to the bar.

"Hey, buddy." Cullen looked up from the drink he was concocting. "I hope you have a nasty deterrent planned so Wonder Woman there doesn't get ideas." He tilted his head toward Andrea who was drawing a beer.

Max knew Uzuri'd worked with Andrea on their "Amazonian" costumes. Andrea's breastplate was red, the leather kilt a dark blue, and she definitely had the figure to pull off the outfit. Max gave her an appreciative look. "Great costume. You know, I think marriage agrees with her."

"With us both. I can't wait until my super heroine attempts to arrest me." With two-day beard scruff and dirty dark clothes, Cullen looked suitably villainous.

"Mmm." Max noticed the golden lasso clipped to Andrea's belt. "Aren't you lucky that Wonder Woman brought her own rope for you to use?"

Cullen grinned, then nodded at the toy bags over Max's shoulder. "Want me to store those behind the bar?"

"Actually, we thought you'd like a bar ornament. Or, perhaps I should say, a bar show."

"Hell, yeah. About time someone decorated my bar." Cullen spread his hands out to encompass the bar area. "*Mi taberna es su taberna*."

"Was that supposed to be Spanish?" Behind him, Andrea made gagging sounds.

Cullen yanked her close. "Silence, wife." Fisting her hair, he took her mouth in an effective silencing technique.

Grinning, Max moved to the end of the bar. To keep observers from infringing on the scene, he set towels and toy bags on the closer bar stools to mark the boundaries. The play would get messy, so he spread disposable barrier cloths on the bar top and the floor below.

Good enough. He shook his head. Poor little Zuri was in for it, tonight.

He looked up. The rafter over the bar held a wealth of heavy chains clipped up out of the way. Reaching high, he unclipped the two closest to the end of the bar so they dangled within easy reach.

A shocked gulp came from his right, and he turned.

Uzuri stood next to Alastair, his hand on her shoulder. Her wide-eyed gaze was on the chains.

"S-sir, what are you *doing*?" The sheer horror in her question told Max the scene was getting off to a fine start.

Perfect. He didn't have the heart to punish her severely, not for high spirits. Not when he enjoyed her pranks. Yet all D/s relationships required a certain level of control from the Dominants. Not responding to outright disobedience would destroy the unspoken contract between them. Would let them all down.

Communication first. "I'm setting up for a scene, little mischief. Unfortunately, our plan for a private sensual session had to be changed."

Her gaze dropped. "I'm sorry."

"So are we." Alastair moved beside Max until their shoulders touched, presenting their subbie with a solid wall of authority. "Tell us why you're in trouble."

Despite her white-knuckled grip on one wrist gauntlet, she straightened her spine and looked up. "I messed with the stuff in your bags."

"Well, that doesn't sound so bad, does it?" Max gave his voice the edge that could frighten hardened criminals.

Her shoulders hunched.

"Can you explain to me why Max seems...annoyed?" The doc's warm *you-can-trust-me, let-me-help* tone had dropped to icy cold.

Her bottom lip trembled. "He t-told me to leave your bags alone, and I didn't."

"Yes, you disobeyed a direct order," Max raised his voice so the people nearby could hear.

"Continue," Alastair said.

"I did it because I was mad," she whispered.

"I would indeed label this a vengeful trick." Alastair's British accent had become clipped. "Continue."

With each *continue*, she shrank more. "I shouldn't have done it here."

"Yes, you planned your misbehavior where the entire club could see," Alastair agreed.

His deliberate wording got through to her. Her head jerked up, and she stared around as if realizing where she was standing—and why. Her face turned a couple of shades lighter.

In a subtle movement, Alastair rubbed his shoulder against Max. *Hand-off.*

"I like the doll, Zuri, but gotta say, I don't like having my dick on display." Max chilled his voice. "Let alone in a cock and ball torture with chains wrapped around my junk."

Nice flinch.

Max removed her cape and lifted her onto the bar. Her tiny nervous yip hardened his shaft.

"Since you like combining chains and genitals, we shall use that as the theme for this session," Alastair said.

Her lovely brown eyes went wide, and she tried to slide off the bar.

"Sit. Still." Alastair said softly, and she froze. Hook by hook, Alastair unfastened her golden Amazon bustier, then laid it on a stool.

Breasts exposed, she sat quietly, all resistance gone.

Break a man's heart, she could. Max removed her shoulder and shin guards, then her gauntlets before putting a hand behind her neck. He pulled her down so he could kiss her trembling lips.

When he stepped back, she peeked at him, quivering with anxiety. "Are you really mad at me?"

"Zuri, do we sound mad?" Max asked. With any luck, she'd never realize they'd never been angered at all.

"Yes. No. Not completely. I...I don't like pain."

Max slid his hand down her long, elegant throat to her bare breast. Lightly, he pinched one velvety nipple, increasing the pressure until she sucked in air.

The dark red of arousal tinged her skin—and both nipples stood up.

"Your body likes pain now and then, baby." He turned his hand over and brushed his knuckles over the hard peaks.

"Would we ever do anything to hurt you past what you can take?"

Without even a hesitation, she shook her head. "No."

"Do you trust us?" He was sorely tempted to ask the other question. *Do you love us?*

"Yes," she whispered.

After kissing her forehead, he glanced at his cousin.

Alastair handed over leather cuffs he'd obtained from behind the bar. Good thing Z kept spares there. No way would any self-respecting Dom use glittering pink ones. *Jesus.* As Max cuffed Zuri's ankles, his cousin fastened cuffs on her wrists.

"Lie back, pet." Alastair positioned Zuri so she lay along the bar with her legs dangling off the end of the oval. He clipped her wrist cuffs together. "Chain?"

Max dug in his bag for the short lengths and handed one over along with a couple of carabiner snap hooks.

Alastair fastened the chain to Zuri's cuffs and pulled her arms over her head. He fastened the other end of the chain to one of the iron rings recessed into the bar surface.

Max grinned. He'd never seen a bar top designed for bondage as well as drinking. He pulled off Zuri's leather kilt, leaving her naked except for the leather cuffs. After clipping one end of a short chain to her right ankle cuff, he lifted her leg and snap-hooked the other end to the chain dangling from the rafter. Her leg was suspended straight up in the air. He did the same to the left and stepped back to enjoy the sight.

Naked submissive, flat on her back on the bar top, arms over her head, legs raised high in a nice wide V. Her ass was conveniently right near the edge where the oval bar curved at the end.

He curled an arm around her leg, kissed her inner thigh, and felt the fine trembling under the soft skin. When he saw the worry on her face, he frowned. "Zuri?"

Was she up for this? They could revise the plan...

Looking at him, she pulled in a slow breath and gave a nod.

Okay. Okay, then.

Alastair huffed a laugh and handed him a subbie blanket. "It is odd how everyone here thinks *I'm* the softhearted Dom."

"They'll soon learn better." Max'd also noticed that the "sadist" had his fingers wrapped around Zuri's forearm in both assessment and reassurance. Half-grinning, Max stuffed the rolled-up blanket under Zuri's ass to raise it up another six inches higher than her head, giving it a good tilt, then adjusted the leg chains again.

Hmm. A waist strap?

Nah.

With the wrist restraints and the legs up and wide, she couldn't go anywhere. He and Alastair enjoyed watching a submissive struggle, and Zuri's body was designed for pretty wiggles. "We're good."

"Isn't she lovely?" Alastair said under his breath as he smiled down at their restrained woman.

"Oh, yeah."

Her eyes were bright, her color slightly darker with arousal, her breathing fast. A little anxious. Not terrified, despite being restrained and having two big guys looming over her. She trusted them.

The knowledge spread warmth through Max's veins.

Alastair leaned down to take a slow kiss and then played with her breasts. Her nipples were soon bunched into jutting peaks.

Max grinned. His cousin did like breasts, no doubt about it, and Uzuri's were especially fine. Max planted his forearms on the bar top, parallel to her upper arm. "I think a warm-up is in order. Your choice, Doc."

Alastair walked over to his bag. "I'd planned to use my softest flogger today, but I don't have time to undo the knots."

Zuri's guilty—and worried—expression was damn cute.

Max squeezed her fingers in reassurance and flattened his

other hand between her bare breasts. Now, that was a fast little heartbeat, wasn't it?

Out of Zuri's field of vision, Alastair opened his bag. He removed the mushroom-headed Hitachi vibrator, quietly plugged it into the electrical socket at the foot of the bar, and laid it to one side. "Perhaps"—he held up a crop—"this might be an adequate alternative."

Max grinned. Trust an Englishman to like something invented for riding. The long black shaft ended in a two-inch wide square of black leather. *No, wait.* The crop had *two* strips of leather rather than the traditional one, which meant it'd make an even louder slapping sound.

Palm on Zuri's chest, Max felt her tense.

Alastair gave her a long look. "What's the safeword here, little mischief?"

Her voice was almost inaudible. "Red. Sir."

"Very good. You sing out if anything starts to hurt too much." Sensitizing her skin, Alastair teased the leather squares of the crop over her right thigh, her mound, then the left thigh—and back again. With each circuit, he'd brush his knuckles over her pussy, keeping her as excited as she was anxious.

Under Max's palm, her heart thudded harder.

Around them, the normal club activities had resumed. Cullen and Andrea were serving drinks and chatting with people near the bar. Conversations hummed with occasional bursts of laughter. From the room's perimeter came the slap of paddles and hands, the thuddier sounds of floggers, cries, and moans. One submissive begged for release in a high voice; a male sub cursed as he sobbed.

Lightly, Alastair flicked the crop up the inside of Zuri's right thigh, checking her face and muscles between each stroke.

Although she'd sucked in a deep breath with the noisy snap of the first blow, she was doing well. Max noticed she wasn't even flinching, despite the noisy slapper crop.

Time to add more sensation.

CHAPTER TWENTY-FIVE

The backs of Uzuri's thighs were stinging from the crop, and her inner thighs had started to burn.

Suddenly the crop flicked the top of her mound with that horrible slapping sound.

"Ah!" The chains clanked as she tried to yank her knees together—without success. Her ankles remained high and wide, leaving her pussy scarily exposed. Erotically exposed.

She lifted her head and looked down her body, seeing Alastair framed by the V of her legs. Keeping with the Halloween theme, he'd worn a scruffy black shirt he'd borrowed from Max and knotted a do-rag over his head like a pirate. He hadn't trimmed his beard for two days, and his darkly shadowed jaw made him look frighteningly dangerous.

When his penetrating gaze met hers, the power in his eyes seemed to shake the entire building. Deliberately holding her gaze, he set his hand over her pussy. At the heat of his palm in her wetness and the pressure over her throbbing clit, need shuddered through her.

A slow smile curved his lips, reminding her that he liked to use pain as one of his instruments.

And then he stepped back and began to crop her again.

The burn on the skin of her legs increased, and she yanked at her ankles again. Uselessly. She growled in frustration.

Laughter resounded around her.

Omigod. She was naked and restrained on a bar. A *bar*. With her legs chained and her pussy exposed. Talk about embarrassing.

"Easy, darlin'." Max squeezed her fingers.

She needed that comfort. The flick, flick, flick of the crop was growing steadily harder, right at the edge of pain. What *did* they plan to do to her? Her mouth was almost too dry to let her swallow. When Max released her hand, she panicked and tried to grab him, but the chain pinning her wrists to the bar top kept her arms over her head. She could feel her heart drumming within her chest. "Wait."

"Easy, princess. I'm not leaving you." Max's voice was a rumbling croon of reassurance. "But I need both hands to play with these beauties." His callused palms were tantalizingly abrasive as he squeezed her breasts, molded them together, and kneaded them. They swelled under his hard hands, and the skin grew achingly taut.

Assessing gaze on her face, he circled each nipple with a wet finger, creating a cool spot in the center of the throbbing heat.

As Alastair hit her harder with the crop, she winced.

Max smiled slowly. "Let me help you with that pain, baby." He bent.

She gasped as his mouth closed around one nipple, engulfing it in heat. His hand captured her other breast, and he rolled the nipple between his fingers.

As a dark hunger roused inside her, the stinging of the crop changed. More like the splashing of hot water, the not-quite-pain sensations streamed straight to her core. Her clit began to throb with a voracious need.

"Better." Max lifted his head and smiled down at her. Palm

along her cheek, thumb under her chin, he held her head immobile as he forcefully took her mouth. His tongue invaded. Possessed. The smooth bar top seemed to drop out from under her.

As Max moved back, Alastair slapped the crop on her mound right above her clit.

The painful—wonderful—sensation shot through her. "Oooh!" Her hips bucked.

With a deep chuckle, Alastair slid his finger over her clit and down inside her entrance, teasing her. Evilly.

Her hips wiggled uncontrollably, unable to do anything else, needing his expert fingers on her clit. His mouth. Something... She made a frustrated sound.

"No, darlin'." Max murmured. "You're not going to move. You're going to take everything we give you—and you're going to take a lot."

"Starting now." Alastair's finger circled her entrance as he glanced at Max. "She's nice and wet. In a good place."

"All right then." Max changed places with Alastair and pulled things she couldn't quite see out of his bag. A bottle of something. A huge zip lock bag of...

"Sir? What's in there?"

"Quarter-inch, stainless steel, sterilized"—Max smiled slowly—"*chain*." He held up one end. She stared. Each heavy link was between one to two inches long.

Oh no. No, no, no. Why had she wrapped that chain around Detective Dragon's dick? Were they going to wrap all that chain around her? Or...whatever they'd planned, she didn't want it. She shook her head. "Sir. No. *Yellow*."

"Sweetheart." Standing at her shoulder, Alastair turned her head toward him. In his powerful, steady gaze was heat as well as... Affection? For her? His lips were warm against hers as he kissed her tenderly. His voice was deep and slow. And strong.

When had she come to rely on his strength? "Although this session is to teach you some boundaries, it's also about trust. You trust us, sweetheart, and we won't break that trust."

Her heart couldn't say no. Not to him. She bit her lip.

"Zuri." Max ran his hand over her inner thigh. The summer's tan made his intense eyes even bluer. "We thought you'd enjoy this more than pain."

The dark beard shadow along his jaw resembled Alastair's. Dangerous. All the same, they were being gentle with her. How many Doms would still be nice if she'd embarrassed them? She pulled in a breath. "You won't hurt me?"

"No, love. This won't hurt." Alastair stroked her cheek. "And we will stop if it gets too much. *Do* you trust us?"

She swallowed and nodded.

Max squirted the stuff from the bottle over the chain links, and the smell of coconut filled the air.

Something clinked. Tensing, she tried to lift her head to see what he was doing.

Alastair chuckled and pushed her head down. "Close your eyes, Uzuri." His smooth baritone could not be disobeyed.

With an unhappy whine, she shut her eyes and tried to relax.

She felt fingers, very slick, rubbing oil along her entrance—and over her clit. Oooh, the sensation made her wiggle.

Max's laugh was low and dark. "Don't worry, princess. You're going to be coming your ears off in a few minutes."

She bit her lip against the wave of excitement—and anxiety. How could he make that sound almost...threatening?

More clinking sounds. Max said, "This is called the chain trick. So you know, I checked the chain myself for any sharp places and sterilized it. Now, sometimes, the links pinch a bit going in." She could hear the smile in his voice when he added, "Just squeak if that happens."

Going *in*? "You're going to put that in me?" In *her*?

Alastair took her hands, and she gripped him hard.

Max glanced at her. "Hang on tight, baby. This is going to fill you as full as fisting would without having to get my hand through a narrow opening." He pushed something cool and slick, thick and nubby, inside her.

And he kept going.

More and more chain settled inside her, and with each additional link, the mass grew heavier.

Max stopped and then his mouth was on her clit, licking and teasing.

Oh, oh, oh. The zinging pleasure made her core contract around...something hard. It weighed her insides down in a disconcertingly frightening, sensuous way.

Max stopped, then something cool and bumpy and slick slid over her clit.

Her eyes flew open, and she lifted her head.

He was dragging the oil-covered links over her clit, up and down, teasing her with the slick, nubby metal.

Each link set the nub to throbbing more. Unnerving heat grew in her center until she squirmed under the onslaught of sensation.

"That's right, baby." With a laugh, Max started pushing more chain inside her.

Still holding her fingers with one hand, Alastair moved his other hand to her breasts to play with her nipples, sending new zings straight to her throbbing clit.

With every inserted link, Max's fingers pushed into her vagina to rub upward against her G-spot. Over and over.

Too many sensations came from inside her. Fullness. Stretching. And so heavy. Her center felt anchored to the bar top; her head felt as if she were floating. Her core ached with need, and still, her breathing slowed.

Max paused. As his perceptive blue eyes assessed her, his concern was heartwarmingly obvious. When he glanced at his cousin, she realized Alastair was watching her as carefully. His fingers lay lightly over her carotid artery. Such a doctor.

A bubbly giggle escaped her, and his eyes lightened to the green color she loved. "All right, love. You're doing fine." He nodded at Max.

She felt Max's fingers press another link inside her pussy. Another. He was going slower. Occasionally, a link pinched her labia with a hot rippling feeling that somehow simply added to the sensations.

More and more.

Her eyes had closed, she realized, and Alastair was licking her nipples, sucking each lightly. She felt incredibly filled and heavy as her entire lower half pulsed with hot pleasure.

Max stopped. After a second, he nuzzled her inner thigh, his beard sensuously abrasive against the tender skin. "That's a couple of feet. I'm not putting any more in. She's all yours now, Doc."

The touches on her breasts stopped, leaving her feeling alone, then a loud humming sounded in the room. That sound. She'd heard it before.

She managed to pry her eyes open.

Max, not Alastair, now stood beside her. He smiled down and laid a warm reassuring hand below her breasts. "Ready, baby?"

Her body seemed to be humming, shimmering with pleasure. "Huh?"

Max nodded toward the end of the bar.

Framed between her legs, Alastair held a Hitachi wand.

Her eyes widened. "Oh, no. No, no—"

"Oh, yeah," Max murmured.

Instead of putting the wand on her clit, Alastair pressed it to her pelvic bone—and the strong vibrations shook her until even the chain inside seemed to be vibrating. A relentless pulsing started deep in her core.

Slowly, he moved it down to her clit—and turned it to high.

"Oh my God!" At the excruciating pleasure, her entire body tightened—and exploded in a shocking storm of sensation. A maelstrom of pleasure crashed over her...and didn't stop. The Hitachi stayed on her clit, sending her over again—and as her vagina rhythmically clenched around the heavy bulk of chain, everything inside her was stretching, pulsating, spiraling up and out of control. Each spasm seized her and shook her. The pleasure was a hot wave of lava, burning through her, and she could feel her arms pulling against the restraints as the world dissolved around her.

She was gasping for breath when Alastair finally lifted the wand. Her body went limp, despite the way her insides were still having tiny contractions. Oh, if this was punishment, she'd take it. "Omigod." Her voice came out husky.

"Fun, right, baby?" A dimple showed in Max's cheek as he smiled at her. "Remember how we made you ask to get off when we played outside?"

She giggled. "I didn't have to beg you this time."

"No, you didn't." A wicked glint showed in his eyes. "Sorry, darlin', but this time you're going to have to beg to stop."

Before she could react, Alastair lowered the Hitachi to her clit again.

The little subbie had bloody good endurance, Alastair thought a while later. Was that her fourth or fifth orgasm? Her body now gleamed with sweat, and her eyes were glazed.

"Please," she whispered. "No more. Please, please, please. Sirs, please."

Max grinned. "Look, she *can* ask for what she needs."

After setting the wand to one side, Alastair joined Max beside her.

When Max glanced over in silent query, Alastair tilted his head to let him take point. Nodding agreement, Max returned his attention to Uzuri. "We want you on your hands and knees now." He gave the little subbie his cop voice. "However, you'll get one more bout with the wand so that you think twice before deliberately disobeying an order again. Right?"

"Yes, Sir. I'm s-sorry I disobeyed." She turned big brown eyes to Alastair and repeated, "I'm sorry, Sir."

Had he ever met anyone more lovable? Alastair bent to kiss her trembling lips. "You're forgiven, Uzuri." As he removed the chains from her wrists, Max released her legs.

When she was freed, Max grinned at him. "Want to do the honors?"

Pull out the chain. "Lazy Yank. If I must." Alastair heaved a loud sigh. "You did the work of putting it in; I should do my part."

"Smartass." As Max moved up, he was laughing.

They both knew that the removal was the best part.

Max turned Uzuri over and positioned her on her hands and knees. As the chain inside moved, she stiffened and moaned with another orgasm. To keep her from going limp, he put one hand under her belly.

At the foot of the bar, Alastair moved her knees widely apart, set a hand on her ass, and closed his other hand around the chain. The bright silver links were stunning against her glossy dark pussy lips. He looked at his cousin.

"Last time with the wand, baby." Max picked up the Hitachi and thumbed it on.

Uzuri didn't have a working muscle left in her body. Unable to even lift her head, she rested her forehead on her hands. With her every movement, the heavy chain inside her shifted, stretching her center and shooting zings of pleasure through every nerve until she wasn't sure if she was still coming or not.

Her arms trembled so hard she'd have slid flat, except for Max's palm under her belly, holding her up.

He'd said something to her, and now a buzz sounded. What was that? Then she realized—and squeaked in protest.

Max set the Hitachi against her clit, pressing it firmly enough that the vibrations set the chain to humming too, and within mere seconds—seconds!—her core gathered, clamped down, and another shuddering climax rippled through her.

Before her orgasm even had a chance to stop...everything inside her started moving.

And the waves of pleasure started anew... "*Nooooo*."

Alastair's deep chuckle sounded as he continued to draw the chain out, slow and steady. Every...single...hard...link bumped right over her G-spot. Every pull moved the heavy mass of chain inside her. Every shift in the weight shuddered through her.

"Oh, *God*." Her center contracted into such intense spasms of pleasure that she was dying. Dying as the devastating pleasure swamped everything around her. She couldn't breathe.

The climax continued and continued even after the chain was gone, and she jerked with each contraction. "Oh, oh, ooooooh."

"Easy, princess." With gentle hands, Max laid her on her side. One hand anchored her in place as his other rubbed her slick, sweaty back.

As she gasped for breath, the buzzing wasn't the Hitachi this time, but the ringing in her ears.

He crouched and smiled into her eyes. "Sweet little mischief. Breathe, Zuri."

Alastair appeared beside him, tucked a blanket around her, and took her hand. "Easy, sweetheart." His gaze was filled with tenderness.

As they touched her, stroked her, watched over her, she felt... cared for. Exhausted, sated, sweaty—and safe. Cherished.

Oh, she loved them so much. Her heart swelled with the emotion until it filled her chest, aching with longing. She looked at Alastair helplessly, and as if he could hear her, he leaned down to kiss her gently.

When he straightened, her eyes filled with tears.

Max made an unhappy noise, and he cupped her cheek. "Baby, what?"

I love you. No words came out.

After a second, he shook his head and gave her a slow, sweet kiss. "Let's get our little mischief home, cuz."

After a shower, Max walked through the quiet house to snag a beer in the kitchen.

When he and Alastair had tucked Uzuri into her bed, she'd barely roused enough to kiss them. They'd both sat beside her until she fell into a deep sleep.

He could have watched her all night. How could simply being with her fill him with such contentment?

Some women were like rushing rivers, always on the move. Some—like Sally—were more like bubbling brooks. Uzuri though...

He had a favorite lake, high in the mountains, where the water was so deep it appeared a midnight blue. During the day, sunlight would sparkle and dance on the surface. At night, he'd count the stars reflected so clearly in the dark, still water...and breathe in the peace.

Yeah, that was their Uzuri.

Carrying his beer, he stepped outside onto the patio.

The tiny solar lights around the garden pond showed Alastair, a glass of whisky in hand. He glanced up. "I see we're in the same mood tonight."

"Seems so." As Max took a chair, Hunter padded over to greet him and settle at his feet. The heat of the day had passed, and the air was damp and cool. The palm trees lining the back fence rustled in the light breeze off Hillsborough Bay.

Eventually, Max broke the silence. "What are we going to do about Zuri?"

"Her two to three weeks of living here is coming to an end, isn't it?"

"Jesus, I forgot we'd put a time frame on that." Max stared at the pond, a sense of urgency growing inside him. They needed to talk this out before it was too late. *Hell.* He opened his mouth. Closed it.

Saying this shit out loud was fucking difficult. At least he could practice on his cousin before laying everything out for Zuri. "I...care. A lot."

"You sound like you're strangling." Alastair chuckled. "You mean you *love* her."

The air emptied from Max's lungs. "Yeah. Yeah, that's right." *Man up, Drago.* "I love her." He sucked back more of the beer. "Fuck, that's hard to say."

"So it appears." Alastair's irritating grin widened.

Max eyed his cousin's chair. Wouldn't take much work to tip it —and Alastair—over. *Nah.* That wouldn't help the discussion, no matter how satisfying. "What about you?"

"Oh, I'm on the same page. I love her." Alastair's smile disappeared as he studied Max carefully. "Can I assume that we want to continue sharing her, or have you found an unexpected possessiveness along with love?"

Max straightened, feeling as if he'd been punched. "What the fuck? You getting second thoughts about a triad?"

"I—no. I love you both." Alastair moved his shoulders. "But those are *my* feelings. Yours might be different, and possessiveness happens. Most of our polyamorous friends have been burned that way at least once."

Max slowly relaxed, and with a long exhalation, sat back in the chair. "Yeah, possessiveness might be a problem for others, but we grew up together. Shared everything—including women. To say you can't have something of mine would be like my right hand getting envious of my left. We share, cuz. That's what I want."

Exactly that. The three of them—a stable ménage. Each giving and receiving. Two Doms to keep Uzuri happy. Fuck knew, she had more than enough love to give back, even if she hadn't admitted it to them yet. In her eyes, he'd seen what she felt.

Alastair nodded. "That's what I want, too."

"Good enough. We share." Max frowned as he examined his feelings. "Huh. Turns out I am possessive after all."

Alastair frowned. "What—"

"If any bastard but you lays a hand on her, he'll draw back a bleeding stub."

Alastair's grin flashed. "Agreed." He *clinked* his glass against Max's bottle, and the deal was sealed.

CHAPTER TWENTY-SIX

Early Monday morning, Uzuri parked in the Brendall's employee lot and headed toward the building. A tiny frisson of nerves made her shiver. The parking lot had never felt safe since she'd been hit by that car.

And there was that weird feeling again, the sense that someone was watching her. The hair raised on the back of her neck.

Hands clenched, she turned in a circle, examining the nearby cars. Two rows down were a couple of other female employees. The manager of the shoe department was hurrying to the door, tie flapping back over his shoulder. Aside from the seagulls perched on the light poles, nothing else moved.

A flicker of light came from the edge of the lot, and she squinted. A man stood behind a car, leaning on it. The flash came again like sunlight reflected off...binoculars? Was someone watching the parking lot with binoculars?

She shivered and, unable to help herself, headed for the store, not...quite...running. Surely he was only some random guy watching birds.

Not Jarvis.

Once inside, she told the guard about the man and was delighted when he walked right out to look. *Look, Dragon Doms, I asked for help.*

In Cincinnati, she'd never sicced a guard on Jarvis. She hadn't been comfortable asking for assistance—and hadn't even realized she was behaving abnormally. If she'd been able to get help, her life might have been different. If nothing else, she wouldn't have felt so helpless.

My Doms, you have changed my life.

In so many ways. *Love.* What an amazing emotion. With a bouncing step, she got into the elevator to the fourth floor. Right now, she felt as if she'd swallowed the sun and was radiating light. She loved them. Both of them. How crazy and wonderful and insane and amazing.

Should she tell them? Or wait? They cared for her...didn't they? She was sure they did.

Insecurity dimmed the glow slightly. What *did* they feel for her?

She'd seen how delusional some people could be—like Jarvis who'd been certain she was supposed to be his. Alyssa in the Shadowlands had been positive she should be Nolan's slave.

Frowning, Uzuri walked down the hallway to her office, nodding absently at her colleagues.

It would be better to...to let Max and Alastair make the first move. They were the Doms, right? Only her time at their house was ending. Did they realize that?

"Ms. Cheval, is there anything you'd like me to set up?"

Uzuri stopped and blinked at the gray-haired administrative assistant. Mrs. Everson had asked her a question. "Set up?"

"For your meeting with the sales associates."

Meeting. "Oh. Thank you. I think everything is ready."

"Very good." Mrs. Everson gave her an encouraging smile. "Good luck with them." The efficient, incredibly dignified woman added under her breath, "The buttheads."

Suppressing her grin, Uzuri strolled into her office to get ready for the meeting.

An hour later, Uzuri stood near the front in Brendall's midsized conference room.

The sales associates from the women's fashion department slowly filled the room. The scowls and cold stares they cast Uzuri's way chilled her blood.

With an effort, she stood tall and kept her face expressionless. This meeting could get ugly. Nevertheless, something had to be done about the situation. Customers were complaining, and the department manager was at her wit's end.

Two more women entered, saw Uzuri, and chose seats near the back, uttering insulting comments. Did they realize several people from upper management were sitting in the back row?

Uzuri pulled in a breath. Although the sales women were admirably loyal, they were also foolish to let their performance on the job suffer, especially for someone like Carole. And if Uzuri couldn't turn this around, those women would be fired.

Her trembling hands felt like ice, but she could do this. She would.

As she moved toward the podium, Alastair, Dan, and Max entered the room, ignoring the puzzled looks from the nearby administrative people.

She turned to stare at them.

Alastair was in one of his beautifully tailored suits. He'd even donned an "adult" tie with not a single cavorting animal. Dan and Max were in their customary detective attire of suit coats and dark jeans.

When they took seats near the door, she realized they'd come to Brendall's simply to give her their support. A lovely warmth entered her veins, melting the icy chill.

Last night, when Max had offered to show up and scare the crap out of any troublemaker in the crowd, she'd thought he was joking. His blue gaze met hers, and he patted his hidden firearm.

The hysterical giggle rising up in her throat almost made her choke. *Bad Max.*

Alastair gave her a firm nod, and she could almost hear his deep voice telling her she could handle anything she put her mind to.

She could. She would. *Thank you, Doc.*

Chin up, spine straight, she stepped behind the podium and surveyed her audience. Mostly hostile.

"Let's get started," she said. "This meeting was called to address concerns about customer service in the women's clothing department. The administration noted when the problems began —and they know the cause."

Uzuri saw faces closing down. The sales associates also knew the cause—and blamed her. "In case you don't know, I'm Uzuri Cheval, a senior fashion buyer. You have undoubtedly heard something about Carole Fuller's problems with me and about her termination. Upper management agreed to let me give you the facts. I know how rumors fly through a department. After all, I spent years as a sales associate."

From the looks of surprise, many hadn't realized she'd started as one of them. Carole had made it sound as if Uzuri had come here, waving her new degree and shoving the veterans around.

"I've been in retail sales since I was sixteen, usually in women's clothing. Over three years ago, I took a sales associate position at Brendall's in St. Pete. Meanwhile, I was taking evening classes at the university. When I obtained my bachelor's degree, I was an assistant fashion buyer there. Last year, I transferred here to Tampa as a senior buyer." She gave them a wry smile. "After a decade of working in retail, I don't think you'd call me an overnight success."

A few return smiles flickered.

"That's my background. Now for the conflict. One day, I was in the women's department to observe what products were selling. A sales associate kept walking away from customers needing help to offer her assistance to women who appeared wealthier. She did this three times while I was watching. Before leaving, I expressed my concern to the floor manager." Uzuri nodded to the manager who stood off to one side.

"Ms. Cheval said exactly that to me. Nothing else." The manager's anger was obvious. "Carole had already racked up complaints about her behavior with customers, many from her own colleagues on the floor. Yes, from you." She pointed to the audience. "I'd already given her two official warnings. That day, I told her if she received any more complaints, she'd be let go. Rather than taking responsibility for her own actions, she blamed Ms. Cheval." The manager's disgust came through loud and clear.

"That was all Uzuri did?" Whispers drifted up from the audience.

"But Carole got fired."

A louder woman protested, "Cheval got her fired."

"Bullshit." Obviously losing patience, Max rose.

Dan stood hastily, set a hand on his shoulder, and spoke instead. "Mrs. Fuller decided talk wasn't enough. She engaged in an act of vandalism one evening. She and another woman flattened a tire on Ms. Cheval's car. They knew Ms. Cheval would leave after dark. Both women confessed, by the way."

He paused, let the murmuring die down, and continued. "It was dark and pouring rain when Ms. Cheval found the flat tire. She tried to return to the building to wait for a tow truck."

Max growled, "And she was run down in the parking lot."

Shock showed on every face.

Dan shook his head. "The driver wasn't Carole Fuller, yet her vindictive vandalism almost got Ms. Cheval killed. Ms. Cheval refused to press charges." Dan's hard face showed he'd have enjoyed tossing Carole behind bars.

A woman whispered, "Those guys don't look like our security guards."

Max set his hands on his hips, which pulled his jacket back enough to show his holstered weapon and badge.

Several women shrank down in their seats. Others gave him interested stares that made Uzuri want to slap them. *Mine.*

Instead, she cleared her throat. "That's the history between me and Mrs. Fuller. Now let's move on to a more serious problem. These are some of the complaints the company has received in the past week."

She handed the microphone to the manager who read three of the letters. One complaint described a rude sales associate so well that the woman cringed.

After finishing, the manager said, "I'll add this. After receiving these letters, verbal complaints, and reviews, the administration is considering terminating every sales associate in our department. They feel they might do better with new staff."

Faces went pale.

Uzuri took the mic. "Administration has two concerns. One, that morale in the department affected treatment of the customers. The second is...well, Carole would only assist a certain subset of the customers on the floor. She's not alone in that preferential behavior."

The audience was silent. Not giving Uzuri anything back.

"I know how tempting it is to help the women who appear to have more to spend. Why waste time on the rest?" Uzuri held her hands wide. "Commissions are what pay the rent, after all. However, customers who are ignored get angry. For every person who actually complains, many more will simply take their business elsewhere. Brendall's can't afford that. Neither can we."

She had them. Expressions were open, showing agreement... and worry.

Alastair, so sensitive to people's emotions, gave her a nod of approval.

Encouraged, she kept going. "Our company policy is that every customer is a star with us. We don't care if the woman can only afford a pair of socks or is buying apparel for a European vacation. If treated fabulously, the woman who buys socks this year will return for her business wardrobe when she scores a fantastic job. We're not only selling for today—we're cultivating our future buyers."

Nods. Omigod, she was getting nods of agreement.

"And as a side note—when I was a sales associate, I learned the hard way that you can't judge a person's wealth by their appearance. Giving *everyone* exceptional service isn't a bad idea, because we really don't know with whom we're dealing. To show that, I thought we'd have some fun to finish off this meeting."

There was a windowed door in the front of the room. Uzuri turned that way and held her hand up to let Jessica know she and the other three could come in.

Uzuri stood stunned as a...a mob entered. *Four. I only asked four people to come.*

Ben led the way in his usual scruffy jeans followed by Marjory, an African-American friend from the university in a red blazer and black dress slacks. Kari was dressed in a suit for parent-teacher conferences.

What was Master Raoul doing here? Heavily muscled, the Hispanic Dom wore his usual jeans and polo shirt.

The next person... Uzuri's breath stuttered to a halt. Master Z's mother, Madeline Grayson, was one of the wealthiest people in the city. Uzuri could deal with rich, but this was Master Z's *mother*. *Omigod.* She hadn't been invited. Moreover, she wore sweat pants and a T-shirt. That was so wrong.

Following her was Vance in his dark *I'm-an-FBI-agent* suit. Gabi was in jeans and sleeveless shirt with her usual blue streaked hair and a new Celtic temp tattoo on her upper arm. Mistress Anne wore casual business attire—tan pants and a blue button-up shirt. Carrying little Sophia, Jessica looked like a stereotypical housewife in jeans and one of her leftover maternity tops.

Uzuri swallowed and tried to remember her speech. Since the manager had given her a list of saleswomen who constantly targeted richer customers, Uzuri selected one. "Phoebe, point out which three would probably get you the best commissions?"

Phoebe chose Kari, Vance, and Marjory. Good, not racist, at least.

Two more made the same choices, although one chose Anne instead of Marjory.

The manager grinned and in an unplanned move, called out three more sales associates. "Ladies, which three would you choose last, let's say?" The manager gave Uzuri a wicked glance.

Oh, score. Two of the women decided Ben, Jessica, and Mrs. Grayson were on the bottom of the list. Another apparently didn't like people of color. Her choices were Master Raoul, Ben, and Marjory.

"We have our contenders." Uzuri smiled at her audience and turned to her friends...and volunteers. "I asked you all to come without changing or dressing up or down. Is this what you normally wear this time of day?"

Nods from everyone—including the people she hadn't invited. Like Madeline Grayson. Jessica's eyes were dancing, the little sneak.

Wanting—totally wanting to start with Mrs. Grayson so she'd leave, Uzuri held firm and started at the end of the line.

She walked to Jessica, kissed Sophia's cheek, and smiled at the fragrance of baby powder and milk. Recognizing Uzuri, the little angel gurgled happily, getting "aww" sounds from the audience. "May I introduce Jessica who is a CPA and whose husband is one of the city's leading psychologists. They live in a stone mansion outside of town where she works from home because of this little bundle of joy."

One of the sales associates muttered, "Mansion? Should have picked her."

Uzuri moved to Mistress Anne. "Anne works as a... Um."

Anne chuckled. "Call it a glorified private detective. I'm certainly not rich."

The woman who'd picked her got teased by her friends.

"This is Gabi." Uzuri got a quick hug. "She works as an FBI victim specialist." The people who hadn't picked her as rich were smiling until Uzuri added, "Her husband is one of the city's prosecuting attorneys."

Eyes were widening.

When Uzuri stopped beside Vance, he bent to kiss her cheek. "Vance is an FBI agent."

Next person. Uzuri froze.

Madeline Grayson made a tiny snorting sound, put an arm around Uzuri, and took the mic. "Please excuse my casual attire." She smiled at Uzuri before speaking into the mic. "I didn't hear about your...party...until my personal trainer had already arrived. I'm delighted that I was able to attend." Her aristocratic voice carried the same intonations as Master Z's.

"Thank you for coming." Uzuri turned to the audience. "This is..." Omigod, how could she introduce Master Z's mama?

Chuckling, Vance said the words Uzuri couldn't possibly utter. "That's Madeline Grayson, who could probably buy Brendall's with pocket change."

"My boy, that sounds quite tacky," Mrs. Grayson said in disapproval, even as laughter filled her eyes.

"Oh my God, I saw her at the inaugural ball, dancing with the governor." Whispers ran around the room.

Uzuri swallowed and took the mic back from Mrs. Grayson. "Thank you."

"You are quite welcome. Continue now; you're doing splendidly."

With the subtle kick in the butt, Uzuri kept going.

"This is Mas—" She stopped abruptly, feeling her cheeks heat. Master Raoul didn't laugh...quite. "This is Raoul who owns an international civil engineering firm."

"That means he's rich," Vance said blandly, and when she glared at him, added, "No, don't hit me, Zuri; I'd have to arrest you."

Laughter ran around the room, and she realized exactly what he'd done. He'd made her human and cute and one of the group.

"This is Kari who is a schoolteacher."

"In a suit?" One of those who picked her made a disbelieving noise.

Kari leaned forward to say into the mic, "I have parent-teacher conferences all day. I always dress up for those, since parents listen better if I wear a suit. I look nice, but I'd be the customer only buying a pair of socks."

The silence said she'd gotten her point across.

"Finally, this is Ben." To her relief, he gave her a hard hug. Mistress Anne must not have tortured him too badly for helping her learn to pick locks. She smiled up at him. "He's rather well known as the photographer BL Haugen."

"Holy shit." The awe in the voices and whispers were so, so satisfying.

"Good job, sweetie," Ben murmured in his rough voice.

Uzuri stepped back, facing her friends...her *friends*...and tried not to let her voice break. "Thank you all for the gift of your time today. I think the next time you visit Brendall's, you'll find that the women's department has the finest customer service in the city."

"Hell with that," one of the associates said. "In the state."

The cheers of agreement chased away the shadows like the sun emerging from behind the clouds.

CHAPTER TWENTY-SEVEN

On Friday morning, Holt got sucked into playing some vigorous two-on-two basketball with the neighborhood teens who had the day off from school. Hey, a game beat jogging any day.

Taking a breather, he glanced at his phone and winced. He still hadn't had breakfast, and Uzuri'd be over in a couple hours for lunch. Before she showed, he needed a bite of something and definitely a shower.

Should probably clean up the place, as well since Nadia was coming over that evening, and she was a neat freak. "Gotta go, guys. Thanks for the game."

"You bet," Duke said.

His taciturn buddy with the multiple piercings added, "Yeah."

"Thanks for showing me that lay-up trick," Wedge said.

"You're welcome." Holt grinned at the three. All about fifteen years old. Too young to drive, too old to play backyard tag with the younger set.

"Tomorrow?" Duke asked.

"Nope. Got work." Holt considered his schedule. "How about Sunday afternoon?"

Duke silently checked with his crew and nodded. "You're on."

Holt gave them a chin lift, tossed Duke the basketball, and headed for home. The exercise had left a nice buzz in his muscles.

Fun game, too. Good kids. They sure as hell hadn't been the ones to fuck with his Harley.

As Holt strolled toward the duplex, he enjoyed the sounds of a peaceful neighborhood—a lawn mower buzzing, children laughing, a beginning pianist mangling "Für Elise". In a front window, a tiny poodle bounced and barked.

Nice area. Although his singles complex made it easy to meet women, the constant parties and noise had grown tiresome. After all, he had a girlfriend now and wasn't "single" any longer.

"Gah!" A toddler "assisting" her mother with weeding held up a dandelion for him.

"Thank you, sweetheart." Winking at the mother, he accepted the flower and studied it gravely. "That's a great flower."

"Gah," the munchkin agreed.

As he stepped off the curb to cross the street, he rubbed his cheek and felt the scrape of beard. Better shave, too. Nadia didn't like him looking scruffy.

Zuri, though, might not even notice. She was distracted these days. Falling head over heels in love would do that.

Max and Alastair were lucky guys. Little Zuri had all the sweetness of a submissive combined with the strength of a person who'd made her own way in life.

He wished them well. The chemistry hadn't been right for Uzuri to be his, but she made a damn fine friend.

Besides, he had a woman of his own. He smiled, hearing his aunt's voice. *"Alexander Sullivan Holt, the woman who wins my wonderful nephew will be a lucky woman."* Only, he'd learned that a man who found a good woman was the lucky one.

Nadia might well be the one for him.

At the duplex, he unlocked the front door and stepped inside...into darkness. Hadn't he left the window blinds open? He turned toward the light switch and heard an angry shout, "Bastard! She's *mine*."

Someone from behind hit Holt high on his shoulder.

Fuck. Someone was in his place. Instinctively, Holt spun and knocked his attacker's arm away. Cold pressure slid across his face. Jerking sideways, he punched out blindly and connected solidly with a chin or cheekbone.

The man bellowed in anger.

Warm liquid poured down Holt's face—and more flowed down his back. Blood. A fiery pain blossomed over his scapula.

Holt spotted a knife in the man's right hand. The fucker had *stabbed* him.

The bastard swung.

Holt jumped back—and was almost sliced by the knife in the man's *left* hand. What the fuck? The bastard had a knife in each hand and had nailed him good. *Shit.*

A knife lifted. "I'm bigger, asshole." The guy lunged.

Holt sidestepped, blocked with his left, and tried to punch. The searing pain in his right shoulder made him gasp, stole the strength from his blow.

"My cock's bigger." A knife slashed Holt's forearm. "I'm better." He kept coming. "You can't satisfy her."

Holt blocked.

The bastard twisted, and a line of fire ran across Holt's forearm as the bastard got him with the other knife. "You touched my bitch. Nobody touches my bitch."

Slice by slice, Holt was forced back. His forearms were being cut to shreds as he tried to keep the knives from his torso. A sidestep gave him a chance to get his balance, and Holt kicked, scored a partial hit on the guy's knee, and gained some space.

His shirt in back was soaked—he was bleeding badly. As his eyes adjusted, he could finally distinguish more of the shadowy form.

Dark skin, dark clothes. Couple inches taller, maybe fifty

pounds heavier. Far too well armed. Holt grabbed a lamp, yanked hard to rip it from the electrical socket, and flung it at the window.

The heavy ceramic punched between the cheap vertical blinds and busted through the window with a crash of glass. Should get attention. "Call 911!" Seeing the guy lunge, Holt jumped back again.

Not far enough. The knife laid open his chin. "Leave my bitch alone, cocksucker."

Glancing behind for obstacles, Holt retreated again. "Who do you mean, man?" *Nadia?* Wait, could this be Zuri's stalker? "You mean Uzuri?"

The roar of rage confirmed it. "You touched what's *mine*."

"You're Jarvis." Dammit, he needed to down this bastard. Holt circled the coffee table and kicked it into the bastard's legs.

Cursing foully, frothing with anger, the guy tossed the coffee table across the room and charged, slashing wildly.

Dodging sideways, Holt punched Jarvis's forearm. That knife dropped.

But Jarvis buried the other blade in Holt's gut.

Fuck.

Holt's legs went weak. Grabbing and anchoring the knife with one hand, he slammed his fist into the guy's face repeatedly.

Jarvis backed up, shaking his head.

Someone pounded on the door. "Holt? Hey, Holt."

"Here!"

Sunlight blazed across the room as the door was flung open.

"No!" Jarvis raced toward the back of the house, flinging furniture out of his way.

As Duke and his friends poured into the room, Holt's knees buckled. He tried to catch himself on the couch—his arm didn't work. Falling, he heard a god-awful *crack* before blackness rushed in.

Humming "Once Upon a Dream", Uzuri did a mini-waltz step as she walked up the sidewalk to her duplex. Holt's car and Harley were in the driveway, so he hadn't been called out for a fire or anything, which occasionally happened, even on his days off.

She couldn't wait to tell him about the meeting on Monday. Even the administrators had been impressed. And this morning, the sales associates had welcomed her when she'd been checking the racks in the petite section. Her admission that Madeline Grayson had shown up without an invitation and scared her to death had put her back on easy terms with everyone. Two of them had taken the time to share their customers' input about the new winter clothing line.

Life was good. She smiled up at the billowy clouds in the blue sky and breathed in the scent of freshly cut grass. A pleasing breeze ruffled the hem of her copper-colored faux wrap dress and made the tall palm trees rustle. The peaceful neighborhood was so quiet, she could hear the low hum of the distant lunch hour traffic.

In fact, it was too quiet.

She frowned. Where were all the children? The only ones she saw were Duke and his fellow jocks gathered on the front porch a few houses down.

How odd. Uzuri walked around the untrimmed plantings by the front door and...

What?

Yellow tape across her doorway made a garish barrier. The front window—the one the landlord had replaced—was all in pieces. Surely, that didn't require *police* tape. Fear ran a cold hand up her spine, and she took several steps back.

"Uzuri!"

She turned to see Duke jog across the street. The linebacker-sized teen skidded to a stop in front of her. "You can't go in. The cops left a few minutes ago, an' they said nobody can go in."

His strained face warned this was more than vandalism, and she grabbed his shoulder. "What happened? Where's Holt?"

"Oh, man, some asshole attacked him. They had a fucking fight right in your place." Duke shuddered. "Like, this lamp came flying out the window. Crashing and glass fucking flying everywhere. Holt yelled about 911. We come through the door, and some huge fucking dude runs out the back."

"Is Holt—" Heart hammering, she couldn't get the words out.

Duke didn't notice. "Sucks that the guy got away. Wedge tried to catch him. No joy. The asshole ran through Mrs. Avery's flowerbed and went over the back fence."

Uzuri shook him. "Where. Is. *Holt*? Did he get hurt? Did he go to the police station?" *Please let him be all right.*

Holt was tough. He could hold his own against anyone.

"Fuck, Uzuri, he was bleeding bad. They took him away in an ambulance, sirens and all."

Following the pink lady's directions, Uzuri hurried down the hospital corridor to the surgery section. Surgery—that couldn't be good. Hands cold, heart thumping in her chest, she burst into the waiting room.

People everywhere. After a second, she recognized Holt's firefighter buddies clustered in one corner. Warren, the one built like a tank, spotted her and walked over. His normally tanned face was pale. "Uzuri, right?"

She stared up at him. "How is he?"

"Seriously fucked up." Warren shook his head, not even seeing her. "Christ Jesus, I've never gone out on a call to one of our own, you know?"

"Warren." She gripped his arm, forcing him to see her. "How *is* he? Is he going to be all right?"

"Dunno. He's in surgery for the gut stab. The kids said he bashed his head on the TV stand. He wasn't tracking right when we brought him in."

"Lost a ton of blood, too." Another firefighter with an Australian accent chimed in.

A ginger-haired guy said, "Whoever attacked him sliced him up like hamburger."

Uzuri swallowed. "Sliced? Like...with a knife?" A *knife*.

"Two knives," Warren said. "One was still in Holt. We found another on the floor."

Jarvis had boasted about using two knives. He'd attacked her dates before. Uzuri couldn't seem to move. All the way to the hospital, she'd told herself not to jump to conclusions. To wait. However, she *knew*.

Jarvis was here. Had attacked Holt—because he was living in her place. Was her friend. *My God, what have I done?* Despair was an avalanche, burying her until she couldn't breathe.

Warren said in a harsh voice, "He's got knife wounds going up his arms. More on his face. Stabbed high in the back." He put his hands on his belly. "Caught one in the gut. Deep enough to—"

The Aussie gripped Warren's shoulder. "Easy on the description, bro. You're talking to a civilian."

"Oh." Warren blinked. "Sorry, Uzuri."

"It's all right." She walked over to lay a hand on the door to the operating rooms. *Oh, Holt.* She needed to be beside him, to give him strength.

To say she was sorry.

She should never have let him move into her place, should never have touched him, should never have been his friend.

She shouldn't have any friends. None.

"They're not going to let you see him, even when he comes

out of surgery," the ginger-haired firefighter said. "He'll be in recovery and in ICU at least overnight and only family's allowed there."

Uzuri turned. "He has a girlfriend. Nadia. Does anyone know how to call her?"

"Hell, that's right." The man pulled out his phone. "My wife'll have her number. She'll call."

Walking over to an isolated corner, Uzuri took a seat. *Jarvis. Here.* Horror clung to her shoulders as even the air in the room darkened. *I'm sorry, Holt.*

He was fighting for his life because Jarvis thought they were together.

Ice slid down her spine. What if Jarvis found out about Alastair and Max? He'd go after them, too. Her heart skipped a beat at the thought of Max being attacked. *"...sliced him up like hamburger."* Or Alastair opening the front door, and Jarvis stabbing him without warning. Hurting him. Kicking him.

Even though she was panting, she couldn't seem to find enough air in the room.

Surely Jarvis didn't know she was staying with them. He'd attacked Holt, not her men. Only...if he checked further, he'd find out. Or he'd trail her from Brendall's to their house. And he'd hurt them.

Maybe kill them.

"Uzuri?" Warren was looking at her.

She realized she'd stood up. Her hands were fisted at her sides.

Jarvis would kill her Doms. She couldn't let him know about them. No matter what happened to her, she had to protect them.

And he'd hurt them if he knew. He would. Oh, God, she had to stay away from them. Chills chasing over her skin, heart pounding, Uzuri ran out of the waiting room.

Soon after lunch, Max pulled into the driveway with Alastair's vehicle in front of him. *Right on time, cuz*. They'd decided to take this afternoon off and set up something special for Uzuri. Their little romantic deserved a treat.

But... Zuri's car was parked under the portico. Well, damn. There went their plans of doing some stage setting. However, if she had the afternoon off, there were other ways to take advantage of all three of them having unexpected time together.

And when they were done, they could sit down and have their talk.

The talk.

To Max's surprise, Alastair didn't pull into the garage. He stopped his car right in the U-shaped drive, and Max had to slam on the brakes to keep from rear-ending the dumbass.

Alastair jumped out of his car and headed toward Uzuri. Fast.

What was going on? Max shut the car down and followed.

Uzuri's car was running, and she was getting in. Her oversized suitcase stood upright in the back seat.

"Uzuri." Alastair lengthened his stride.

"What the hell?" Max broke into a run.

Uzuri hesitated and straightened.

"What is going on?" Alastair asked as he neared the car.

Her hand on the open car door was visibly shaking. She bit her lip, then raised her chin. "I've been here well over two weeks. It's time for me to go home."

"Is it now?" It was plain Alastair was trying to keep his voice level, but Max heard the shocked pain.

Yeah, it fucking hurt. Max stared at her. "So you're sneaking out without even talking to us. Did you leave us a note?"

She winced.

Yeah, she'd obviously left a fucking note in her room.

Her grip visibly tightened on the door. "I thought a note would be easier for all of us."

His anger was growing from sparks into a full-fledged wildfire, one that would send any animal in its path fleeing. "Easier for you, maybe. Me, I'd rather have some fucking answers. When you left this morning, you were all hugs and kisses. Now you're walking out?"

The pain in the doc's eyes sent Max's rage flaring higher.

It felt as if someone was using a heavy drill bit on his heart. All day, he'd been thinking of how she'd react, what she'd say, when he and Alastair told her how much they cared. And asked her to stay.

Meantime, she'd been packing her bags.

"Zuri." He struggled to keep his voice reasonable. Talk about reasonable—this wasn't. Hell, this was totally unlike their little Miss Politeness. He softened his voice. "Zuri, did we do something to upset you?"

"Sir. Um, Max. There isn't anything to talk about and I appreciate the help and this...whatever this is...was...is over." The words didn't even sound like her.

She wouldn't look either of them in the eye.

Did she think they'd hit her or something?

Jesus.

Alastair took a slow, careful step forward, as if she were one of his terrified kid patients. His gaze stayed on her. "I think you should talk with us, pet. It's obvious there is something wrong."

Yeah. Something was fucking wrong. This wasn't her.

"No. We're done. Forever." Her wide eyes filled with tears. Looking hopeless, looking *helpless*, she slid into her seat, slammed the door, and stomped on the gas.

As her car shot down the drive, Max glanced at Alastair. He looked as stunned as Max felt.

Max scrubbed his hands over his face. "We'd better look at that note."

At Brendall's, Uzuri left her bags with the security guard and headed upstairs. Not to work. She simply needed a place to think where she'd be safe. As she walked through the hallway and into the reception area, the sense of unreality tugged at her. But being here helped her feel more stable. In fact, she'd felt stronger simply walking through the door. *My store. My life.*

As she strode toward *her* office, she knew she wasn't going to cut and run again. No, this time, she'd fight. Somehow.

The administrative assistant gave her a worried frown. "Ms. Cheval, you don't look well at all. Are you ill?"

"Something at lunch didn't agree with me, but I'll be fine."

After managing a smile, she stepped inside her office, closed the door, and leaned against it. The air-conditioned room felt cold and dry with a faint scent of cleansers.

Oh, she wanted to run back home—to Max and Alastair's house. To breathe in the comfort and safety and—and love—that was there. Her Dragon Doms' home would hold the brisk fragrance of the sea, the perfume from the tropical flowers in the yard, a hint of chlorine from the pool—and sometimes more than a hint of wet dog.

The TV room would smell of leather and more recently, the vanilla candles she'd lined up on the mantle.

In the mornings, the kitchen smelled like coffee and the bacon that Max loved—and that Alastair considered a fast road to a heart attack. Or sometimes popcorn in the evenings.

Her eyes burned. *Not good, girl. Not when even the memory of a smell makes you choke up.*

She walked to the window and looked out over the sunlit parking lot. With all that light, why did she feel engulfed in darkness? As she set her forehead against the cool glass, the condensation of her breath fogged the view.

Alastair had been hurt. *She'd* hurt him. And he'd still been gentle.

Max had been angry. Then concerned. Worried.

Yes, she'd hurt them both. Wasn't it funny that she could love them so, so much and give them only pain?

There was nothing else she could have done. Never, ever would she let them be hurt like Holt.

Oh, Holt. Everything inside her urged her to go to him—but she couldn't get in to see him. She huffed an angry growl. The hospital wouldn't even give her any information. She'd had to call Warren. Holt was out of surgery and in recovery. The doctor wasn't offering odds, but said it looked good.

Uzuri pulled herself straight. She needed to talk with Anne—to let her know about Holt so he had friends to be with him.

And...if the attacker was Jarvis—and it *was*—the police needed to be told. Only they wouldn't believe her, not with Jarvis living in Cincinnati. They'd treat her like the Cincinnati police had for months and months—as if she were some paranoid idiot. She'd learned her lesson.

But Max and Dan were police. They'd believe her. Only...she couldn't see Max, and Dan was his partner. Oh, this was such a mess.

First, she needed to see where Jarvis was.

Pulling out her phone, Uzuri winced. No phone calls showed in the history...because she'd blocked her Dragon Doms' numbers. If she heard Alastair or Max, her resolve might waver. Waver? It would disintegrate like centuries old fabric.

In her ear, the ringing stopped. "Hey, Uzuri. What's up?"

"Anne." Uzuri straightened her shoulders. "Can you do a quick check for me? On Jarvis?"

"I'm already at the computer. Hold on a second." There was silence on the line. "He's still employed at the factory job."

"Oh." Uzuri felt a rush of relief, then her fingers tightened on the phone. That didn't rule him out. Employed didn't mean actually there.

"Uzuri." Anne's voice took on the authority that made her a Domme. "What's happened to spook you?"

"It's Holt. He was staying in my duplex, and someone attacked him—with two knives—and that's how Jarvis fights." Uzuri swallowed against the throat-clogging guilt. "Jarvis might have thought Holt and I were together. In Cincinnati, he attacked every man I dated."

My fault. All my fault.

"Knives? Fuck. Is Holt going to be all right?"

"He had surgery and is in recovery and then goes to ICU."

"Got it." Anne growled something under her breath. "I'm not liking the feel of this. First, I'm going to see if Kassab really is at work. Or not. It'll take me a while, though. Are you somewhere safe? Please tell me you're with the Dragos and not at the hospital."

"I'm safe, thank you. Can you...t-tell the others about Holt. So he has people there?"

"I will. And I'll check on Kassab. I'll get right back to you."

Ten minutes later, Uzuri had her answers.

Jarvis had called in sick yesterday and today. He was *here.* In Tampa. Her hands closed into fists. How long had he been coming to Tampa? What about those times she'd felt she was being watched and called herself paranoid? Had he been stalking her for months?

Her stomach knotted, and bile rose into her throat.

What about those petty, nasty incidents she'd attributed to teens? The garbage on her doorstep, the dead mouse... She stiffened. Could he have been the one to run her down in the parking lot? Before his conviction, he'd been a trucker and skilled with vehicles. He'd have liked damaging her.

And he wouldn't want her to die quickly.

He'd screamed that at her in the courtroom as he was being dragged away. *"I'll cut you to pieces. Watch you die, bitch. Die slowly."*

He'd tried to cut Holt to pieces. Her hands shook as she clasped them in front of her on the desk. He must never, ever find out about Max and Alastair.

That's why she'd left her car in the duplex driveway beside Holt's Harley. At first, she'd thought to stay in the duplex and let Jarvis come after her, but that was stupid and would let him win. So she'd left in a taxi, making sure she wasn't followed before coming to the store.

Now...now she needed to figure out how to help the police catch him. Before he hurt someone else.

I'm so sorry, Holt. She closed her eyes as she thought of the different pain she'd brought to her two Masters. How they must hate her now. "You're better without me."

How funny. She'd thought she'd packed everything, but somehow, her heart was still there.

Seated in the breakfast nook that afternoon, Alastair read over the note they'd found as if reading it again and again would help. His heart ached for all of them.

Dear Alastair and Max,

Alastair almost smiled. Trust Uzuri to conform to the etiquette of a note.

I'm sorry for leaving you so abruptly and without speaking with you first. Several words were crossed out. **I think Jarvis is in town. Holt was attacked at the duplex and is in the hospital. If Jarvis finds out that I'm with you, you both will be in terrible danger.**

I've moved out and you won't see me again. This is best for everyone.

Please...please be careful. More words were scribbled out.
With love,
Uzuri

Tucking his phone into his pocket, Max walked into the room with Hunter at his heels. "Cullen called the fire station and got an update. Holt's doing well. Unfortunately, he isn't coherent enough to tell anyone what happened. He'll spend the night in the ICU, so he'll be safe enough."

"That's good." Alastair shook his head. "What about Uzuri?"

Max's mouth tightened, the pain almost radiating from him. The little submissive had inflicted a hard blow to the cop's soft heart.

Alastair knew exactly how much he was hurting.

Bloody hell. In her attempt to save them, Uzuri had dealt out a whole different kind of pain. "Any other news?"

Max nodded. "Yeah. Dan checked with the detectives on the case. The neighborhood kids saw the attacker. Description fits Kassab. Sliced Holt to pieces, left a knife in Holt's gut, and another one on the floor."

Alastair felt the wrongness. As a firefighter, Holt faced danger, but to be attacked in his own home? "I assume they didn't catch him?"

"No." Max shook his head. "One other thing. Uzuri's car is now parked in the driveway. She's not there; her car is."

"Why leave her vehicle there?"

Max rose and paced across the room. "Because..." He paced back. "*Dammit*. She's hoping the vindictive bastard will think she still lives there."

Alastair felt the same fury. And fear. She was out there alone rather than here under their protection. That wasn't to be tolerated. Silently, Alastair watched his cousin.

After stalking around the room two more times, Max dropped into a chair, anger gone. Alastair appreciated the trait. Max's temper, once roused, could remove a person's hide, but he forgave as readily as he yelled. After a second, Max bent and ruffled Hunter's ears. "Got any ideas?"

"I do." Alastair tapped the phone on the table. "Galen boasts he can find anyone. It appears to be true. Uzuri is at Brendall's."

"Is she now," Max breathed. "So, cuz, are we going to let our little subbie get away with this kind of behavior?"

"No." Alastair smiled slowly, pleased they were of the same mind. "No, we are not."

CHAPTER TWENTY-EIGHT

U zuri could hear the first few people leaving for home. The department tended to clear out early on Fridays. At her desk, she stared down at the notepad filled with ideas. None of them looked logical or smart or anything a cop would take seriously.

She needed to call the police now and talk with them—although Anne had said she'd let Dan know.

What now? Rubbing her forehead, she sighed. She felt so tired that she might slide right into a heap on the floor.

Leaning her head against the high chair back, she closed her eyes. Would the police listen to her if she asked them to let her help catch Jarvis?

"*Excuse* me. I need to announce you." Outside the door, the administrative assistant sounded annoyed as well as amused. "If you'll wait..." The sentence cut off.

At the sound of her door opening, Uzuri opened her eyes. And jerked upright.

Max was closing the office door. Alastair stood beside him, frowning at her.

Uzuri put her hand to her throat. "What are you..."

As if choreographed, they strode across her office. One on each side, they rounded her desk, blockading any escape. In a button-down, aquamarine shirt and stone-colored pants, Alastair set a hip on her desktop, making himself comfortable. Max crossed his arms over his black T-shirt-covered chest and leaned his butt against her desk.

They stared down at her like alley cats cornering a mouse.

She hated that she had to clear her throat before she could speak. "What are you doing here? I thought we'd decided we were...um...finished. Not together."

"I don't believe *we* had reached a consensus on that," Alastair said quietly.

"Imagine our surprise to read that your buddy Kassab is in town." Max's voice was flat. Cop voice. The one that said she'd was in oh, so much trouble.

She tried to push her chair back, but one of the *jerks* had put a foot behind the wheel. She pulled in a breath. *All right.* They were angry. She got it. Nonetheless, they needed to understand their danger. "Now that you know about Jarvis, you know you have to stay away from me. He's targeting anyone—any guy—I might be interested in. He's done it before, but never..." She swallowed, remembering the firefighter's expression when he'd described Holt's injuries. "Jarvis has never been so violent before."

"Only with you," Max snapped.

"But I never lived with anyone before." She set her left hand on Alastair's thigh and her right on Max's. "He doesn't know about you two. If you stay away from me, you should be fine."

Max curled his hand around hers, his grip unbreakable, as his blue eyes bored into hers. "Do you honestly figure we're worried about being *fine*?" He said the word as if it were the worst of insults.

The pit of her stomach dropped. What had she been thinking? Jarvis's violence had driven her Cincinnati friends away, but they hadn't been Doms, let alone overprotective-to-an-insane-degree Shadowlands *Masters*.

"You tried to protect us. That's heartwarming, love." Alastair laid his big hand on hers. "However, I think, instead, we should try to ensure your safety. That is *our* job, after all."

She couldn't speak as the utter loneliness, the emptiness inside her began to fill with their presence. The feeling that swept through her was indescribable, one she'd never felt before—the realization that she didn't have to carry the entire load herself, make all the decisions, be afraid all the time. Tears filled her eyes.

"No, don't you start that shit," Max growled, worry crossing his features.

"What kind of tough cop can't deal with a crying woman?" Laughing shakily, she wiped her eyes. "Better?"

"Fuck, yes." He bent forward and planted a hard kiss on her lips. "Workday's over, baby. We're taking you home now."

"B-but…" Uzuri set her mouth. "No. You need to stay away from me."

"She told us no?" Max gave his cousin an incredulous look. "Our subbie said no?"

"The soundproofing appears to be adequate." Amusement didn't hide the iron underlying Alastair's deep voice. "If I spank her, the secretary won't hear. Perhaps."

Outrage welled inside her. "Spank me. Here? You wouldn't dare."

A slow smile curved Alastair's lips. He glanced at Max.

As she started to rise, Max yanked her, face down, over her own desk and pulled her dress up over her ass.

"I quite like her undergarments." Alastair ran a finger along the edge of her lacy apricot-colored thong before his hand stuck her mostly bare bottom.

Slap. The sound echoed off the wall a second before she felt the sting.

Her yelp of pain was muffled by Max's calloused hand. Her

instinctive attempt to bite netted her a painful squeeze on her cheeks.

"That swat was for saying no to us." Alastair sounded as if he were listing off grocery items: bread, flour, sugar. "She lied to us at the car. Three more."

Her swearwords came out muffled. "Mmmmph, mmmph, mmmph."

"Glad I don't know what she's calling us," Max commented.

Slap, slap, slap.

The spanking hurt. Alastair wasn't going easy on her at all. His anger had been obvious beneath his resonant tone.

She'd hurt them both.

"Gonna yell any more?" Max asked.

She shook her head. When his hand was gone, she whispered, "I'm sorry."

"Are you?" Max didn't sound as if he believed her.

"I want you safe. The thought of losing you... I didn't mean to hurt you. I'd never..." She choked as sobs rose in her throat.

"Ah. There we go." Alastair helped her up and into his arms. Breathing in the fragrance of his sun-scented aftershave and cuddling against his hard chest was like coming home.

She felt Max tugging her skirt down.

A minute later, Alastair kissed the top of her head and turned her. Max was sitting on her desk. Without a word, he pulled her between his legs and wrapped his arms around her. Another wide, firm chest and his embrace was equally hard. Almost punishing.

"You scared the fuck out of me. Don't do that again," he growled in her ear.

Don't do that. "Max, it's not safe. Really." Fear for them swept through her again. She turned her head. Surely, Alastair would be reasonable. "It's better if I stay away from you."

"Love, that's not going to happen. We're staying close to you." Slow, British-accented words. And he was being totally unreasonable.

"Doesn't matter if you don't agree. You stay with us." Max's voice held an inflexible iron undertone. "Got it?"

Oh, she loved them so much. She blinked hard.

With a huff, Max kissed the tip of her nose. "You cry and I'll beat on you."

"Such a threat." Such a fake. She squeezed him hard. "Now what?"

"We'll go home and make arrangements." Alastair glanced around the office. "Is there anything you need?"

"No. My suitcase is downstairs in the security office." As they crossed the office, she stopped at the mirror on the back of the door to swipe away the smudges beneath her eyes and put her hair in place.

Max grinned. "Our high maintenance woman. Nothing messes you up."

At one time, his words would have hurt. At one time, he'd have said the words with a different attitude. Now, his tenderness and...appreciation...came across clearly.

She sniffed at him. "Scruffy cop. I'm going to start buying your clothes for you."

Score. Now his gaze held true worry.

Pleased, she walked through the door that Alastair held open and stopped.

Most of the buyers' section was packed into the reception room. All women. Apparently Mrs. Everson had mentioned Uzuri's gorgeous visitors.

Silence fell over the room as the Dragon Doms followed Uzuri out. Two entirely different types of males, both supreme eye-candy. Uzuri could have sworn every woman in the room ovulated.

Mrs. Everson smiled at her. "I hope it was all right not to call security. These gentlemen said they were...*yours*?"

"Both of them?" one woman whispered in a hoarse voice.

"That would be correct. Please log her out for the day." Alastair put his hand on Uzuri's lower back to move her forward.

Max frowned at his cousin. "I thought *she* was *ours*."

"It's the same thing, I believe." Alastair's lips twitched.

"All right then." Max ran a slow finger down Uzuri's cheek, his eyes crinkled with a smile—and several sighs wafted around the room. "Guess that works."

On the way back to the house, Max drove, keeping a close eye out for any vehicles that might be following them. If Kassab had gone crazy enough to attack Holt, God only knew what he'd try next.

In the back seat with Uzuri, the doc was fielding phone calls.

"Yes, she's safe. She's fine. She's with us." Being a smart guy, Alastair resorted to texting whenever possible.

"Who...?" Uzuri asked.

"Jesus, everyone." Max glanced at her confused expression in the rearview mirror before returning his attention to the road.

Alastair explained, "People want to know what they can do to help, whether it's to give you a place to stay, to serve on guard duty, or to set a trap."

"For me?" The stunned note in her voice could break a man's heart. Didn't she know how much she was loved? "But—you said, *set a trap?*"

Alastair said, "We're trying to think of how to do that without risking your safety. Kassab needs to be caught."

"Oh, yes," she said. "That's what I was thinking, too. I can be bait if the police will help me figure out how."

Max felt his teeth grind together. "Only if we can do it in a way where you'll be completely safe."

"Only if," Alastair agreed.

Without slowing, Max pulled into the garage, barely leaving room enough for the door to clear the car's roof. "Keep her here," he told Alastair as he slid out of the car. Hand on his weapon, he checked the garage, then stepped inside the house and turned off the alarm system. The readout showed no one had entered since they'd left.

Everything secure, he went outside. Hunter abandoned his doghouse in the backyard and ran over. "C'mon, buddy. See who's home."

After Hunter had given Zuri a you've-been-gone-for-years greeting, which she enthusiastically returned, Max led her toward the stairs.

Her feet dragged. "I want to go to the hospital to see Holt."

"He'll be in ICU all night. You can't see him." He glanced down at her, smiling as the light from the windows glowed on her face. Smooth skin. Big, worried, velvety eyes.

He and Alastair needed to wear her out now so she could get a good night's rest. Really, fucking her into exhaustion was what a kind-hearted Dom would do.

Alastair chuckled. "Let's go to your room, Max."

They were definitely on the same page. "Oh, yeah." He turned away from the stairs and headed toward his rooms at the back of the house.

He felt Uzuri's little hand tense. "Why Max's room? Why not mine?"

Max tilted his head down to whisper in her ear. "You'll see."

They usually spent nights in the little subbie's room. After all, females liked having their girly shit close and having their own bathroom. She had a thing about satin pillowcases, too.

Twice he'd taken her to his room to play, but he'd never shown her *everything*. He gave her hand to Alastair and headed across the room.

"Strip completely," Alastair told her.

"But..."

Argument? Max turned in time to see her eyes lower, to see her lovely surrender. She started to unbutton her blouse.

The situation with her stalker was a mess, yet contentment hummed in Max's veins.

Zuri was back with them.

Smiling, he slid open the glass door to let in the fresh, mois-ture-laden air. The wind was beginning to pick up, the harbinger of the incoming tropical storm due tomorrow.

An hour later, Uzuri lay on the blue and brown flannel bedspread, sweat cooling on her body, and utterly limp after another orgasm. How many had that been?

Propped up on an elbow, Alastair lay beside her, stroking her gently. The tenderness he showed now was a startling contrast from how he'd hurt her only minutes before. How did he know so surely which painful sensations would drive her pleasure higher and higher?

Two Doms. One a master of pain, one a master of pleasure. Her clit was exquisitely sensitive from the vibrator Max had used. Her pussy and back hole still throbbed from the double-headed dildo.

Pain and pleasure. Her Dragon Doms were really, really scary.

She turned her head to locate Max.

There he was beside the bed. As he removed his shirt, muscles rippled beneath his tanned skin.

"You're so pretty." Her voice came out hoarse.

Catching her watching, Max simply grinned.

She turned to look at Alastair.

His aquamarine shirt was unbuttoned, and the smooth, dark expanse of streamlined muscle was a feast for her eyes.

"You, too." When had she come to adore how big her Doms were?

"Why, thank you, sweetheart." Openly amused, Alastair ran a finger over her lower lip, before bending to kiss her lightly.

The bed sagged as Max lay down beside her. He started

playing with her hair, pulling a braid apart and combing the strands out with his fingers.

She couldn't summon up the energy to swat his fingers. "Don't make me hurt you, white boy." Her eyes started to drift shut.

Max chuckled...and didn't stop messing with her hair. "I look forward to the battle, black girl."

Without opening her eyes, she smiled. It was odd how closeness could transform uncomfortable words into an expression of affection.

But if he called her his *Nubian princess* again, she'd put his flogger through the office shredder.

"Don't go to sleep, Uzuri," Alastair warned. "We're not through with you."

Pleased, she roused. They'd played with her, but hadn't... taken...her yet. Neither Dom had gotten off. "I was wondering when we'd get to the good stuff."

He smiled. "We will, indeed, get to the good stuff. First, there is something you should know."

"Oh. All right." Warm and sated, cuddled between the two strong bodies, Uzuri figured she could take anything they wanted to say. "Shoot, Sir."

He picked up her hand. His trimmed dark beard framed lips that had done devastating things to her mere minutes past. His eyes, deep brown in the dim light, met hers. "We love you, Uzuri."

"What?" Her heart stopped. Simply skipped a whole slew of beats. She stared. "You love me?"

"Told you she hadn't caught on." Max cupped her chin in his big, callused hand and turned her head. "Look at me, little mischief."

Her eyes met his.

Cop eyes. Piercing. Determined. His voice held a low growl as he said, "I love you with everything in me. I want you as my woman. My lover. And my submissive."

Love? She couldn't find enough air, and her voice came out a whisper. "Yours?"

"Mine—and *ours*." Max looked over her head at his cousin.

With a hand on her cheek, Alastair turned her head toward him. "I love you, Uzuri. You are mine—and *ours*. We want you here with us."

At the warmth—the *love*—in his eyes, her heart swelled, filling her chest, filling her world. "You love me." Impossible. Amazing. Wonderful.

The earth itself seemed to tremble as joy resounded through her world. They loved her. Alastair and Max loved *her*. And wanted her to stay. She could have them both.

Could take care of them.

Could go to them when she was troubled or upset. Could comfort them when they had problems. Push them to talk.

Could tuck one in at night and sleep with the other. Wake up with muscular arms around her. Because they loved her. "Omigod." Her fingers closed around Alastair's hand, and her left hand groped for and found Max's. "Omigod."

"Yeah, there. I think she got it." The laughter in Max's voice brought her gaze to his face.

"I love you, too," she whispered.

The amusement in Max's eyes transmuted to blue heat.

She turned to look into Alastair's dark face. Clean lines, square jaw, strength in every feature. "I love you."

"I know." He kissed her gently, tenderly, coaxing her full response. His firm hand held her in place as his kiss deepened, possessed—and gradually turned so carnal that her toes curled under the wave of heat.

When Alastair pulled back, Max rubbed his knuckles down her cheek. "Are you ready to take us both this time?"

Both? At once? Her mouth went dry. However, although still frightening, the idea was exciting, too. Her Doms claiming her together. She shivered. "Yes."

"Very good." Alastair leaned over and took her lips again. The room spun around her as she gave him everything he wanted. Although she felt Max leave the bed, she didn't move. Couldn't move.

Sometime later, she heard Max call, "Ready, cuz."

Releasing her, Alastair rose to stand beside the bed and stripped off his clothes.

She sighed with pleasure. Broad shoulders, flat stomach, long, long erection. Neatly shaved groin—he'd made her shave him last time. Maybe Max would trust her to do the same someday. Unable to resist, she stroked her hand down his stomach.

"Come here, beautiful." He scooped her off the bed, making her squeak, and carried her toward the sliding glass doors. The chocolate brown drapes were pulled back. On the patio outside, the last rays of the setting sun danced off the pond waters.

Max waited near the corner inside the doors. Completely, powerfully male—and magnificently erect.

Several leather straps dangled from chains anchored to a big bolt in the ceiling.

"Didn't something else hang there?" She eyed the ceiling and looked around. Yes, a pot of trailing golden pothos had hung in the bedroom corner previously.

"Good memory." Max held open a strap.

Alastair slid her right leg into the opening. After they did the same with her left leg, Max fitted the straps to her upper thighs. As Alastair turned her in his arms, Max encircled her upper arms with other straps. A final leather band ran between two chains to support her back.

Alastair moved her hands to the chains beside her shoulders. "Hang on."

When she complied, Max secured her wrists to the chains with Velcro straps. "We'll just make sure your hands stay out of our way."

Her pulse kicked up a notch. Both of them at once. In a... This was a *sex* swing.

As Alastair released her and moved away, she stared at the straps around her thighs. The sex swing in the Shadowlands resembled a leather hammock in which the submissive would lay almost flat.

This one, though...

With her weight supported by the thigh straps, she was sitting almost upright. This was like a real swing.

She'd always liked swing sets.

With an uncontrollable giggle, she tried to set it to rocking.

Max chuckled. "Don't worry, mischief. We'll have everything moving real soon." When he pushed her legs apart and stepped between her thighs, she realized the height of the swing was perfect for...for insertion.

Her laughter vanished.

His intense blue gaze met hers. "You ready?"

For two cocks at once. She bit her lip.

"Uzuri." Standing beside her, Alastair ran his hand over her loose hair. "We want you to try this once. If you don't like it, we won't play this way again."

But what if... Her voice emerged, shaking. "Will you still—"

"Love you?" Alastair's expression turned tender. "Would you still love me if I didn't like oral sex?"

"Of course. That doesn't have anything to do with—" When Max snorted, she got it. "Oh."

"Exactly." Gripping her hair, Max tilted her head back and kissed her slowly, taking his time. Oh, he could kiss so well.

When he stopped, she felt Alastair behind her. His hard chest warmed her back. Oh, oh, oh, they were going to *start*. She wasn't *ready*.

"Better begin, cuz, before our princess gets too anxious." Max's gaze lingered on her face, then her hands where she had a death grip on the chains. "Breathe, darlin'."

She tried, she did, only she heard Alastair donning a condom, and he pressed his erection against her anus, and it felt ever so much bigger than the plug. She was still slick from the lubricant they'd applied earlier, and—

When Max skimmed one finger over her swollen, sensitive clit, she jerked as the stunning pleasure blazed into a flashing fire. "Oh, moooore..."

"You'll get more, baby."

Pressure built against her anus. "Push back against me," Alastair murmured.

She tried, knowing it would help, and after an uncomfortable moment, the head of his cock slipped in. He was *huge*. She tried to turn, to push him away—but her wrists were restrained. She struggled, feeling impaled. Helpless.

And the realization sent a wave of heat through her.

"Easy, love." His crooning baritone soothed her nerves. Slowly, gently, he worked his way in. When she squirmed, Alastair cupped her right breast. His other hand closed tighter on her hip, holding her as his cock continued the merciless penetration until his groin pressed against her buttocks.

He bent to kiss the curve between her shoulder and neck. "All in, sweetheart."

"Okay." Her backside throbbed painfully around the intrusion. Her voice cracked as she revised her answer. "Y-yes, Sir."

In front of her, Max was studying her again. "I know it's uncomfortable, but it'll get better."

Alastair's voice rumbled in her ear. "No hurry, love. Get used to the feeling." He didn't move.

Panting slightly, she remained frozen, feeling Alastair's warm hand on her breast, the pressure of Max's hand cupping her pussy...and the impossible searing ache in her backside.

Gradually, the discomfort eased to a milder burn, and...more. Something wanton and hot quickened in her core, and a disconcerting arousal wakened.

Max's keen gaze lifted from her face to his cousin, and he nodded.

"Excellent." Unhurriedly, Alastair pulled back, and she heard him apply more lubricant before he pressed back in. His slick cock was cool as it entered her, and then heated inside her. As he eased in and out, the leisurely sliding sent electricity sizzling directly to her core.

As need lit a fire in her veins, she trembled.

"There we go." With one hand, Alastair rolled her left nipple. When his fingers pinched harder, a shocking zing shot through her, and her anus clenched, making him laugh. "Max, let's see how it goes."

As Alastair gripped her hips firmly, she knew how well they had positioned her to be taken. Her pussy and anus were at exactly the right height. Her hands were restrained high and out of the way.

Standing between her open thighs, Max kissed her lightly. "Little mischief." She met his intense eyes. "You tell us if something hurts."

Nodding, she braced herself. Not that there was anything at all she could do to help or to hinder. And somehow, her helplessness only added to the erotic heat and set up a flutter in her stomach.

Alastair's hands on her hips tightened as he slid out of her back hole. At the same time, Max steadily pressed into her vagina until his cock was seated to the hilt.

Her breathing caught as she stretched around the hot, thick invasion.

Without stopping, Max withdrew as deliberately.

Alastair thrust in. The feeling—oh God, the feeling of being taken by the two of them was overwhelming. Everything down there was stretching. The two cocks were sliding in and out, separated by only the thinnest of membranes. Pleasure swelled, billowing outward, until it was simply devastating.

Her moan filled the room, and Alastair chuckled.

As he drew out, Max bent to kiss her lightly, his steady b[l]ue gaze on her face. "She can take more, cuz."

Alastair pulled back; Max surged in.

"Then let's give her more." Keeping one hand on her right h[ip,] Alastair reached around to cup her mound. His fingers brush[ed] over her clit. At the hot rush of sensation, everything inside [her] clamped around Max's rigid shaft.

Max laughed. "Oh, yeah." His right hand gripped her left h[ip,] holding her in place. With the other hand, he started to tease [her] nipples into distended, aching peaks.

As the Doms alternated thrusting and withdrawing, [the] exquisite torment grew so intense, she started to shake. Her c[ore] steadily tightened around them until every tiny movem[ent] consumed her world.

Alastair's finger relentlessly circled her clit.

Her body gathered, each muscle tensing as her insides sh[iv]-ered around the Doms' rhythmic penetrations: front, back, fr[ont,] back... "Oh, oh, oh."

"Let go, love," Alastair whispered, and as if her body [just] required permission, she climaxed...and each successive wave [of] pleasure grew more and more overwhelming. Her core spasr[ned] around one thick shaft, then the other, and her cries ech[oed] around the room.

As the contractions diminished, and her heart thum[ped] crazily in her chest, the men slowed further, giving her tim[e to] recover. The swing was rocking slightly. Her sweaty palms w[ere] slick on the chains.

"Thank you for trusting us, sweetheart." Alastair kissed [the] top of her head.

"Mmmhmm." Oh, how she loved them. She saw Max [also] smiling, and the way he looked at her, as if she delighted his [eyes,] simply made her bones melt.

on tight, darlin'." Max glanced over her head at
e

at?" Uzuri gripped the chains.
rl." Alastair chuckled. "Yes, now, Max."

nds tightened on her hips, and suddenly, their speed
lastair's long shaft thrust into her anus—and with-
s Max's thickness pressed into her pussy. Her Doms
er, fast and hard, ruthlessly alternating so she was
t a cock inside her.

arched as the glorious sensations pulsed through her,
pleasure to new, impossible heights, and drowning
f the world.

orgasm erupted in dazzling explosions, shuddering
o intensely that the room flashed white. Her fingers,
her *hair* tingled with the pulse of her climax.

mbled his pleasure, pressed in deeply, even as Max
and the two filled her to the point of pain. As she
the impossible, soul-shattering pleasure, they
arms around her, squeezing her between them as
well. All three. Together.

nse of their love and loving was the greatest joy she
n.

CHAPTER TWENTY-NINE

"Yeah, well, I'll be here. Sorry." Holt hung up before he descended into rudeness. The scheduler at the fire station hated adjusting for injuries—especially ones incurred off the job—and Holt's Saturday afternoon call hadn't made him happy at all. Too bad. Considering the entire station knew about the attack, the dumbass'd had enough warning.

Holt clicked the phone off. At least he was out of ICU and in a regular hospital room where he could see people and make phone calls. Turning slightly, he reached to set the phone on the over-the-bed tray table. *Christ.* Moving only that much set off explosions of pain in Holt's gut and back.

A sound had him turning toward the door. *Pain.* He muffled a groan. *Yeah, don't move so fast, idiot.*

"Oh my God." Barely inside the room, Nadia stared at him, green eyes shocked. "Warren said you'd been hurt. I hadn't realized. Look at you."

Thanks, no. He glanced down anyway. Gauze was wrapped around his arms to keep him from irritating all the newly closed knife wounds up and down his forearms. At least the butt-ugly hospital gown covered the bigger dressings on his back and belly.

Only...she wasn't looking at anything except his face.

Her gaze was locked on the long slice from cheekbone to jaw and the gash on his chin. Without thinking, Holt fingered the line of knotted off stitches. The stiff ends of the thread felt like fucking fishing line. Attempting a smile, he said lightly, "Sorry about the mess. The guy had a big knife."

Why the fuck was he apologizing?

No, cut her a break. She'd had a shock. He could read every emotion crossing her face. Definitely a shock.

There was also a hell of a lot of revulsion.

Holt cleared his throat. "Nadia. Did you come with a friend?"

"Uh. Yes." She waved toward the door. "Di brought me so we could go on and have drinks. It's happy hour."

"I see." Hadn't planned to stay long, had she? A knot of pain unrelated to his injuries took up residence under his ribs. He'd thought they had something...more...but apparently not. She was intelligent and fun to talk with, personable, interesting, and good in bed. It seemed he'd forgotten to look for compassion. Perhaps he'd gotten spoiled by the generous nature of the Shadowlands submissives.

"So, are you doing all right?" She hesitated and added reluctantly, "Is there anything you'd like me to bring you?"

He wouldn't mind if she brought him a lover who wouldn't bail when the going got rough. However, that wasn't what she wanted to know.

Holt shook his head. "I'll be fine. You go ahead and enjoy your evening."

"Sounds good." The relief in her smile told him everything he needed to know. Hell, she hadn't even touched him.

Before she could get out the door, he went ahead and bit the bullet. "Nadia."

She turned, tensed as if she was worried that he'd ask her to stay.

Not in this lifetime.

"I'll mail you the things you left at my place." In case she had any doubts as to what he was saying, he added, "I hope you find a guy who can make you happy."

Mouth open, she flushed, then paled...and walked out the door.

Well. He had to say—*that sucked.*

After contemplating his dismal luck with females, he realized he was gritting his teeth. Because he hurt. Should he punch the IV button for a hit of pain medication or gut through it?

Before he could decide, a little whirlwind rushed into the room.

"Holt." Uzuri skidded to a stop beside his bed. Her expression held the same appalled shock as Nadia's—and then her eyes filled with tears. "Oh, boo." She took his hand, ever so carefully, barely moving after she saw the heavy dressings on his wrist and arms.

His fingers tightened around hers, and the ache in his chest grew. He'd wanted this from Nadia. Sure it was best to realize early on he'd made a mistake about her, but now there was an...emptiness.

"Does it hurt?" she whispered. "How bad? Can I get you anything? Should you have a pain pill or something? Or...since it's boring in hospitals, I should go get you some books or your iPod or—"

"Hey." Fuck, it hurt to laugh. Seriously hurt. He did need some pain med. Unfortunately, the damn button for the medication was clipped next to his pillow. No way to hit it unobtrusively. Damned if he'd admit to pain and increase the worry in her big eyes. "No, it doesn't hurt. I'm doing fine." His brows drew together. "You're not here by yourself, are you?"

"She came with us." Max stood inside the door.

A movement behind Uzuri caught Holt's attention. Alastair stood next to the head of the bed. He glanced at the pain control button, and his eyebrow lifted in a silent inquiry. Clever guy, the doc.

Holt nodded enough to agree without letting Uzuri notice. He squeezed her fingers instead. "I figured you two might be close."

Alastair shook his head. The poor bastard had lied to Uzuri about not hurting. He was almost gritting his teeth with pain.

Best Uzuri not know or she'd burst into tears. She felt bad enough thinking she was to blame for Kassab's attack on him.

Alastair glanced at the bright bouquet in the window. "Uzuri, who sent the flowers? Can you check?"

"Sure."

As she walked around the bed to the flowers, Alastair quietly set the button in Holt's hand and re-clipped the cord in a better location.

The firefighter squeezed the button and gave Alastair a grateful look.

"They're from your firehouse." Uzuri returned and took Holt's hand as if she could somehow take away all his pain.

The stubborn little minx. Bloody hell, he didn't like having her anywhere outside their home. Not until Kassab was behind bars.

But she wasn't going to listen to them. He and Max had told her it wasn't safe to visit Holt and offered alternatives. Skype, phone calls.

Alastair hadn't known she could yell that loud. In fact, she'd had a total shit-fit, as Max had called it. She'd insisted she had to see her friend for herself, to make sure he was cared for, to be there if he needed her, to find out if he wanted anything, to bring him some goodies if he could have them, and on and on.

As rain spattered against the window in furious gusts, Alastair moved to lean against the sill beside Max. Their woman might think she wasn't brave, but he pitied any poor bastard who got between her and someone she loved.

And she loved *them*. The joy of it sang through his veins like a massive infusion of endorphins. She was going to stay.

Which was a good thing, since he and Max would have trouble ever letting her go. Her response to taking them both had been dazzling, not only reaffirming the love they'd given to her, but also deepening the bond he had with Max. Sharing with his cousin had always felt right; sharing someone they both loved was...more. With her mischief, energy, and sweetness, she filled the missing place in the triangle in a way that no one else could.

And she loved them. Loved *him*.

He listened to the wind screaming outside and the hammering of rain on the windows and watched his woman. How did she keep getting more beautiful?

Her lips were swollen, and her cheeks were beard-burned from almost twenty-four hours of lovemaking. Worried they'd change their minds about visiting Holt, she hadn't taken time to apply makeup or spent much time on her hair.

Alastair half-smiled. Max had undone her braids during their play, and her hair had stuck out in all directions. After glaring at the cop, she'd quickly bunched her hair up, made a long roll from crown to nape, and ruthlessly bobby-pinned it all in place.

Quite impressive, actually.

"Alastair, Max." Veering around a short male janitor who was talking on a cell phone, Dan Sawyer walked into the room, glanced at Uzuri, and back at them. "You two are smiling. I take it the reacquisition of your subbie went well?"

"You're as nosy as a girl, pard," Max muttered. "Did you talk with the Captain about Zuri and this bastard stalker?"

"Yeah. He's all for setting up a trap. In fact, he's staying late to meet with the four of us once we leave here."

"Dan, are you here to talk to me?" Holt asked.

Dan turned. "Good to see you awake. And yeah, I have a few questions."

"I figured. Although a couple of detectives interviewed me earlier, I had a feeling I'd see you and Max." Holt squeezed Uzuri's hand. "Let me get this over with, sweetie."

"Okay to talk with him, Doc?" Max asked.

Alastair checked. The medication had kicked in, and the tight muscles around Holt's eyes and mouth had relaxed. He was moving, rather than holding himself stiffly immobile. Alastair nodded at Max.

"All right, then." Max stepped closer to the bed, Dan beside him.

As Uzuri came to stand beside Alastair, he frowned at her slumped shoulders. "You can stop worrying now, love. He's doing well."

She nodded without looking up.

Hmm. He lifted her chin. Tears had filled her eyes. Curving his hand around her nape, he asked softly. "What's wrong, pet?"

"His face. He'll have scars, won't he?"

Alastair hesitated. The truth would hurt her. Nevertheless, honesty was what he gave his friends, his patients, his lovers. Everyone. "Yes. None of the deeper nerves were damaged, so his movement isn't impaired, but he'll have some loss of sensation for a while." Holt's mouth didn't droop. His lips curved up equally on both sides. "The scars will fade slowly until all that will remain will be white lines."

"They won't go away completely though. He'll never look the same." She drew in a shuddering breath. "Because of me."

"No. This wasn't your fault."

"I shouldn't have come to Tampa. Or I shouldn't have made friends. I should have known Jarvis wouldn't give up, that he'd come after me. I shouldn't have let Holt move into my place."

The anguish in her voice squeezed his heart, and he pulled her closer. "If Kassab didn't come after you, wouldn't he go after someone else? Maybe someone more vulnerable?"

"Maybe." Her gaze dropped. "Probably."

"Well then." Alastair saw Max lean forward intently as Holt answered a question.

What were they talking about?

"*She's mine.* Kassab said that...a lot." Holt tried to scratch his cheek and winced when his fingers hit the stitches. With an annoyed grunt, he dropped his hand. "Got a comment about him being better than me."

"Better how?" Dan asked.

Holt saw Uzuri watching, and he grinned at her. "I'd say he meant better in bed since he followed up with the size of his dick. And how I couldn't satisfy her."

Max snorted and glanced at their little submissive. "Usually get that shit from insecure bastards. What do you say, princess? Is he insecure?"

The skin on her cheeks darkened slightly. "If you mean was he better or bigger, then the answer is no."

"Go on."

Uzuri gave him an exasperated look. "Seriously?"

Max waggled his fingers in a *give-me-more* gesture.

"Oh, fine. He was, um, average length, and...um, a pencil dick? And he could last pretty good, but his idea of skill was to get on and pump." She hid her face against Alastair's chest.

He kissed her head. "Thank you, love." The entire discussion had knotted his gut, and yet he felt a trickle of amusement at her embarrassment.

The corner of Max's mouth tipped up as he met Alastair's gaze.

Dan chuckled. "Odd how women can discuss sex exhaustively with their buddies and get fucking embarrassed with anyone else."

"No shit. Have you heard those Shadowkittens?" Max shook his head. "Could give a guy a complex."

Holt laughed, grabbed his side, and groaned. "Fuck, Drago, if you're going to be funny, do it elsewhere."

"Sorry." Max glanced at Uzuri. "But it's good to know what triggers the asshole has. Never know when it might come in handy during the interview process."

"Gotta say, those interviews must make for interesting reading." Holt grinned. "You donut munchers are just plain weird."

Uzuri giggled, and Holt grinned at her.

Max shook his head. "Least we're not always playing with our hoses like you nozzle jockeys."

When Holt reached up to scratch his face, Alastair warned, "Uh-uh."

Holt scowled. "It itches."

Under Alastair's arm, Uzuri turned to look and made a helpless sound.

Holt's expression softened. "Zuri, it's simply a cut. Nothing to get upset about."

"It's going to scar," she whispered.

"It will," he agreed evenly. "Do you think I care?"

"But... Women will..."

"If Alastair got a scar on his pretty face, would you turn away from him?"

"Of course not." Her fingers fisted Alastair's shirt. "Don't say that. Don't ever say anything like that!"

"Well, sweets, that's the kind of woman I want. If the shallow ones fall by the wayside, I don't see it as a problem."

After a moment, Uzuri's shoulders relaxed. Alastair gave Holt a nod of gratitude. Well handled. On the other hand, had there been bitterness there? Hadn't Uzuri mentioned the Dom had a lady friend?

Dan checked his watch. "We need to get going."

"Yeah." Max glanced at Holt. "You gonna get out of this place soon?"

"Couple of days. Because of the gut stab, they're dumping in antibiotics for a while." Holt smiled. "The landlord finishes the remodeling tomorrow, so my apartment will be quiet."

"We'll take care of packing your stuff at Uzuri's and bringing it over," Alastair said.

Dan grinned. "You realize you'll be swamped with Shadowkittens for a while, right?"

"Like I'd object to help with cooking and cleaning?" Holt's lips curved. "Be good friends and send the single ones. And have them wear those little ruffled aprons Z keeps in the costume boxes. Only the aprons."

Max snorted. "Yeah, he's feeling better."

Naked submissives? That sounded like Holt, Uzuri thought, and still...last week, he'd said he was serious about that redhead. Uzuri frowned. "Should we send an apron for Nadia?"

Holt's face went still before he said lightly, "Hey, I play the field. Remember?"

Play the field. Right. That girlfriend—that bitch—had dumped him, hadn't she? Had left him when he was down and hurting.

Uzuri clenched her hand. If she ever ran into the woman, there was going to be some hair pulling. Or punching. She knew how to punch now.

Forcing a smile, she gave Holt what he needed. "Holt, you play the field better than any gambler betting on horses. I'll ask Master Z to round you up some gorgeous fillies."

His lips curved up, although no smile showed in his blue eyes. "You're a good friend, Zuri."

Her heart felt as if it was cracking in half. "I'll be back tomorrow. What can I bring you?"

"Be safer if you stayed away." His gaze turned to Max. "Keep her—"

"I *will* be here." Her voice came out hard and mean—how rude was that? She lightened up. She needed to buy him a comfortingly fuzzy bathrobe—steel blue to match his eyes, of course. What else? "What should I get for you?"

Max snorted. "Might as well tell her. She threatened to disappear if we try to keep her from seeing you."

Her Dragon Doms. Uzuri glared at them. They'd actually discussed locking her away. For her own good.

"Stubborn subbie," Holt muttered. He grinned at her. "In that case, how about my eReader from the duplex?" Then he shook his head. "No, come to think of it, it's at work. Since they won't let me eat real food for a couple of days, can you bring me a milk-shake? Strawberry."

"Sure." Uzuri kissed him lightly on the cheek. His eReader was at the duplex—she'd seen it. However, like her Dragon Doms, he didn't want her to go to the duplex where Jarvis had been. Rather than feeling crowded, all these protectors made her feel safe and... and cared for.

They'd all go together to get his eReader.

"Come, pet. Let's be on our way." Alastair held out his hand.

Taking his hand, she glanced out the window. Lighting flashed erratically in the pitch-black clouds. Thunder rumbled almost continuously, and rain slammed against the window in ugly gusts. They'd have to make a run for the car.

Outside the room, Dan led the way. Without missing a step, Max and Alastair bracketed Uzuri as they walked down the hospital corridor to the elevator. Uzuri loved how everyone from janitors to MDs greeted Alastair with smiles, comments, and jokes.

"Drago. Got a second?" In the first floor hallway on the way to the lobby, a short, gray-haired doctor stopped them. "I have a question about the med regimen Laring is taking."

"Of course." Alastair cast them all an apologetic look and bent slightly to listen to his colleague.

Putting a hand behind Uzuri's back, Max guided her out of the way of the people going by.

Dan followed. "I meant to ask you, did you hear about the body they found in St. Pete? It might tie into one of ours. The coroner's report says..."

As the two cops discussed the grisly murder, Uzuri quickly stepped out of hearing. *Ewww.* The contents of a person's stomach shouldn't be a topic of conversation.

Her phone chimed with an incoming message, and she pulled it out of her small purse, taking another step away. The caller ID said RAINIE—and text messages from Rainie and Sally could be extremely...perverted.

Uzuri thumbed the message open.

"*IF YOU DON'T WANT THAT CUNT RAINIE TO DIE, GET YOUR ASS ACROSS THE PARKING LOT TO THE BLACK VAN*."

What? Cold stabbed into her chest like an icy dagger. She read the message again. Cunt? Rainie?

The message had come from Rainie's phone...knowledge swept through her like an icy wind. Jarvis had sent the message.

He had Rainie. Her knees threatened to buckle.

He wanted her outside.

He'd hurt her.

Kill her. Her mouth went dry, and her hands started shaking so hard she almost dropped her phone. *I can't.*

Gripping the phone hard, she turned toward Max, holding the phone out. She opened her mouth.

Her cell chimed, and words scrolled up the screen.

"*IF I DON'T SEE YOU RIGHT FUCKING NOW, I DRIVE AWAY. HOW HIGH WILL THE BITCH BOUNCE*?"

Bounce? He'd run over Rainie or do something horrible.

If Max and Dan came with her, he'd see them. He'd kill Rainie before leaving. *My Rainie.* The big-hearted woman who had dropped everything to stay with Uzuri after the attack at Mistress Anne's house. Like Holt, Rainie would get hurt or killed only because she knew Uzuri. *I can't let that happen.*

But what could she do? Go outside? To Jarvis?

He'll kill me. Uzuri stood paralyzed. Her heart felt as if it'd beat out of her chest, and she couldn't breathe. *I'm a coward.*

She couldn't afford to be a coward. Rainie needed her.

"Courage is endurance for one moment more." She could do this.

The men would stop her. There was no time to talk. To explain. She lurched into a run.

"Uzuri," Max sounded startled. "What—"

She turned and threw the phone at Dan. "Dan, Jarvis has *Rainie*. Make the Dragons be smart."

As she dashed out, running full tilt into the lobby, she glanced back. Dan caught her phone in one hand and grabbed Max's shirt with the other. Alastair was just turning around.

Uzuri ran out the front door and came to a stop as a crack of thunder shook the ground. Like crashing waves, rain spattered the ground, eased, and increased, whipped by the gusting wind. The palm trees lining the edges of the parking lot bowed under the onslaught.

The sun was blotted out, as if night had set already.

Terrified Max or Alastair would catch her, Uzuri hurried farther away from the entrance, then stopped to scan the dark parking area for black vans. Go left or right?

Arbitrarily, she chose right. Halfway down the first line of cars, she slowed. *There.*

A woman stood motionless behind the open cargo door of a black van as the exhaust formed a white fog around her. In an oversized man's raincoat with the hood and collar up, Rainie was barely recognizable.

Oh no. Hands clenched tightly, Uzuri crossed the sidewalk and stepped off the curb. Rain drenched her clothes and hair as she crossed the lane toward the line of cars—toward where Jarvis must be. Her legs, her body, everything inside her screamed a protest. Each step forward was hard-won.

Run, Rainie.

Why didn't she run?

In a few more steps, Uzuri saw a leather dog collar was cinched around Rainie's neck. The collar was attached to a heavy metal chain that ran into the van. The raincoat's sleeves hung empty. Did she have her hands tied behind her back?

Uzuri was close enough to see how the hood's bottom had been pulled shut to conceal the duct tape over Rainie's mouth. In the pouring rain, no one would even notice. If they did, Jarvis would probably kill them.

Seeing her, Rainie shook her head frantically and then jerked her head for Uzuri to get away.

And if Uzuri left? The message text had asked, "How high will the bitch bounce?" If Jarvis drove away, Rainie would be dragged behind the van. By her neck.

Leave you here? Never.

When Dan grabbed his shirt, Max turned, fist lifted. "Let *go*."

"Wait, Drago, dammit. Alastair, get over here!" Dan dragged Max down the hall. As he stepped into the lobby, far enough to see out the huge windows, he slapped Uzuri's phone into Max's hand. "Read that."

Max's gut tightened. "Jesus, no."

Alastair leaned over Max's shoulder to read. "Kassab has Rainie?"

"Wait. Uzuri's crossing toward the cars. Toward a black van. That might be Rainie at the rear." Releasing Max, Dan narrowed his eyes. "Why isn't Rainie moving? Is she tied to it? Is that why the threat?"

Max scowled. Once Kassab grabbed Zuri, he'd take off. However, he'd also drive away if he felt threatened—like if Max and Dan ran out of the building toward him.

Dammit, what was the little sub thinking?

Alastair gripped his shoulder. "Uzuri will try to stall."

Light bulb moment. Of course, she would. She'd know they'd come after her. She would do what she could. Max edged into the lobby far enough to assess the parking lot. The van was parked so the rear faced the hospital. If Kassab was in the driver's seat, the only shot possible would be through a side window.

"Yeah, she'll stall." Max glanced at Dan. "Alastair and I will draw his attention on the left. You go to the right. If we can get the drop, we will. You take a shot if you have one."

Phone to his ear, calling for backup, Dan nodded.

Expression grim and determined, Alastair met Max's gaze.

"We'll get her, cuz. Let's go." Fear-sweat slicked his palms as Max led the way across the lobby. When the entrance doors slid back, he and Alastair sauntered out. Cold, hard rain slapped at him. The wind whipped his hair as he turned to the right.

There was the van in the line of cars. It'd been pulled far enough forward to block the space in front, too. The clever bastard. He'd be able to drive forward instead of backing out. The white exhaust showed the engine was running. "Let's use that umbrella of yours."

Alastair opened up his huge umbrella, covering them both.

A glance at the hospital door showed Dan was coming out. Max stopped. "Hold, cuz." Every cell in his body wanted to charge Kassab and get Uzuri back. Instead, he waited.

Turning his collar up against the rain, Dan moved past.

Slowly, Uzuri walked up to Rainie and patted her shoulder. "Hey, girl." Maybe she could remove the collar?

No. A shiny new padlock locked the collar and attached the chain to the D-ring.

"'Bout time you got here, you stupid-ass cunt." The hammering rain and the gusting wind almost drowned out the rasping voice.

But not quite. The vile satisfaction she heard turned her skin icy cold and her mouth dry. Her feet wouldn't move.

"Get in here, bitch." His shout probably couldn't be heard by anyone more than a few feet from the van.

A whimper escaped her.

Again, Rainie jerked her head and made a muffled sound past the duct tape. *"Run."*

Leave Rainie to die? *Never.* The fear didn't recede, but she could move again. She was shaking so hard the ground itself felt wobbly. Pacify him. "On my way. Sir."

Stall. Her Doms would come; she knew it. She had to make sure Jarvis stayed here. *I have to do this.* Ever so slowly, she moved past Rainie and climbed into the back of the van, scraping her knees on the rough edge.

She remembered what Max had said. *"Going into a fight, you know you might get hurt, but baby, I want you fucking determined that you'll be the only one standing at the end."*

Just watch me, Sir. When she pushed to her feet, her head brushed the ceiling. The sliding side door was open on the left, and a series of lightning flashes illuminated the inside. The cargo van was empty except for a long truck toolbox along the window-less right wall. Rainie's chain ran across the floor and padlocked to a metal bolt above the toolbox.

Light glinted off the shaved scalp of the man in the van. A wave of fear froze her in place. *Oh, God, no.* Seeing him again was like walking into a nightmare. Bullet head, thick neck, bullish build. Ragged jeans and a stained black tank.

The low ceiling forced him to crouch slightly. He was tossing a pistol from hand to hand.

She couldn't pull her eyes from it. A gun. He had a *gun*.

"Yeah, there you are. Uppity bitch. Think you're too good for me. Too smart for me." His face twisted, his top lip lifting in a snarl. "Sent me to *prison*. Who's smart now, cunt? Been driving down here for months, an' you never caught on. Did ya like the dead mouse?"

"I'm here, Jarvis. What did you want?" She stood out of his reach, so terrified she could hardly breathe. *Please come now, Sirs.*

"Fucking stupid, aren't you? I want you. And now I got you." His laugh was an ugly, grating sound. Straightening slightly, he shoved the pistol under his belt in back.

And lunged for her.

She jerked back, instinctively blocked and moved sideways, and somehow, her foot thumped him hard in the knee.

"Bitch!" He didn't go down.

Not hard enough. Max's voice reprimanded her. *"Hit me like you mean it."* Jarvis turned toward her, and she stepped in and punched him in the eye with all her might.

"Fucking cunt!"

Her momentary victory ended when his fist caught her in the cheek and knocked her against the passenger seat.

Pain seared across her face, and she shook her head. In the dark van, she heard him move and stuck out blindly. Her fist slammed into his stomach.

He grunted.

She ducked sideways.

His backhand caught her shoulder instead of her face—and still sent her to the floor. He kicked her in the belly, curling her into a ball of pain.

She gasped for air, hurting, hurting.

At the rear, Rainie tried frantically to climb in. Hands restrained behind her back, she couldn't boost herself in.

Grabbing Uzuri's shirt, Jarvis yanked her up and threw her toward the toolbox. Her hip hit the metal edge with a tearing pain. Half sprawled across the box, she lifted her legs and kicked and kicked. She got his thigh, his knee, his—

He slapped her, knocked her back, and grabbed her wrist. A handcuff closed over it.

With her free hand, she punched him in the mouth, felt his teeth against her knuckles.

"Fucking bitch." Grabbing her hair, he slammed her head against the van wall, once, twice.

Stunned, dizzy, hurting, she collapsed onto the toolbox.

"I'm gonna enjoy slicing you into pieces. Goddamn cunt." Roughly, he cuffed her other wrist, and she realized the heavy chain padlocked to the van wall ran between her arms—and then out to Rainie.

"There you go, you stupid slut. That's how I like you."

The toolbox was cold beneath her thighs. Dizzily, she closed her hands around the chain for support. *Stall.* "You'll never get away with this, you dumbass." She kicked him, unable to get any leverage. Knowing he'd hurt her. Fairly certain he wouldn't stab—or shoot—her. Yet.

His backhand whipped her head to one side.

The pain... Oh God, it hurt. As blood trickled hotly down her chin, fear rose like a conflagration inside her, and she cowered away from him.

"That's more like it. Don't fucking call me names. Ever." Straightening, he grabbed her hair again and yanked her head back and forth.

Her rain-soaked hair, so carefully rolled, tucked, and pinned, fell down in her face. The slap of wetness on her burning cheek sent her anger flickering back to life.

Bastard.

A lightning bolt lit the van and showed her Rainie still standing outside the back door.

Must. Keep. Going. Pain or not, fear or not. *"Courage is endurance for one moment more."* Her Doms were coming. And, although the fight had seemed to last forever, it probably hadn't been more than a couple of minutes.

She couldn't let him get in the driver's seat. What could she do?

Scream? With an empty parking lot and hammering rain, no one would come. He'd drive away.

Seduce him? Hysterical laughter welled up in her. He wouldn't believe any seduction, not now.

Talk? He liked to talk.

"Jarvis." She put a trembling whine into her voice. Or maybe it was already there. "Let Rainie go. I did what you said. Please."

"You are the stupidest cunt." Sneering at her, he pulled his pistol from behind his back and walked toward the rear of the van.

"No. No—don't shoot her." Uzuri struggled to stand.

And from beside the toolbox came a tiny whine. A lightning

flash revealed a small nose poking out of the shadows beside the toolbox. A tiny tongue licked her ankle. What was a puppy doing in the van?

She gently pushed the puppy back in the shadows. *Hide, baby.*

Near the rear, Jarvis looked out the back door.

Just outside, Rainie stood still, shivering with cold. When she saw Jarvis, her chin lifted.

"Think you're brave?" He pointed his pistol at Rainie. "Don't move, bitch, or it'll be bang, bang, *bang.*"

Uzuri caught her breath, trying not to cry, trying not to scream. He would shoot Rainie, given the slightest reason. *Hurry, Sirs.*

Jarvis walked back, grabbed Uzuri's handcuffs, and yanked. "Good enough. You can sit and watch your big bitch bounce along behind the van. Watch her die."

Uzuri fought to get a breath. "You bastard. Don't you—"

"Yeah, she was a damn good lay." Max's voice came from somewhere close. His words were slurred, his voice loud enough to be heard over the rain. He sounded drunk. "For a black girl. What was her name? U-Zur-something?"

"What?" Eyes widening, Jarvis spun and jumped to the open side door.

Fear iced through Uzuri as he held the pistol next to his leg. *Max, oh God, Max. He'll shoot you. Get away!*

And if Max was out there, so was Alastair. For her. *No, no, no!*

Panic was a rising tide, ripping her thoughts to shreds as she frantically yanked at the chain that kept her from attacking Jarvis.

The lightning flashed, and her gaze met Rainie's.

Rainie, still standing outside the van. Chained.

Chained.

Fingers trembling, Uzuri reached up and yanked the bobby pins from her hair.

Delay, Alastair thought. There was a car between them and the black cargo van. They were near enough to be heard, not close enough to spook the bastard. He angled the umbrella to keep their faces in shadow without obstructing their view of the van.

The inside of Kassab's vehicle was dark. Occasional lightning flashes showed movement inside. A man stood in the open side door.

"Fuck, that's a pistol he's holding." Max raised his voice again. "Shoulda been there, buddy. The bitch could fuck."

On the other side of the van was a lighter blotch. Was that Uzuri's pale shirt? She was in a line behind Kassab. Alastair wanted to curse. Max couldn't shoot without a high risk of hitting Uzuri. Dan would have to find a clear shot somehow.

Push the man's buttons, Max had instructed—and Holt's story had given them a few. "I do like dark meat." Alastair spoke loudly and slurred his words in an imitation of Max's drunken act. "You're a lucky bastard. Did U-Zur-something enjoy herself?" He tossed Max the verbal cue, knowing his cousin would run with it.

"Oh, hell yeah, she enjoyed." Max puffed up his chest. "Said I had the thickest cock she'd ever seen. Loved all over my dick, and hey, she sucks cock like a Hoover vacuum."

From the corner of his eye, Alastair saw the form in the van straighten. *The fish was hooked.* He slapped Max's back. "Way to go. God knows you're big enough to make her happy."

Max roared with laughter, authentically enough that probably only Alastair could hear the tension under it. "She sure appreciated my repertoire. Most bitches do, you know."

Alastair tried to drag out his response. "What do you mean?"

"Gotta do more than missionary, ya know. Seems some idiots think fucking is only climbing on and pumping. Dumbasses."

Alastair could feel the waves of fury from the van. However, Kassab hadn't moved. Was standing right there in the door. Dan should be in position about—

"Holy fuck, does that guy have a gun?" The man's yell from the other side of the van said Dan must have been spotted. Bloody hell.

Max cursed and reached for his weapon.

"Bastards!" Kassab raised his pistol.

Max slammed into Alastair, knocking him into a car.

The sharp crack of Kassab's weapon was followed by a metallic smack when the bullet hit a vehicle.

Even as the van's side door slammed shut, Max dashed toward the driver's side.

Rainie. Alastair raced toward the back of the van.

The van's engine had been running—and the bastard floored the gas. The van shot forward.

Alastair raced after it.

Another pistol fired. Louder.

The van veered—sloppily—to miss an oncoming car and turned to the left. Fishtailed.

Max fired.

The roar of the engine halted. The idling van slowed to a snail's pace.

Alastair grabbed the swinging back door, fearing to see Rainie's body.

No body.

No Rainie.

No Uzuri, either.

The back of the van was empty.

Alastair turned and looked around. No bodies on the pavement.

The passenger door opened. Dan reached up and turned on the overhead light. He shook his head at whatever lay hidden from Alastair's view by the driver's seat. "Hell."

Max opened the driver's side, and his face tightened. He glanced back at Alastair. "You can't help here, cuz. It was a head shot."

As Alastair turned away, Dan asked, "Where're our girls?"

That was an excellent question.

Puppy in her arms, Uzuri huddled against a tire, shaking and hurting. Was it over? Fear for her men was a cold stream running through her veins. She'd heard the crack of firearms. Were they hurt? Nevertheless, after hearing Max and Dan's rants about civilians injured in shoot-outs, she knew to keep her head down.

"Uzuri!" That was Alastair's voice. He was alive.

She whimpered in relief.

Rainie rose from where she'd been crouched. "C'mon, girl-friend, sounds like the war is over. That dickheaded douche-bag of a dipwad is done." After gathering the long length of chain in loops over one arm, she held out her hand. Her wrist showed bleeding abrasions from the ropes Jarvis had used to tie her arms behind her back.

Uzuri had scraped her fingers raw undoing the knots. Of course, they'd both been hysterical right then. What was probably only minutes ago seemed like hours. She secured the shivering puppy, gritted her teeth as the handcuffs bruised her wrists, and grabbed Rainie's hand.

Rainie pulled her up.

Pain. Pain everywhere. Her stomach and right leg and shoulder hurt like...like a lot. And her hip, too. Her face.

And it didn't matter at all. Why hadn't Max called out? Where was he?

Limping, she hurried after Rainie. As she exited the row of cars, she looked toward Jarvis's black van. It'd moved, was in a regular lane.

A ways from it, Alastair walked on one side, Dan on another, obviously searching the parking lot. Her Alastair was all right. *Thank you, Lord.*

And there—there was Max, too. Both her men. Her legs weak-ened at the rush of relief.

Max spotted her. "Zuri!"

She broke into a halting run and met him partway, thumping into him so hard she knocked him back a step. His arms closed around her, painfully, all iron muscle and strength—and safety. *Here. Here was home.*

Half crying, her face buried against his hard chest, she realized his cheek was against the top of her head as he murmured endearments and curses. "Fuck, you scared the hell out of me." "I love you." "You should be spanked."

Her giggle came out high and hysterical, but better than totally sobbing. She lifted her head and saw that Dan had Rainie held close against him with his phone in the other hand. Probably calling Jake.

A step away from Max, Alastair was waving down the police cars streaming into the parking lot. Seeing her looking at him, he opened his arms.

After pushing the puppy into Max's arms, she fell against Alastair, shaking against his solid frame. So warm. The rumble of his voice in his chest was the most comforting sound in the world. She breathed in his wonderfully masculine scent as he cuddled her even closer.

"I was so scared for you two," she whispered. So scared.

In fact, more scared than she should have been. Scowling, she pulled back, and her voice came out high and angry. "What were you *thinking*? You practically asked him to shoot you!"

Alastair's deep laugh boomed out. "We needed time to get Dan in place—and to keep him from taking off with you." He squeezed her back against him, kissing her firmly.

"Wouldn't it figure some concerned civilian had to poke his nose in," Max muttered.

"Is he..." Uzuri glanced at the van.

"He's dead, sweetheart," Alastair murmured.

Uzuri leaned her forehead against his chest. Dead. She would mourn the loss of Jarvis' life, maybe someday. All she could feel right now was relief.

Dan was talking to Rainie, sounding even gruffer than normal.

"You were chained to the van. When it took off, I figured we'd find you..."

Find her dead.

The thought made Uzuri shake harder.

"Me, too." Rainie's attempt at a laugh came out a strained rasp. "But Uzuri picked the padlock holding the chain to the van."

"She what?" Dan turned to look at her.

Rainie nodded. "She got the lock off—and was running toward the door as the van took off."

"I fell right out of the van," Uzuri grumbled. Some graceful heroine she was. With handcuffs on and the puppy in her arms, she couldn't catch herself at all.

"Picked the lock?" Dan asked. "Where the hell did you learn how to do that?"

"Ben showed me." The day she'd been so delighted to get into her Sirs' bags seemed years in the past. She held her wrists out. "I couldn't get the handcuffs off."

"Picked the lock. Brilliant." Alastair hugged her hard enough to squeeze the breath from her body. "And brave."

Max nodded. His pride and approval were enough to set up a small sun inside her chest.

Rainie's gaze was soft. "You could have left me there. You came." She shuddered and blinked hard before giving Uzuri a firm nod. "Thank you."

They thought she was brave.

Courage is enduring one moment more.

She *had* been brave.

Max pulled his key ring out of his pocket. "I keep a spare key. Give me your wrists." After handing the puppy to Alastair, he undid her handcuffs. His expression tightened when he saw the bleeding scrapes.

"Think we owe Ben a steak dinner," Max muttered to Alastair.

"Agreed." Then, as the puppy started wiggling to get back to

Uzuri, Alastair frowned as if realizing what Max had handed him. "Why do I have a puppy? Where did it come from?"

"I don't know." Uzuri took the puppy back, and it bathed her neck in delight.

"It was bait, and he used it to get me." Rainie gave an annoyed growl. "He carried it into the vet clinic and said he had three more to bring in for shots. They'd busted open the box holding them and would I help him carry them in?"

Dan grunted. "Of course, you went right out."

"Well, yeah." Rainie looked disgruntled. "He opened the side, said, "Grab that one," and when I leaned forward to look, that was that."

Uzuri held the puppy toward her. "Here, you earned him."

Rainie shook her head. "Jake won't let me have more dogs and"—she smiled—"he's bonded to you. Can't you tell?"

"I can't..."

Max grinned. "Seems fair. I think you've missed having a little dog."

"But you already have a dog."

"*We* already have a dog," Alastair corrected. "Hunter will enjoy a friend. Looks like this one is small."

"Terrier-poodle mix, I'd say," Rainie said. "You'll have a total fluff ball that will stay lap-sized."

Uzuri gathered the puppy close, feeling her heart brimming over.

Max looked at Alastair. "Don't know if you saw how she's limping. You need to check her over. Rainie, too."

Alastair smiled over at Rainie. "We'll swing by the ER." Then he touched Uzuri's cheek gently. "Once we get released from this mess, we'll discuss how our submissive scared us to death. If she's not too injured, I'll only spank her a little before we release our worries in another way."

"Spank me?" She scowled up at him.

And then, as she saw the smoldering heat in his eyes, her

anger sputtered out, and a flame ignited low in her belly. Come to think of it, she had a few worries to release, as well.

Still… "Excuse me, oh wonderful Dragon Doms, but I *did* call for help, didn't I? And I knew you'd come."

"Well, that's true. You trusted us to come after you, and you were very brave. You get a pass on the spanking." Max touched her bruised face gently. "She's cold, cuz. Let's get her checked out and get her home. Then we'll warm her from the inside out." He leaned down and whispered, "Because I need to be buried deep inside you…fucking deep."

Uzuri's knees almost buckled.

Alastair's laugh shook her. "We have a plan. Something to look forward to." He touched his mouth to hers. "Do you know how much we love you, our brave little mischief?"

They'd risked their lives to save her.

Yes. She knew.

CHAPTER THIRTY

A week before Thanksgiving, Uzuri pulled into the driveway and parked inside the garage. Even as she got out of the car, she was mentally ticking off everything she had to accomplish before they headed up to Colorado for the holiday.

At the Drago family ranch. With all of the Dragos.

Way to terrify a girl.

What did people wear on a ranch in Colorado?

Before she reached the door from the dark garage to the kitchen, she heard a flurry of high yips and Hunter's lower bark. Dior's little paws scrabbled on the other side of the door as the puppy tried to dig his way through.

She heard Max's relaxed laugh. "Easy, mutt. She's coming."

He opened the door for her, and she stepped through into light and warmth. The scent of ginger and garlic swirled around her. Chinese. Alastair must be cooking.

"'Bout time you got home. Trade you." In his usual black T-shirt and jeans, Max took her purse and briefcase. He dumped the fluffy puppy in her arms, then grabbed himself a kiss, even as Dior frantically licked her neck.

"Mmm, you taste good," he murmured. He pulled her closer and took a deeper kiss. "Welcome home—and you're late."

"Late?" She frowned at him, then bent to give Hunter some hugs and scratches. "I'm not late. I always get home now."

In a cream-colored, short-sleeved shirt and khakis, Alastair walked over and handed her a glass of wine. He also took a kiss, taking full advantage of the fact that she had a poodle and wine in her hands. "We missed you, therefore you're late."

"Oh." Oddly enough, that almost made sense. "I missed you, too, so I guess I am."

"Supper will be in about half an hour," Alastair said. "In the meantime, we left something for you by the garden pond."

"Oh. Okay." Had she ordered something and forgotten? After a sip or two or three of wine, she kissed Dior, set him down, and headed out onto the patio. This late in the day, the sun was setting, and pink was coloring the puffy clouds in the dark blue.

The air was cool with mist from the splashing pond. *Hmm.* Were those Barbie dolls arrayed on the rocks by the water?

Uh-oh. The last time the guys had messed with her dolls was after she'd reprogrammed their phones' ring tones to play "It's a Small World." That time, Dr. Dragon had held a paddle; Detective Dragon had been leaning on a massive dildo.

That had been a great night.

But she hadn't played any tricks recently. After taking another sip of wine for courage, she set her glass on a table and approached the pond.

Her Zuri-doll was naked and kneeling. Okay, that wasn't scary. She was submissive, after all.

Dressed in a short-sleeve shirt and khakis, Dr. Dragon stood over Zuri-doll, holding out a gold cuff-style bracelet. A *real* bracelet. The gold head was shaped like a dragon with ruby eyes and diamond brows. The tail held more diamonds.

In jeans and a black T-shirt, Detective Dragon gripped a tiny heart-shaped gold padlock also studded with diamonds.

"What is this?" she whispered.

"We don't have a Masters and slave relationship, not a twenty-four-hour one, and yet...we wanted something to symbolize what we share." Smiling slightly, Alastair had followed silently. He reached around her and took the bracelet from his replica. "We didn't think you would like a traditional slave collar."

Just as silently, Max appeared to stand beside his cousin. "Traditional or not, we wanted a way to show—and for us all to remember—that you belong to your dragon Doms."

Alastair's voice deepened. "Strip, love."

She stared at them. She'd been living with them a month, had been their submissive for a month, and believed their relationship was...defined.

She hadn't thought anything was missing, so how had they known she wanted something more tangible? The words and the symbols.

Her heart started pounding as she took off her pumps. Her dress, her bra, her thong followed. As each item of clothing was removed, she slid further into the soft place where decisions were no longer hers.

"Kneel for us, princess." The edge of steel in Max's voice was gentled by the warmth. The love.

Her legs didn't want to hold her up anyway, and she went down on her knees, right there on the patio...only to find that one of them had put a cushion there first.

Alastair's gaze was tender and steady as he studied her face, then held out his hand.

When she set her left hand in his, he kissed her fingers in the way that always thrilled her, then fastened the bracelet around her wrist. "The bracelet is a symbol of your submission to us, Uzuri." He leaned down and took her lips in a long luxurious kiss.

"And a symbol that we cherish your surrender and will love you and protect you. You are ours—as we are yours." Max bent and kissed her, slow and firm. "We love you, Zuri."

When he straightened, he took the padlock from his doll, put it on the bracelet, and clicked it shut. The laugh lines beside his blue eyes crinkled. "Even you might find it difficult to pick a padlock with one hand."

She couldn't speak for a moment, couldn't even see for the tears in her eyes. Wiping her cheeks, she felt the weight on her wrist and saw the sparkle of the diamonds. The dragon watched her with its flashing eyes. "I-I. It's beautiful."

After a moment, she managed to whisper, "I love you. Love you both." She looked up at her Dragon Doms, side by side, both smiling, and the warmth and love flowed from them to wrap around her.

When Alastair bent to offer her a hand, she frowned. "Wait... Aren't you supposed to *ask* me?"

"You need us." Max gave her a smug smile. "It's our job as your Doms to give you what you need."

She scowled.

Chuckling, Alastair lifted her to her feet and hugged her. "We all know you'd say yes."

Oh. "Good point."

Max leaned against her from behind, squeezing her between her two Doms. "I think we should celebrate, don't you?"

He was hard against her. Alastair was just as hard in front. And she was beginning to melt right into pure lust. Unable to resist, she reached down and undid Alastair's pants, then pushed back enough to get room to let his cock out to play.

Glancing down, she choked. *Oh...oops.* She'd forgotten what she'd done as she was waking the guys up this morning. Omigod, she was in trouble.

At the sound she made, Alastair followed her gaze to where her hand was wrapped around his cock.

Although Alastair's smile disappeared, his cock's wide silvery smile—and round eyes—remained.

She eyed her happy face artwork. It looked good, considering how quickly she'd had to work before the guys had awakened this morning. The silvery marker she'd used to draw the eyes and big grin on the head of Alastair's cock showed up...extremely well. The urethral slit made a perfect nose. Perhaps the grin was a little demented, but seemed very happy.

Wasn't it nice a cock normally pointed downward so her Dom hadn't noticed the face until getting an erection now? After all, Alastair discovering his happy face at a public urinal might have been bad. For *her*.

"What?" Max leaned forward to peer over her shoulder. He burst out laughing. "Good to see you feeling cheerful, Doc."

"We were both in her bed this morning," Alastair pointed out ever so politely.

Uzuri looked away. *Uh-oh.*

Max's laughter sputtered to a stop. "You didn't..."

When he stepped back, she turned.

He opened his jeans. His dick bounced out enthusiastically— which seemed only right since it had an adorable grin in black marker.

This time it was Alastair who roared his head off.

Despite Max's stern expression, she could see his lips twitching with his attempt not to smile. "It was bad enough to have dolls painted to look like us. This? No."

Her Dragon Doms moved to stand shoulder-to-shoulder, arms folded over their chests. Both with the same grim expressions.

The ground she stood on seemed to take a fast elevator ride straight downward. "Um. Your dicks look really happy."

"Mmm. I think mine would be happier being faceless." Even Max's stern control couldn't keep the laughter out of his voice.

Alastair nodded. "I believe a blowjob would be an effective method of removal." His gaze rested on her, amusement dancing in his warm hazel eyes. "You may continue until the faces are gone."

Oh, they tried so hard to look mean, until Alastair busted out laughing again, and she was in his arms, pressed between them both. As the setting sun glinted over her beautiful bracelet, she was kissed and hugged and filled to overflowing with love.

She sighed happily.

Coming home truly was the finest part of the day.

ALSO BY CHERISE SINCLAIR

Masters of the Shadowlands Series

Club Shadowlands

Dark Citadel

Breaking Free

Lean on Me

Make Me, Sir

To Command and Collar

This Is Who I Am

If Only

Show Me, Baby

Servicing the Target

Protecting His Own

Mischief and the Masters

Beneath the Scars

Defiance

The Effing List

It'll Be An Adventure

Mountain Masters & Dark Haven Series

Master of the Mountain

Simon Says: Mine

Master of the Abyss

Master of the Dark Side

My Liege of Dark Haven

Edge of the Enforcer

Master of Freedom

Master of Solitude

I Will Not Beg

The Wild Hunt Legacy

Hour of the Lion

Winter of the Wolf

Eventide of the Bear

Leap of the Lion

Healing of the Wolf

Heart of the Wolf

Sons of the Survivalist Series

Not a Hero

Lethal Balance

What You See

Soar High

Standalone Books

The Dom's Dungeon

The Starlight Rite

ABOUT THE AUTHOR

Cherise Sinclair is a *New York Times* and *USA Today* bestselling author of emotional, suspenseful romance. She loves to match up devastatingly powerful males with heroines who can hold their own against the subtle—and not-so-subtle—alpha male pressure.

Fledglings having flown the nest, Cherise, her beloved husband, an eighty-pound lap-puppy, and one fussy feline live in the Pacific Northwest where nothing is cozier than a rainy day spent writing.